A Blaze of Poppies

A Blaze of Poppies

A novel about New Mexico during World War 1

by Jennifer Bohnhhoff

This book is a work of fiction.
Any reference to historical events, real people, or real locales is used fictitiously.
Other names, characters, places and incidents are the product of the author's imagination, and any resemblance to actual events, locales or persons, living or dead, is entirely coincidental.

ISBN-13: 9798465104562

Cover Design by https://weftandweave.weebly.com/

Dedication

To my feisty mother, Kay Swedberg,
a natural born story teller
who came to New Mexico in 1957
to doggedly follow her dreams.
I am forever grateful for your example
and your continued love.

Acknowledgements

Writing may be a lonely endeavor, but it would be impossible if the writer were completely alone. I had a lot of help and a lot of emotional support in the writing of this book. These are the people I am most indebted to:

To my tour guides:

Csaba Köves, who goes by Charlie, guided me through World War I Battlefields. If you ever want a tour of military sites in Europe, he's your guy. https://www.phoenixcustomtours.com/

Iain Roy McHenry is THE best guide for the Belgian/Flanders/Ypres portion of the war, and has authored a book on the underground portions of the war. https://www.tothefrontline.com/

To my authority:

Paul Peeples is a marine, an historical interpreter, and the guy you want watching your back for all those little details.

To my editors and early readers:

To **Patrice Locke Lewis** https://www.bypatricelocke.com/ and **Chris Eboch** http://www.krisbock.com/, both better writers than I am, who read my early manuscripts and suggested the changes that really gave the story life.

To **Suzanne Balthaser**, **Jean Wilkinson-Rodney and Lois Haag**, who found all those annoying typos, compound words that weren't, and the like, and to rancher and educator **Eileen Wood**, who helped me saddle up and ride straight. I thank you all.

Part One

A Town Ablaze

1916

Chapter One

Agnes Day rode into the yard at the Sunrise Ranch as the sky blushed peach and crimson. Ernesto Bernal waited, curry comb in hand, at the tack room door. He chewed the tip of his mustache.

She screwed up her face and spit in a way that wasn't at all ladylike. "What is it this time? Weanlings got blackleg? Locusts predicted?" She and the ranch manager conversed in Spanglish, the jumbled mix of Spanish and English that was common on both sides of the border. Agnes grew up speaking it with him and his wife, Lupe, who ran the kitchen. Since *mama* is the same in both languages, no one knew with any certainty whether her first word was in English or Spanish.

"No problems on the range. The problems, they are here." Ernesto jerked his head at the big adobe house. "*La Dama*, she is very upset with you."

"Because?" Agnes swung down and steadied her wobbly legs. Her shoulders felt stiff, her face sun sore. After a long day in the saddle, she didn't need her mother's hysterical drama. She needed a tall glass of Lupe's sweet tea and a long soak in the tub.

"Because you are so late."

Agnes pulled off her leather gloves and slapped them against her dungarees, kicking up a cloud of dust. "She knew I was riding fence today. That takes time. Why should she be angry?"

"Because," Ernesto said with a grim smile, "today is your birthday. She had Lupe make a cake. And there are guests."

"Men?" Agnes asked.

Ernesto nodded. "Men. They have already drunk all of Lupe's punch. Now, they are drinking tea."

Agnes groaned. She hated parties, especially those with eligible bachelors. Mildred Day was determined to marry off her fifth and final daughter before she became a spinster.

Agnes drew a hand over her face, gritty with salt crystals left when sweat dried in the thin, arid desert air. She was no spinster. She was a rancher, determined to follow in her father's footsteps. The Sunrise Ranch was her passion and her destiny, and it took all her time and effort. She didn't have time for courting.

Agnes yearned to draw herself a luxurious bubble bath and read magazines until her toes were as wrinkled as black walnuts. But mother was a force to be reckoned with. There was nothing for it but to clean herself up as best as she could on short notice and attend her own party. She gave Diablo a pat on his rump, and walked stiffly into the kitchen, where she shrugged out of her barn coat and hung it and her grey man's Stetson with a Montana peak beside her father's black Stetson on the pegs by the back door.

Three other hats, a man's straw boater and the two campaign hats occupied the other pegs. That meant her party guests were a civilian and two soldiers, probably from nearby Camp Columbus. Was mother so desperate that she had given up on the local boys and was inviting soldiers now?

Lupe, a tall, big-boned woman, stood in a cloud of steam, stirring something on the wood-burning stove. It was February, but the kitchen was as hot as the Fourth of July. Agnes' birthday cake, an extravagant affair frosted in pink marshmallow creme, rested on the kitchen table next to a basket heaped high and covered by a napkin. Agnes smiled at the cake. Lupe insisted on whipping one up once a year even though she had long since outgrown such fripperies. The hot, flaky biscuits she knew were under the napkin were more to her liking now. She was just slipping one out when Lupe's wooden spoon smacked her hand.

"Ouch!" Agnes brought the stinging hand to her mouth.

Lupe brandished her spoon at her. "No snacking for you, *mija*. Not when there are guests waiting. Your mother, she is . . "

"I know," Agnes interrupted. "Furious. Ernesto told me. I'll go!" Hands up in surrender, she backed out of the room, then dashed up the stairs two at a time. Agnes leaned her elbows on her windowsill and looked at the range stretching to the horizon. A red Oldsmobile 44 sat next to the windmill. Any man foolish enough to park such a beautiful car near the stock tank, where curious cattle could bump into it and leave it covered with nose prints wasn't the man for her.

She had kicked off one of her boots when Lupe backed into the room carrying a pitcher of warm water. Agnes chuckled and shook her head as Lupe filled the bowl that sat on the washstand.

Lupe wagged her finger at Agnes. "I know you want to soak in that big, white, tub the *Señor* put in for you, but you don' have the time. Your neck, mija. It is red under all that dirt. Why didn't you wear a bandana?"

"I did, but I took it off to wipe my face and lost it somewhere."

Lupe clucked her tongue. "Somewhere out there is a coyote wearing a red bandana and feeling he is *muy guapo*. And you: wear this dress. It is good with your eyes, no?" Lupe rummaged through the chifforobe and pulled out a pleated, cornflower blue dress that had a fashionably hobbled skirt and lace at the collar and cuffs. Agnes shimmied out of her dusty flannel shirt and dungarees. She splashed water on her face, then ran a washcloth over her neck, legs and arms, wiping away dust.

Agnes sat at her vanity and looked into the mirror. The girl who stared back was no beauty. She was a rancher. With that position came responsibilities that led to wind-chapped skin and calloused hands. But the set of her chin and eyebrows showed a steely determination. Not many people as small as she - only 5′3″ and not quite a hundred pounds - could rope a steer and bring him down. Her best feature, her eyes, were clear, direct, and bluer than the high desert sky, but her dull, light brown hair was cropped in a functional bob. Agnes dipped her brush into the wash water, then drove it through her hair until the dent where her hat had crushed it disappeared.

She opened the white jar of Peredixo Cream that her sister Elsie had given her. The cream failed at making her complexion white and smooth, but it cooled her burned, chapped skin. Her toilet, such as it was, complete, Agnes threw on her dress, adjusted the lace at the collar, then slipped on a pair of low pumps and tied bows in the ribbons that held them on.

She scowled at the mirror, tried on her most intimidating, condescending smile, then her haughtiest look, determined to scare away the would-be suitors waiting in the parlor below. After an encouraging nod to herself, Agnes strode forward and nearly fell over, hampered by the pegged skirt. She took a deep breath, recollected herself, and walked out into the hall.

Agnes was halfway down the stairs when she heard a loud, crow-like guffaw erupt from the parlor. It was a laugh she hadn't heard for years but recognized instantly. Heinrich Dieter, her old schoolmate and the man her mother had always pinned her hopes on, was back from college.

Chapter Two

Agnes pushed the palm of her hand into her forehead in an attempt to stave off a headache. Heinrich Dieter was part of her mother's master plan to position her daughters into the upper echelons of power in the new state of New Mexico. It was a plan Agnes wanted no part of.

When Agnes' mother married John Day, she left the booming and modern railroad town of Las Vegas, New Mexico and moved to the territory's backward, desolate bootheel. To console herself, she'd immediately begun transforming the Big House at Sunrise Ranch. The centuries-old hacienda had been built more for protection from Indians and weather than for refinement. Mildred turned it into the stately mansion expected of the mistress of a cattle empire. If one didn't look at the flat desolation outside the windows, one could believe that she was in a proper Victorian manor house in the middle of a verdant English garden.

The house complete, Mildred then focused on the next step of her plan. She made her husband sit on every board and join every organization that brought prestige. She had married four of her five daughters to rich and influential men. Agnes was the last, and Heinrich Dieter was, in her mother's opinion, perfect for her. His father owned a prosperous mercantile in the nearby town of Columbus, and had sent his son to college. Harvard, no less. Rich, well connected and going places: He was exactly what Mildred wanted for her daughter. Too bad he didn't know enough about cattle than to leave his shiny red car near the water tank.

Agnes paused in the parlor doorway and studied the assembled party. Her father sat stiffly erect in his wing-back armchair, looking uncomfortable in the high collar, starched shirt front, and spats that he only wore for special occasions. Mother sat next to him on her ornately carved lady's chair, her teacup poised daintily halfway to her mouth as if she were waiting for someone to say something so that she could respond. Across from them, three men perched shoulder to shoulder on the edge of the overstuffed horsehair settee, teacups balanced precariously on their knees.

"Ah! There's our Aggie!" Heinrich Dieter said.

Agnes winced, embarrassed by the familiarity of her childhood nickname.

"So it is!" Mildred chirped enthusiastically. "Agnes, dear! Come in and greet our guests! You remember Heinrich, don't you? He's back from school! With a law degree! And he's brought some friends to help you celebrate your birthday! Isn't that nice?"

Agnes entered the room to the clatter of teacups as the men stood. She kissed her father, bent to kiss her mother, then turned to the three men. They were so different from each other that the image of the three monkeys: speak no evil, see no evil, and hear no evil, popped into her mind and, though she tried hard to look intimidatingly stern, she couldn't suppress a grin.

As if encouraged by her smile, Heinrich held out his arms. "Aggie! Long time, no see! How about a birthday kiss?" Heinrich was tall and rangy. His eyes were brilliant blue, and his honey blond hair cropped short except for the fashionable fringe of bang that fell into his eyes and caused him to throw his head like a petulant pony. If not for the acne, he might have been as handsome as he obviously thought he was. His college sweater made him look so all-American that no one would guess he was the son of an immigrant who spoke English with such a heavy German accent that half his customers couldn't understand him.

Agnes took a step to the side, putting the coffee table between them. She gave his hand an authoritative shake, which she made extra strong when she felt how fish-like his hand felt in hers.

"Heinrich."

"Your mother suggested I bring along a couple of friends. I thought it the perfect opportunity to help out some of the troops stationed at Camp Columbus. They so rarely get to do anything with good company, you know. Allow me to introduce Corporal David Benavides. He's a dispatch rider with the National Guard."

Agnes released Heinrich's hand and offered hers to Benavides. The Corporal glanced up, gave Agnes' hand one quick pump, then wiped his palm on his khaki trousers. His dark brown eyes stared at his feet and he shifted his weight back and forth as if there was something disconcerting on the carpet. Benavides was small and thin, a good prospect if someone was looking for a jockey. Agnes, though small herself, was sure she outweighed him. His straight, black hair was cropped short, and his skin was so dark that Agnes wondered if he was Mexican, Indian, Negro, or some combination of the three.

The third man was taller than she, with broad shoulders, and coloring that made him look like a faded memory instead of a flesh-and-bones person. His coffee-with-cream skin almost matched his close-cropped hair and his uniform. His eyes, a strange, light color somewhere between brown and gray, had a piercing quality, like a coyote's. She could not look away from them.

"And this is Private Guillermo Bowers. He's National Guard, too. A machine gunner. Aggie here's an old friend of mine. We went to grade school together. Didn't we, Aggie?"

"Yes, Heinrich. You dipped my braid in the inkwell when we were in fourth grade."

Aggie shook the machine gunner's hand. Despite his ethereal look, his grip was firm and sure, his warm skin as calloused as any cowboy's.

"Ha!" Heinrich gave another raucous guffaw. "Aggie here was so mad, she chased me from the schoolhouse, threw me down in the dirt, and sat on me! But I said I liked her sitting on me, so she climbed off and walloped me instead!"

Mildred laughed, as if appreciating the memory. When no one else joined her, her twittering died out, replaced by an awkward silence.

"I go by Will." The machine gunner's voice was low and smooth. Agnes felt like he was talking only to her. "No one calls me Guillermo."

"No one calls me Aggie, either."

Heinrich's laugh broke the silence, awakening Agnes to her surroundings. She pulled her hand from Will's and took a step back, bumping her calves into her mother's knees.

"The ink grew out, Aggie. No harm done. You didn't have to get it bobbed, or anything. At least not then. Bobbed hair like yours is very fashionable now, though. I saw a lot of it on the girls in Boston, where Harvard is. You would fit right in."

"I don't care a continental about fashion, and I don't care about fitting in." Agnes watched with some satisfaction as Heinrich blushed.

"Our Agnes is a practical girl. She bobbed her hair so it won't get into her eyes when she's riding," Mildred said in a conciliatory tone. "Well, dear, why don't you sit down and join us in a cup of tea?"

Agnes gave her mother a pitying look. "I've kept you waiting so long. I'm sure our guests are positively swimming in the stuff. Lupe would be relieved if we ate dinner before it got even more overcooked."

"Let's get a picture first, to commemorate the occasion. Look what I got when I was back east. They're all the rage now." Heinrich pulled a small, boxy apparatus from his pocket. It was no bigger than a cigarette case, but when he pulled on it, metal struts opened up and a leather, accordion-like tube appeared.

"What's that?" Agnes' father, who had been his usual silent and disinterested self, suddenly perked up.

"It's a vest pocket autographic, Mr. Day. It's Kodak's newest, smallest camera. And it has a nifty feature: it's autographic. I can use this little pencil to write in this box and it shows up on the film. Shall we take a picture?"

"Let's let the maid do it!" Mildred said, and called Lupe into the room. They bunched up in front of the fireplace and Lupe snapped the picture. Afterwards, they went to the dining room for what turned into a very uncomfortable dinner. Mildred talked far too much. Heinrich simpered and guffawed, and Corporal Benavides glowered at his plate. With the exception of the time John Day looked up and said "This is good, Mother," Agnes' father didn't say a word. Agnes, too, ate in silence, but she was less settled than her father, for every time she looked up, she caught Private Bowers' pale eyes staring at her. The Private answered Mildred's few questions in a calm, quiet voice, hesitating as if he had to think long and hard about even the simplest of questions.

An hour later, the three Days stood on the front porch and waved at the red tail lights as Heinrich's fancy red Oldsmobile 44 disappeared into the night.

"Well, I never! If I'd known Heinrich was even considering bringing Mexicans to dinner, I'd have talked with him first." Even though the temperature had dropped as soon as the sun set, Mildred snapped her fan open and began fluttering it violently. "Don't get me wrong: some of my best friends are Mexicans. They have, after all, been in this country longer than we have. But Heinrich could come up with more suitable companions. These two weren't good prospects as suitors. Why, neither of them spoke more than four words apiece."

"Still waters run deep," said Agnes' father, who'd also been quiet throughout dinner. John Day was a man of few words and usually let his wife do all the talking.

Agnes threw herself onto the porch swing. "Maybe still waters run deep in your case, Papa. But with those two? Their still waters were more than likely just mud slick atop quicksand. Heinrich Dieter brought them to make himself look good by comparison!"

Mildred hopped onto the swing next to her daughter. She was so petite that her feet didn't touch the porch. "He doesn't need to do that. His father's store is the best general merchandise store in Columbus. And now that he has a law degree, I expect Heinrich'll campaign for a seat in the legislature. Just think, Agnes! You could be Mrs. Heinrich Dieter, with a house in Columbus and another in Santa Fe!"

"You know that's not what I want, Mother."

"Well, you can't stay here! Not alone! It's not safe anymore!"

For the past six years, revolution had been raging in Mexico. The names Francisco Madero, Pascual Orozco, Pancho Villa and Emiliano Zapata were all linked to violence, some of which was aimed at American business interests. Only last month Villistas, followers of General Villa, had stopped a train carrying American employees of a mining company in Santa Ysabel. The Villistas had robbed, stripped and shot the Americans, one of whom had lived to tell the tale by playing dead.

"Now Mother," John said, "you know the revolutionaries don't dare cross the border. As long as we stay on our side, we're perfectly safe."

"A woman can't run a ranch on her own!" Mildred's hand beat double time as she fanned away her frustration.

John took a seat on Agnes' other side. His boots pressed the porch floor boards and the swing swung into motion. "Leave our Ag alone, Mother. She can make her own decisions."

"She postpones much longer, she'll be a spinster!"

John put his arm around Agnes so that he could pat his wife on the back. "We have plenty of time. We'll find a suitable solution before I'm too old to run this place."

"In the meantime, I am going to give myself a nice, warm, relaxing bath." Agnes leaped off the swing and slipped back into the house before she said something that would really put her mother into a snit. She was almost to the base of the stairs when the tone of her mother's voice stopped her.

"John Day! I can't believe you let her just walk away like that! And in the middle of an important discussion! All I want is for her to be safe and secure. I want what's best for her."

"You want what you think is best for her, Mother. But our Ag thinks differently." Her father's voice was so measured and calm that it made Agnes relax. She hoped it had the same effect on her mother. "Every herd has its maverick. Ag is ours. The harder you try to make her cut right, the more determined she is to cut left. I say, let her go. She'll find her own way. It may not be the safe and secure way, but it'll be what's best for her. Have faith."

Agnes smiled as she tiptoed up the stairs. As long as she had her father's support, everything would be fine. She eased herself into the enormous clawfoot tub, sighing as the rising water relaxed her, then reached over the side and blindly fumbled around on the little wicker table that sat beside the tub. Her fingers found the well-thumbed copy of Everybody's Magazine that had been passed from ranch house to ranch house for the past two years. She propped her elbows on the rim of the tub and opened the magazine to an advertisement.

Do You Want a Job Where You Have The "Say So"
Instead of the "Do So"?
The International School of Correspondence has trained
thousands of men who are now drawing large salaries.

Agnes scanned the list of courses available: Electrical Engineer, Building Contractor, Telephone Expert, Book Keeping, Teacher. The list went on and on. Agnes snorted, feeling a little pity for anyone who had to take any of those courses.

She didn't need to take a correspondence course to do what she planned to do. Agnes would stay right here on the Sunrise Ranch. She would ride the range each morning and fall into bed each evening, tired and satisfied that she had done her best by the cattle she owned and the land that nurtured them. It was her destiny. She and her father knew it. It was just a matter of time before her mother would give up and accept it, too.

But just because Agnes wanted to stay on the ranch didn't mean she didn't want to learn new things, especially when they were practical. Agnes flipped backwards through the pages until the title *Our Invisible Allies caught* her attention. She was on the third page of the article when the door opened and Lupe entered the bathroom.

"Lupe, did you know there're little animals called leukocytes? They eat bacteria, and that keeps us from getting sick. And you didn't have to come help me. I'm doing fine."

"I never seen no leukocytes or bacteria around here. And I'm not here to help you. I'm here to help me. I don't want to have to iron this." Lupe picked Agnes' blue dress off the floor and gave it a shake.

"Oh, they're here. You don't see them because they're really tiny," Agnes said.

"Smaller than no-see-ums? I won't worry about them, then. If they're too small to see, they're too small to worry about."

Agnes shook the magazine. "It says right here that maybe we could use them to cure polio and tuberculosis, and other diseases."

Lupe frowned. "It would be hard to train so small an animal to do anything. But I guess it could be done. I once saw trained fleas at a circus. They rode little bikes and carried tiny little umbrellas. But I don't think you could get them to cure a sick person."

Agnes laughed and put the magazine back on the wicker stand. "Maybe not. Say, Lupe, are Octavio and Miguel coming back for branding this year?"

Lupe smiled, happy to have a chance to talk about her sons. They had grown up with Agnes, but had gone north to mine copper in Santa Rita, coming back for holidays and special events on the ranch. "They always come back. They like to help *El Don*."

"Mother says a woman can't run a ranch by herself, but that's what I aim to do. I'll need good workers."

Lupe sat on the edge of the tub and smiled down at Agnes. "The Bernals will stay at Sunrise Ranch as long as there are Days that need us. When Ernesto and I are too old to manage this ranch, Miguel will move back and take over for us. Then we will get him a wife from Mexico, the way Ernesto got me. Now get to bed. The sun isn't going to rise any later tomorrow just because you lazed around in a tub all night." Lupe gathered up the rest of

Agnes' clothes and left the room. Agnes laid her head back and frowned at the ceiling. She needed to convince her mother that she didn't need a husband to assure her future. She had The Sunrise, and that was all she needed and all she wanted.

Miles away, coyotes with eyes like Private Will Bowers sang eerie harmonies for the listening moon, as if longing for something more.

Chapter Three

Agnes laid her forehead against the kitchen window and frowned at the rain that pummeled the windows. Ranchers loved soft rains that soaked the ground and turned the brown and yellow land the pale green of spring. Gully washers like this dug deep arroyos and pooled in lagunitas, little lakes that were potential death traps for livestock.

She slipped into her oilskin coat and went out the back door without saying a word to anyone. She was throwing a saddle blanket over Diablo's back when Ernesto walked up.

"¿A dónde vas, señorita?"

"I'm going to check the herd, make sure there aren't any stuck in *las lagunitas*. I won't be long," Agnes answered.

"La Dama, she won't like it. She will worry."

Agnes smiled wryly as she tightened the cinch beneath Diablo's belly. "My mother is the reason I'm going. She thinks I can't run a ranch on my own. I'm showing her I can."

"I'll get a *vaquero* to ride with you." Ernesto turned toward the bunkhouse, but Agnes held out a hand.

"They're probably in the middle of a rip-roaring poker game. I promise you: if I find any stuck cattle, I'll come back for help."

Ernesto gave a shrug and a wave, obviously resigned to letting Agnes do what she wanted, and she was glad of it. She really didn't want to be contrary, and she didn't like to argue, but once her mind was set on something, there was little point in arguing. She appreciated people who understood that about her.

As soon as she passed out of the yard, the weight of being cooped up indoors lifted off her shoulders. The rain slacked into a fine mist that freshened the air and gave it an earthy, green sage smell. Diablo's hooves made soft, splooshing sounds. His breath came out in roiling clouds that reminded her of the locomotive that passed on its way to Columbus.

She had been out about an hour when she came to a cow that was buried in mud up to her hocks and bellowing her discomfort. Agnes checked the cow's side for the lazy D that was the Sunrise Ranch's brand, then sighed and looked back toward the ranch house. She had never pulled a bogged cow alone. It was hard to do, even with a partner. But the prospect of riding back, then having to listen to an irate cowboy complain about being taken from a good poker game just to ride through the rain and rescue a cow too dumb to keep out of trouble seemed too unpleasant to countenance. Agnes looped one end of her saddle rope around the saddle horn, dismounted, and gave Diablo a pat. "We've never done this on our own, but I think we can. You're a smart enough horse to pull when I give you the signal, aren't you boy?"

"Stay with your horse. I'll go in after the cow."

The voice made Agnes whirl around, her heart pounding with a sudden rush of adrenaline. Here she was in the middle of the flat plain. She could see for miles. How in the world had anyone snuck up on her without her seeing him from a long way off? Agnes felt irritated that she could have been so oblivious to her surroundings. The irritation was replaced by fear. If this stranger meant to do her harm, no one would hear her cries for help.

Determined to make herself as intimidating as possible, Agnes glared at the man who was standing just on the other side of Diablo.

"Who are you? What are you doing on my land? And get away from my horse."

The man took a step back from Diablo, took off his hat and held it humbly at his chest. "I'm sorry, Miss Day. Didn't mean to give you a fright. I'm Will Bowers. Remember me? I was at your birthday party eleven days ago."

Agnes recognized the man with the coffee and cream skin and the pale brown eyes and her knees nearly buckled with relief. This wasn't a bandit or one of the dangerous drifters that came through on occasion. Still, she was embarrassed that she had been caught so unawares. "You've been keeping count of the days, Private Bowers?"

"Well, no." Will looked at his hat, which he turned like a steering wheel making a hard right. His flustered look melted Agnes' irritation.

"You still didn't tell me what you're doing here," she added in a tone that was just a trifle softer.

"Just walking. I was going stir crazy sitting around in the barracks."

"Walking? All the way out here? That's got to be, what? Six miles? Seven?" Agnes wanted to laugh with the absurdity. Ranchers never walked if they could help it. They rode. She wasn't even sure she could walk six miles. Not without blisters and sore feet. Agnes looked west, towards Camp Columbus. She saw nothing. Not even smoke from the chimneys.

Agnes remounted Diablo, then handed Will the coiled saddle rope. "Well, if you're offering, I'd be a fool not to take your help. You know how to do this?"

"I've done it a time or two. Here. Hold my hat."

She watched him wade into the water, skeining out the rope behind him, his arms wide as he balanced through the muck. When he reached the cow, he looped the end of the saddle rope around her horns. He bent down to claw her feet free of mud, then moved behind her and wrapped her tail around his hands.

"Ready? Watch out for rope burn," he called.

Agnes snorted. "I know what I'm doing." She gave Diablo a nudge with her heels and he strained forward, taking all the slack from the rope. Will pulled and heaved at the cow's rear as she bellowed and floundered, sometimes kneeling and sometimes gaining a foothold, her hooves making sucking sounds as the rope dragged her forward. They moved, inch by inch, until finally the cow found firm footing and stumbled onto dry land.

"Watch yourself. She's bound to be irritated and take it out on the wrong person," Agnes said. Will just nodded. Obviously, he knew exactly what he was doing.

As he wadded back onto dry land, the cow charged him, but she was wobbly and weak from her time in the mud. "Now, now, sister. None of that!" Will seized the angry cow by the horns. He gave her head a quick twist and she went down on her side. "Sorry, girl."

Will thanked Agnes for holding his hat. He reached out for it, saw how muddy his hands were, then wiped them on his shirtfront, which was just as muddy.

Agnes laughed and set the hat on Will's head. "Thank you for freeing my cow. Come back to the ranch house and I'll reward you with a cup of coffee and a slice of cake. Lupe, our cook, made a nice chocolate one yesterday."

He looked down, his hands out, open palmed, indicating how muddy he was. "Thank you. But I'm in no condition to pay a social visit."

"Pshaw. This isn't a social visit. I'd offer the same to any of my cowhands."

"Well, then, all right." He turned toward the ranch, but Agnes blocked his way with Diablo. She slapped the skirt behind the cantle of her saddle.

"You've already walked six miles today. It's another couple to the Big House. Cowboys don't walk. Climb up."

"I'm no cowboy. I'm a soldier, and they walk plenty. Besides, I'm muddy."

Agnes rolled her eyes. The ranch hands might grumble at what she told them to do, but they would never argue. "You know how to pull bog. That makes you a cowboy, even if you are a soldier. Climb up."

"But . . . "

"Don't argue with me." Agnes narrowed her eyes and spat in a very unladylike way. Will shrugged, then surprised her by springing into place without putting a foot on a stirrup. She sensed him holding himself erect and away from her, his hands gripping the cantle for balance. It was obvious he'd been around a horse or two. Just how much of a horseman was he? She kicked Diablo into a trot, then a canter to find out. Will stayed put behind her, moving with the horse as if he were a part of it.

"You know your way around livestock. You worked on a ranch?" she asked.

"I've done a little of everything," he answered.

"Like what?" Agnes waited, but Will didn't elaborate.

As usual, Ernesto waited at the tack room door. This time he wasn't chewing on his mustache, but tapping the toe of his boot, his arms crossed tightly across his chest. "You told me you would come back if you needed help. And what are you doing, riding double on Diablo? You want to hurt him? And with a stranger, no less!" Ernesto's Spanish came out angry, fast and hard. Agnes glanced at Will to see if he'd understood, but Will's face was passive and calm as he slipped off the back of the horse. He hadn't touched her, not even bumped against her the whole ride, leaving her as clean as he was dirty. She dismounted and answered Ernesto in Spanish.

"I had all the help I needed, and Diablo's fine. Ernesto, this is Private Bowers. He's been to the house for dinner before, so he's no stranger. Tell Lupe that I'd like to reward Private Bowers with a slice of that excellent cake she made yesterday. We'll wait for it on the porch."

Ernesto raised an eyebrow and opened his mouth as if to argue, but then he clamped his lips together and made for the kitchen, leaving Agnes and Will to unsaddle Diablo. When they were seated side by side on the porch swing, neither of them talking, Lupe came onto the porch.

"*¿Le gustaría un café o té, señor?*" Lupe asked in an imperious tone that was unlike anything Agnes had ever heard from her before. Had her mother put her up to it, and for what purpose? She was about to translate for him when Will stood up and took off his hat as if addressing a fine lady. "*Café,* *por favor, con un poco de azúcar. Gracias señora. Tengo muchas ganas de probar tu maravilloso pastel."*

Lupe melted into a fluttery, giggly girl. "You decide whether my cake is marvelous after you taste it, *Señor*. So, a little sugar in your coffee, coming up." She retreated to the kitchen.

"I don't think Lupe expected you to be able to answer her," Agnes said. "I certainly didn't. How come you didn't speak when Ernesto was lecturing me?"

Will shrugged. "That wasn't my argument. I thought you'd be embarrassed if I intervened. Was Lupe testing me? I wonder if being able to speak Spanish means I passed or failed."

"I know how to find out." Agnes pulled the front door open and found her mother standing on the other side, her ear pressed against the door. She took Mildred by the elbow and led her deeper into the house, where Will couldn't hear their conversation. "Mother! What do you think you're doing?"

"I might ask the same of you," Mildred answered. "The two of you! Riding double! And him, covered with mud!"

"I found a bogged cow. Private Bowers helped me haul her out."

Mildred rolled her eyes. "And what was he doing out there in the rain, I'd like to know. I tell you, Aggie: he's not suitable for you.

"Suitable for what, Mother? We rescued a cow. We didn't apply for a marriage license."

Mildred harrumphed. "Do you know anything about him at all?"

"I know that he can pull a cow from a pothole."

"Does he have money? Is he from a good family? What are his prospects? Why is he just a private? And how does he know Spanish that well?"

"I speak Spanish just as well as he does. So do you. It doesn't mean anything. And I'm not interested in him as a marriage prospect. I just want to give him a piece of cake as a reward for helping me. You know I'd do the same with any of our cowhands."

Mildred's eyes narrowed. It was clear to Agnes that her mother didn't believe her. But it was true.

Agnes sighed. "Mother, he just happened to be in the right place at the right time. I promise you he's no marriage prospect. I wouldn't be interested in him if he was. The Army moves men around. I'm staying here, on the ranch, for the rest of my life."

"So, you need a man who will stay here with you?" Mildred asked.

"Yes. I mean, no! Mother, I don't need a man. Not one who travels. Not one who stays put. I can do this by myself. And stop putting words in my mouth that I didn't say." Agnes scowled at her mother, who beamed gleefully back at her. She turned on her heels and escaped to the porch, where she found Will leaning against the railing, looking out over the desert. His shoulders were slumped and when she stood by his side and looked up at his face, it looked tight and drawn. "I'm sorry," he said in a voice that sounded close to breaking, "I didn't mean to cause problems between you and your mother."

Agnes laid her hand on his. "You didn't cause any problems. This argument between my mother and me is ongoing. It's about. . . "

The door slammed open. Out walked Mildred carrying a tray. "Mind if John and I join you? We could use a bit of company!"

She set the tray down on a side table and called back into the house. "Yoo-hoo! John, dear! We're ready on the porch!"

Mildred gave Will a critical look. The corners of her mouth drooped disapprovingly. "There's a basin out back, near the kitchen door. I've put one of John's shirts out there, too, if you'd care to change. Lupe can wash it after you've gone. . ."

Will thanked Mildred, then bolted down the stairs so quickly that Agnes wondered if he might run all the way back to Camp Columbus and never come back. She glared at her mother, who just shrugged.

"Well, Aggie, if you're going to bring young men home, your father and I have to make them feel welcome."

Before Agnes could think up a suitable retort, her father stepped through the door. He wore his good suit and stroked his mustache, a habit he had when something bothered him. Mildred bustled around, pulling up two rockers and pushing her husband onto the swing.

Will returned, his face and hands pink and shiny from scrubbing. He wore a shirt that was slightly too big for him, the cuffs rolled back, but it was clean. John stood up and shook his hand before he and Mildred took the swing and Agnes and Will seated themselves in the rockers.

"Agnes tells us that the two of you saved one of our cows," Mildred began.

"Pulling bog is no easy feat, son. Takes some practice to do it right. You raised on a ranch?" John asked.

Will, who'd taken off his hat and was studying its bill as if it were the most interesting thing in the world, barely mumbled an answer. "No, sir, but I moved around a bit before I joined the military. Had a number of jobs. Spent some time on a ranch up Springer way."

"Springer has fine ranches! Did you know the Sandlins? Here, have a piece of cake," Mildred said in a chirpy voice. She placed a slice of cake and a fork on each luncheon plate and handed them all round, then poured cups of coffee.

"No, Ma'am. Can't say that I did." Will set aside his hat and accepted the plate, which looked like a plate from a child's tea set in his big hand. He placed the cup and saucer on the little table between him and Agnes.

"What else did you do? Besides ranch work, I mean." John's mustache was full of crumbs and smears of chocolate icing.

Will swallowed hard before answering, then took up the coffee cup. "Worked on engines for the railroad in Belen. In Albuquerque I chauffeured awhile, then worked as an auto mechanic. I've done a bit of construction, too. Roofing."

"My, what a full resume. You weren't raised on a ranch. What did your father do?"

Will swallowed hard, as if the cake had suddenly stuck in his throat. "He managed a business."

"Ah! But you moved frequently. I don't suppose every business man can manage like Frederick Dieter has. The Dieters have been here for years. Established themselves and became a part of the community." Mildred gave her daughter a coy look, letting Agnes know that she had compared the two would-be suitors and found this one lacking. "I don't suppose you've found time to go to college like your friend, Mr. Dieter?"

"No, ma'am. Didn't make it past the eighth grade."

Mildred gasped, but John nodded and started stroking the crumbs out of his mustache.

"Neither did I, son. Sounds like you've made yourself handy, though. Like working with your hands?"

"I like keeping busy. Being useful." Will put down his plate and got to his feet. "Glad I could be of service today. Thank you, Mrs. Day, for your hospitality. Please give *Señora Bernal* my compliments. Mr. Day. Miss Day."

He nodded to each of them and they rose to their feet to see him off. John shook Will's hand solemnly. As Will was going down the stairs, Mildred called after him.

"Tomorrow's Sunday. You'll attend chapel with us at 11 o'clock? And bring that friend of yours! Corporal Bustamante, was it? Sunday dinner follows immediately afterwards."

Will stopped walking, his shoulders hunched up like someone who was avoiding a beating. He turned slowly and took off his hat. "Thank you for the invitation, ma'am. We'll come if we can get leave."

As soon as Will was out of earshot, Mildred Day shook her head and murmured. "Didn't even give back John's shirt. We'll see if he has any better manners tomorrow."

Agnes stared at her mother, wondering what she was up to.

Chapter Four

By the next morning, Agnes was sure she knew exactly what her mother was up to: Mildred Day was determined to embarrass her daughter into never wanting to see Private William Bowers ever again. Agnes had decided that two could play this game. She was determined to embarrass her mother into never wanting to invite any young suitors over. She waited in the courtyard with the hired hands, who were smoking one last round of cigarettes before they had to go in and sit on the flat, hard pews that felt nowhere as comfortable nor as familiar as their saddles. They had all cleaned up, trimmed their whiskers, and were wearing their Sunday best. For a bunch of rough-necked cowboys, they didn't look too bad.

Agnes glanced west. She was not interested in Will Bowers, even if he had proved himself to be a competent horseman who knew a thing or two about cattle. Still, the flat, barren plain that separated the Sunrise Ranch from Columbus looked more empty than usual this morning. For some reason she felt oddly disappointed.

"¡*Señorita! Eres una tía otra vez*!" Ernesto jabbed a thumb over his shoulder, towards the stables.

Agnes smiled as she leaned against the corner of the stables, her arms crossed over her chest. The two tiny javelina piglings were so new that their umbilical cords dragged along.

"Aren't they cute!"

The voice made Agnes jump. She turned and found Private Will Bowers standing there, his campaign hat in one hand, a brown paper package in the other. Agnes looked up and down his clean and freshly ironed uniform as her nerves calmed. "Must you always sneak up on me?"

"That wasn't my intention. Either time. Seems whenever there're animals around, you're so focused on them that you don't notice anything else." He jerked his chin towards the javelinas. "Surprised they're so tame."

"She's come with her babies every spring for as long as I can remember, like it's her intention to introduce me to the new ones. Does that make me part of the family? Ernesto thinks so. When I was little, he called me *Tia Cerdo."*

"Aunt Pig?" Will laughed. "He call you Aunt Cow, too?"

Agnes joined in Will's laughter. She pointed at the javelina, who was licking her babies clean. "Look at what a good mother she is."

Will's face darkened into a frown. "Even wild pigs have better mothers," he muttered, so low that she barely heard him.

The bitterness in his voice made Agnes gasp. "Are you talking about my mother?"

Will's face went even darker. "Yours? Why, no! Miss Day, I apologize that you even thought that. Please, forget I said that. It just came out; a thought, but not something I should have shared."

They watched the pigs in an uneasy silence, the mood ruined. What had he been referring to, and why would he not want to talk about it?

"So," Agnes said, trying to change the subject and bring them back to a comfortable place, "How long have you and Heinrich been friends?"

"We aren't really," Will said. "David, the Corporal who came to your party, went into town to buy something at the dry goods, and Dieter invited him to have supper with a local. He really had no idea what he was getting into, but the thought of home cooking appealed to him. He invited me to come along."

"So you had no idea what you were getting into, either?"

Will shook his head. "Absolutely none. Just looking out for a friend."

The chapel bell rang, and as they turned to go, Will touched Agnes' arm tentatively. "What's chapel like?"

Agnes shrugged. "Like any other church service."

"That's the thing: I've never been in a church."

Agnes stopped walking and stared at Will as if he'd said he was born on the moon. She had never known anyone who hadn't been to church, didn't even know that it was possible.

"I don't come from a family of church goers," Will said apologetically, "but that doesn't mean I can't start now, does it? I'm still allowed in, right?"

Agnes smiled broadly and took his arm. "Of course you are. Don't worry. I'll help you. And I'll help Corporal Bustamante, too, if you convinced him to return."

"His name's Benavides, not Bustamante, and no, he didn't come. I brought someone else. I think you'll like him." As they entered the courtyard, Agnes noticed that her father was talking to a soldier who towered over him. That was a rarity. John Day was well over six feet, but this soldier was even taller. Agnes' mother stood by on tiptoes, as if her words couldn't possibly reach such heights otherwise. Agnes noted the chevrons on the man's sleeve.

Will pulled off his hat. "Good morning, Mrs. Day. Mr. Day. I see you've met Sergeant Dobbs. Sergeant, this is Miss Day."

Sergeant Dobbs doffed his hat and smiled, showing off two dimples in his pink- tinged cheeks. He had chocolate brown eyes and a smattering of freckles across his nose that made him look like a schoolboy. A very big schoolboy. "I was telling your mother how nice it was of her to include us. I hope it's not too much trouble."

Mildred laughed and eyed the brown paper package in Will's hand. "With all the hands we have on the ranch, a couple more mouths won't matter, not one little bit. Did you bring us a present? That wasn't necessary."

Will's cream and coffee skin flushed as he handed over the package. "It's no present. It's Mr. Day's shirt."

Mildred tugged apart the paper and looked inside. "All clean, pressed, and folded up right. Does the Army have a laundry service that does this?"

Will's face went even redder. "It does, ma'am. But they're not open Saturday evenings."

"Oh! Aren't we the handy one! Let's go in, shall we?" Mildred placed the shirt and its brown paper wrappings on the porch, then they crossed into the chapel's cool, whitewashed interior. They walked up the center aisle, past four rows of pews. As she guided the two soldiers into the front row, Agnes watched Will's head pan the front of the church, following her father as he took his place behind the lectern on the left, then her mother as she scooted onto the organ bench behind the tall, foot-pump pipe organ that sat at an angle on the right. He looked somber, overawed by the little chapel. She glanced up at Sergeant Dobbs, who beamed down at her appreciatively, smiling as if he were thoroughly enjoying himself.

"Number three hundred ten," Mildred called out. Agnes made a show of taking the hymnal from the rack under the pew while Bowers and Dobbs copied her. She turned to the hymn and immediately wondered if her mother had chosen it specifically for the two men sitting on either side of her.

Be an overcomer, only cowards yield
When the foe they meet on the battlefield;
We are blood-bought princes of the royal host,
And must falter not, nor desert our post.

Never yield a step in the hottest fight,
God will send you help from the realms of light;
In Jehovah's might put the foe to flight,
And the victor's crown you shall wear at last.

Be an overcomer, forward boldly go,
You are strong enough if you count it so—
Strong enough to conquer through sustaining grace,
And to overcome every foe you face.

Everyone sang, even the ranch hand who was known for his ability to sing only two notes, both of them flat. The hands jokingly called it singing for their supper, for only those who attended chapel could eat Lupe's famous Sunday dinner. Agnes worried that her two guests wouldn't know what to do, but when Sergeant Dobbs picked up the bass line and Private Bowers began to sing tenor, she happily switched to alto. The blending of their harmonies encouraged the others to sing even louder. Agnes watched her mother's smile broaden.

After three more hymns, Agnes' father stepped behind the lectern, put on a pair of reading glasses, and cleared his throat. "A reading from Romans, the thirteenth chapter, verse four: *For the one in authority is God's servant for your good. But if you do wrong, be afraid, for rulers do not bear the sword for no reason. They are God's servants, agents of wrath to bring punishment down on the wrongdoers.*" John slammed the big Bible closed with such force that the sound of it echoed like a thunderclap and made everyone jump. He took off his glasses and scowled at the two men sitting on either side of Agnes for a long while before he went on to talk about obeying authority. Agnes was sure it was a warning, and that her mother had put her father up to the fire and brimstone sermon that followed. Mildred Day must have invited Will so that John would scare him away.

Agnes glanced sideways, first at Will and then at Sergeant Dobbs. Neither man squirmed. In fact, the sergeant was smiling and nodding, and Will looked thoughtful and interested. Agnes smiled and chuckled inwardly, pleased that they had enough backbone to not be intimidated. If they were willing to play along at a game they didn't even know they were playing, she was going to make her mother very uncomfortable.

Mildred led the congregation in a rousing rendition of *Onward, Christian Soldiers* before John dismissed them. Agnes hooked one hand in Will's arm and the other in the Sergeant's and they walked three abreast down the aisle. "For someone who claims he's never been in a church, you're pretty good at the hymn singing."

"I wasn't familiar with any of those songs, but I can read music well enough," Will said.

"Me, I'm used to old-timey hymn sings. I was raised Methodist. My mother plays the piano at my church. We have something in common." Sergeant Dobbs smiled down at her. She couldn't help but smile back. His cheeks were so pink that she was tempted to pinch them.

"You both have excellent voices," Agnes said.

"Bowers and I are in the Company glee club. Will's also our back-up pianist. He plays ragtime like nobody can," Sergeant Dobbs added.

Agnes turned to Will to comment, but his face had darkened again, like it had when they were watching the javelinas. She swallowed her words, confused and unsure what was bothering him.

"My! What singers the two of you are!" Mildred said when she caught up with the trio outside the chapel. She smiled brightly, not seeming to notice that Agnes' arms were intertwined with both men.

"Thank you, ma'am! Singing is easy when one has an accomplished accompanist to lead the way." Sergeant Dobbs' comment left Mildred spluttering and tongue-tied for only a moment.

"Well, now! I hope you've worked up a good appetite. Our Lupe makes a Sunday dinner so big that the house can't contain it." Mildred gestured towards the barn, which, like every Sunday, had been swept out, its occupants put out to pasture. Ernesto and some of the hands had laid planks over sawhorses and collected every chair and stool in the entire compound. Because she thought it was a little brazen and would mortify her mother, Agnes seated herself between the soldiers. Her mother and father sat across from them. When everyone was seated, Lupe carried out platters of roasts, bowls of beaten potatoes, canned corn, beans, baskets of biscuits, and four kinds of pie. Will offered to help her, but she waved him off: Sunday dinner was Lupe's chance to shine for the extended family that was the Sunrise Ranch.

Agnes didn't speak much: she was too busy watching the Sergeant ingratiate himself with her mother. Sergeant Dobbs was charming and witty, and it was clear that her mother enjoyed talking with him about his childhood on a farm and his exploits in the Army. John was his usual, quiet self, but on occasion he, too, would nod and comment appreciatively about something the Sergeant said. Will, on Agnes' other side, was largely silent. Once Agnes glanced over at him and saw him watching her face carefully, his pale brown coyote eyes boring into her.

"He's good company, isn't he?" Will's voice was so quiet that no one else could have heard.

"My mother seems quite taken with him," Agnes answered.

"And you?"

"I'm glad you brought him."

Will nodded and averted his eyes, while Agnes wondered what that was all about. Had he and her mother made some kind of a pact to find a suitable match for her? The idea annoyed her so much she wanted to spit, but doing so would bring a torrent of objections from her mother. She fought the urge to tell him off, right there and then, in front of everybody. She didn't need him or her mother finding a spouse for her. She was fine on her own.

"Having dinner in the barn is a brilliant idea!" The Sergeant waved his fork around, as if blessing the place with his good opinion.

"When Agnes' sisters were still at home, we used to do quite a bit of entertaining here," Mildred said. "Of course, we had our formal dinners in the dining room, but the barn was perfect for the informal affairs that young people love. Oh! The ice cream socials we would have! And the dances! Weren't they fun, John?"

Mildred turned to her husband, who had been silently slicing his meat and chewing thoughtfully, his eyes on his plate. He looked up and grunted an acknowledgement. "Yes, Mother. Those were the days."

"Say! Why don't we have a dance, John! It's been so long! And times have changed. Instead of just square dance sets, let's let the young people do some of the more popular dances. What's popular now? The Foxtrot?"

"If you say so, Mother." John nodded and put another forkful of meat into his mouth.

Mildred turned towards Agnes and the two soldiers. "We'll invite every young person in the county. Let's set a date, say, not this Saturday, but Saturday next? Won't that be fun? That would be, what? . . . March twelfth?"

"March eleventh, ma'am. And fun? I should say so!" Sergeant Dobbs turned to Agnes, his face radiant. "Miss Day, would you do me the honor of the first dance?"

Agnes felt herself blushing. "I'd be delighted to, as will all the girls in the county. I'm sure your name will be on every dance card." Agnes turned to Will. The irritation she felt at his feeble attempts at matchmaking came through in her voice, which was even sharper than she had intended. "And how about you, Will? Care to dance the second dance with me?"

Will looked up, and his eyes were full of pain. "I don't dance."

Agnes balled up her napkin and was trying to decide whose face to throw it in: her mother's, Will's, or the Sergeant's, when she looked at her father. John Day narrowed one of his eyes ever so slightly. He shook his head a tiny bit, letting her know that he saw she was about to have a snit and wanted none of it. Agnes closed her eyes and took a deep breath, smoothing the napkin over her thighs.

"Fine. I didn't want to dance with you, anyway," she muttered at Will, whose only response was to stare harder at his plate.

"Bowers, here, can play for us! He's crackerjack at the keyboard! Mrs. Day, do you have a piano we could bring into the barn?" Sergeant Dobbs and Mildred continued to make plans, oblivious of Agnes' narrowly avoided eruption.

Agnes turned to Will, but he wouldn't meet her gaze. For the rest of the meal, Agnes wondered how her plan to mortify her mother had gone so wrong. All she wanted was to be left alone to manage the ranch. She didn't want a husband. So why did she feel humiliated and rejected by a lowly Private who was trying to set her up with his friend the sergeant? She didn't know whether she wanted to cry or shout, but one thing she did know: if her mother's plan was to humiliate her and make her want to never see Private William Bowers again, then she had succeeded.

Chapter Five

Agnes awoke in the middle of a dream.

Pop . . . pop . . . pop, pop . . . pop.

What was that? Fireworks? It wasn't July Fourth. Popcorn? She fumbled for her alarm clock. It read half-past four.

The intermittent popping changed into a continuous barrage, like the purr of a contented cat. It stopped, then started again, stopped, and started.

The horizon glowed. Sunrise, Agnes thought groggily, then shook her head. She was looking west, towards the town of Columbus.

Agnes' mind woke with one, sickening lurch of reason. The sun didn't rise in the west. The glow had to be a fire. And the pops and purrs weren't fireworks. They were firearms and machine guns.

Heinrich had said that Will was a machine gunner. Camp Columbus was just south and west of the town.

Target practice, she told herself, but that didn't seem right, either.

She had to know what was happening. Agnes leaped out of bed and into her clothes. She raced downstairs, grabbed her coat and hat in the kitchen, and rushed to the stables. Diablo's nostrils flared and his flanks quivered as she slid his bit into his mouth, threw on his saddle, cinched it down, and mounted. Diablo spun around and bolted west. Agnes, usually so careful to warm him up before he ran, gave him his head, trusting him. They thundered down the dark dirt road until Diablo had worn out his nervousness. He slowed, blowing air and sweating in the cold night air.

Agnes, too, felt herself pulling back. The popping and purring were gone, the night silent. Yet the lurid glow remained. She began to feel very foolish for being out alone at night, and riding towards who knows what. Her mother was going to be furious at her.

She reached where the road passed just a few hundred yards north of Camp Columbus and saw tents lit from the inside like boxy Chinese lanterns. Dark silhouettes raced between the tents, shouting at each other. Agnes sensed the frenzy of the movement, the desperation to bring a situation under control. She had felt that herself as she threw on her clothes. Now she was seeing and hearing it multiplied by an army. Diablo, too, sensed it. He pawed the ground, snorting, his nose flared. She swallowed hard and reached down to pat his neck, encouraging both him and herself. Diablo danced in a circle as if asking her if she wanted to go forward, turn into the camp, or return home. The glow over Columbus compelled her toward it. The phrase 'like a moth to a flame' crossed her mind and she brushed it aside, refusing to consider it. She wouldn't return to the Sunrise until she knew what the popping and the glow was.

Behind her the sky lightened and took on a glow that mirrored the one in the west. Dawn was coming, and with it, she hoped, clarity. Surely everything would be easier to understand in the clear light of day. The lurid light from the fire paled in the dawn. A column of black, roiling smoke appeared.

As she neared the town, and the sound of the men in the camp faded, a dull roar and crackle took its place. Several houses and stores were on fire. Flames leapt from the roof of the Commercial Hotel. The entire building, one of the tallest in town, was engulfed. Every window framed an inferno. As she watched, one window shattered, spilling glass onto the street and filling the air with sparks. Piles of clothing lay on the road. Had people thrown them from the hotel windows?

Agnes set the scene to rights in her mind. While tragic, fires were not that uncommon, especially in places like hotels, where people weren't settled into a routine as they were at home. All it took was someone leaving an article of clothing too close to a gas lamp, a cigar ash dropping into the bedclothes, and a fire was the sure result. Had the Commercial been storing ammunition for the Camp? That would explain the gunfire.

A group, presumably the occupants of the Hotel, huddled together in the street. Agnes rode toward them. William Ritchie, the proprietor, was a friend of her father's. She could only imagine the desolation he must be feeling as he watched his entire establishment disappear into a pile of ashes.

"Mr. Ritchie?" At her voice the men, who had been looking toward the Hotel, jumped and turned towards her, swiveling something in their midst.

A machine gun.

Agnes threw her hands into the air, startling Diablo, who reared. She scrambled to regain the reins.

"Identify yourself." A man stepped toward Agnes. He was barefoot, his military tunic hung unbuttoned over his pants. Gold bars on his shoulder epaulets identified him as a lieutenant.

"Agnes Day. I'm from the Sunrise Ranch, just east of here. Where's Mr. Ritchie? The man who owns this hotel. He get his boarders out all right?"

Will stood up and stepped toward her, separating himself from the other men. He wore nothing but a red union suit. Agnes broke into hysterical laughter at the absurdity. A machine gun? In Columbus? Will Bowers in long johns? It made no sense. Will glanced down at himself, then went into a hunch, turning sideways.

"Private Bowers, you know this woman? See that she gets home safely!" the Lieutenant ordered.

Will snapped a sharp salute. "Yes, sir. Permission to dress and get a mount, Lieutenant Lucas?"

"Granted, but be quick about it." The lieutenant waved his hand and his men formed a protective circle around Agnes while Will ran towards camp. "You shouldn't be here, Miss. Too dangerous."

"I'm sorry. I saw the light. It's visible a long way away."

Lieutenant Lucas nodded. "I should think so. We've had quite a night here. Go home. Don't return until you receive official word that Columbus is safe. If you're worried for your safety out on the ranch, we could set up a perimeter."

"Against what?" Agnes asked.

"Villistas," the lieutenant said. "It's time we do a sweep of the town. Can someone escort this woman to camp so she can reconnoiter with Private Bowers?"

"I'll do that, Lieutenant." Agnes recognized the short, dark soldier who snapped a salute as Corporal Benavides, the other man who had accompanied Heinrich Dieter to her birthday dinner. Lucas gave his head a jerk, indicating that she should follow him back up the road.

"What did he mean, Villistas?" Agnes asked Benavides as soon as they were moving.

"You've endangered everyone," he said brusquely.

Agnes sighed, exasperated by all the answers that weren't answers at all. "A hotel burned down. Was it storing ammunition? Is that what caused all that racket?"

Corporal Benavides glared up at her. "Are you really that dense? Columbus was attacked by Mexican revolutionaries last night. General Villa's men."

Agnes shook her head, as if denying his words would make them untrue. "My father says revolutionaries wouldn't dare cross the border and attack Americans."

"Your father's wrong." Benavides spat the words out. "They did. Looted stores. Stole horses. Killed people. Didn't you see the bodies in the street in front of the hotel?"

Agnes pulled Diablo to a halt. Those bundles of clothes in front of the hotel - were they bundles? Or bodies? How had she missed that? Was it the dim light, or her own stubborn unwillingness to see what she didn't want to see? Her hand started to shake, making Diablo dance and snort. She stuffed her fist into her mouth to suppress another hysterical laugh. Or maybe a scream, she wasn't sure which. "Who? Who died?"

Benavides scowled at her. "I don't think you'd know the soldiers' names, and I don't know the names of the civilians. At least not yet. There'll be a formal report that'll sort it all out. But we got more of them than they got us. There's Bowers. Let him answer your questions."

Will Bowers rode up on an Army mule. He was dressed in his uniform, and looked composed and solemn. He and Benavides nodded at each other, and the Corporal turned back to join his platoon. Will held out his hand, offering Agnes the lead, then fell into place beside her.

"I didn't know," Agnes said, her tiny voice edging into despair.

"Of course you didn't. It surprised us all." Will hesitated a moment, then added. "You've got to be more careful. Don't rush into danger. I don't want you hurt."

Agnes nodded, acknowledging the wisdom of his words without really thinking about what he'd said. "Corporal Benavides said people died."

She looked over at Will, who was staring at the hand that clenched his reins.

"Lots of people. More Villistas than Americans. There'll be a full report." Will leaned his head back, looking up at the morning sky. The sun had risen completely, and meadowlarks sang from the mesquite bushes. Riding east, the morning looked beautiful, fresh, and full of promise. Over their shoulders, black smoke billowed from the Commercial Hotel like a bruise on a child's pink cheek. "It happened so fast, and it was dark, chaotic. I think the proprietor of that hotel got it. And some of his guests."

Tears sprang to Agnes' eyes. William Richey had been to her house for dinner many times. He was a congenial man, quick to laugh, with a good eye for both business and making life pleasurable. It would hurt her father to know that his friend was dead. She heard a sob and looked, astonished, at Will, who quickly wiped his face and looked away.

"And Dobbs," he added.

"Sergeant Dobbs? The man who came to chapel with you?"

Will nodded. "Shot through the body, but he wouldn't leave us. Continued firing the machine gun until he'd bled out."

Agnes convulsed into wracking sobs of loss and fear, embarrassment and relief. She cried for Mr. Richey, who had enlivened the little town of Columbus, and for Sergeant Dobbs, the pink-cheeked giant with the beautiful voice. She cried for the destruction of the hotel, and the terror that the occupants must have felt. She cried that people could be so angry, or so desperate, or so cruel that they would flow over the border and do this. And she cried out of humiliation that she had ridden into a hornet's nest without thinking of what damage she might have caused. When was she going to learn to not rush impetuously into situations? But mostly, she cried for the young man who rode beside her, tears streaming down his face. She had no words to support him that didn't seem trivial or insensitive.

Agnes saw a small figure on horseback heading west, toward them, and riding hard. As he neared, Agnes recognized Ernesto. He drew up, pulling on the reins as he slowed his lathered horse.

"*Gracias a Dios* I find you," Ernesto said breathlessly, mixing English and Spanish as he did when he was flustered. "We have been looking everywhere. Your father, he has had a heart attack."

"No!" The word came out as a shriek. Just before she kicked Diablo into a gallop, she heard Will shout that he would go for the doctor, but she was in too much of a rush to answer. Agnes rode, hell-bent, for home, leaving Will and Ernesto in her dust.

When Will rode up to the Big House, Agnes was standing on the porch, her arms wrapped around the post. Sweat streaked his dust-covered face, and his mule's sides were lathered from the hard run. "Doctor Pritchard's on his way," he said as he reined in, just in front of her. "I helped him hitch up his carriage, then rode back quick as I could. How's your father?"

Agnes opened her mouth to answer. Nothing came out but an anguished sob. She closed her eyes and leaned her forehead against the post, hugging it so tightly that its corners bit into her arms. In a moment, he had dismounted and was by her, his hand resting gently on her shoulder. "He's gone, Private Bowers. Lying there as if he were asleep, but cold. My mother wanted me to stay with him, but I couldn't! I just couldn't!"

She let go of the pole and turned towards him, searching his eyes for comfort. Instead, she saw her own misery and pain reflected back at her. "It's my fault. All my fault. If I'd been here instead of chasing a glow in the sky, I could have saved him."

"How?" Will asked. Agnes opened her mouth to answer, but could think of nothing to say. She didn't know the first thing about stopping a heart attack. Still, if she'd stayed in her bed, where she belonged, perhaps her father never would have had a heart attack in the first place. Sobs overwhelmed her, and she buried her head in his chest.

The door opened and Lupe stepped out onto the porch, shielding her eyes from the sun as she looked at the dust cloud on the dirt road. "Who's that in the carriage? We will not have mourners yet, no?"

"It's the doctor. The one from town," Will answered.

"Bueno. I will tell La Dama, and she will come down to meet him. She will not like seeing the two of you like that." Lupe smiled a little apologetically, then disappeared back into the house. Agnes pulled herself out of Will's arms and wiped tears from her face with the sleeve of her shirt. She suspected she looked just as disheveled and streaked as he did, but she didn't care. "What am I going to do? I don't know anything about the business side of running a ranch."

"Plenty of people will help you. Ernesto, for starters." Will looked at the carriage that was closing in on them. "I'll take the doctor's horse and my mule to the stables and attend to them. Where's your horse?"

Agnes shrugged. "I left him right here when I got home. Maybe Ernesto took care of him? Maybe he wandered back to the stables on his own?"

Will nodded. "I'll see to him." He stepped off the porch and shook the doctor's hand, thanking him for coming, then unhitched the doctor's horse and led it and his mule away.

Doctor Pritchard barely crossed the threshold before Mildred clambered down the stairs and threw himself into his arms. "Oh, Doctor! Thank God you're here! You can't imagine what a shock it was to my system to wake up and find my husband, lying there cold and stiff. I! Sleeping next to a dead man! You cannot imagine the horror! The shock to my system!"

"Indeed, I cannot." Doctor Pritchard pulled out his stethoscope and listened to Mildred's chest, his bushy eyebrows knit together in concern. "It's a good thing, Mrs. Day, that you have a sound constitution."

"I screamed for Agnes until I was hoarse. When she didn't come, I ran to Ernesto's place. Barefoot! In nothing but my nightgown! My hair streaming out behind me! Doubtless I looked like a madwoman!"

"Then it is a good thing no one was here to see you." Doctor Pritchard patted Mildred's shoulder. "Shock or no, your heart is fine and your health good. I suggest you put your feet up and let Lupe get you a nice cup of tea while I go in and take a look at John."

As soon as he had climbed the stairs, Mildred scowled at Agnes. "He certainly didn't show much sympathy."

"He's got a lot on his mind right now. Columbus is in a shambles" Agnes settled her mother into one of the upholstered chairs. She held her hand while Mildred continued to babble on about the shock, and how horrible it was to be left alone. Agnes winced, knowing that her mother blamed her for not being there just as much as she blamed herself.

Doctor Pritchard reentered the parlor much quicker than Agnes had expected and dropped rather wearily into the big leather chair.

"That's John's chair," Mildred said sharply.

"So it is. You'll have to excuse me. It's been a long day already." Doctor Pritchard hauled himself upright. He looked around, then folded his big frame so that he could sit on the footstool. "Mrs. Day, you can be comforted by the fact that your husband passed away peacefully in his sleep. It appears he had a heart attack, hours before the first shot was fired in Columbus. I'm sure he didn't feel a thing."

He turned and looked at Agnes. "It was those shots, was it not Miss Day, that roused you from your sleep?"

"It was," Agnes said.

The doctor nodded. "Your father was dead long before you left the house. Now, I'm not saying that there's anything prudent in a young woman leaving her house in the middle of the night, especially to chase after sounds she can't identify. You were lucky that you didn't get yourself killed. But I am saying it had no bearing whatsoever in your father's demise."

Agnes slumped and began crying again, this time from relief.

"You should be crying, after all the terror you caused me. When will you ever learn to think before you act?" Mildred stopped talking and Agnes, following her mother's gaze, saw Will standing in the doorway, his hat in his hands. "Private Bowers, you will go to Dieter's Dry goods and send some telegrams. John had a lot of friends and business partners who'll want to know about this. And the girls and their families. I will make a list." Mildred rummaged through the desk while Agnes escorted the Doctor and Will out.

"Thank you for coming," she said numbly, then almost laughed at the absurdity of the phrase. She knew it was what she was supposed to say, but it seemed so trite. But what else was there to say? What could she say that wouldn't start her wailing again? Both men muttered that it was their pleasure and then went to the stables. They'd harnessed up the Doctor's carriage before Mildred came out with her list. Will tucked it into his breast pocket and the two men went back to town. Agnes leaned against the doorframe and watched them go. Behind her, her mother wailed miserably. Agnes could not bring herself to comfort her, not when she felt her mother accused her of bringing on this misery. She had never felt so alone.

Chapter Six

For the next week, as the community of Columbus occupied itself with funerals, wakes, and burials, Agnes tried to put her grief aside and begin the process of taking over the family business. Due to their own bereavement, Mildred refused to let anyone from the Day household leave the property. The Day family was so integral to the community that it came to her. Within days, half the prominent families in the county had come to pay their respects. They lounged about on the front porch and occupied every seat in the dining room and the parlor. Cigar-smoking men on the front porch and women crowded into the kitchen argued about who was to blame for Columbus' pillaging, for the weather, the economy, and countless other annoyances and tragedies, great and small. Agnes watched the sea of faces, looking for a sign that people blamed her for her father's death and for leaving her mother alone. Doc Pritchard's assurances hadn't assuaged her guilt for her father's death and for leaving her mother alone.

She distracted herself from her guilt and from the crowds by taking her father's account books and letters up to her room and trying to learn all she could about the business of running a ranch, but the rows of figures flummoxed and overwhelmed her. Fear of her own inadequacies drove her back out to the range. Agnes changed out of the dress her mother made her wear, and into her beloved dungarees and flannel shirt. In the saddle her shoulders relaxed and she could breathe again.

In spite of loving them, Agnes was not looking forward to her sisters returning to the Sunrise. They were older, and tended to lecture Agnes as if she were still a child. Furthermore, it was hard to argue with their success, even if it was not the kind of success she wanted.

Charlotte arrived first. Agnes watched her neighbors flow down the porch steps and crowd the fancy new, two door Chevrolet touring car that Charlotte had rode up in with her two sons and her husband. Charlotte elbowed her way through the crowd of gawkers. She hugged Agnes tightly. "How are you holding up? How's mother?" she whispered in Agnes' ear even though everyone was too distracted by the car to hear them.

"I'm all right, I guess. It's been hard. Mother is pretty shaken."

"As she should be. Married nearly forty years, and now alone."

The word *alone* made Agnes wince. Did Charlotte mean it as a barb?

"And as if father dying wasn't enough! You know the Columbus attack has made all the papers. Even nationally. It's horrible," Charlotte said, yet her face didn't look stricken. Agnes nodded but didn't know what to say. For days she had listened to people talk about it as if it were some exciting story and not a tragic reality. She supposed she would have seen more grief had she been able to attend one of the funerals in town, but she hadn't. The distance between here and town was enough to distance people from the horror.

"I heard the Dieter family cowered in the back of a deep closet as their dry goods store was looted. When are you going to start taking care of your hair?" Charlotte pinched a few bobbed locks in her fingers and frowned.

Agnes pulled back and brushed the hair from her face. "I keep it washed and clean. What more do you want? And hiding was the smart thing to do. Mr. Moore and C.C. Miller both tried to defend their stores. They got shot, and both the mercantile and the drug store were set ablaze."

"Something more attractive than a bob. You look like Buster Brown." Charlotte chucked Agnes under the chin. "I'm glad Heinrich wasn't hurt. I suppose he's been around, consoling you?"

Agnes slapped Charlotte's hand away and made the excuse that she needed to help Ernesto wrangle Charlotte's trunks up the stairs.

Beatrice, her husband and their three sons followed later that afternoon, having driven from Dona Ana in a Studebaker carriage whose roof was laden with so many trunks that it looked like an overland stagecoach delivering a year's worth of goods.

"Are you being kind to Mama?" Beatrice asked as she gave Agnes a two-cheek kiss that made Agnes feel like her sister was putting on French airs.

Agnes nodded. "I'm trying not to ask her too many questions about running the ranch. There's so much I don't know."

Beatrice's husband Stanley, raised an eyebrow. "All the more reason to get rid of the place."

"Sell the Sunrise? It's our legacy. There's still a lot for me to learn, but Ernesto and Lupe are here to help. Maybe in a few years, one of the nephews will want to join me. It's in their blood, after all."

Stanley didn't argue, but a knowing look passed between him and Beatrice, adding to the growing sense of paranoia Agnes had felt since her father died.

The next day, sister Maude came down from Las Vegas in a hired wagon with her husband and two boys. A few hours later Elsie, her husband and the final nephew showed up at the train station after a ten-hour ride from Albuquerque. Agnes didn't go downstairs to greet them. She watched her sisters stroll about the dusty yard in their fine, lace trimmed dresses and thought they didn't belong here anymore. Each sister had married a man with a bright future: A banker with aspirations to be a senator, a civil engineer who designed roads for the state, a railroad executive, and a professor of architecture at the College of Agriculture and Mechanical Arts. None were the least interested in the Sunrise Ranch. It was up to her, and her alone, to keep the place going.

It was a heavy burden. Going through the papers and accounts, she found running the Sunrise harder than she had imagined. Agnes stared out the window at the expanse of sagebrush and wished she could just ride fence and bring in the herd, like one of the hands.

She noticed Will and Ernesto draping the chapel with black crepe. They seemed to be together a lot lately. She had seen them fixing a fence once. Another time, she turned the corner and found Will feeding the chickens, a job that was usually Lupe's. She found comfort in watching him work. He was so much like her father: quiet and steady, dependable and hardworking. There was nothing flashy about him, nothing awkward like Dietrich's guffaw. He knew hoof stock and was handy around the buildings. It was a shame that he was in the Army and would be moving on soon. If he were willing to stay, he might be just the kind of man she needed.

The next day L.B. Fowler, the family attorney, and his wife arrived from Silver City. While Mr. Fowler and Mildred locked themselves away in the study, Agnes sat with her sisters and Mrs. Fowler, listening to visitors from Columbus talk about how they had defended themselves with rifles and shotguns. They claimed that four machine gun emplacements had fired an astonishing 20,000 rounds during the 90-minute fight. Agnes listened to the thunder of eight sets of boys' boots running up and down the stairs, and thought it sounded much like the *pop pop pop* of machine guns. People gleefully related how, after Villa left his dead and wounded and slipped back into Mexico, they had dragged dead Villistas and their horses to a pit, doused them with kerosene, and set them on fire. It made Agnes shudder, remembering the bundles of clothing that hadn't been bundles at all. She looked around at faces bright with conversation and felt a little sick to her stomach. If they had been there and seen what she had seen, they wouldn't be speaking of it as if it was an event in some dime store novel.

The funeral service occurred on a stultifyingly warm afternoon. As she lined up with her sisters, Agnes told herself that the ordeal was almost over. Service, burial, reception. She could count the events she had to endure on one hand, with fingers to spare. Then the crowd would go away, her sisters return to their homes, and she could truly settle into managing the ranch.

She looked forward to the solitude and silence. Without the constant chatter or conversation and the chaos of her nephews underfoot she would be able to think.

Someone said it was time, and the group walked through the front door of the Big House and through the crowd that lingered in the chapel's doorway. Ernesto and Will had packed the chapel with every chair the family owned, making the aisle down which they marched so narrow that they had to go single file, and the whole procession had to wait as Charlotte and Maude elbowed each other for the privilege of walking behind their mother to support her. They packed into the front pew. Agnes felt a trickle of sweat run down her back like a tear. She squeezed her eyes tightly closed and felt the sting of salty sweat in them.

Beatrice's husband, the college professor, gave the oration. Each of the other husbands and several business associates and fellow ranchers added their own remembrances. The nephews wiggled and whispered. Their mothers shushed them. Mildred insisted on playing the organ. When she broke down halfway through the second verse of *Abide with Me,* Will slid beside her on the organ bench and finished the hymn. Agnes watched the muscles of his back move under his pressed khaki shirt. The harmonies in his rendition did not match what was written in the hymnal, but they were lovely.

After the speechifying and hymn singing, the brothers-in-law carried the coffin to a small plot ringed by a white picket fence. Agnes studied the four fine granite stones of her grandmother, her two uncles, and an aunt who had died young. Her father had been born on the Sunrise Ranch in the summer of 1861, just before grandfather had ridden off to join the Confederate Army. He had never returned. Agnes' grandmother had struggled to keep the ranch going. She'd brought Ernesto's father and mother up from Mexico to help. When he was old enough, her father had taken over. Now the ranch was her responsibility. She threw her handful of dirt onto the coffin and promised her father that she would continue to build on his legacy.

While Will and Ernesto tamped down the dirt, the family wandered back to the barn. Lupe, who usually insisted on doing all the cooking, had allowed the local chapter of The Daughters of the Confederacy to help. Together they had laid out a huge spread of pulled pork and buns, coleslaw and pies. Agnes hesitated in the doorway, studying the swirling crowd. It looked more like the food tent at the County Fair than a funeral. Everyone who was anyone in southwestern New Mexico was there, many to see and be seen rather than to honor a great man who had touched many lives. She picked out the family lawyer, the local doctor, the Commander of Camp Columbus, the President of the Agricultural College, even the second lieutenant who had been the barefoot hero of the machine gun emplacements. None looked very bereaved. Agnes turned her back to the tent and spat in disgust.

She turned back around and studied the crowd until she picked out her own family. Surrounded by her daughters, Mildred, draped in black silk and wearing a veiled hat with enormous, glossy black feathers, was once again regaling an audience with the pitiful tale of how she awoke to find her husband cold and dead, and no one - no one! - was there to help her. Agnes squeezed her eyes shut to keep the tears from flowing. Her mother had become a sympathetic, tragic figure, and, even though no one had said it, she was sure that it was all at her expense. Surely everyone looked at her and saw what a thoughtless, heartless person she was. If only she'd stayed home the night of the Columbus Raid. None of this would have happened.

Frederick Dieter and his wife Sophie, dressed in clothes that would have looked fine at the opera, were there with their son, Heinrich, who was wearing a gray sack suit that Agnes was sure must be fashionable back east, although she'd never seen anything like it out here in New Mexico. The three of them worked the room, shaking hands like this was a political campaign, not a funeral. Heinrich looked up and his eyes caught Agnes'. He excused himself from his parents and came to her, his hand fishing in his vest pocket until he brought out an envelope.

"I made copies for you, your sisters, and your mother," he said. "I thought you might all want a print."

Agnes opened the envelope and looked at the photograph that Lupe had taken on her birthday. Her father was off in the left-hand corner of the print, yet it was his face that drew her attention first, his eyes serious and serene, his grave smile barely discernible beneath his mustache. She tore her eyes from him and looked at herself, bored and petulant in the middle of the grouping. Heinrich beamed on her right. Next to him, Corporal David Benavides, the National Guard dispatch rider, glowered at the camera as if picking a fight with it. Will stood beside him, and a little distant from the group. He looked lost and distant as he stared off into space instead of at the camera. He must have moved, for his image was a little blurred.

Her eyes trailed back to the left, where her mother, obviously preening and in love with the camera, stood between her and her father. Next to him, the words "Aggie's b-day 2-15-16' were scrawled in Heinrich's handwriting on a white area. Agnes swallowed the lump in her throat. Her father looked so much like her memory of him, so serious and silent. Her eyes lingered on him, as if she expected her father's black and white image to open its mouth and tell her that she hadn't caused his death, that everything would turn out all right.

"Thank you, Heinrich," Agnes' voice choked on the lump in her throat.

"What are friends for?" he answered.

The noise and laughter bubbling out of the room suddenly seemed too incongruous, too bright. Agnes turned her back on Heinrich before he could see the tears welling in her eyes. She escaped to the back of the stables, to the same spot where she had seen the mother javelina show off her babies only two short weeks ago.

Will Bowers stepped up beside her and leaned his shovel against the wall. "Ernesto and I are done. He tells me Lupe's going to plant marigolds. It's going to look really pretty."

Agnes tried to smile, to thank Will for his help, but an aching melancholy blocked her words.

"I didn't make you jump this time." Will slapped his hands together, then rolled down his shirt sleeves and buttoned the cuffs.

Agnes shrugged. "No baby pigs to distract me."

Will gave her a little jab with his elbow. "And here I thought maybe you were just getting used to me sneaking up on you."

"I've got a lot of things to get used to. I don't think I can do it."

"You can do it. You're a strong woman. Stubborn, and determined," Will said.

Agnes leaned her cheek against Will's shoulder and breathed in the smell of earth and salt on clean skin. "When I was little, sitting in chapel, I thought that my Father was God. Later, I figured out that he was just a man. Still, whenever I picture God, he's got that same deep, mellow voice, the same stern look. I can't let that image fade! I can't forget what he looked like. What he sounded like." Agnes buried her face in Will's chest and he enveloped her in his arms. His warmth radiated through the khaki cloth, and the measured beating of his heart comforted her.

"It's terrible to lose a father, especially one who was such a good and wholesome part of your life."

"Is your father still alive?" Agnes looked up and watched his face darken, his brows draw together in what looked like anger but may have been something else.

"I don't want to talk about my father, and it's not why I sought you out." Will pulled back until his hands clasped her shoulders. "I came to tell you that I have to leave for a few days. Sergeant Dobbs is being loaded onto a train this afternoon. Tomorrow he'll be buried at Fort Bliss. I'm in his honor guard. I don't like leaving you. Not after all you've been through. I'd feel better if you were inside the barn with the others instead of out here on your own."

"Then that's what I'll do, Private Bowers." Agnes looked up at the man who'd been silently standing by, supporting her and the family for the last few days, and her heart swelled with so much gratitude that, without even knowing she was going to do it, she got up on tiptoes and kissed the tip of his nose. He jerked back, surprised, then beamed an enormous smile and kissed her forehead before walking off.

When she walked into the barn, Agnes was smiling and thinking how lucky she was to have Will Bowers' support and protection. Her mother smiled back at her, then stood up and tapped her spoon against her glass until the entire room quieted and every eye was on her.

"Now that we're all here, I have an announcement." Mildred clasped her black-gloved hands, looking like she was going to burst into song. Her eyes glinted with steely determination. "The Sunrise Ranch is too big an enterprise for a widow like me. I am putting It on the market. You all represent most of the movers and shakers in this county, and I would appreciate your help in finding an appropriate purchaser for the property."

"You can't do that!" Agnes's shout interrupted surprised voices that had risen up from all corners of the room. Everyone had an opinion on the selling of a great ranch, but they all quieted and stared at Agnes, who felt as if she were about to faint. Her heart pounded so hard that her breath came in pants. "What about me? What am I going to do if you sell the Sunrise?"

"You don't own the ranch. I do, and I am moving back to Las Vegas in two weeks' time. Maude needs help with the boys, and I want to be back in society, not out here, alone, in a barren wilderness." Mildred gave a nod, as if to dismiss the conversation. She sat down and picked up her fork.

Agnes realized a sea of eyes focused on her. This was no place to have this argument. Not with all of Columbus and every influential person from the southern part of the state looking on. She marched to her mother and sisters and bent her face close to theirs. "You can't do that!" she hissed.

"She can, and she did," Charlotte, the oldest sister said.

"Mama never liked it here," Beatrice added. "Too remote. Too arid. You can't think it fair that she languishes here, all alone, just because you want it."

"She'll be much happier living with me back in Las Vegas. That's where all her old friends are. And some of her grandsons," Maude said.

"Fine," Agnes said. "I can see your point. Go ahead and move in with Maude, Mother, but leave the Sunrise in the family. I'll handle it until one of the nephews is old enough to take over."

"Don't be silly," Agne's mother said.

"And stop being so selfish," Elsie added. "We're all Daddy's girls. We all deserve a piece of his empire."

Mildred wagged her finger at Agnes. "Don't say you're surprised. I've tried and tried to talk with you about your future. This is for your own good. This way you'll give up these foolish ideas about running a ranch and settle down like your sisters."

Agnes balled her hands into fists of indignation and stared, one at a time, at each of her sisters. Each smiled back at her, looking for all the world like four cats who'd swallowed their canaries. This is why the men had raised their eyebrows whenever she talked about the ranch. They had decided that they were going to sell it, and they didn't want any arguments from her. Agnes steeled herself against the tears that threatened to burst from her eyes.

"I will fight this."

"I don't see how." Her mother gave one more self-satisfied smile before spearing a potato and popping it into her mouth.

Chapter Seven

Agnes felt a rage of tears building in her. She rushed from the barn before it exploded out. The barrage of voices behind her stung like a windstorm in the desert. She hunched her back against it. How could her mother and sisters wrest the only thing that she wanted from her? Why hadn't she seen it coming? Looking back, the signs were everywhere, as obvious as the brown cloud in the west that always presaged a windstorm. She was angry at herself for being caught unawares, angry at her mother and sisters for bringing this upon her, and angry at everyone else in the barn for laughing and talking in the midst of this tragedy. It was bad enough to lose one's father. Must she lose his legacy, the Sunrise, too?

Unlike a dust storm, Agnes couldn't just hunker down and wait this out. If she did, the ranch would be gone. She would be homeless. Directionless. Forced, perhaps, to do what her mother wanted her to do: marry Heinrich Dieter. She had to fight back. But how? The sound of laughter, the clink of forks against plates distracted her. She couldn't think here. She needed to get on the range where the only sound was wind through the mesquite and the occasional lowing of a cow or call of a hawk. She needed room and quiet to think.

Agnes walked through the empty kitchen, grateful that Lupe was too busy serving in the barn to confront her here. Upstairs in her room she pulled off her dress and, like a soldier preparing for battle, pulled on her canvas trousers, a plaid flannel shirt, and the vest with pockets full of her extra gear. She tied a bandana around her neck and made for the kitchen, where she slipped into her boots and rammed her hat on her head. She felt herself again: strong and ready for anything.

The shadows were growing long when she saddled up Diablo, but the voices in the barn and the number of carriages and cars in the yard told her she wouldn't be missed for a long while yet.

Agnes rode with the sun in her eyes until she realized that she was heading toward Camp Columbus. She shook her head. Will wasn't going to be there. Even if he was, what could he do to help her now? She wished she had him to talk to. He spoke so little, but what he said was practical, measured, thoughtful: a good balance to her emotional impetuousness. She turned Diablo south, then followed the railroad tracks until she heard the low rumble that meant a train was coming. She pulled off to the side and held Diablo still, standing in the stirrups with her hand over her heart as the train rumbled by. She wasn't sure if this was the right train, but she could pay her respects to Sergeant Dobbs anyway. A face in a window flashed by and her heart constricted. She was sure it was Will's face, a flash that disappeared into the distance, leaving her alone.

She wanted to shout at the train, to shake her fist in frustration. *You were wrong to think I would be safer inside the barn than alone outside, Will. The barn held a den of vipers.* She stood in the stirrups until the train disappeared in the east and the rumbling died into silence.

Agnes dropped back into the saddle, and Diablo turned north at a leisurely trot. She had no idea where he was going, but since she didn't know where she wanted to go, there seemed little point in not giving him his head and letting him lead her on.

The sun dropped lower, but she was not afraid. She knew the way home, even in the dark. Let Diablo go where he wanted; she could turn him whenever she needed.

An idea flashed across Agnes' mind, as startling as the muzzle flash of a gun. Diablo was traveling north. If he continued, they would pass through Deming and arrive at Silver City, where the family attorney, L.B. Fowler lived. In times of stress and financial hardship, Fowler was the man to whom her father turned. Surely, he knew that John Day wanted Sunrise Ranch to stay in the family. He would know what to do.

Fowler was back in the barn right now. She had seen him there. But that barn wasn't the place to talk with him. Not with her sisters to listen in. She would meet him in his office the next day.

Agnes knew she was being both foolhardy and impetuous. Silver City, after all, was 86 miles away. But once Agnes made up her mind, it was set. She patted the rolled blanket tied to the back of her saddle, then checked to make sure she had two canteens and some beef jerky in her saddle bags. She would ride all night, but years of riding the range and sleeping under the stars had prepared her for this journey.

Darkness fell. Agnes allowed Diablo to pick his pace and his path, occasionally checking the Pole Star to make sure they weren't too far off course. Afraid that someone might recognize her and force her to return home, she skirted the town of Deming. Agnes smiled as she thought about how much her mother was probably worrying about her. Let her worry. She'd wanted Agnes off the ranch, and now she was off the ranch, at least for the night. Then she thought of all the guests crowding the barn, and her sisters and their sons crowding the Big House. Would her mother even notice that she was gone?

A little way out of town she stopped at a stock tank, where she and Diablo both drank deeply and she refilled her canteens. When she was too tired to stay in the saddle, she hobbled Diablo near a good patch of buffalo grass, rolled herself in her blanket, and slept. The stars were fading in a pearl-gray sky when she awoke.

Agnes rode into Silver City in the middle of the afternoon. The town was born some forty years ago, when silver and other ores were discovered nearby. It had gone through a rowdy adolescence of rough and tumble miners, card sharks, and ruffians and matured into a prosperous commercial center full of stately mansions. The bustle here intimidated Agnes. Everyone in town seemed in a rush.

Agnes turned west at the intersection of Bullard and Broadway. At its far end, the imposing County Courthouse blocked the road, as if suggesting that no one could get around the law. Agnes scowled at the building. Maybe her mother had the law on her side, but Agnes was going to find a way to keep the Sunrise. What was right and what was legal weren't always the same.

Just before the courthouse sat a tall house with mustard yellow shingles, stained glass in the tops of the windows, and a sign outside that said *L.B. Fowler, Attorney* at Law in fancy gold script. She hitched Diablo to the porch rail, climbed the steps, and turned a bell key.

A maid in white cap and apron answered the door. Her eyes looked Agnes up and down, and then she pulled the door nearly closed, so that just her face appeared. "Go around to the kitchen door if you want a handout," the girl said.

Agnes let out a guffaw as she thought of what she must look like, She pulled off her hat and slapped it against her thigh, causing a billow of dust to hang in the air. "I'm not the vagrant you think I am. I'm Agnes Day, of the Sunrise Ranch. Mr. Fowler represents my family. I'd like a word with him."

The maid's mouth formed an O. She told Agnes to wait a moment and slammed the door. When it opened again, the maid, who still wore a look of astonishment, stood on tiptoes to look over the shoulder of a dapper young man in a black sack suit. The man's dark hair was slicked back, and a little mustache twitched beneath his pointy nose, making him look somewhat like a weasel. He looked up and down Agnes appraisingly, and his nostrils flared as if he did not like what he saw. "Miss Day? I'm Arthur

Howard, Mr. Fowler's clerk. Mr. Fowler's at the Court House right now, in a hearing. Would you care to wait in his office?"

"Do you have a stable out back? I'd like to unsaddle my horse first."

Mr. Howard snorted contemptuously. "We had stables. They've been converted into a garage, but I'm sure we could find some room for your horse in there. However, letting a lady unsaddle her own horse would never do. I'll get a boy from the livery stable down the road to attend to it if you would care to come in."

Agnes resisted the urge to tell him that she was no lady. Insult the clerk and it might be harder to get what she wanted from his boss. She followed him down the hallway, and he pointed out that the first door on the left was the office. Beyond, he said, was a powder room with a sink and toilet, where he suggested she wash up before sitting on the furniture. The maid handed her some towels, then left her in peace. Agnes looked in the mirror and laughed out loud. Her eyes looked startlingly blue staring out of her dust-covered face. No wonder she had scared the maid. Agnes washed her face, neck, and hands. She dampened her hands and ran them through her hair so it wasn't so hat-flattened, then she beat her clothes with a towel until she'd gotten most of the dust out of them. She would have to apologize to the maid for making a muddy mess out of the powder room.

Back in the office, Agnes looked around. A tall roll top desk, its surfaces piled with papers and books, stood against a wall that was covered with ornate wallpaper and framed certificates that looked very official and important. Two other walls held floor to ceiling bookcases filled with leather-bound books. The fourth had a bow window hung with crimson velvet curtains that looked out to the front of the house. In front of the window, the law clerk sat transcribing notes at a little desk piled high with papers.

"Ah, I see you clean up rather well. I fancy you would look quite lovely in a dress." Mr. Howard indicated that Agnes should sit in one of the upholstered chairs that surrounded a conference table in the middle of the room. His rudeness flabbergasted Agnes, and for a moment she fought the urge to wallop him. She had told herself that she had to be polite to Mr. Fowler's clerk, but this was too much.

"And I fancy you would, too," Agnes countered. She watched his mouth open and close, like a fish out of water. He gathered his papers and scurried out, closing the twin French doors behind him and leaving Agnes in peace. Agnes eased herself into the chair with a sigh. She hadn't realized just how tired and saddle-worn she was. She took a cookie from the plate that sat in the middle of the conference table, and downed it with three glasses of cool water from the pitcher.

She must have dozed off because she woke with a jerk when L.B. Fowler opened the French doors and strode in. He wore a rumpled black suit and string tie that made him look like he belonged in the Wild Old West instead of the Twentieth Century. Bushy gray hair stuck out over his ears, framing the bald crown of his head. Halfway in age between Agnes' father and grandfather, a very young Fowler had been wounded while serving in a division of Texas infantry during the Civil War. He still walked with a limp. As soon as Agnes looked at him, Fowler's habitual scowl softened into something that might be mistaken for a smile.

"Good afternoon, Miss Day. What a pleasure to see you two days in a row. Your father's funeral was a nice affair, wasn't it? Brought most of the county together."

"My mother says she is selling the Sunrise," Agnes answered. She hadn't ridden all night just to exchange small talk.

"That is what she intends." Mr. Fowler rifled through the piles on the roll top desk, extracted a sheaf of papers, then took a seat opposite Agnes.

"But she can't! It's been in the family for two generations. I plan to lead it into its third. You must stop her!"

Fowler pulled a set of wire-rimmed spectacles from his breast pocket and threaded the earpieces over his ears. "I'm afraid your father's will names your mother as executor. As such, she can do whatever she wishes with the property, including sell it."

"My sisters want their share." Agnes noted desperation in her voice and tried to control it. She needed to sound reasonable and strong.

"Well, it's not strictly true that they have a share. Neither do you. The entire estate goes to your mother. The only way you, or any of your sisters, for that matter, have a right to anything is if your mother decides to gift it to you, or if she were to die - a solution I am not in any way advocating you undertake, understand." He chuckled at his own joke, then looked at her over the top of his spectacles, waiting for her to respond.

"Is my only option to buy the ranch from my mother?" Agnes asked.

L.B. Fowler chuckled again. "My dear Miss Day, that is indeed an option, but not for you. You do not have the means to entertain such a proposal."

"Then, I shall find a job that pays a good salary."

Fowler shook his head. "There's no job in America that pays that kind of wage, especially for you. Women don't command that kind of earnings. Between you and me, we know what your Mother wants, do we not? Might Heinrich Dieter have the money to buy the ranch for you?"

Agnes ran a hand over her face. "Why does everyone think I should marry that man?"

Fowler chuckled. "Mildred Day has never been good at holding her cards close to her chest. She told me she was doing this to force your hand."

Agnes clutched the chair arms as if she expected it to buck and throw her. "I've known Heinrich my whole life. Believe me, there is no spark between us. Furthermore, he's not the least bit interested in ranching. I marry him, I lose not only the ranch, but my freedom. I follow him to Santa Fe, maybe Washington. Mr. Fowler, I will die before I do that. My whole life, I've wanted nothing other than to work the Sunrise. I will find a way, with or without your help."

The lawyer pulled his spectacles up until they rested on the top of his head. The compassion in his rheumy eyes made her throat knot up. "Let me lay my cards on the table, metaphorically speaking. I have been charged with selling the ranch. I have not been given a deadline, per se. The market is very depressed right now: what with Mexican revolutionaries crossing the border and burning settlements, no investor is interested in these borderlands. Additionally, people are worried about the war in Europe and whether America will get involved."

"You're telling me it's not a good time to sell." Agnes scooted forward in her chair, anxious to understand the implications.

Mr. Fowler nodded. "The best thing I can do to preserve the Day estate is to hold onto the property until peace and prosperity returns."

"You'll need someone to manage the property," Agnes noted.

"I plan to keep on Ernesto and Lupe Bernal. As caretakers."

"And the other hands?"

The lawyer frowned and shook his head. "Scuttlebutt has it that the population of Camp Columbus is about to explode. Since an army travels on its stomach, I should be able to get a pretty penny per head for those beeves. If cattle go, the ranch hands would have to move on. Being the rowdy young men that they are, I would expect most to abandon the ranch if war was declared anyway."

Agnes nodded. "Probably true. Without the hands, though, Ernesto will need an assistant. The fences will still need to remain intact, and the buildings maintained. His wife can't do all that. I'm sure the Bernals could offer room and board. Closing up the Big House and the Bunk House will save heating money."

"True." Mr. Fowler leaned back and studied the ceiling. Agnes felt hope flutter in her stomach. "Miss Day, I don't suppose you have someone in mind for this position?"

"Yes, I do," Agnes said. She was perched so far forward in her seat that she risked slipping off and landing unceremoniously on the floor. "Me."

Mr. Fowler threaded his fingers together over his large stomach. "Who knows what the future might hold? These are uncertain times. I promise to keep John's estate as intact as possible for as long as possible. Until it finds a new owner, there's no reason to force out the daughter of the old one."

Agnes nodded. "Especially when she's determined to find a way to stay on. Sell the cattle if you must. If it keeps my mother and sisters satisfied, sell the furniture. But please, may I keep Diablo?"

"That black filly who's munching hay next to my Oldsmobile?"

Agnes giggled. "He's a gelding, not a filly."

"And I'm a lawyer, not a rancher," Mr. Fowler said with a smile, "and I marched with the infantry, not rode with the cavalry. You'll have to talk with your mother about that. I'm sure she'll let you keep one little horse as a consolation prize. I'm surprised she let you ride up here on him."

Agnes felt her face go red. "She didn't. I left without telling her."

Mr. Fowler shook his head and whistled. "Knowing Mildred, she's practically appoplexic over it. We'll have Arthur, my clerk, send a telegram so she'll stop worrying. Tomorrow he'll rent a horse trailer and take you and that horse of yours home in the Oldsmobile. Now, let's you and I take Mrs. Fowler out to dinner at the Palace Hotel. Your appearance is going to raise a lot of eyebrows; people are going to wonder where I found a ruffian from the old days."

Agnes smiled slyly at both the clerk and the maid as she passed them in the hall. It felt good to let these city folks know that, dirty and disheveled as she looked, she still had influence. During the course of a nice steak dinner, the matronly Mrs. Fowler said that Agnes' father had been like a son to her and her husband. That made Agnes a granddaughter of some sorts. When they returned home, Mrs. Fowler drew a lovely bath for Agnes and loaned her a nightgown before tucking her into a pillowy-soft four poster bed. Agnes hadn't been treated in this manner for so long that she half expected a bedtime story.

At four in the morning, Agnes wrote a short note thanking the Fowlers for their hospitality before she slipped out, saddled Diablo, and rode away. A full day in the saddle was far better than a four-hour ride with the pretentious Arthur Howard.

Chapter Eight

The sun set several hours before Agnes rode into the Sunrise Ranch. Diablo's head hung. His back feet dragged, and he stumbled as he walked. Agnes felt just as tired, but a sense of exhilaration and power kept her in the saddle. She had ridden all the way to Silver City and stated her case to a lawyer, and he had responded favorably. Keeping the ranch was not guaranteed. Not yet, but the agreement she had struck with Mr. Fowler had bought her time. She'd figure out something to keep the Sunrise in the family.

Agnes sighed in relief when she saw a shadowy figure waiting by the tack room. Good and faithful Ernesto. He was always there for her! She was too tired to carry the saddle to its rack. Ernesto would do it for her.

But it wasn't Ernesto. Heinrich Dieter came forward, his smile shining out of the darkness.

"Aggie! Thank God you're home! I was growing tired of waiting."

"No one asked you to wait here." Agnes swung herself down. She hung onto the saddle's fender as her legs adjusted, terrified that she would collapse in a heap.

Heinrich did not reach out to support her. He didn't even seem to notice that she was having difficulties. He continued in his chipper way. "I've had a long talk with your mother. She thinks we should get married."

Agnes pressed her eyes closed and rubbed her face, too tired to process Heinrich's jabber. "You're marrying my mother?"

He laughed. "No silly. Your mother thinks I should marry you."

Agnes slipped the bridle off Diablo's head and hung it on her shoulder. She knew Diablo was too tired to move around, so she didn't bother to halter him. "Heinrich, I'm too tired to joke with you right now."

"It's no joke! You are from one of the area's premier ranching families. I'm from one of the most successful mercantile families. Together, we command a lot of respect. It'd be easy for us to find a place in politics."

Agnes lifted the saddle flap and unbuckled the girth. She dragged the saddle off Diablo's back and shouldered her way past Heinrich. "I'm not the girl for you."

"Sure you are! Ever since you sat on me in the school playground . . ."

Heinrich didn't have a chance to finish his sentence before Agnes interrupted him. "Having been sat on is no criteria in picking a wife. I thank you for your consideration, and I appreciate your friendship, but I am not the woman to help you get into politics. Open that door, will you?"

Heinrich jumped into action, opening the tack room door with a flourish that Agnes was sure he thought chivalrous. She carried in her gear and stored it while Heinrich followed her around as awkwardly as a puppy.

"Besides," he added, "your mother says you need a place to go, now that the ranch is on the market."

Agnes staggered to a stop. She closed her eyes and took a deep breath to compose herself before she answered. While she had no intention of marrying Heinrich Dieter, the thought of crushing him emotionally was repugnant to her. They had known each other too long, and the community was too closely knit for her to spurn him without both of them ending up the worse for it. "Yes, well, I just got back from having a talk with our lawyer. He doesn't think it'll sell anytime soon, and says I can stay here and manage the ranch. I'm not as desperate as my mother would have you believe."

Heinrich followed her out of the tack room and into the stable, where he hovered as she put Diablo in a stall, gave him water and hay, and brushed him. "So you won't marry me?"

"No, Heinrich. I won't marry you."

"Please? My parents are going to be so disappointed." Heinrich's voice raised several octaves. He sounded like a small boy who was almost ready to cry.

"Well, I'll take that as a compliment, but it doesn't change my decision."

Heinrich seemed to wilt, his long frame crushed under the weight of rejection. It broke Agnes' heart to see him so downcast. "But we can still be friends," she offered as a consolation, "Friends forever, and I'll sit on you anytime you need sitting on."

"Really?" Henrich said with a sniff.

"Just tell your parents that I'm a foolish girl who doesn't know what's good for her. Tell them you can do better than me. You'll find a girl who loves politics, and wants all the finer things in life."

"Will I?"

"Of course you will. And maybe, just maybe, she'll let you sit on her."

"Great!" Heinrich's teeth flashed in an enormous smile. They shook hands, and Heinrich climbed into his car and drove back to Columbus through the dark. Agnes was too tired to watch him go. As she stumbled towards the house, she was not sure if she was relieved that he hadn't taken her rejection badly, or a little disappointed that he was so quick to give up on her.

As Agnes entered the dark, still house, a figure rose from a front parlor chair. Before she had a chance to react, her mother enveloped her in a fierce embrace that nearly squeezed the air out of her.

"I've been so worried for you! Riding all that way! On your own! Do you realize what might have happened to you? Bandits! Revolutionistas! Rattlesnakes! This is terrible country, full of danger."

Agnes sagged into her mother, breathing in the comforting smell of soap, starch, and roses that always surrounded her. "I was fine, Mama. I've been riding alone all my life. You know I can take care of myself."

Mildred Day clasped her daughter by the shoulders, holding her out to look at her, although in the darkened room Agnes was sure she couldn't see anything. "That's the real issue, isn't it? You think you can take care of yourself. Trust me: this world is not a place for an unattached woman. You simply cannot go about on your own, riding wherever you will. You need a man to protect you. Your father is no longer here to do it."

Agnes dropped into a chair and pressed the toe of one boot into the heel of the other, wearily pulling it off. "Is that why you had Heinrich Dieter ambush me?"

Mildred snorted. "I did no such thing!" Her voice brightened with hope. "But wait! You talked with Heinrich Dieter? When? Where?"

"I did. Just now. Out by the stables."

"And he proposed?"

"He did." Agnes leaned back in her chair and waited for her mother to stop squealing. "And I turned him down."

Mildred collapsed into a chair. "He was your ticket out of here! The kind of man you need."

"I don't need a man," Agnes said, "and I don't need a ticket out of here. I'm staying here. This ranch is my legacy."

"You'll do no such thing! This ranch will be your ruination. I am selling it to protect you from such foolishness. So, you had better find a man and marry before you end up a homeless wanderer."

"Enough. I don't have the energy to argue with you." Agnes dragged herself out of the chair and plodded up stairs that seemed to have grown steeper and longer in the past two days. She dropped onto the bed and fell asleep without even taking her clothes off.

Agnes thought she might sleep forever. She had never been so bone-tired, never pushed herself to the limits of her endurance. But old habits are hard to break, and even sleep-deprived and physically exhausted, Agnes' internal clock woke her early the next morning. She crept out of the quiet house without bothering to change out of the rumpled, dusty clothes she had ridden home in, and was on the range before the sun crested the horizon.

One look at Diablo told her that he wasn't ready to ride out yet, so she selected a little buckskin from the string of horses the ranch kept. The land she rode through was just beginning to show its spring colors, the first of the Mexican poppies dotting the landscape yellow. She was stapling up a fence when a movement caught her eye, and she stopped to watch a herd of pronghorns blaze across the eastern horizon. They ran so swiftly that no horse could keep up with them, their gait so smooth they seemed to float along, a cloud of dust floating in their wake.

"They're beautiful, aren't they?"

The voice made Agnes gasp and jump, dropping her hammer. She spun around, furious. "Will Bowers! When are you going to learn that sneaking up on me is neither wise nor kind?"

Will shrugged and indicated the vast, flat expanse behind him. "I don't see how crossing that expanse, in plain sight, is sneaking up on you. Where's Blackie?"

"Blackie?"

"That feisty gelding you always ride."

"His name is Diablo. And I suggest you learn to whistle as you walk, so you don't surprise people." Agnes picked up the hammer and went back to pounding staples into the post, intending to use the movement to hide her shaking hands. She couldn't understand why someone so quiet, whose movements were so deliberate, could make her heart race, but race it did.

"I'll try that next time," he said, before staring off at the distant, drifting line of pronghorns for so long that Agnes wasn't sure he would ever speak again. "I hear that your mother is selling the ranch."

"Bad news travels fast." Agnes pounded in more staples than the post really needed. "You hear that in Texas?"

Will shook his head. "As soon as I got back, which was late last night. What are you going to do?"

"I went to see the family lawyer. He says the political climate isn't good for selling ranches this close to Mexico right now, and I can stay as long as I want."

"But when it sells?"

Agnes stopped hammering. She looked into Will's earnest face and convinced herself that he was asking out of genuine concern. But she was angry, tired, and sore, and had little patience for anything. What she wanted was to be left alone to do the thousand trivial chores it took to keep a ranch running. She didn't want to think.

"If you must know, I will earn a small salary for keeping up the ranch. I intend to find some other means of making money. If I'm lucky, the economy will stay bad long enough for me to make a bid on the ranch myself."

"You know that I'm a certified marksman, don't you?"

Agnes laughed. Wasn't that just like a man, to want to be at the center of attention? "Well, good for you, Will."

"That means I make extra pay. An extra $8 a month. I can support you."

Agnes stared at Will. "Support me? On $8 a month? You think that's what I'm worth?" She watched Will's face darken until he was redder than a desert sunset.

"I didn't mean . . . I meant . . . I . . ." Will stuttered, took a deep breath, then dropped to one knee. "I meant, marry me. Then you won't have to worry about what happens to you when - if - the ranch sells."

"You think marrying you is some kind of consolation prize for losing a ranch? That I can't take care of myself?"

"You've got to be prepared," Will spluttered. "Terrible things can happen to a woman on her own."

All the rage and pain that Agnes had bottled up erupted. "What is it with all you men asking poor, pitiful orphan me to marry them?"

Will staggered back as if he'd been slapped. "All us men?"

"You this morning. Heinrich Dieter last night. Did my mother put you up to it like she did Heinrich? Is this some kind of competition between the two of you? Who can make a conquest of me?"

Will's face turned even redder. "No, I didn't speak with your mother. She wouldn't want me as a son-in-law, anyway. And I didn't come out here planning to ask you anything. I came to say goodbye. The Punitive Expedition is organizing to enter Mexico. I'll be going with it."

"Before, you told me that you came out here just to walk. Now you're telling me you were stalking me?" Agnes shrieked.

"I wasn't stalking you, but I wasn't just walking, either. I came to be with you. I was wasting my time. I wish you and Heinrich all the best." Will retreated through the mesquite.

"Come back here! We're not done," Agnes called, but he waved one hand dismissively, hunched his shoulders, and continued on. She watched until he was just a speck on the horizon. The smaller he grew, the larger the empty space in her heart. Although she hadn't known him long, Will had been a faithful friend, supporting her through a difficult time. What was she going to do without him around?

It bothered her that he thought she'd chosen Heinrich over him. She wished he understood that she hadn't. What she'd chosen was freedom and the ability to choose her own destiny over being tied to a man - any man. And that included Will.

Agnes packed up her tools and rode back to the big house, fighting the urge to cry. He was going to leave someday, anyway. He was a soldier. They moved from camp to camp. There was no sense getting attached to him, not when she wasn't willing to move whenever he did. Still, his coyote eyes lingered in her memory. She passed the chickens in the yard and remembered him feeding them, went into the stables and remembered seeing him currying one of the horses. His touch seemed to be on everything.

She drew a tub full of hot water and eased herself into it, then reached over the side, found the well-thumbed copy of Everybody's Magazine on the little wicker table. It fell open to the *International School of Correspondence* advertisement and she felt a little pang remembering how smug she'd felt, thinking she didn't need to train to become a rancher. Now she wondered how much money could she make if she had a certificate from this school. Enough to make a down payment on the Sunrise? The advertisement claimed the school had trained thousands of men in large-salaried jobs.

Men. There it was again. Men got the good paying jobs. Women were supposed to depend on them.

She flipped to the job ads, looking for ones open to women. Nannies. Maids. Cooks. None paid much more than room and board. Discouraged, Agnes leafed through the magazine until she found the dog-eared article on germs that she had once found so interesting. As she skimmed the page, an idea sparked in her mind.

Nursing.

She flipped back to the *International School of Correspondence* advertisement and scanned the list of professions for which it trained.

No nursing. Agnes tore through the pages of *Everybody's* until she found the ad with the serious woman in a white cap and collar staring out at her. "Become a Nurse," the banner read. "The Chautauqua School of Nursing has trained thousands of women in their own homes to earn $10 to $25 a week as nurses."

Agnes threw the magazine aside and reached for her towel. Tomorrow, she would write for more information, then talk to Doctor Pritchard about becoming a county extension nurse in addition to a ranch hand.

Chapter Nine

Mildred's hand hovered over the packing crate, holding a paper-wrapped tea cup. "Maybe we should plan one last party before we pack?" Agnes looked up from the mess of wood shavings she was using to cushion the china. She wiggled her nose to keep from sneezing. "Why would you want to do that?"

"Everyone who's anyone has put aside their mourning and hosted General Pershing since he's taken over Camp Columbus. He's very well connected, you know. Might even be President someday. And he's single."

Agnes stared at her mother, shocked that she could be thinking such a thing so soon after her father's funeral. Black Jack Pershing was handsome, with the trim mustache, ramrod posture, and the refined manners and gentlemanly composure of a West Point graduate. At fifty-five, he remained young and spry. The fact that he was single seemed more a tragedy than an opportunity to her. His wife and daughters had been killed in a house fire, leaving him with a six-year-old son to raise. "Mother! Surely, it's too soon to think about things like that. Both you and the General should still be reeling from your losses."

Mildred chuckled. "Not for me, dear. I was thinking of introducing the General to you."

Agnes' shock turned to horror. Black Jack was old enough to be her father. She looked around for a way to deflect the argument. "The parlor pictures are packed. Think he'll be impressed by the dark rectangles they left behind on the wallpaper?"

Mildred tapped a finger against her lips thoughtfully, then signed and placed the teacup in the crate. "I suppose you're right. Promise me that you'll accept any invitation to meet him. I worry you'll become an eccentric hermit once I'm gone."

"I promise," Agnes held up her hand as if swearing an oath.

"To become an eccentric hermit?" Her mother smiled. She had been less of a harpy since deciding to move to Las Vegas. The two were more relaxed around each other, and that had made these last few days easy and sweet.

"I promise to do everything I can to marry Black Jack Pershing when he returns from Mexico. But I won't rush the wedding. You'll have plenty of time to buy a gorgeous gown. It might be my wedding, but all eyes will be on you."

While Mildred chuckled, Agnes studied the boxes and crates piled in the corner of the kitchen, each tagged for its final destination. The china was to go to one of Agnes' sisters, to be passed down in due time to another generation of Day women. In recognition of her years of service, Lupe would receive many of the kitchen tools, pots and pans, and some of the linen. The furniture would stay shrouded in dust cloths in the big house, either to be sold along with it, or sold elsewhere. Maude's house, large as it was, could not absorb another complete household.

"You're lying. You didn't go to the parade when the General arrived, and you're not planning to see the Army march south tomorrow," Mildred said cheerily.

"I am not lying to you," Agnes protested. "I plan to use the two-prong approach to ensnare Black Jack. As soon as the Punitive Expedition returns, I'll go to every celebratory dinner party and tea that he's invited to, provided I'm invited myself. And I'll also go to every event that the public is invited to at the Camp. Every parade. Every lecture. Every ceremony."

Agnes smiled at her mother. Pershing planned to use a two-prong approach, leading a 2,000-man contingent south from the New Mexican border town of Hachita while a larger contingent of lumbering supply wagons left Columbus. She had no intention of following a two-pronged approach to capture anyone's heart. She was too busy figuring out how to keep the Sunrise.

"Then why not come with me tomorrow?" Mildred asked.

"Really, mother, how likely is it that Black Jack will pick me out of the crowd? Say to himself 'Now, there's a pretty young girl. I think I'll marry her when I come back from Mexico'?" Agnes turned her back to her mother, afraid of the emotion that surely must be playing across her face. She wasn't afraid that Black Jack Pershing would pick her out of the crowd, but that Will might.

In the week since Agnes had turned down his offer of marriage, she had not heard from him. The silence left an awful gap in Agnes' days and in her heart. She missed his steady, practical presence. She wished that she could explain that her outburst was the result of grieving and exhaustion, that her life had been turned upside down by her father's death, and that marriage was out of the question, but she couldn't face seeing pain in his coyote brown eyes. She wished she'd found a kinder, gentler way to let him down.

Agnes considered all the upheaval at the ranch. As L.B. Fowler has predicted, the Army bought the ranch's beeves at a premium. The hands, seeing the writing on the wall, had drifted away singly and in pairs soon after driving the herd to Camp Columbus. Only four people: she, her mother, Ernesto, and Lupe, remained. After Ernesto negotiated the sale of the ranch's horses, the only animals left would be Lupe's chickens and hogs, and a few horses. Soon, her brother-in-law would arrive with a nice carriage and a couple of buckboards to escort Mildred and all her belongings to Las Vegas. Then Agnes would lock up the big house and move in with Lupe and Ernesto.

While the number of people at the Sunrise Ranch shrank, the population of Camp Columbus exploded. Two Cavalry brigades, an infantry brigade, two companies of engineers, two of waggoneers, one of ambulances, and a detachment of the signal corps had swelled the ranks of Camp Columbus to over 6,000 men in the past few weeks. The sounds of engines, shouting, and the ring of hammers filled the desert air. Even after the column moved south tomorrow, Camp Columbus would continue to grow. A new quartermaster, charged with building a railroad depot and an airfield, was expected soon. Camp Columbus and the town that shared its name, had risen from the ashes.

Agnes brushed aside a tear and straightened her shoulders. It was good that Will was leaving with the Punitive Expedition and her mother moving to Las Vegas. She needed time to focus on her own goals. She had written to the Chautauqua Correspondence School of Nursing. Once her materials arrived, Agnes' plan was to work on ranch upkeep in the cool morning hours, then study in the heat of the day. Becoming a nurse would enable her to pay some earnest money towards the Sunrise. If she could stall her mother, perhaps she could rebuild the herd and make the ranch profitable again. If her mother and sisters received hefty dividends, would they agree not to sell after all?

"It's more likely that Black Jack will see you if you're out and about," Mildred said, bringing the conversation back around. "Promise me you'll go into town. Attend events. I'll leave you the gig carriage and a carriage horse if you promise me."

"I can ride Diablo," Agnes argued, but Mildred shook her head.

"You'll look more lady like in the gig. And it's so easy to drive, even a woman can do it."

Agnes chuckled. She could drive any wagon or carriage on the farm, even the big buckboard, but this was not a point worth arguing. Better to let her mother think of her as a weak young lady who would need Ernesto's help than get into another argument about how she was capable of taking care of herself.

After her mother left to see off the troops the next day, Agnes stood at her bedroom window and watched the dust column slowly move south as tears ran down her cheeks. When Will returned, she would look into those coyote eyes and apologize. Maybe they could become friends again.

That night at supper, Mildred's cheeks were flushed pink and she couldn't stop talking about all the handsome young officers. For the next week, she shared the local news every night at dinner. Two spurs had been added to the rail. A depot had been built. A YMCA was being erected. The 1st Aero Squadron had arrived and were taking up residence in a field between Columbus and the Sunrise Ranch. The squadron had eight airplanes and six motorcycles. They made noise that scared the horses, but the pilots were so dashing! All college boys who'd volunteered! Agnes wondered how her mother would bear to leave all the excitement behind to move to Las Vegas, but a week later, she, Ernesto and Lupe stood on the front porch waving handkerchiefs as her mother rode away in a caravan of wagons carrying everything she couldn't live without.

Agnes chuckled. "I wish I could see the look on Maude's face when she sees all the gewgaws and bric-a-brac Mother's bringing."

"You knew she wouldn't be able to part with her trinkets," Lupe said. "So many memories."

When even the dust cloud had gone, Lupe and Agnes stopped waving and went back into the big house, checked the windows, and draped the remaining furniture in dust cloths. The mantel clock's tic tocs echoed down the hall. Agnes stopped the clock, then went out to the porch, where Ernesto had already loaded her one steamer trunk and the piano into the wagon for the brief ride across the yard to the manager's house. Agnes laughed, remembering her mother's insistence that the piano move with Agnes, lest disuse warp it so that it couldn't hold a tune. She wasn't sure who would play. It certainly wouldn't be her, and as far as she knew, Ernesto and Lupe had never sat at a piano.

When Agnes awoke the next morning, the sun had already cleared the horizon. Agnes sat on the edge of her bed and rubbed her face, angry at herself for sleeping in. She shrugged herself into her robe, shoved her feet into slippers, and staggered into the kitchen.

Lupe took one look at her and clucked her tongue. "*¡Buenas dias cariña*! Here, my darling: you need this. You didn't sleep well last night?"

Agnes gratefully accepted the steaming cup of coffee. It had more cream and sugar than she usually used, but it tasted like a warm, sweet hug. "Your house creaks and groans differently than the Big House."

Lupe nodded. "It's always hard to sleep in a new place, mija, even if it is your own bed you sleep in. I remember when Ernesto first brought me here. I didn't think I'd ever sleep again without the bells from the church ringing the hours. It was too quiet." She picked up her *rodillo* and returned to rolling out tortillas

"I don't know if it was that, or the fact that I didn't have any reason to get out of bed. It's like I'm waiting for life to start again. I really need to keep myself busy. Where's Ernesto?"

"*Mi* poor *esposo*. Like you, he doesn't know what to do now that he doesn't roust the hands. This morning he rode to the post office! He will wait long before Meester Dieter leaves his breakfast table and comes downstairs to open the store."

Agnes imagined Ernesto drumming his fingers on the saddle horn while the Dieters peered down at him. Lupe handed her a basket of tortillas and a bowl of canned plums, and she ate them because she knew she needed nourishment, even if she wasn't hungry. She changed into working clothes even though she had no work to do. She was listlessly hanging clothes on pegs when she heard the jingle of harness and looked out the window to see Ernesto riding back into the courtyard, a parcel tucked under his arm.

Agnes clambered down the stairs and burst into the kitchen.

"Are those my books?" Agnes lunged for the package. Ernesto twisted to hide it.

"Y buenos días para ti también."

Agnes gave him a peck on the cheek.

"Forgive my rudeness. You deserve better. I was just. . . "

"I know. So excited. Here, my little scholar." He handed over the package and she ripped off the brown paper wrapping while he sat at the kitchen table.

"Bueno!" Lupe said. "And now you begin training los bugs?"

"What?" Agnes asked, genuinely confused.

"The no-see-ums that you train to kill the tuberculosis. Remember? You read about them in that magazine of yours."

Agnes laughed. "It's a little more complicated than that."

"What could be more complicated than teaching little bugs?" Lupe set a plate of beans and eggs in front of Ernesto. "Any news?"

Ernesto tucked a napkin into his shirt and scooped up beans with a tortilla. "The expedition had its first engagement. At a place called Guerrero."

Agnes felt the blood drain from her face. "Were any soldiers hurt?"

"Five of ours wounded. But they killed 56 Villistas and wounded another 35. I'd say we slaughtered them."

She watched Ernesto, dumbfounded. How could he eat with news like that? "What if one of them was Will?"

"Will's fine," Ernesto said, and shoveled in more beans. But how would he know? Wasn't he worried? It was too much. Agnes crashed through the kitchen door, saddled Diablo, and was galloping towards the camp in a matter of minutes. Her heart pounded with the rhythm of Diablo's hooves, which seemed with every strike to condemn her for treating Will so badly the last time they had seen each other. Why hadn't she ridden to camp and apologized for rejecting him? Why hadn't she gone to see him off?

David Benavides, the sulky little dispatch rider that Heinrich had brought to her birthday party on the day she met Will, was standing near the motorcycle pool. The Corporal glanced up, a scowl reducing his dark brown eyes to slits.

Agnes reined in Diablo. "Any news from Guerrero?"

David scowled even more, his dark skin turning darker still. He nodded. "Why do you always show up when there's a disaster?"

"Hear from Will? Is he all right?"

David Benavides let out a long, impatient sigh and rolled his eyes heavenward, then crooked his finger, indicating that she should follow him. Agnes swung down from the saddle. She handed the reins to a private who stood with his jaw hanging loose, obviously confused by this harpy on a horse. "You. Loosen his cinch and give him a bucket of water."

"But," he said. Agnes put up a hand to stop him as she scurried after the retreating Corporal. They passed a long row of tents and came to the motor pool, where dozens of trucks and cars in various stages of completion were parked.

"Ask him yourself." Benavides pointed at a massive truck. Agnes saw a man bent double, his upper half deep in the engine cavity, his butt stuck in the air, his feet resting atop the wheel.

"Will!" Agnes shrieked his name in delight and relief. Will Bowers straightened, smashing his head into the hood.

"Ow! Agnes! What are you doing here?"

"You're not dead!" Agnes said, stating the obvious.

"No, I'm not. But I'm seeing stars." Rubbing the top of his head, he stepped down off the wheel and bent double. "What are you doing, sneaking up on me like that?"

"You're the one who sneaks up on people!"

Corporal Benavides snickered. Will and Agnes glared at him until he turned red and slunk away.

"Go check on Diablo!" Agnes shouted after him. She turned to Will and glared. "I thought you were in Mexico! When I heard there was a battle, I worried you might have gotten killed."

"I wanted to be in Mexico," Will said. "Then these Jefferys came: 27 of them. The wagon bodies were separate, with no tools to attach them to the truck chassis. Someone had to figure out how to get them up and running."

"And that someone was you?"

Will nodded. "One can be too handy. I said I'd worked on cars before, so I got the job. While I was rooting around for a solution, the 1st Aero squadron came in by train. They had a portable machine shop."

"So, you've been here? Safe? all along?" Agnes felt her relief fading into irritation, "How come you didn't tell me?"

Will pulled a handkerchief from his back pocket, pressed it to the top of his head, and looked at the blood on it. "I didn't think you'd care. Not after our last meet-up."

"Well, I do, William Bowers." Agnes pulled the handkerchief from Will's hand. She climbed up on the truck's fender and began dabbing at his cut scalp.

Will grinned, his eyes sparkling. "Now that I know that I'll keep you posted on my whereabouts. I've missed you. And the Bernals. I've talked with Ernesto a few times, when our paths have crossed in town."

"Ah," Agnes muttered as she dabbed at the wound. That explained why Ernesto hadn't been concerned about Will and the battle. She would have to scold him for not telling her where Will was.

"Lupe's invited me to dinner a number of times. Mind if I accept the next time she offers?"

"I would like that," Agnes said, smiling back. "Just don't make any more marriage proposals."

"I wouldn't do that. Lupe's already got a husband." Will grinned even more broadly. Agnes laughed and stuffed his handkerchief into his chest pocket. She was still laughing when she returned to the bewildered Private who was watching Diablo.

Chapter Ten

Agnes' head slammed into the binder lying on her desk. She jerked awake, blinking to clear her head. The binder's cover had *Chautauqua Correspondence Course* embossed on it above a logo that read

'I Will'
Conquers
While
'I May'
Fails

Agnes ran her fingers over the words *I Will. I will* stay awake, she told herself, and *I will* pass this course, even if it kills me.

Before she'd plunked down her $75.00 enrollment fee, Agnes had checked with Doctor Pritchard, who'd assured her that Chautauqua was one of the largest and most reputable of the correspondence schools. The brochure said that thousands of women had completed the course. How hard could it be, if thousands had succeeded? Now, a month into her studies, Agnes wondered if thousands of women were smarter than she was.

The box Ernesto had brought home from the post office on the day she'd learned that Will was still at Camp Columbus contained the first portion of the three-part nursing course in a binder that had a printed book plate inside of the front cover that read

These lectures are issued to
Miss Agnes Day
who is enrolled as
a Student in this Institution.
The lectures are her property.
She, however, agreeing to reserve them
solely for her individual study.

Every time her determination wavered, Agnes opened her notebook and read the book plate. She was determined to complete the course in one year, rather than the 15 months that it took most women. The sooner she had her nursing certificate, the sooner she could put away money for a down payment on the ranch.

Agnes skimmed through the lessons. Titles such as *Nursing a Case of Septicemia Under Difficulties, My First Surgical Case, Nursing Pleurisy Patients, Typhoid Cases, Respiratory Infections. Pure Air in Pneumonia,* and *Nursing Contagious Cases: Measles Complicated by Broncho-Pneumonia* were intimidating, filled with words she didn't know, black-and-white photographs, sometimes of gruesome injuries, and diagrams she struggled to interpret. Even though the tests were taken open-note, she mailed them off in their postage-paid envelopes with some trepidation. So far, none had come back with a failing mark.

Agnes found herself studying to the exclusion of everything else. Lupe roused Agnes from her studies so that she could eat, and sometimes reminded her to turn off the light and sleep. Mildred would have been horrified. Her daughter really was becoming a hermit.

A rap at her door caused Agnes to jerk awake again. Lupe peered in, her face alight with a broad smile.

"*Mija,* it's time for supper. Freshen up and come down. Our special boy is here." Lupe used the special pet name she had for Agnes. *Mija,* my daughter, sounded sweet in Agnes' ears. Lupe was far more than a cook and maid. She had raised Agnes while her mother was busy decorating the house and attending society functions with her older daughters.

Agnes stood up, knocking the chair back into the bed. She straightened it, then ran her fingers through her hair, which hadn't been trimmed since before her father died. She really was becoming a recluse. "Isn't this the second time this week?"

"Third," Lupe answered. "It's a good thing. You wouldn't talk to anyone if it weren't for him."

"He just likes your cooking," Agnes felt her cheeks flushing. She tucked her shirt into her dungarees, then followed Lupe down the stairs. Agnes was pleased that Will was, once again, a frequent guest at the ranch. Not one to stand on ceremony, always willing to dry a dish or replace a broken board on the porch, Will had an easy, unassuming way of fitting in. He made a willing fourth when Ernesto wanted to play cards on a rainy afternoon, and Lupe delighted when he plunked out a tune on the piano. It was clear that Lupe and Ernesto adored him. Maybe, Agnes thought, he reminded them of their own sons.

Will got up from the kitchen table when Agnes entered the room. Agnes smiled back, taking in the soft, pale eyes that were somewhere between brown and gray, so close in color to his coffee and cream skin, his close-cropped hair, and his khaki uniform that he looked like a sepia-tinted photograph come to life.

"Good of you to come all this way to have Sunday Supper with us," Agnes said, a little tease in her voice.

Lupe looked up from the pot she'd been stirring. "He and Ernesto's been up on the roof all afternoon. Didn't you hear them up there?"

Agnes shook her head. "I heard something, but I guess I was concentrating too deeply about the treatment of pleurisy to give it any mind. What's wrong with the roof?"

"*Mija,* didn't you hear the wind last night? So strong it ripped off tiles." Agnes shook her head and Lupe shook a wooden spoon at her. "It isn't good, *mija*. Who is going to trust you to take care of them if you can't take care of yourself? You need the fresh air. Go for a ride with Will after supper."

"We could ride to the airfield," Will offered. "Have you seen the new planes?"

"I've never seen an airplane, period; old or new," Agnes admitted.

After dinner they rode to the new airfield that lay east of Camp Columbus. Will explained that the Army had sent eight biplanes called Curtiss JN-3s to Mexico, where they were supposed to be used for reconnaissance. Their 90 horsepower engines had proved too weak to climb over the 12,000-foot mountains of northern Chihuahua or deal with the erratic winds in the mountain passes. One plane developed engine problems. Another got lost in the desert. Four crashed. Pershing had sent the remaining two back to Camp Columbus, where they were retrofitted with more powerful engines. Now they carried mail between Columbus and Camp Dublan.

They rode into a dip in the land that was filled with brilliant yellow, papery blooms, like a bowl of sunshine amid the tan and sage desert. The entire landscape looked ablaze in yellow flame. "Will you look at that? I hadn't noticed the poppies were in bloom," Agnes said.

"Where've you been? Hiding under a rock?" Will said.

"Under a book is more like it," Agnes admitted. "I'd planned to ride out every morning, but with the cattle gone, there's not much to do. So I've focused on my studies. They're harder than I thought they'd be."

Will pointed at a section of fence. "I worked on that section yesterday. Four poles were down. Spring rains and wind, I guess."

Agnes felt a tinge of irritation. "I could have done that."

"I know that," Will said, "I figured I had more time than you."

Agnes clamped her lips together. She appreciated the help, but not the suggestion that she wasn't doing her job or that she couldn't keep up.

The airfield wasn't much to look at: a broad, flat area that had been leveled and cleared of shrubs and prairie dog holes. A line of very large tents along one side served as hangers for the planes. Smaller tents and wooden buildings housed the nearly 100 officers and enlisted men who served in the 1st Aero Squadron. Agnes sat spellbound, watching the frail little machines bob through the air, touching down in a practice landing, then roaring up into the air again. They sounded alternately like mosquitos and what she imagined a lion's purr might be like, the noise fading as they became tiny spots in the sky, then growing deafening as they approached.

When the pilots went into the mess hall for dinner, Agnes and Will rode up to one of the parked planes. She was surprised to find its body was just canvas stretched taut over a light, wooden frame. How could something so inconsequential stay aloft? What would it be like up there, above the ground? Would she be able to see the whole ranch at once? What would the house look like from above?

Will just shook his head. He had never been in a plane and didn't have any idea what it was like.

Agnes rode back to Sunrise Ranch in silence, the buzz of plane engines ringing in her ears.

"Penny for your thoughts," Will asked.

"Do they ever give rides? I mean, to civilians like me?" she asked.

Will nodded. "The pilots have been taking every child or pretty girl who asked on for a joyride They're the local heroes right now."

"Could you ask for me?"

"I could if I wasn't heading to Camp Dublan in the morning," Will said.

Agnes pulled up on the reins, stopping Diablo. She stared at Will, dumbfounded. "Camp Dublan? In Mexico? Why?"

Will sighed. "The trucks are assembled. It's time I rejoined my company."

"I wished you'd told me," Agnes said.

Will smiled a little ruefully. "Ernesto, Lupe and I have talked about it at dinner the last three times I've been to the Sunrise."

Tears welled in Agnes' eyes. "I've been so preoccupied with my nursing course, I guess I didn't hear you. I can be pretty self-absorbed." She bit her lip to stop herself from crying. She could see by the crestfallen look on Will's face that her misery was affecting him, too.

"You're not self-absorbed. You're goal-oriented. When you decide you're going to do something, you focus on it, sometimes to the exclusion of everything else."

"Like a bulldog," Agnes said wryly.

"I guess you could say that."

Agnes clucked her tongue and Diablo broke into a trot that Will's mount matched. "How about you, Will? You don't strike me as a bulldog."

Will rubbed his chin and stared at the horizon. "I'm no bulldog. I'm a working dog, maybe a cattle dog. I work better for others than I do for myself, and I'm happiest when I've made the people around me happy."

"Those aren't bad traits."

"Neither's yours. It'll get you through this nursing course. And get you the ranch."

"I wish you didn't have to go." Agnes' voice sounded ragged, on the edge of tears.

He sighed. "When I joined the Army, I gave my pledge to do my duty. I wouldn't be much of a man if I walked away from it now."

"I understand." Agnes sniffed and gave Will a fleeting, hesitant smile. "I have to become a nurse so I can save the Sunrise. You have to fulfill your duties. Just don't forget me."

Will swung his horse around so that they were knee to knee. His left hand cradled the back of her head as he pulled her face close and kissed her gently on the tip of her nose, then tilted her head down and brushed his lips against her forehead. "That," he said, "is something I could never do.".

Part Two

A World A Blaze

1917-1918

Chapter Eleven

Agnes tied Diablo to the railing in front of Dieter's Dry goods store and pulled the door shut behind her to keep out the sharp February wind.

"Aggie! What a pleasant surprise to see you here!" Heinrich smiled brightly and leaned his forearms on the counter of the square little booth in the corner that served as a post office.

"It is a surprise," she answered, a bit flustered, "I've never known you to work in the post office before."

Heinrich shrugged. "First time for everything. What with the troubles with Mexico, and the war in Europe, business is kind of depressed these days. I've sent a lot of letters to law firms around the state, but haven't had any luck finding one that needs an associate right now. I see you've been sending a lot of letters, too. And getting responses." He pulled a stack of envelopes out of a cubbyhole and studied them. "Here's one from your mother. How's she doing these days? Enjoying Las Vegas? And your sister Charlotte. And one from the Correspondence School. Hope it's good news. And all these Mexican stamps! You should start a stamp collection."

"Yes, well." Agnes felt her face turning pink. She took the stack from Heinrich, then handed him one to post.

Heinrich studied the address. He looked up, his eyes serious and pleading, like a puppy waiting for its bowl to be set down. "Is it the uniform? Is that what you find so attractive?"

"Oh, Heinrich! Private Bowers is just a friend of the family. He helped Ernesto with chores around the ranch."

Heinrich nodded. "Sure. Ernesto? Is he your ranch foreman?"

"He is. He and Lupe, his wife, have been there my whole life." It surprised her to realize that he didn't even know their names, although he'd been to the ranch dozens of times. How many times had he accepted a plate of food from Lupe and not even bothered to look at her because she was a servant, and a Mexican at that?

Heinrich nodded. "I know the couple you're talking about. Hardworking. You're lucky to have them. My parents have a devil of a time keeping good help. Well, Aggie, I'll see you next time you ride in. Or I could drive your mail out, make myself useful while I'm there. I may not be as handy as this Bowers fellow, but I could help out with chores too, you know. That is, until I find more suitable employment."

"No doubt that will happen soon." Agnes patted his hand sympathetically, then escaped into the cold, February air. She dropped the bundle of mail into her saddle bag. When she got home later that day, she would race upstairs and tear open the letters from Will. The others, from her mother and sister and the one from the correspondence school, would have to wait.

Agnes had made Will promise to write to her, and write he did. His letters surprised her with their erudition. The soft spoken, unassuming man had a way with the written word that she hadn't expected from a mechanic and general roustabout who hadn't made it past the eighth grade. There was nothing intimate or personal in his letters, but as she read them, she heard his sonorous voice and saw the world through his eyes. Sometimes, she even felt his lips on her forehead. She closed her eyes and tilted her face up, as if the memory of that kiss could brush her lips. She tucked his letters neatly away in her desk, and reread them over and over.

Agnes responded with letters of her own, pouring out her hopes for the ranch, the weather and changing seasons. She described her medical visits throughout the community with as much humor and compassion as she could muster. Because his letters were breezy and impersonal, she was careful to keep hers the same. Every time she was tempted to mention the kiss, or the future, she put down her pen and went for a long, hard ride. If he wasn't going to mention such things, then neither was she.

Besides, Agnes told herself she didn't have time for a relationship with Will. She had a ranch to save, a nursing certificate to earn, and a part-time job as Doctor Pritchard's assistant to keep her busy. And she didn't want him hanging around, fixing things for her. She had to prove that she could do this on her own.

Will's letters suggested that life at Camp Dublan was comfortable and monotonous. The newspapers depicted a different story. Instead of hunting down Villa, the Expedition's mission had become protecting itself in an increasingly hostile environment. Mexican soldiers were joining forces with the Villistas while demonstrators marched in opposition to the U.S. expedition. U.S. soldiers were being captured and killed. Agnes was sure Will was trying to protect her from worry. It wasn't working.

Agnes walked Diablo to the livery stable, where he would stay while she worked for Doctor Pritchard. A couple of men in uniform whistled at her as she passed. She ignored them.

The Doctor looked over the top of his wire-rimmed glasses as Agnes came into his office. He set aside the medical journal and pushed away from his desk, then pulled his watch from its pocket and studied it. "Right on time. I appreciate punctuality."

"I try." Agnes took her white apron off its peg and tied it on over her dungarees, grateful that the doctor didn't insist she wear a skirt and blouse.

"I worry when you're not here on time, you know. Banditos are still coming over the border. "

Agnes made a dismissive sound as she helped the doctor into his lab coat. "I'd be more concerned about the guardsmen and all the camp laborers. I can't even walk down the street without catcalls."

"They are an undisciplined bunch of hooligans," the Doctor agreed. "The town jail's always full of rowdies who've gotten into fights. A girl like you can't be too careful."

"It'll all change tomorrow," Agnes said.

Tomorrow, General Black Jack Pershing was to cross into the United States and parade triumphantly through the streets of Columbus. With him would be some 2,700 refugees: Americans who had owned ranches south of the border, Chinese immigrants who faced discrimination in Mexico, and Mexican citizens escaping the violence of their country's long civil war. There would also be well over 10,000 soldiers, including a certain Private William Bowers.

Doctor Pritchard washed his hands with harsh lye soap and plenty of hot water. He rinsed them, then shook them, three times as always. Agnes handed him the towel.

"Would it be all right if I didn't come in tomorrow?" she asked as she took the towel from him and hung it to dry.

Doctor Pritchard smiled, the skin around his eyes creasing beneath the gleam of his wire-rimmed glasses. His mouth lay buried behind the huge walrus mustache that hid both amusement and displeasure from patients and nurses alike. "I suppose we have no appointments?"

"None. All cancelled when the Expedition's return was announced."

"I assume you wish to see the parade?" He turned toward her, the lenses of his glasses reflecting her image back at her, obscuring his watery blue eyes.

"Yes, doctor."

Doctor Pritchard harrumphed, which was his way of biding time while he gathered his thoughts. His eyebrows met in a peak above the bridge of his nose. Eyebrows, especially those as full as Doctor Pritchard's, could say a great deal. "I suppose there's a returning soldier you would like to see?"

Agnes felt her cheeks grow red and wished her own face wasn't so readable.

"Miss Day, I gave you this job so that you could gain clinical experience concurrent with your studies. Nursing is a high and noble calling, but it is not a profession at which you can dabble. You must take it seriously. If you are just biding time as you wait for a proposal from a soldier, I shall not provide you with a recommendation for a position, even if you manage to complete your studies. This could be the end of your nursing career before it's even begun."

Agnes' eyes flashed to the doctor's face. "Oh! No, sir! I want the afternoon off to help assign refugees to tents. I've volunteered with the women's auxiliary to make sure those tents remain healthy and hygienic."

The Doctor's mustache tilted to the side, a sure sign of skepticism. "Well, then, seeing as we have no appointments and the records are caught up, I suppose you can take a day to volunteer with the women's auxiliary's effort to assuage refugees. That's the kind of service that will look good on your resume."

The next afternoon, Agnes rode Diablo into town while Lupe and Ernesto took the gig. Lupe wore her Sunday-best dress and a flower-trimmed hat with a brim so broad that it covered both her and Ernesto, who sat half a head shorter than his wife, but respectable in his best suit. Instead of her usual dungarees and flannel shirt, Agnes wore a flowery dress with a skirt that was too full to be fashionable, but allowed her to ride. She told herself that wearing a dress would make the male refugees respect her more than wearing what they might consider a man's get up, but her hand kept drifting to her forehead, where Will had kissed her.

The town of Columbus was bedecked with bunting and flags, ready to greet the returning soldiers with a parade, followed by a chicken dinner so large that it had to be served from planks on sawhorses set up in the middle of Taft Street. The women's auxiliary of Columbus had prepared for the refugees as well, setting up a camp outfitted with surplus army tents and provisioned with local produce and canned goods. Lupe had donated half of last summer's canned peaches. As the hygiene and health liaison for the women's auxiliary, Agnes would help assign tents to families and groups of single men. She was charged with making sure the refugees were healthy enough to leave after a few months, when the camp would be disbanded.

Ernesto, Lupe and Agnes joined the crowds lining Broadway. They accepted the little flags that were handed out by clerks from A.D. Frost's Hardware and Furniture Store, and by Dieter's Dry goods. As soldiers marched by, Agnes stood on tiptoe, trying to find one with a cafe au lait complexion. She wished she were taller, or the man in front of her would realize that he was blocking her view.

"There he is, *mija*! I see him! "Just when she was sure she had missed him, Lupe squealed and flapped her flag so violently that the man in front of Agnes stepped aside. Agnes' heart leaped. The sun had burnished Will's face, but his eyes and his bearing were unmistakable. She shouted his name and his eyes jerked in her direction. A slight smile crossed his face. He had seen her! Wave upon wave of handsome young soldiers wearing clean uniforms, brown Montana-peaked hats, and glossy black boots flowed past. Agnes settled back and waited, sure that Will knew where to find her when the column reached the end of the parade route and dispersed.

"There he is!" Lupe shouted again, this time nearly smacking Agnes on the head with her flag. A flotilla of brown Montana hats floated over the sea of spectators and it was moving in their direction.

Ernesto took Lupe's arm. "Come, Lupe. Let's see if they need any help setting up for dinner."

"But I want to see Will!" Lupe wailed.

"You will see him soon enough." Ernesto whispered something into Lupe's ear. She giggled, her hand covering her mouth, and allowed him to lead her away.

Agnes found herself tiptoeing to get her face above the sea of people, her eyes darting from round, brown hat to round, brown hat. She felt a touch on her elbow, whirled around, and there he was, so close that she could smell his salty earthiness. For a moment, the noise of the crowd faded into silence and she forgot about anyone but Will.

Will placed his hand on the small of her back and pulled her close. She threw her arms around his neck, and their lips met, sending a jolt through her that made her weak in the knees. He squeezed her tighter, holding her against his strong, warm body.

Someone jostled into them and suddenly she remembered where they were. Agnes pushed against Will's chest. She cupped her cheeks with her hands and felt them burning in embarrassment. She erupted in laughter. "Why are you always sneaking up on me?"

"Sorry. I didn't mean to." He pulled off his hat and sheepishly stepped back, regret and embarrassment playing across his face.

"Oh! No! I didn't mean that! I mean, it's all right. I mean . . ." Agnes didn't know what she meant, but she did know that she didn't want to discourage him. She had waited a long time for that kiss, and it had been everything she had dreamed of. Agnes glanced around for the disapproving eyes of Doctor Pritchard. He wasn't there. No one seemed scandalized by a girl kissing a soldier in broad daylight. She smiled slyly at him. "I've been thinking about doing that for a long time."

Will flushed under his tan. "So have I."

They grinned at each other. Agnes felt a wave of shyness. Suddenly his boots became very interesting.

"Miss Day. Agnes. May I call you Agnes?" Will's voice made her look again at his face, where a million emotions seemed to compete. Will looked relieved and worried, happy and miserable, all at the same time. And those eyes! Why had she ever thought they were the eyes of a coyote? Clearly, they were cattle dog eyes: perceptive, intelligent, filled with both intention and attention and desperate to please her. She was so enraptured that she barely heard him speak. "I hear there's a chicken dinner on Taft Street, in front of the Clark Hotel. I would be honored if you would allow me to accompany you to it."

Agnes felt herself flush. "I can't." She watched his face fall, and quickly grabbed his forearm. "I'm on the committee to help refugees. I have to settle them in. But Ernesto and Lupe are there! At the chicken dinner, I mean, not at the refugee camp. They're anxious to see you. Eat with them. I'll catch up as soon as I can. Will."

At the sound of his name, Will's face lost all its tension. She planted a peck of a kiss on his cheek, and with an encouraging smile, turned and elbowed her way through the crowd, unsure whether her feet were actually touching the ground.

Three hours later, Agnes hobbled towards Taft Street as fast as her pretty, button up boots with the wobbly little heels allowed. The refugee camp had been a tangle of terrified and confused people, all acting badly. Babies, exhausted from the drama of the day, wailed inconsolably. Their cranky older siblings whined. Men demanded. Women, in sobbing voices, wanted to tell about all the lovely and irreplaceable heirlooms they had left behind. Families that'd brought wagons full of household items wanted to know where they could store them. Families with nothing but the clothes on their backs wanted to know where they could get new things. No one, it seemed, wanted to just give the names of their family members and then retire to a tent.

Now it was evening, the February temperatures were dropping to freezing. She was tired to the bone, her feet hurt and her back ached. She wished she had worn her regular work boots. They were so much easier to walk in. But, truth be told, Agnes had to admit to herself that she really wasn't a walker at all. She never went anywhere if not on horseback.

Agnes had worried about how she was going to find Will in the crowd. She turned the corner and, instead, found Taft Street deserted. Not even the planks and sawhorses remained to show that anything had happened here. Agnes bit back her disappointment and silently cursed whatever civic minded thought had made her volunteer to help refugees on the day the troops returned. Now, she was sure, Will was back at Camp Columbus. Who knew when he would get leave again? She limped back to the livery stable, found Diablo, then rode home.

Agnes' emotions swung wildly as she rode through the gathering twilight. She shivered and wished she was wearing something other than a flimsy little dress. Her feet hurt. Her head ached. But she had been kissed! And what a kiss! Agnes shook her head, wondering why that kiss made her heart race. It didn't get her any closer to owning the Sunrise. Didn't help her complete her nursing course. Yet, just thinking about it made her giddy.

She was close to the house when she heard someone playing the piano, and her heart soared. Ernesto came out of the stable. Despite the darkness, she could see he was smiling.

"It is good to have him back," he said as he reached for Diablo's bridle.

"That it is," Agnes agreed. She swung down and gave Ernesto a hug. "Thank you for keeping him busy until I got back here."

Ernesto laughed. "That was not difficult. Lupe has been talking to him all afternoon. And filling him with cake. He's like an extra son to us."

Agnes thought about that as she crossed the porch, her little heels clicking on the floorboards. Will fit in at the Sunrise as if he'd always been a part of the family. His presence felt comfortable. But there was something beyond that comfort, something that made her heart leap when she saw him. She wanted to explore that extra something. She entered the parlor and slipped onto the piano bench next to Will. Lupe, who had been drumming her fingers on the armrest of an upholstered chair, made an excuse about cleaning up the kitchen and left the room.

"That's a jaunty tune," Agnes said, one hand keeping time in the air. "A march, is it? I feel I should know the name."

"It's *The Girl I Left Behind Me,*" Will answered. "It's an old song. I think it's been sung in every war that America's ever been in. Probably was British before that."

"Does it have lyrics?"

Will nodded. "Lots of 'em. All different. Here's one version; an Irish one." He closed his eyes and sang in that fine, tenor voice that she had missed. Since she didn't know the words, Agnes hummed along in harmony.

All the dames of France are fond and free
And Flemish lips are really willing
Very soft the maids of Italy
And Spanish eyes are so thrilling

Still, although I bask beneath their smile,
Their charms will fail to bind me
And my heart falls back to Erin's isle
To the girl I left behind me.

"Very nice, Private Bowers," she said when he had played the last chord and his hands rested in his lap. "So, you sang about the girls in France and Flanders, and Spain. How about the ones in Mexico?"

"I wouldn't know," he said.

Agnes had meant this as a joke, but Will's face darkened into a scowl. Embarrassed and not knowing how to dig herself out, she plunged on, moving from joke to nursing lesson.

"Doctor Pritchard says General Pershing kept the Mexican prostitutes in a special barbed-wire stockade, and that soldiers who visited them were required to take a prophylactic."

Will scowled. "The Doctor shouldn't be saying such things to a lady."

"I'm not a lady, I'm a nursing student, and this is an interesting case." Months of reading medical studies had turned the subject clinical, to be analyzed, not moralized. "He said that the strict sanitary regulations led to one of the lowest venereal disease rates that any army, anywhere, has ever known. Was it really as well run as Doctor Pritchard says?"

Will pulled his fingers off the keyboard and tucked them into his armpits, his arms folded defensively over his chest. "You think I'm the kind of man who goes to cathouses?"

"I'm just curious," Agnes said. "I wasn't accusing you of . . . "

She never got to finish. Will stood up so quickly that he nearly knocked over the bench, with Agnes on it. "Not any more. Not for a long time. It's getting late," he muttered, and gathering his hat at the door, stormed out.

Agnes stood on the porch and watched him blend into the darkness. Lupe appeared beside her, wiping her hands on a dishtowel. "He did not say goodbye?"

"I think I got him mad," Agnes said. "All I did was ask him about how Pershing managed the prostitution operations in Mexico."

Lupe stopped wiping her hands and stared at Agnes. The look of disappointment in her eyes made Agnes want to curl up in a ball. "Oh Mija! How could you insult an honorable man like that? Sometimes I think you are too smart for your own good. You have to learn to think *con tu corazon, no con tu cabeza."*

Agnes laid her face in her hands against the doorframe and cried, ashamed of herself, and determined to learn to think with her heart instead of her head.

Chapter Twelve

The trail of dust along the road showed that someone was in an awful hurry to get to the Sunrise Ranch. Agnes wished it was Will. He hadn't been there in two weeks: not since the day of the parade, and she desperately wanted to apologize and make things good between them. She had ridden to Camp Columbus the day after their argument, only to have Corporal Benavides suggest she give him more time to cool off. But two weeks? It made her heart ache, just thinking about it.

During those two weeks, Agnes had admitted to herself that she had begun envisioning a life with Will in it. She had missed him so much while he was in Mexico, missed his easy, gentle way of supporting and encouraging her, how he fit in like he'd always belonged and made all of them, Lupe and Ernesto included, happy. If only she was sure she would be able to keep the Sunrise!

The swirling dust cloud moved closer. A red Oldsmobile appeared. Agnes' heart sank as she recognized Heinrich Dieter's car. HIs window was down and his arm was out, waving something large and white and rectangular that folded and bent in the wind.

Lupe came to the doorway. "What's that in his hand?" She wiped her hands on the front of her apron, then reached behind her to untie the apron strings.

Agnes winced. "I'm hoping it's my certificate, and I'm wishing he wasn't bending it all to heck."

Heinrich stuck his head out the window and shouted something that was lost under the growl of the engine and the rumble of wheels on gravel. Just as he pulled up at the Big House, the paper escaped his grasp and fluttered like a wounded pigeon into a bush.

Agnes sighed and went down the porch stairs.

Heinrich climbed out of the car and retrieved the envelope. With a little flourish, he held it out to Agnes. "For you, m'lady. I was so excited, I had to deliver this myself."

"Did you have to go and bend it, too?" Agnes ripped it from Heinrich's hand and studied the return address. 371 Mainstreet, Jamestown, New York. Her heart beat so hard she was sure Heinrich could hear it over the idling engine. She carried it back to the house, cradling it against her chest as if it were the Holy Bible.

"Is it? Is it?" Heinrich tagged along, leaping from one side of her to the other to gaze at her face.

"Hope so." Agnes walked into the kitchen, grabbed a paring knife, and slit the envelope, careful not to damage its contents. She slid out a certificate on stiff, cream-colored paper from the Chautauqua School of Nursing certifying that Miss Agnes Day had successfully completed its nursing course. Behind it, another stiff sheet of paper bore her nursing license. Agnes let out a long breath and dropped into a chair, relieved and a little surprised that the long ordeal was over. She'd done it! She'd passed the final exam!

She shook her head and reminded herself that the long ordeal wasn't really over. Getting her nursing license was hard, but it was just a stepping stone to a job that would enable her to earn the money for a down payment on the ranch. She still had a long way to go to achieve her goals. Suddenly her head felt heavy. She propped it up in her hand, wondering if she had the strength to go on. She wished Will was there. He'd know what to say to shake her from her torpor.

Heinrich pumped his fist in the air. "I knew it! Ever since we were school chums! I knew you were going to do great things. Let's take a picture to commemorate the moment! He pulled his little camera from his pocket. Agnes held up the certificate and tried to smile through her exhaustion.

"Let's throw a party to celebrate! We can do it at the store! Invite the whole town!"

"That's not necessary," Agnes said.

"What are old friends for? Really! How about Sunday afternoon? Really, Aggie: this is really just too big an achievement not to warrant a party."

"You really are too kind, Heinrich. Really. I'll really think about it and get back to you," Agnes said, mimicking the excitement in his voice while she parroted his *reallys* back at him. She escorted him out the front door, thanked him for delivering the envelope, and promised he'd hear from her. She leaned against the door and let out an exasperated sigh. Really, that boy was too much. If she was a bulldog and Will was a cattle dog, Heinrich was an overgrown puppy.

"What was that all about?" Lupe popped her head out of the parlor, where she had retreated when Agnes and Heinrich had exploded through the front door. Agnes waved her into the kitchen and showed her the two papers embossed with gold seals and ribbons. Lupe ran her hand along one of them and made a small *ooo* of appreciation. "*Mija,* I couldn't be prouder if you were my own daughter. I throw a party for you, no?"

"Exactly what Heinrich wanted to do."

"And you said?"

"No, of course. I don't want him to feel I owe him."

Lupe threw up her hands. "He has been your friend your whole life. His father has the money. Let him do this."

"Honestly, Lupe! You sound just like my mother!"

"No, Mija. Just because a friend gives you a party doesn't mean you have to marry him. I know Mr. Heinrich is not the one for you. If he were, you would have known it long ago. Like me and my Ernesto. The first time I laid eyes on him: *eee-jo-lah*!"

"No," Agnes said. "No *eee-jo-lah* from Heinrich. And no party, either. I don't want to encourage him."

The next day, Agnes rode into town intending to thank Heinrich for his kind offer, but say she wanted no party. She found every power pole and wall in town plastered with a handbill advertising a celebratory reception for Miss Agnes Day, at Dieter's Dry Goods, on Sunday. She rode back to the Sunrise Ranch knowing she could no more stop the party than hold back the waters of the Red Sea.

At the party, Agnes picked up a finger sandwich held together with a toothpick topped with an American flag, then edged between sparkling glass display cases. Every bit of wood in Dieter's Dry goods had been polished to a bright luster. Red, white and blue bunting decorated the walls and the tops of the windows, and a framed picture of Agnes holding her certificate and dazedly smiling into the camera stood right next to the punch bowl. The Dieters had gone to a great deal of trouble preparing for this party. Half the town and camp were there, all wearing their Sunday best and displaying their best manners. She hadn't expected anyone to care this much. Perhaps they didn't. Perhaps they just liked an excuse to dress up and celebrate after all of last year's funerals. It didn't matter. Agnes would make the rounds, then go home, change out of her dress, and return to being a rancher. One day of celebrity was enough.

She elbowed her way to Mr. Dieter who ladled punch into little glass cups that a sign said could be purchased as a set or singly, as souvenirs of the day. A starched white apron wrapped around his considerable paunch, making him look slightly ridiculous.

"This was very kind of you. You went to considerable bother," Agnes said.

Mr. Dieter beamed. "Nothing is too good for our Aggie! Our families, yours and mine, we have been friends and business partners since before you and our little Heinrich were born!"

"Ja, ja! Good Americans we are!" Mrs. Dieter said. She held out a tray of pimento-cheese stuffed celery and smiled nervously, obviously uncomfortable with the crowd. Her English wasn't good, and she usually stayed upstairs in the family's apartments.

Agnes made her way through the crowd, stopping here and there to talk with someone, but determined to get to the corner where she'd caught a glimpse of Will and Corporal Benavides huddled together. Her stomach kept doing flips as she struggled to keep her face impassive and serene. She didn't know whether she wanted to throw herself into Will's arms and apologize or scream at him for being absent so long. She was afraid of making a scene in front of half the town.

"Private Bowers. Corporal Benavides," she said stiffly, nodding at each when she'd finally caught up with them.

"Miss Day. Lovely party. Congratulations on finishing your program." Will responded. Corporal Benavides scowled at the floor.

"I haven't seen either of you at the Sunrise lately." Agnes tried to keep her voice as casual as she could, but she could hear the edge in it. Why, when she liked this man so much, did she always end up fighting with him?

"You know where to find me if you need me," Will answered.

"I came to the camp once," Agnes replied. "Corporal Benavides suggested you didn't want to see me."

"He did?' Will raised one eyebrow and looked at his friend, who glared even harder at the floor but said nothing.

"Please do come. We need to talk. And I need to apologize." Agnes held out her hand. It was trembling. Will stared at it for a second, then he looked up at her face and she saw mirth dancing in his eyes. Her stomach stopped dancing, and she smiled back at him.

"I consider that an invitation, Miss Day." He took her hand in his and she squeezed it, feeling its warmth and strength surge up her arm.

"Please. Call me Agnes."

"There you are Aggie! Come here! I have someone you need to meet!" Heinrich Dieter wedged himself between Agnes and Will, then placed his hand on the small of her back and guided her through the crowd, discussing her plans for the future.

"Stop it!" she hissed through clenched teeth while her lips still smiled. "People are going to think we are engaged."

"Would that be so bad?" Heinrich whispered back.

"Yes! Yes, it would." Agnes looked over her shoulder, embarrassed that Will might be watching and getting the wrong idea. She couldn't see him in the crowd. "

"Just play along. Don't you know how good this is for business? For my folks?"

Agnes glared at him. The Dieters were good friends of the family, and they had gone to a lot of trouble, all for her. But after half an hour of this she couldn't wait to escape the party and return to the silence and emptiness of the ranch.

"Whose party is this, anyway? That's it! I'm going home."

Agnes broke free and elbowed her way towards the door. She passed through a knot of men she didn't recognize. They were rough looking, with hair that needed cutting and a shifty way of looking around a room that made her wonder if they were pickpockets. One of them thrust a copy of that morning's newspaper into her hands.

"Lookie here! The no-good Kraut Zimmermann has finally admitted that his cable was genuine." The man spat the words out, making Agnes pull back to avoid his whiskey-tainted breath. Agnes remembered hearing about the telegram, sent to a Mexican official by a German Foreign Secretary named Arthur Zimmermann, but intercepted and published in American papers. The telegram had proposed a military alliance between Germany and Mexico, promising to give Mexico its former provinces of Texas, Arizona, and New Mexico if it entered the war. She hadn't paid it much attention. She was too busy with her coursework and the ranch.

The man jabbed his finger at a political cartoon in which a man labeled Neutrality lay sprawled at the foot of an American flag, a knife sticking out of his back. "That's what that telegram did, Missie. We'll be in it soon. Let's see which side that boyfriend of yours joins up on." Agnes spun around, looking for Will. Then she realized that they were talking about Heinrich, whose face had gone ashen, and who was backing towards his parents.

"This means war!" another of the rowdies shouted. "Let's string up every Kraut we can get our hands on! Before they get the chance to shoot our boys!"

"Please!" Mr. Dieter held out his hands in a gesture of peace and calm, "We are here to celebrate Miss Day's achievements. Let us not allow politics to darken the atmosphere."

The drunken man pointed a finger at Mr. Dieter. "'Course you don't want us speaking against the Krauts! You are one!"

Another drunkard stepped forward. "Your store didn't burn during the raid, did it? You a colluder? Maybe a spy!"

"I am a loyal American! I love my country! Look! I have parties. With bunting." Mr. Dieter's finger jabbed first at the bunting, then at the flags on the sandwiches. Mrs. Dieter, her eyes so wide that the whites stood out, squeezed into the space between him and the counter.

Agnes remembered that two weeks ago, while she was riding past to work, she had noticed Heinrich putting a new pane in the store window. At the time, she hadn't thought much of it. Now, she wondered if someone had thrown a rock through the window. Were the Dieters being harassed because they were German? The crowd began to grumble. If she didn't do something, her party would turn into a lynching.

Agnes' heart raced as she elbowed through the ring of rowdies that had surrounded Mr. Dieter. She climbed onto a chair, and gave the crowd her most brilliant smile. "Is everyone having a lovely time?" she shouted.

The crowd answered with a sprinkling of applause. "Good! I'm so glad to hear it. The Day family has known the Dieter family since they moved to the area. Decades ago. They are the kind of people we need in our town: Hardworking people who charge a fair price and keep our economy going. And look what kind neighbors the Dieters are! Handing out flags so we can welcome our boys back with a parade! Throwing this party for the whole town!"

"It's your party, Ag, not ours," a man shouted, and a few others laughed.

Agnes shook her head. "The Dieters could have invited just me over for dinner. All this," she waved her arm, encompassing the punch bowl, cakes, and sandwiches, "is for you." Agnes pointed her finger, then moved it around, looking every face in the eye.

The applause was louder this time. Agnes took a breath to steady herself, then smiled the flashiest grin she could manage. "And this isn't the only time the Dieters have shown themselves good citizens of the community. I know for a fact that Mr. Dieter willingly extends credit to neighbors who need it." She raised her hands and was answered with cheers and more applause. "And good American that he is, he pitched in when the rest of you generously helped the refugees." The crowd broke into roars. Agnes knew that they were cheering for themselves, but she also saw that the fight had gone out of them. The drunkards seemed to have sensed that their chance had ebbed, too. She watched them slip away and felt her body relax.

"It's been a long day, and the sun doesn't wait for a rancher who parties the night away. I'll be going now, but not before thanking the Dieters for this lovely event." Agnes turned towards the couple and began clapping. The crowd roared. People began thanking the Dieters and taking their leave. Agnes gathered a few plates, handed them to Mrs. Dieter, then walked out the door. She was exhausted; standing up to a crowd had drained her.

She found Corporal Benavides waiting outside. His scowl told her that he was still determined not to enjoy himself. Agnes gave him her sweetest smile anyways. Corporal Benavides reciprocated with a respectful nod of the head.

"That was very brave of you, Miss Day, talking down a whole gang of roughnecks."

She shrugged. "I was never in any kind of danger."

"You were in more danger than you knew," he replied. "You still are. Those men aren't the kind that respect women, even when they haven't been passing a flask. I'll see you home."

She unhitched Diablo from the rail and swung up so that she was looking down on him.

"You're going to walk?"

He nodded. "I'm going to walk."

"There's no need," she said. "I ride alone all the time."

"Not after ruining a group of hooligans' fun." He hooked his fingers through Diablo's halter and began leading both horse and rider toward home.

"Really, there's no need," Agnes said.

"Orders is orders," he said.

"You were ordered to escort me home? By whom?"

"Bowers."

Agnes smiled teasingly at Benavides, whose face had grown even darker with irritation. "Private Bowers is giving orders to Corporal Benavides? Is this punishment for you not letting me see him last time I rode to camp?"

"He's my friend," Benavides said. "I wouldn't do it otherwise."

"Where is he?" Agnes asked.

"Sentry duty. Made me promise I'd see you home."

Agnes stored away the fact that Will had watched after her even when he couldn't do it himself. "This telegram: do you think it will really cause us to enter the war?"

"That's what they're saying. The whole camp is abuzz."

Agnes shook her head. It seemed crazy to send American boys all the way to Europe, especially when they were needed right here. Was the United States Army really going to abandon the borderlands to fight on a distant continent?

"I suppose this means you and Will have to go?" Agnes felt an ache of emptiness inside. She had known that Will was going to move on. All soldiers did. But he had established a rather permanent base in her heart.

Benavides shook his head. "We aren't regular Army. We're National Guard."

"So, you're staying here?" Agnes asked.

Benavides shook his head. "We demobilize next month."

"And then what?"

"We go home. Back to our regular jobs until we're called up again."

"And home is?"

"Roswell for me."

"And for Will?"

Benavides scowled up at Agnes disdainfully. "How should I know? Men don't sit around talking about things like that."

"You're going home. Might Will decide to stay here?" A tiny bit of hope glimmered in Agnes' heart like the evening star hovering on the far horizon. If Will didn't have to continue following the Army, might he stay on the Sunrise? He was certainly welcome.

David Benavides glared at Agnes for several steps before he spoke. "Will's no one man army. Other troops will rotate in. They're not going to leave the border unprotected. Or maybe you don't need an army. Maybe you can climb onto a chair and stop the next raid yourself."

Hurt by his sarcasm, Agnes shut her mouth and let him stew in silence the rest of the way home. This was Will's friend, and he seemed determined to keep them apart. Why? What had he seen in her that was so reprehensible? She remembered the first time she met Benavides and Will. She had not been very impressed with either of them. But things had changed. She had changed. Agnes touched her lips, remembering how he kissed her on the day he returned.

They arrived at the Bernal's house and Corporal Benavides turned to go.

"What have I ever done, that you despise me so?" Agnes asked.

Corporal Benavides took off his hat. He looked up at Agnes, and for the first time she didn't see anger and hatred in his eyes. She saw pain. "My Dolores. Every time I go home to Roswell, she's pregnant. None of the kids look like me. But she's got the widest smile and the sweetest eyes, and I can never bring myself to get angry at her. Private Bowers is a good man. He deserves a good life. Don't toy with him."

"He is. He does. I won't," Agnes said, holding her hand up as if making a pledge. The Corporal lifted one eyebrow, showing he doubted her word, then he turned on his heel and walked back down the road to Camp Columbus.

When she was safe in her little bedroom in the Bernal's house, Agnes opened the drawer of her desk and withdrew a newspaper editorial written by New Mexico's governor, Ezequiel C. de Baca in the February 3 edition of the New York World.

> *New Mexico will stand loyally behind the president and hold up his hands. We endorse the action already taken. We believe the avenues of trade on the high seas should be kept open to commerce in accordance with the law of nations and that the armed force of the United States should be used for that purpose if necessary.*

Agnes read through the words again, then set them back in the drawer and closed it, hoping that hiding the words away made them less true. She wasn't sure if she wanted New Mexico to stand loyally behind the United States, not if the United States wasn't going to stand behind New Mexico. How could the Army leave southern New Mexico when Germany was offering the state to Mexico for the taking? And how could she allow Will to leave again?

Chapter Thirteen

Agnes rushed home from Doctor Pritchard's office to help Lupe prepare a special meal to celebrate the demobilization of the National Guard. Since he was not part of the small contingent that would remain at Camp Columbus, Will could no longer stay at the camp. Where he would go next remained a mystery. Agnes was determined to make sure he knew that staying at the Sunrise was an option.

In the month since her party at the Dry goods store, Will had become a regular dinner guest again, and that pleased her. But he had remained formal and distant, and that had not. Will acted like a friend of the family, not Agnes' love interest. He called her Miss Day, and offered her gentlemanly courtesies. On rare occasions, though, his mask would slip, and she glimpsed a more intimate Will, the one who called her Agnes and smiled at her with those gray-brown eyes. The Will who had kissed her. She watched the dusty road between the Sunrise and Camp Columbus, silently practicing what she was going to say to coax Will back to her. The cutlery she clutched in her sweaty hand grew hot and slick.

A lone figure appeared, small against the vastness of the desert.

"There he is, Lupe," she called over her shoulder.

"*Bueno.* Time to put in biscuits."

The Bernals ate at a worn table in the center of the kitchen. Once, the table had been painted white, but hundreds of plates and cups dragged back and forth across it had taken much of the paint off, exposing weathered pine. She set the table, then glanced out the open door. Will was close enough now to see that he wore a tweed cap, a simple white cotton shirt, a pair of gray trousers, and shouldered a duffle bag heavy enough to make him lean.

Ernesto emerged from the stable as Will came into the yard. Will dropped his bag and the two men shook hands. They talked for what seemed an eternity.

Agnes sighed. "What in the world can those two be talking about that's taking so long?"

Lupe chuckled. "The condition of the roof. How much rain we might get once the monsoons start. Why the chickens aren't laying. Men can always find something to talk about instead of what's important."

It was true, Agnes thought. Men talked about the weather, the animals, the economy. Women talked about the men, their children, and their feelings. She wished she knew what Will felt, what he planned.

Agnes's hand trailed to her lips. She remembered the kiss they had shared the day he returned from Mexico. One mention of the whorehouse at Camp Dublan, and he had clammed up. Was he prudish? Hiding something? Or was it the clinical way she'd discussed it? Was he opposed to her becoming a nurse? There were so many questions she wanted to ask, but they all stuck in her throat. Over a month had gone by, and the questions had remained unasked. It was strange, this sense of intimacy and yet distance. She had known him over a year, knew his character, his trustworthy nature Yet what did she know of his past? What were his plans for the future? Did they include her?

When he and Ernesto finally came in, Will took off his hat and handed Agnes a fist full of poppies. "*Buenas Tardes,* Lupe, Miss Day. Here. These are for you," he said in the Spanglish that everyone on the border spoke. As

Agnes filled a glass with water to put the poppies in, Lupe enveloped Will in a motherly hug that made Agnes' own arms twitch with jealousy. She remembered the feeling of those arms around her.

"Good evening, Private Bowers. We're so glad you could join us for one last meal before you move on," Agnes said pointedly, watching Will's face for a reaction. Anything, a wince or a smile, would have been better than the stoic nothingness she saw there. "I'm not sure I would have recognized you. I don't think I've ever seen you out of uniform before."

Will looked down, as if surprised to see what he was wearing. "I'm a civilian now. I bought these from Dieter's Dry Goods. Like 'em?"

She did. The white shirt set off Will's coffee and cream skin and made his shoulders look even broader, while the pants hugged his slim hips. But before Agnes could answer, Lupe motioned them to the table and set out bowls and platters of fried chicken, tamales, biscuits, beans, gravy and coleslaw: the usual mix of food from her childhood and from the Days'. "How are things at the camp, *mijo*? Pretty empty?"

"It was crowded during the changeover, but us old ones are all gone now, and the new men are settling in." Will held out a chair for Agnes, then stood until Lupe had seated herself. Agnes looked sideways at Lupe, a bit annoyed that she was asking questions. She had her own questions to ask: her own script that she had gone over and over in her head. Lupe's questions weren't a part of it.

"Pretty empty around here, too," she said, improvising so it wouldn't look so obvious. "If we're going to get this place up and running again, we'll need another hand."

Will poured gravy over his chicken and beans, then offered the gravy pitcher to Agnes. "Want some gravy? How's the job hunt going, Miss Day?"

Agnes passed the gravy to Lupe. "I've never been much of a gravy fan. It's salsa over gravy every time for me. Sent in my application to be an extension home nurse quite some time ago. Haven't heard back from the state, though. I figure while I'm waiting would be a good time to get some work done around here. Maybe start building up the herd again, if I can find a cowboy to help me work them."

She waited for Will to volunteer. Instead, he used a biscuit to load his spoon with beans. "Lupe, this is excellent, as always," he said before shoveling them in.

"Whoever stayed on to help would get Lupe's cooking all the time. Doctor Pritchard only pays me $7 a month. At that rate it's going to take me a long time to make a down payment. I could make more money if I ran a hundred head or so. But I could use more help than just Ernesto can give me."

Ernesto's head snapped up. "*Señorita*! Do not put me out to pasture yet. I am not that long in the tooth."

Agnes unfurled her napkin and set it in her lap as she waited for Will to volunteer to stay on the Sunrise. Watching him shovel in beans exasperated her. Honestly, where was he going to find a better deal than she was offering him? A chance to stay on the Sunrise and ride the range? What could be better?

"Write us a list," Will said.

Agnes' jaw dropped. "What?"

Will looked up. She saw the mirth in his eyes and realized that he had been playing with her. Had he planned all along to take her up on her offer? "I said, write us a list. Ernesto and I can do anything you put on it."

Ernesto broke into a grin. Clearly, he was in on this joke. "Si. This old man and this boy, we'll get this place up and running again. Will's going to stay on with us for a while."

"Mijo!" Lupe said, and rapped Will's head with her spoon, obviously delighted.

"That's great news!" Joy ran through Agnes like electricity. She reached for a tamale, and peeled off its cornhusk shell. Convincing Will had been easier than she thought. She knew she was grinning like a fool, but she couldn't help herself. "Now that the Expedition's over, I bet a lot of ranches will settle back into business as usual. Your friend, Corporal Benavides: He has a ranch down by Roswell, doesn't he? Now that peace is finally here, is he going to increase the size of his herd?" She picked up the bowl of beans, intending to serve herself, then pass it to Ernesto. Something about the look on Will's face stopped her, the bowl suspended in air. "What?"

Will looked at Ernesto. "They don't know, do they?"

Ernesto shook his head. "I didn't, either. Not until you told me."

Agnes set the bowl down, her mouth suddenly dry and her appetite gone. "Know what?"

Will took a deep breath. "If Benavides goes home, it'll just be for a short stay. President Wilson declared war on Germany today. We'll be called back up."

Agnes gasped. "Surely President Wilson doesn't expect Benavides to go to Europe! He just got back from Mexico! He's got a ranch to run!"

Ernesto chuckled. "I don't think President Wilson cares about Benavides' ranch. He's got a war to fight."

Will served himself a second helping of beans. She was sure he was intentionally avoiding her gaze. Suddenly she realized that Ernesto had said Will was staying for a while. Not forever, or a year, or even a season. Her heart lurched in her chest. "You're going, too. But Will, I need you here."

"You don't need me. You have Ernesto," Will said. "Pass me the chicken."

"I told you! Ernesto is old," Agnes's voice rose to almost a wail. She noticed Ernesto wincing. She tried to calm down and speak reasonably, logically. "Sorry, Ernesto, but it's true. You need Will just as much as I do."

Will stared at the ceiling, considering. "Do you remember what attracted you to Columbus on the night that Villa attacked?"

Agnes nodded even if she didn't understand the connection. "The fire?"

"You couldn't see flames or smoke, but you knew it was there."

"There was a glow. In the sky," Agnes remembered.

"It attracted you. You raced Diablo toward it."

Agnes felt her face flush. "I was just curious."

Will nodded. "You knew there was a conflagration. You knew there was danger. But it called you. You couldn't wait until morning. You didn't want to arrive too late and find nothing but ashes."

It dawned on her that Will was explaining how he felt about the war. He wanted to go, wanted to see it for himself, and was afraid that it would be over before he got there if he didn't go quickly. "This isn't your fight."

"That wasn't your fire," Will answered.

Agnes took a deep breath before she began again. "This is a European war. We don't have to get involved."

Ernesto reached over to the sideboard drawer, and pulled out a newspaper clipping. In his stilted English, he read New Mexico Governor C de Baca's editorial, the same one that Agnes had in her desk drawer. He looked up, squinting at Agnes as if to see if she understood. "This President sent troops to protect us from Pancho Villa. If he wants us to go to war, we will go. New Mexicans need to show that we are *Americanos* too!"

"But not Will. He doesn't have to go," Agnes argued.

"What if I want to?" Will's voice was so low that Agnes was not quite sure she had heard it. She looked into his eyes and saw the desire to be a part of this great adventure, and she knew there was nothing she could do to stop him from going.

"When are you leaving?" she asked.

"I don't know. The new recruiting campaign hasn't even begun. But when it does, I want to be first in line."

Agnes stared, dumbfounded, at Ernesto, and then at Will. Tears of frustration and loss brimmed her eyes and she brushed them away. This was not how she'd expected the dinner to go. Will was going to stay, but not for forever, and when he went, it was to a place far away and very, very scary. She needed to change his mind, but she didn't know how much time she had to do it, or if she was brave enough to listen to his answers if she asked the questions that were needling her.

As they cleared the table after dinner, Agnes held up the glass filled with the poppies Will had brought her. "Oh, look. They're already wilting."

"Poppies are here for a short time, then gone," Will said.

"Like you?" The words caught in Agnes' throat. They came out as a whisper.

Will looked up, his eyes filled with pain. "I've been on the move all my life. I've never stayed anywhere very long. You can't expect that to change."

Will stayed with the Bernals for two months, during which he helped Ernesto split wood, mend fences, paint, reset the glass in the windows, and a dozen other little chores. Agnes came home from work every day hoping that evening would be the one Will again opened up to her and she would be able to share her thoughts and dreams with him. He was polite and kind. Some days, as they sat on the front porch and watched the shadow of the earth creep up the eastern sky until the world turned dark and the stars came out, she was almost sure that he was close to a declaration. But it never happened.

Nor did she develop the bravery to confront him. Agnes wanted to understand why he had withdrawn from her, but she was afraid that asking him would push him even further away. She was angry at herself for being such a coward. She came close a few times, screwing up her courage and beginning a sentence that might have led to a deep discussion, but each time she saw the pain in his eyes and her question died on her lips. At night she lay in bed, knowing that he lay on a mattress in the front room, just below her. She listened to the little sounds in the house, hoping to hear Will talk out in his sleep and, perhaps, call her by name. Outside, the crickets chirped. Inside, Ernesto snored. But for all the sound he made, Will could have been in Europe already.

The day in early June came when Will was to leave. Will and Agnes stood on the front porch while Ernesto brought out the carriage and Lupe fussed with the duffel bag Will had carried on his shoulder when he left Camp Columbus. It held everything he owned in this world: a few changes of clothes, a few books, a hairbrush, and a penknife, and she wanted to make sure that the hard edges of the books wouldn't poke Will as he carried it.

Will's plan was to board the train to El Paso in Columbus, then switch trains and go north to Albuquerque, where a camp for new recruits was being established on the eastern edge of the University of New Mexico's campus. Because he was still a civilian, he wore the simple white shirt and gray trousers that he had bought from Dieter's store.

"Ernesto, *mi esposo*! We can't all ride in that!" Lupe wailed as her husband halted the gig carriage in front of the porch.

"Si, Lupe. Will wants Agnes alone to take him to Columbus." Ernesto climbed down from the seat. Lupe's grumble turned to a chuckle, and Agnes wondered if Lupe was thinking romantic thoughts. She pulled in a breath and hoped that Lupe was right.

"Right then! We'd best be going." Agnes gave Lupe a nervous smile, then ignoring Ernesto and Will's outstretched hands, climbed up to the seat. Agnes tucked her hands into her lap so that no one would see them trembling. They rode out, and neither talked for a long while. Finally, Agnes swallowed hard. She had little time left, and a lot of ground she needed to cover.

"Is it because I pursued a nursing certificate?"

"Is what because you pursued a nursing certificate?"

"What ruined things between us. When I asked about sanitary practices at the brothel at Camp Dublan, I was curious about . . ."

Will cut her off. "I'm proud of you for becoming a nurse. Proud of your inquiring, intelligent mind. Proud of you for working. But I'll never talk with you about brothels."

"Why not?" Agnes asked, aware that she was probably just being dense or naive. There was a lot about men and women that she didn't know.

"I think the world of you, Miss Day. I would hate to lose your good opinion."

"But that's just it. You're calling me Miss Day. You used to call me Agnes."

Will snorted but didn't reply, so she continued.

"Remember right after my father died? You offered to marry me."

"I was worried for you. Shouldn't have been. You can manage just about anything."

Agnes swallowed hard. "I've always been independent. And stubborn, I admit. But we work well together. And you like it here on the ranch, don't you?"

"The Sunrise is heaven on earth. No place I'd rather be."

"Then stay. Work with me." Agnes placed a shaking hand on Will's thigh. She twisted to look into his face. His eyes, impassive and hard, stayed on the road. His jaw was clenched.

"Be a kept man? I don't think so. Won't work for me any more than it would have worked for you." Will's voice sounded grave and choked. The pain in it made Agnes' own throat close up. What was it, she wondered, that kept them at arm's length from each other?

At the station they faced one another and Agnes saw regret and anticipation battle in Will's face. She could tell that he was fighting to keep himself from vaulting onto the train that was to propel him away, but politeness and, she hoped, fondness for her kept him rooted.

"I've never been out of New Mexico, so I can't tell you what it's going to be like over there," she said, smiling to keep the tears from flowing.

"I'll write and let you know, if you'll let me," he said.

"Let you? Of course, I'll let you!" Agnes nearly laughed out loud at his statement, but then the seriousness in Will's face made her stomach knot, and she pressed her lips together to stop herself from saying something that might shut him down entirely. She fumbled in the back pocket of her dungarees and pulled out an envelope. "I've written my address in here, just in case. And I've included a print of the photograph that Heinrich took on my birthday. So you don't forget what I look like."

Will grasped Agnes by both elbows and looked deeply into her eyes. "I've asked Heinrich to watch after you. He's a good man; comes from a good family and has a bright future in front of him. He'd do anything for you. Miss Day, you are the most amazing woman I have ever met. You deserve a good life. You deserve the ranch. You are determined. I wish you all the best. Good-bye."

Agnes stared at Will. Was he taking leave of her forever? Did he want no part of her life? What made him sure that she would be happy with another man, especially Henrich Dieter, the bumbling boy she'd gone to grade school with? "You'll be back, won't you?"

Will shook his head. "You deserve better than me. A man with a good background and a promising future. I have neither. But I will help you in any way I can."

"Then stay! How can you help me if you are half a world away?"

Before he could reply, the train whistle blew its warning. Will kissed her on the forehead, grabbed his bag, and bounded onto the train, leaving her standing bewildered and crying on the platform. Agnes climbed back into the gig and shook the reins. By the time she was halfway home, she had wiped the tears from her face and set her jaw determinedly. How dare Will Bowers decide for her which man to have in her life! She hadn't wanted a man in her life anyway. She could go on without him.

Agnes marched into Doctor Pritchard's office the next morning, her face set in a look of determination, her fists clenched as if she were climbing into the ring. "Doctor Pritchard, how do I join the Army Nursing Corps and go to France?"

He looked up at her, his bushy eyebrows quizzically forming an arch beneath his furrowed brow. "And good morning to you, too, Nurse Day."

"I'm serious. Do you know to whom I apply for the ANC?"

Doctor Pritchard sighed and set down the book he had been reading. Agnes was sure there was a frown under his mustache.

"I see no periorbital hyperpigmentation."

Agnes smiled. "No bags under my eyes. And they're not red rimmed, either. Doctor, I am tired, I admit, but I haven't been mooning away. I was awake most of the night, thinking."

"That young man of yours: the soldier. He shipped for France?"

Agnes took a deep breath. "Private Bowers shipped out, yes, and yes, I saw him off. But I'm not chasing after him. My reasons are twofold."

Agnes held up two fingers, spreading her feet as if preparing for an argument. Doctor Pritchard sat back, folding his hands over his belly, obviously amused.

"Twofold, huh? Go on."

"One," Agnes brandished one finger, looking like an umpire calling strikes, "the pay is good, much better than being your assistant. If the state isn't going to offer me an extension home nursing position, and I've been waiting for months, then I must have this job. I need more money if I am ever going to have a hope of buying the Sunrise Ranch."

"Logical," Doctor Pritchard said. "Go on."

"Two," Agnes said, holding up a second finger, "New Mexico is a new state. We are duty bound to show our allegiance to our country, especially since it came to our aide in our time of need."

The doctor chuckled. "How noble of you. You are aware, are you not, that France is a big country? There's no guarantee you'll be posted anywhere near that soldier of yours."

"I assure you, I am not following a man," Agnes said. She swallowed the quaver in her voice. She didn't want to admit it out loud, but Will was lost to her forever. He had given her over to Heinrich Dieter, left her with nothing more than a brotherly kiss on the forehead. He had said he would help her, but he didn't mean it. If he had, he would still be there, not off on a lark to France so he could watch it burn to the ground. If she were going to keep the Sunrise, she would have to rely on herself alone.

Doctor Pritchard shook his head, but there was a glimmer in his eye that showed he was more amused than unsupportive. "I'm not used to sending young ladies into the jaws of death, but knowing you, you'll find a way to go with or without my assistance. Has anyone ever told you what a bulldog you are?"

Agnes smiled, remembering Will once calling her that. She'd show him.

The doctor nodded. "'ll make some inquiries on your behalf."

Less than a week later, the Doctor called her into his office and had her sit across from him, in the big leather chair he reserved for patients. "I did some research, and I think I can tell you what you need to know about serving overseas," he said.

Agnes leaned forward, her hands clasped as if she were praying. "And?"

"The Surgeon General has called for volunteers. They're being brought into service through the American Red Cross, and through a base hospital system that the Army's recently created. Six base hospitals, with more than four hundred nurses, have already sailed for France and are serving the British Expeditionary Forces."

Agnes squeezed her hands together until her knuckles turned white. "Does that mean I'm too late?"

The Doctor shook his head. "I assure you, a great many more units will follow once we start shipping our boys over. But, much as the Army wants nurses, it's not making joining easy. You'll have to buy your own uniforms and camp equipment, and you must bring $50 in gold coin with you"

"What for?" Agnes asked.

"So, you can buy your way home when you've had enough. They won't pay to send back shirkers. Plus, you hold no rank. Even orderlies can and will treat you like a servant. Miss Day, you're not the type to be bullied around."

He was right: Agnes was known for her bulldogged determination. She had never let anyone bully her. The first time an officer shouted at her, she would have to fight down the urge to spit in his face. "I can do what I have to do."

"Then there's the subject of your salary. Until you complete your training, you will only receive $15 a month. Depending on your specialty and theater of action, it could go up to $60 a month.

"Theater of action?" Agnes asked.

"Where you are stationed. The closer to the front, the more your pay."

Agnes grinned. "Even during training, I will get twice what I do here. Forgive me, Doctor, but that's no deterrent."

Doctor Pritchard turned a bit purple and spluttered before he answered. "I think you will find conditions - and treatment - much harder. I may have paid you less, but I treated you better. And I have two more warnings for you, or shall we call them considerations. One: You'll be required to sign on for the duration of the conflict."

Agnes shrugged, nonplussed. "Once our boys get over there, it should be over pretty soon."

"That's what they said in 1914," Doctor Pritchard said. "And two: your mother will be beside herself. Are you sure you want to face her wrath?"

"My mother, or an army of Huns. I think I'll take the Huns." Agnes and the Doctor smiled at each other.

By the end of September, Doctor Pritchard had found a training position at Fort Bayard for Agnes. The old fort was in the Pinos Altos Mountains, seventy-five miles north of Columbus. It had been built for the Apache Wars, but was now a hospital for soldiers suffering from tuberculosis.

Agnes was packing her bags when she heard the whine of a car engine and looked out her window to see Heinrich Dieter's red Oldsmobile 44 pulling into the yard. She hoped he was delivering a package from his father's store to Lupe. Heinrich had been a frequent caller since Will's departure, always announcing that he was there to help, but never actually doing anything more than follow Agnes, or Lupe, or Ernesto around as they did their chores. He talked plaintively about how badly things were going, sometimes slipping into near tears. It seemed to Agnes that he was trying to woo her through his own helplessness.

And while she was sure he was exaggerating to gain her pity, it was true that Dieter's Dry Goods had not been doing well since President Wilson declared war. Throughout the nation, people questioned the loyalty of German Americans, just as the gang of drunkards had at Agnes' party. In July a barge exploded at Mare Island Naval Shipyard near San Francisco, and newspapers suggested it was the work of a German spy who sabotaged the barge to destroy munitions destined for the western front. Suddenly, every American of German extraction was suspected of treason and intrigue.

Lupe appeared in the doorway. "*Mija*? Mr. Heinrich Dieter is close to tears, *pobrecito*," Lupe said, using the word for *poor child*. Agnes set the sweater she had been folding onto the bed and clumped down the stairs followed by Lupe, mumbling something about making up a plate of cookies.

Heinrich looked lost in deep and troubling thought when Agnes entered the kitchen. He looked up and his face lightened into a tremulous smile. He held out his arms as if expecting once again the hug he never got. "Aggie!

How good of you to see me! I know you must be terribly busy with packing and all."

"That I am, old friend." Agnes held out her hand. He shook it enthusiastically before his face went back to the sober look it had when she entered the room. She gestured for him to take a seat at the kitchen table, then sat opposite him. Lupe set a plate of *biscochitos,* two mugs of coffee, a sugar bowl, and a can of evaporated milk between them.

Heinrich added several spoonfuls and a large dollop of milk to his coffee and stirred it so vigorously that it sloshed over the rim.

"May I say that the Dieter family, all of us, are so very proud of you. I know it's been hard since your father passed, but you've shown real pluck."

Agnes gave a little shrug, a sort of 'awe, shucks' movement which she hoped would be an acceptance of his praise without making her look too vain. She reached for a *biscochito,* the flaky, cinnamon-and- sugar-coated cookies that Lupe made by the hundreds.

"In fact, my father is so impressed that I've decided to follow in your footsteps."

"My footsteps?" Agnes froze, her cookie suspended above her coffee cup. "You're going to correspondence school to become a nurse?"

He shook his head. "Not exactly. But I promised Will I'd look after you, and it seems to me the only way to do that is to follow you into the service. I've been talking to a recruiter, about entering the medical corps. I don't have the training you do, but I could be a stretcher bearer, or some kind of aide, or an ambulance driver: anything to keep me out of the trenches."

Heinrich's eyes held a terror that she had never seen before. Her heart ached for the laughably gawky boy, so smart and yet so awkward, so full of laughter.

"You know, you don't have to do this. You could stay back and help Lupe and Ernesto. I'm sure your father needs you in the store, too." Agnes looked up at Lupe, who was standing stiffly at the kitchen sink, a look of horror on her face.

Heinrich smiled ruefully. "You know as well as I do that I'm not much help here on the ranch. I don't know one side of a cow from the other. And father doesn't need help, not with business down. Besides, he says a stint in the military will look good on my resume. Everyone supports our troops these days. They'll be voting enthusiastically for veterans in the next elections. And this will prove our loyalty to America. We're tired of being called Kaiser-loving Huns."

Agnes put her hand comfortingly atop Henrich's. "Those all sound like good reasons. But you know, there's no guarantee you'll be posted anywhere near me. France is a big country."

Heinrich's face crumbled into a mask of misery. "I guess so, but I've got to try, don't I? I've got to do what's right. For you. For my father. For my country. But I'm scared, Aggie. You've always been so brave. I'm not. I'm terrified."

Heinrich burst into tears. Agnes fought the urge to slap some sense into him. "We may not end up at the same field hospital, but if we get leave, we can arrange to meet."

Heinrich pulled out his handkerchief and blew his nose. "The thought of you and me in Paris will be a comfort."

Agnes patted Heinrich on the back. She looked up at Lupe, who was dabbing her eyes with the hem of her apron, and wondered how she was going to manage.

Chapter Fourteen

Agnes stepped out the front door of L.B. Fowler's gracious Silver City house and, remembering a day when she had arrived so dirty and disheveled that the maid had thought her a beggar, smiled at the sign with his name in fancy gold script. So much had changed in the two years since her father had died. She was ready for the next part of her life to begin.

"Thank you again for another lovely weekend. There's no other place I'd rather be," she said to Mrs. Fowler, who beamed at the compliment.

"With the exception of the Sunrise?" Mr. Fowler, his reading glasses gleaming on the top of his head, stepped around his wife and shook Agnes' hand.

"Well, true," Agnes said, laughing. "But the Sunrise is too far when I only have 24 hours leave. Still, it's nice to get away from Fort Bayard once in a while: eat food that isn't hospital food, sleep on that downy mattress and lounge in your tub."

"You're like a granddaughter to us," Mrs. Fowler said. "Thanks for listening to all of Papa's stories about your grandmother, and what your father was like as a child. They must get tedious."

"Not at all," Agnes said. She saw the stableboy walking Diablo down Bullard Street, so she gave Mrs. Fowler a quick kiss and walked down the porch stairs to meet him and begin the six-mile ride back to the hospital. Determined to get as much training as possible during her six months at Fort Bayard, Agnes had studied and worked with the same diligence and focus that she had used to gain her nursing certificate. She'd discovered that the cool, dry air of the mountains was good for the 300 soldiers who were hospitalized for tuberculosis. In addition to tuberculosis, Agnes expected to see cases of pneumonia and soldiers whose lungs were compromised by poison gas attacks once she was posted to France. She had learned a lot and was anxious to get the letter saying that the Army Nursing Corps was ready to take her. It was time to go from trainee to real, practicing nurse: time to get the extra salary that she could sock away for the down payment on the ranch.

The road to the Fort passed east, through fields that again were golden with Mexican poppies, reminding her of the time she and Will went to see the planes practicing their take offs and landings on the Columbus airfield. Had that really been a year ago? When Will first left for training, he'd written frequently. It had been six months since she'd gotten the last one, that said his unit would sail for La Havre, France, on Christmas Eve. By now, he could be anywhere. Or dead. Dead or alive, Will Bowers had shown that he wasn't interested in a future with her. He'd given her over to Heinrich Dieter, written a few letters, then gone on with his life. She shook her head and spat, telling herself to buck up and be brave. She didn't need Private William Bowers to help her keep the Sunrise. She could do it on her own.

Agnes dropped Diablo off at the fort's stables, then went to her dorm room and changed from her dungarees into her nurses' uniform. The white dress with its crisp, white apron and headscarf made her feel emotionally crisp, and alert, transforming her from a tough cowgirl to a wise and capable nurse. She checked herself in the mirror, then walked across the parade ground to the administration building.

"Hello, Edna! Reporting back for duty," Agnes called as she went through the double doors. Edna Gilbert, the competent young receptionist with the finger curls that made her look like the actress Pearl White, looked up from her paperwork and coyly gave Agnes a sidelong smile. "Glad to have you back! Have I got a boatload of mail for you!"

Agnes' heart leaped with hope. A boatload! If only one of those letters had really been on a boat! Edna went to the bank of cubbyholes, pulled a stack of mail from one, and handed it to Agnes, who quickly rifled through it. Two letters from her mother, no doubt lectures on how to conduct herself and despairing of her daughter gallivanting across Europe while there was a war on, one letter from Heinrich, who had been training at Camp Funsten in Kansas, but was obviously on the move because the postmark was from Philadelphia, and one large, official-looking envelope. No letter from Will. Agnes felt a stab of disappointment before elation took over, and she ripped open the big envelope.

"Those your orders?" Edna asked. She stood on tiptoe, trying to read the letter upside down from her side of the counter.

"Yup," Agnes recited the details as she scanned the letter. "Depart New York City. Aboard the Leviathan. April 24th.

"April 24th? Of this year?"

Agnes nodded. April 24, 1918."

"Isn't that just like the Army! Leave you hanging for months, then want you to move in just weeks."

"Yup. Hurry up and wait, wait and hurry up." Agnes rifled through information about what to bring, where to meet Mrs. Theodora Abrim, the head nurse in charge of getting the women safely ensconced in American hospitals overseas, and what was expected of her. She looked up, her head whirling and her heart pounding with nerves and excitement. "So much to do to get ready!"

"Tell you what," Edna said, "You make a list. I'll send it to a dry goods in Silver City, just tell me which one. Then, next time you have leave, take one of our carts to pick it all up."

Agnes dashed off a quick note to Mr. Fowler asking for an advance on the money that had been set aside for her support. She drew up a list for Edna that included a large steamer trunk in which to pack all the clothing and supplies for a year in France. When she went into town to pick up her supplies, she bought her train ticket and wired her travel information to New York so someone could meet her at the station. She sent letters to Lupe and Ernesto, her mother, her sisters, Heinrich, and to Will, with her new contact information.

When all was ready, Agnes began to worry that she didn't know enough and wasn't strong enough of mind to do this. She remembered how rattled she had been by the bodies in Columbus on the day that Pancho Villa raided the town, and how she could not bring herself to sit with her dead father. Could she really handle the horrors of war?

Agnes rode the train with her nose pressed to the window, a feeling like a stranger in a strange land. She had never been outside of the Chihuahuan Desert before, hadn't realized that other places looked so different. The land became greener, the skies grayer, and the rivers wider the farther east she went. Familiar gravelly sand gave way to dark, rich soil. The creosote bush, yucca, and ocotillo disappeared, replaced by bushes she could not name. Soon the grass was not blue grama, but something lush and thick, the grazing cows fatter and sleeker than the ones at home. She vowed to return to each town that whizzed past her window on her return trip. Trinidad, Colorado, Topeka and Kansas City, Chicago, Toledo: each had something that Columbus and Silver City didn't. She wondered what that something was, and why people would choose it.

The train hugged a flat expanse of water so large that Agnes could not see the other side. There were no hills to break it up, no mountains to draw the eye: just a wide, flat gray monotony that made the barren desert look varied and interesting in comparison.

"Excuse me," she said to a conductor as he passed by, "that water? Have we already reached the Atlantic?"

The conductor bent down to glance out the window. He chuckled. "That's Lake Erie, Miss. Look close enough and you can see Canada on the far shore."

"Really? Another country!" She spent an hour trying to catch a glimpse of Canada. The lake narrowed as it went east, and she finally got her glimpse of a foreign shore as the train neared Buffalo.

When staring out the window became too tedious, Agnes pulled out the photograph that Heinrich had taken on her birthday. She studied the faces, trying to recall the timber of each of their voices. Then, knowing that their relationship was over, she pulled out her letters from Will and read and reread them, looking for clues as to what had gone wrong. Just like the ones from Mexico, Will's letters were informative and well written, but showed no emotion towards her. The first had come soon after he arrived in Albuquerque. He said that Camp Kitchener, on the eastern edge of the University of New Mexico campus, was no more than a field with stacks of lumber. Officers lived in a student dormitory that had emptied due to enlistments. Enlisted men slept in overcrowded tents. Each company identified 100 men to build barracks, and since he had prior experience, he had been chosen to be among them.

Before the end of June, his second letter said he had finished his construction work. When he got time off, he walked the mile downhill to Albuquerque, a thriving town with a railroad depot and four and five story brick buildings, where he met up with old friends. Once he went to the Sandia Mountains, east of the town, and hiked among tall pines.

Three weeks later, Will wrote that he had been assigned to the 1st New Mexico Artillery Battery A, which had been stationed at Camp Columbus, so he knew many of the men. Their Captain, Charles M de Bremond, was a Swiss immigrant who was teaching his men French. This unit had received so many accolades in Mexico that Pershing had selected it to be among the first American artillery units to reach France. Agnes smiled, looking at all the exclamation points.

Will's fourth letter had an August date and was postmarked at Camp Greene, in Charlotte, North Carolina and told Agnes that the 1st New

Mexico Artillery had become part of the 66th Field Artillery Brigade. Then his last letter, from September, said that the 66th was being sent to Camp Mills, on Long Island, in New York. They would sail for La Havre, France, on Christmas Eve.

Agnes brushed back a tear. Where was he? Why had he stopped writing? Since she had written to him at the Camp Mills address and told him that she was training at Fort Bayard, she had heard nothing from him. Had he been lying when he said he was proud of her for becoming a nurse? She folded up his letters and stuffed them back in her valise, wondering why he had written to her at all. Fine. If Will had gone on with his life, so would she. She had better things to think about than Will. She was nearing New York City, where she would board a ship and cross an ocean that was even bigger than Lake Erie, to a country even stranger and more foreign than what she'd seen out the window of the train. With shaking hands, she clutched her valise tightly and told herself that she was ready.

The train pulled into New York City's Penn Station. Agnes disembarked, paid a porter for lugging down her trunk, then looked around for someone who might be Mrs. Theodora Abrim. Men in business suits pulled out their pocket watches and compared them to the enormous clock hanging from the center of the ceiling. Nannies pushed prams with howling babies. Beggars, peddlers, and street urchins who looked like they'd just as soon steal your purse as doff their hats passed by, too close for comfort. Other street urchins hawked newspapers with splashy headlines. The noise and smells and movement accosted her senses. More people milled and rushed through the station than she had ever seen in her life. Surely that one building alone held more people than all the citizens of New Mexico. But nobody looked like they were looking for a new nurse.

Wishing for a way out of the chaos, Agnes sat down on her steamer trunk and turned her eyes to the immense vaults of glass in the station's ceiling. The panes looked impossibly suspended against the scuttling gray clouds, a marvel of modern engineering every bit as impressive as the automobile and the airplane. The sky, hemmed in by steel beams, looked like mere shards and rectangles of itself. She missed the vast expanse. A few pigeons wheeled in the air, searching for a way out. Agnes was considering finding a police officer or an information desk when she heard someone calling her name.

"Yoo-hoo! Miss Day! Miss Day, is that you?"

A woman waved her arms as if performing a frantic semaphore. She strode across the lobby with a gait that was both ungainly and spritely, all elbows and knees, like a young filly trying to run. She was about the same age as Agnes, but her wide smile gave her a childlike appearance. Her hair, the color of cornsilk, escaped her bun and danced about her face. Her periwinkle eyes sparkled, and her cheeks were flushed.

"Whew!" the woman said when she was finally next to Agnes. "You're Miss Agnes Day?"

"I am. And you are Mrs. Abrim?" Agnes held out her hand, but the woman laughed, then lunged forward and caught her in a hug that almost took her breath away.

"Nope! And I'm Sadie Sundvuist. I've been looking for you for ages! I got distracted! By this keen street performer! He had the cutest little monkey on a chain, and it was hopping around and picking people's pockets! All in good fun! Everyone was laughing about it!"

"I thought a Mrs. Theodora Abrim was to meet me," Agnes said, puzzled by the flood of words.

"Mrs. Abrim's busy, so she sent me, and I would have been here on time, I really would have! But there was this street performer." Sadie's infectious enthusiasm melted away the tension and worry of the trip. Agnes was still unsure what lay ahead, but if Sadie was any indication, it would be a great adventure.

"With a cute little monkey," Agnes said with a smile.

Sadie's eyes widened. "And how! You saw him?"

"No, silly," Agnes said, "You just told me about him."

Sadie whacked herself on the forehead with her open palm. "Boy, can I be a simp! Here! Let me get your bag. We've got to get you back to meet the others. You're going to like them! They're a swell group of girls! Most arrived in the past two days. We're just waiting for a few stragglers. Oh, porter! Porter!" Sadie whirled around and semaphored a group of uniformed black men lounging in a corner. One half dragged, half carried the steamer trunk to the curb, where he brusquely hailed a horse-drawn taxi cab. He helped them settle inside, then stored Agnes' trunk in the back. Sadie rewarded him with both a coin and a kiss on his withered cheek. He scowled. As they pulled away from the curb, Agnes watched him pull out a handkerchief and vigorously scrub his cheek.

Agnes chuckled. "I don't think he approved of your forward behavior."

"Pshaw! What man doesn't like a little peck on the cheek?" Sadie leaned forward and continued to prattle. Agnes sat back and let Sadie's words flow over her, catching a phrase here and a statement there, but most of the time focusing on the street scenes flowing by and her own emotions. At the Sunrise Ranch it was possible to ride for an entire day and not see another person. Even in the bustling towns of Deming and Silver City, a five-minute ride out of town would take a person out of sight and hearing range of others. She looked up as a train clattered overhead on an impossibly thin metal track. The ground began to rumble and Agnes looked down, expecting it to break open.

“Earthquake!” she shouted over the road.

“Subway!” Sadie shouted back. “Underground! Right beneath us! Hundreds of people, just whizzing by! Ain’t it grand?!”

Agnes shook her head, overwhelmed by the layers of humanity. Rumbling subways, beneath the congested streets. Elevated trains above. It was enough to make her head spin, especially with Sadie's babble.

It took the cab about fifteen minutes to make the half-mile trip and for Agnes to learn that Sadie was the fifth of three daughters and two sons born into a Swedish father and Norwegian mother in a tiny, farming community in Iowa, and that her father had let her go on this adventure because his ears needed a rest. She had never done well in school, but she was a hard worker and wanted to go places and do things that her parents had never considered doing, but then Sadie contradicted herself by saying that both her parents had bravely left their villages when they were just teenagers, crossed the Atlantic, met each other, and settled into a place where they knew no one and didn't speak the language. They couldn't even speak to each other when they were first married! And her sisters and brothers were all so sober and hardworking! A whole family of stoic Scandinavians! Sadie found she had to do the talking for all of them! Agnes smiled and nodded, and let Sadie ramble on.

The cab pulled up in front of Hotel Martha Washington, a women's-only hotel that, at $1.50 a day, was a reasonable and safe place for single women of high moral character. While Sadie paid the driver, a bellhop wrestled Agnes' trunk into a lobby that was much larger and nicer than she had expected. Sadie explained that about a hundred of the women now staying at the hotel were in their group.

Sadie continued to babble while Agnes checked in at the registration desk. All of a sudden, Sadie went silent. Agnes turned and found a matronly woman with graying temples standing where Sadie had been. The woman had steely gray eyes that bugged out and deep wrinkles leading down from the corners of her mouth, a combination that brought to mind ventriloquist dummies. Agnes fought to control a giggle.

"I take it you are Nurse Day," the woman said, not at all amused. She had a Boston Brahmin accent that Agnes recognized because Heinrich had jokingly emulated it when talking about his years at Harvard, but Agnes found difficult to understand. The woman offered her hand and Agnes shook it, surprised at the vise-like grip. "I am Mrs. Theodora Abrim, and I am to escort you and the rest of these women through France until such time that each of you has been placed in a suitable position. It's our mission to fill gaps in the staffing of a string of casualty clearing stations. Attrition among the ranks, you know."

"Yes, Mrs. Abrim. A pleasure to meet you," Agnes said, suddenly sober.

"I take it you and Nurse Sundvuist have become friends?"

"Oh, yes," Agnes answered, "She made me feel quite welcome."

Mrs. Abrim frowned, deepening the wrinkles around her mouth. "Let us not become too friendly. I expect my nurses to take their jobs seriously. Very seriously, indeed. And let us not forget that we shall be spread out across the battle lines. We are not like regular nursing units, who have trained together and work together in a single field hospital. We are replacements. Best not to get too friendly with any of these women. It will make separating from them that much more difficult."

She squeezed her eyes and studied Agnes critically. "You are, if I remember, the one from Mexico? You don't look like a Mexican."

"New Mexico," Agnes corrected. "We became a state five years ago. There are a lot of Anglo-Saxons in New Mexico."

Mrs. Abrim nodded. "You are a rancher's daughter? Used to primitive conditions?"

"Yes, ma'am. And strong. And willing to work hard."

"And not in this for romantic reasons? This line of work is not pretty, regardless of what the recruiting posters would indicate. You are highly unlikely to find a suitable marriage prospect among the wounded."

"Romance is the last thing on my mind. I'm here to earn money for my ranch," Agnes said, and watched the head nurses' frown deepen. In spite of the first impression Sadie had given her, this was going to be serious business.

"There must be easier ways to do that," Mrs. Abrim said before she turned away to lecture another young nurse.

On the day of embarkation, Agnes and the other nurses watched a hired wagon set out with their luggage, then they marched to the wharf with Mrs. Abrim leading the way. They all wore their newly-issued khaki uniforms. The smart-fitting jackets and tight, peg skirts made them all, even Sadie, look dignified and official. People cheered and wished them well as they passed, and Agnes remembered the day she had waved an American flag and greeted Will back from Mexico. It seemed so long ago. She reached up and brushed back a tear.

When the Leviathan finally came into view, Agnes gasped. Originally built in Germany and christened the *Vaterland,* she was the world's largest ocean liner, bigger than ten locomotive engines put together: larger, even, than most of the buildings in New York City.

"She isn't as grand as one would suppose," Mrs. Abrim announced as she turned and stopped the women. "When we entered the war and seized her, she was retrofitted for wartime use. Note the big caliber guns mounted on the decks, and the depth charge chute erected on the stern. This isn't a pleasure cruise. The passage may be dangerous."

Agnes glanced sideways, wondering if any others might join the few who had lost their nerve and returned home.

"They sure did paint her funny," Sadie said. She was right. The paint made her look like something between a circus tent and a herd of zebras.

"That, Nurse Sundvuist, is called dazzle camouflage. It is designed to make her appear to be going a different direction than she actually is, to throw German U-boats off our trail. Wait here. I will get direction for us."

As Mrs. Abrim elbowed her way through the crowd, Agnes leaned on a railing and watched huge crates of material for infantry, field artillery, and machine gun battalions float past in huge cargo nets. Soldiers led horses up a gangplank and onto the deck, where each horse was strapped into a sling and lowered through a hole into what she assumed were stables below. She was amazed at how calm the horses were. Diablo would never have submitted to such treatment, even with the blinders that covered the horses' eyes. Whoever had broken them and enabled them to trust their handlers implicitly knew what he was doing.

Mrs. Abrim returned, her face red with the exertion of pushing through the crush of people. "We wait until the cargo is stowed. Nurses, you will find when we board that this liner is no longer luxurious. Do not expect fine wines and gourmet dining. The ballroom had been converted into a hospital, the gymnasium into an isolation ward for contagious cases. You will be expected to serve in both."

Agnes nodded. Good. The more she worked, the less she would worry about the ranch selling before she could buy it, or about why Will had stopped writing. Mrs. Abrim continued her lecture.

"The walls between the staterooms have been ripped out. The inside spaces are huge: about the size of a football field. The women on this ship, and there are four hundred of us, will occupy one of these. I expect you to remain in it when you are not working or eating in the mess hall, which on a ship is called a galley."

Galley, Agnes thought. Kitchen. Head meant toilet. Starboard and port. Ships had a lot of words that weren't used on the ranch. She had committed them to memory, along with lots of new nursing words. Septicemia. Pleurisy. Debridement.

Mrs. Abrim continued. "While you may go on deck for air, you must keep out of the sailor's way. They are busy sailing this ship and watching for the enemy. And no fraternizing with the nine thousand men aboard. We must be professional."

Agnes nodded. She had no intention of fraternizing with anyone. She was here to work.

"Remember, your steamer trunks will be stowed in the hold and all you will have at your disposal during the crossing is what you've packed in your valises," Mrs. Abrim said.

Sadie jerked as if awakened from sleep. "My brush! I bet I forgot to get it out of my trunk!" She clambered onto the cart that had carried their baggage and began digging through the pile of trunks.

Finally, a man with a megaphone shouted that passengers were invited aboard. While a band played *The Tiger Rag,* personnel for several field hospital staffs and what seemed soldiers beyond number streamed up the gangplank. It was as if all of Camp Columbus had been encased in steel and set on the river. When Agnes thought no more people could fit, a fidgety sailor with a clipboard led Mrs. Abrim and her charges up a gangplank, down several sets of stairs, along a few passages, and past a place that he called "the ladies' head" and pointed to it as if it were significant. He stood aside and waved them into a cavernous room.

Agnes felt her jaw drop as she looked up at a forest of open iron frame bunks with canvas bottoms, stacked four high. "Are we supposed to sleep on those?"

"Nacherly," another woman said. "They's called 'standees.' Now pick one, or you'll get left with the leavin's." Agnes threw her carpet bag on an upper middle bunk, thinking that the top was frighteningly high and the bottom claustrophobic. Sadie chose the bunk right next to hers, so they could sleep head-to-head and whisper all night. Around her, a sea of women chattered and argued as they settled in. Most of the women were nurses, but there were also secretaries, 'Hello Girls' to man telephone switchboards, and others. A few head nurses and matrons were trying to keep everything orderly and proper, but it was clear to Agnes that squabbling and tears were going to be an inevitable part of the trip. Some of the women, to the consternation of the matrons, were already talking about finding where the soldiers or the officers were bunking. Agnes shook her head. She had no interest in meeting men.

"This is going to be one giant slumber party!" Sadie said, smacking Agnes with her pillow.

"Stop it," Agnes said as she tried to control her laughter at the absurdity of the situation. It was comical, really, watching so many young women settle in, and clear that for many of them, this voyage was a first time away from the confines of home, an adventure of epic proportions. Agnes wished she felt more excited, but the crowds, the noise, the confinement of the space, big as it was, intimidated her. She was suddenly homesick for the open range.

When everyone had found a bed, the whole group marched to the head, which proved to be a lavatory with wash basins and toilets and definitely not designed for four hundred occupants. They freshened up, then marched up to the main deck, where they crowded the railings. Soldiers pressed in against them and the mood became festive. Somebody produced streamers and confetti. Soon the entire deck was cheering as the ship pulled away from the dock.

"I was wrong! This isn't just a slumber party! The whole voyage is going to be one, big floating party! With doughboys!" Sadie shouted over the tumult.

As the city sank into the ocean, the crowd dispersed, drifting away one by one and in clusters. Agnes told herself that New York wasn't really sinking; the curvature of the earth made it look that way. It was astounding to think that she could see that far. Even on the vast, flat plain, little rises, lone mountains, sometimes distant ranges disrupted the horizon. For the first time since she had left home, Agnes felt like no one was within ten miles of her. It felt wonderful. She closed her eyes and breathed the tang of salt, so different than the bite of sage in the air at the Sunrise. The sun slipped into the ocean and the horizon disappeared as water and sky blended into velvety nothingness.

But it wasn't nothingness. It was a whole world, and while it was hidden from her, it was very much alive. Will was out there somewhere in the night in front of her. Her mother, her sisters, Ernesto, Lupe, and everyone she had ever known and loved were behind that curving horizon, where the sun still shone and the dry air smelled of yucca blossom, sage and mesquite.

"Miss? Are you alright?"

The question jerked Agnes back into the present. She wiped a hand across her face and realized that she was crying. "Yes, I'm fine. It's all just so beautiful," she said to the young sailor who had taken hold of her elbow. The look of concern on his face made her want to start crying all over again.

He looked a little confused and she was sure he wondered what beauty she could possibly see in all that darkness and nothingness, but he nodded and gave her a little smile. "Perhaps, Miss, you'd like to go down below? They've begun serving dinner in the galleys. They do it in shifts; there's too many of you to sit all at once."

Agnes nodded and thanked the young sailor for his kindness. She returned to the stairwell and tried to retrace her steps, but became lost in the labyrinth of passages. She passed smoking lounges and galleys full of men, not seeing a single other woman. Was she on the wrong level of this multi-leveled ship?

She passed one door and heard a piano playing a familiar song, and it gave her pause. It was *The Girl I Left Behind Me*. Tears brimmed in Agnes' eyes as she remembered Will playing that on her parents' piano, singing sweet words in his lyrical tenor voice.

All the dames of France are fond and free
And Flemish lips are really willing
Very soft the maids of Italy
And Spanish eyes are so thrilling

Still, although I bask beneath their smile,
Their charms will fail to bind me
And my heart falls back to Erin's isle
To the girl I left behind me.

The song was a march, but Will had played it in a minor key, with such longing that it sounded as if whoever was marching was homesick and wanted to return to his love. It stung to think Will probably had none of those feelings. He had left. Stopped writing. Had he found someone new? One of those fond and free French dames? A willing set of Flemish lips?

Whoever was playing now wasn't playing with the same sweetness. Instead of a march, the pianist laid down a ragged, jazzy time, and the men sang along boisterously. Agnes focused on the lyrics. They were completely different.

Kaiser Bill is feeling ill,
the Crown Prince has gone barmy,
We don't give a chuck for old von Kluck
And all his bleedin' army.

She marched into the room, determined to make the men respect the lovely song and sing it right. And then she saw the piano player, and her blood really boiled.

Chapter Fifteen

The piano player had a broad, square back and hands that danced over the keys. The close-cropped hair on the back of his head nearly matched his khaki uniform.

That was all it took. Agnes saw red. She stormed across the room and slugged Will in the jaw. Hard.

He sprang to his feet, the bench clattering over behind him, his fist pulled back, ready to return the blow. Then he froze.

The singing grew ragged, then petered out entirely. The entire room stared.

Delight, embarrassment, and confusion ran across Will's face. His clenched hand opened and massaged his jaw. "Miss Day! What are you doing here?"

"I might ask the same of you," Agnes replied through clenched teeth.

"Look at Bowers!" one of the crowd shouted, "On ship two hours and already got a floozie mad at him!"

Will looked at the sea of hooting, catcalling faces and frowned. "We're making a spectacle of ourselves. Let's get out of here." He tried to take Agnes' elbow, but she pulled away and shoved him. They scuffled all the way to the door as the room howled with laughter. Once they were gone, the room burst into song as if nothing had interrupted their revelry.

Agnes pulled away from him. "You told me you shipped out in December with Battery A."

“Keep moving,” Will said. “What we need is air. And privacy.”

Agnes continued to splutter and argue as Will herded her down the passage and up a companionway. Every time he touched her, she slapped his hand away. Months of anxiety spilled out, disguised as rage when really it was relief. Will was alive! But he still had a lot of explaining to do.

When they were in the open, he rubbed his jaw and grinned at her. “And you always complained about me sneaking up on you! For a little woman, you pack a powerful punch.”

“I asked you a question. Why aren’t you in France?” Agnes demanded, ignoring his smile.

Will's forehead wrinkled. "I was supposed to be. My orders changed.”

“Why didn’t you tell me?” Agnes bit her lip to keep it from trembling. It was a question she’d wanted answered for a long time, but she was still afraid of the answer.

“I did. Didn’t you get that letter?”

Agnes shook her head. Every word out of Will’s mouth quelled her anxiety a little more. Months of worry eroded away, but slowly, like wind on sandstone. She calmed a little and took a shaky breath. “Last letter I got was before I went to Fort Bayard.”

Will blinked. “Fort Bayard? Have you been ill?” He placed his hand on her forehead as if he could tell now whether she had taken ill all those months ago.

“I’m fine. I was training there. For the ANC. Since September.” Agnes reached up and brushed his hand away, but she did so gently.

“Last I heard, you were working for Doc Pritchard and looking for a county extension job. You’re with the ANC now?”

Agnes nodded "More money. To buy the ranch. So, you didn’t stop writing me in September?” Agnes’ heart fluttered. After months of feeling abandoned, the realization that it was all just a misunderstanding made her want to laugh out loud.

"Not in September. Kept sending them to the P.O. box in Columbus. I eventually did stop, though, because I stopped getting letters from you. I assumed you'd moved on, found a way to buy the ranch. Maybe gave your heart to Heinrich."

"I'm going to give Heinrich a black eye next time I see him. I bet he's the one who didn't forward your letters. Oh Will! I'm so sorry. That I hit you. That I didn't believe. I should never have lost faith." She gazed at the man before her, his face so open and honest, humble and generous. She wanted to kiss him, to make up for lost time and for months of feelings of hurt and abandonment, but a wave of shyness overtook her. How did one resume a relationship after so much time? So much angst? Agnes palmed Will's cheek, which was still red from her fist. Her hand trailed down the side of his neck, along his shoulders and down his arm, where it found a patch embroidered with half a golden sun, like the lazy D brand from the Sunrise Ranch, set in a red sky. A stripe of blue, like the ocean in front of them, lay along the bottom.

"A sunrise!"

Will smiled. "Sunset, actually. It's the 41st's patch. They call us The Sunset Division."

"Sunrise, sunset. They both look like a lazy D. Maybe I'll add rays to the brand when I buy the ranch.

Will smiled. "Maybe that'll give me luck. Your letters to me are probably at Camp Mills, on Long Island. Or maybe the Army forwarded them to France. I'd be there already if I weren't so handy."

"What do you mean?" Agnes asked.

Will put his arm around Agnes' shoulder and the two of them looked out at the vast blackness. "Seems the more I know, the longer I have to wait to do what I want. If I didn't know engines and monkey wrenches, I would have been with Black Jack in Mexico a lot sooner. This time, they learned I know how to break horses. When the Brigade embarked, me and a few others were detached and sent to Camp Hill, near Newport News. We're bringing the horses to Camp de Souge, in Bordeaux. Oh! Speaking of horses." He reached into his pocket and brought out a small, black horse."

"Is this Diablo?" she asked.

"Yep. I carved it while sitting around one day. Blackened it with boot polish. I've kept it to remind me of you. Maybe you'd like to keep it, now? To remind you of me?"

Agnes tucked it away in the pocket of her dress. "I'd like that very much. Funny thing: I watched the horses being loaded. Admired whoever'd trained them. Hadn't guessed it was you." She felt so secure with his arm around her, his warmth protecting her from the chill night air. She told him about Doctor Pritchard's campaign to find her a position in the ANC, the tuberculosis wards at Fort Bayard, the long ride across the country, and the new group of nurses who would be doled out along the line to any hospital that had lost staff. When she finished, they lapsed into a warm and comfortable silence. Agnes listened to the hum of the engines, the rush of waters breaking against the ship and the slow, steady beat of Will's heart and felt contentment for the first time in months.

"And I thought you'd given up on me," she said.

"It's you who should give up on me," Will answered. "I'm not good enough for you."

"And why is that?" Agnes looked up at Will, who seemed to be holding back both words and tears. Music drifted up the stairwell. It wasn't the rowdy music that had made Agnes so angry. This was a waltz, and it seemed the perfect, lyrical, lulling music for the moment.

Will wiped a hand across his face, as if erasing his thoughts. "Let's not talk about it tonight. Let's just enjoy being together again. Someone told me the nurses would be joining us after dinner, and there'd be dancing. Would you like to go in and join them?"

Agnes shook her head. "I'm sure my unit isn't dancing. Our head nurse said we weren't allowed to fraternize with soldiers. Besides, I like it out here. It's like home. A horizon. Stars. Quiet."

"Remember the dance your mother planned before the Villa raid turned our whole world topsy-turvy?"

Agnes nodded. She felt a pang of homesickness for a time that seemed so very long ago.

"I wanted to hold you in my arms way back then. Never got the chance." Will took her right hand in his and put his left hand at the small of her back.

"You told me then you didn't dance," Agnes said.

"That's so you'd dance with Dobbs," he said.

"Why did you try to pawn me off on Sergeant Dobbs?" Agnes asked, pulling her head back so she could see his face.

"He was the better man," Will answered. "You would have been better off with him."

Agnes shook her head. "That wasn't your decision to make." She rested her cheek on his chest and breathed in his scent. She felt safe and secure, the questions gone. They danced in the dark long after the music had ceased and the musicians gone to bed.

"There you are! I been searching all over for you!" At the sound of Sadie Sundvuist's bubbly voice, Agnes and Will pulled apart. Sadie squeezed between the two of them. She looked up and down Will as if appraising a statue, then coyly ran a hand through the blond wisps that had escaped her bun. "Well, hoopty-do!! You been holding out on me, Agnes. You didn't tell me you had a beau! And a handsome one, at that. How'd you arrange to cross over on the same ship?"

Agnes' jaw sawed back and forth as she searched for the right thing to say. Should she claim Will as a beau, or should she deny it?.

Sadie laughed. "Don't tell me you just met the guy!"

Agnes shook herself out of her reverie. "No! Of course not! Sadie Sundvuist, this is Private William Bowers. We knew each other back in New Mexico. He helped around the ranch. Private Bowers, this is Sadie Sundvuist, from Iowa. She's part of my nursing unit.

"Pleased, I'm sure," Sadie said in a flirtatious voice. She held out her hand, palm down, as if she expected Will to take it and bring it to his lips. He shook it instead. Sadie gave a little toss of her head and turned to Agnes. "Mrs. Abrim's mad as a wet hen. You weren't there for night-time roll call.

She wanted to tuck us all in nighty-night and read us a bed-time story, but you weren't there."

Agnes felt her stomach clench. She had worked so hard to get here, and now she was jeopardizing everything. Could she give up seeing Will to protect her position? If she didn't, would she be sent home, and all her training go for naught? She looked between Will and Sadie, then swallowed. "Please tell Mrs. Abrim that the quiet and the wide-open spaces lured me out here. They remind me of the desert," Agnes said.

"Some desert," Sadie swept her arm across the darkness, "but nope, I'm not making excuses for you while you waltz around on deck. Time for you to get below before Abrim comes looking for you." Sadie hooked her arm into Agnes', and dragged Agnes off, but Agnes noticed that Sadie looked back over her shoulder and winked at Will.

Will was frequently down in the cargo holds checking on the horses and making sure that the loads of artillery wagons, automobile trucks, and shell cases his detachment was responsible for hadn't shifted. Agnes found herself busy with rounds in the hospitals and in training sessions led by Mrs. Abrim. When they were both free, they managed to find each other on the open decks, where they watched flying-fish stream along in the ship's wake. The sailors commented that the weather for this crossing was exceptionally mild. They asked Agnes and Will to keep their eyes peeled for breaching whales, which looked so much like the wake of a periscope as they glided through the water that the two were frequently confused.

They were standing at the railing one day when they heard someone harumph behind them and turned to find Head Nurse Abrim glaring at them, her fists on her hips. "And just what are the two of you doing?" she demanded.

Agnes stared at Will. They hadn't even been touching. Was this going to get her sent back to the States? Will pulled off his cap off. "Ma'am, we're helping the sailors keep an eye out for enemy vessels."

"Oh?" Mrs. Abrim raised an eyebrow. "No hanky-panky?"

"None, ma'am," Will answered. "I'm Private William Bowers. I served in Columbus, New Mexico during the Punitive Expedition. I met Miss Day then, and spent some time helping on her ranch." He held out his hand. Mrs. Abrim studied it a minute before shaking it.

"Make sure you always meet out here in the open, where everyone can see what you two are doing. And no holding hands or smooching! You'll be a bad influence on the other girls. You got me?"

"Yes, ma'am," Agnes said, smiling in relief as she watched the older woman walk away. Maybe Mrs. Abrim was not as stern as she had originally made herself out to be.

In the galley the next morning, Sadie and Agnes shuffled through the chow line with their tin trays. Agnes took canned peaches and dry toast, but Sadie asked not only for her own sausage and cream gravy, but Agnes' as well.

"I don't know why you don't like this stuff. It's better than what my mother used to give us kids for breakfast. I may be Scandinavian, but pickled herring and brunost cheese just don't cut it."

"I've never been much of a gravy fan," Agnes said, "and when they go and call it 'shit on a shingle,' it takes away any interest I might have had. I wish they had green chile or salsa."

"Never heard of them." Sadie stuffed her mouth full. Agnes ate thoughtfully, remembering Lupe's breakfast burritos and wishing she was back at the Sunrise. Patience, she told herself. Do the work. Earn the money. Then savor the results. She went back to the lavatory and brushed her teeth, then spent a whole day in the hospital ward. An hour before dinner, she went to the foredeck, where she found Will standing at the railing, watching the sea.

"Hey, kids!" Sadie slipped into the space between Agnes and Will, which was far too narrow even for her thin shoulders. Will and Agnes scooted apart while Sadie smiled dazzlingly at each of them in turn, then brought up a hand and brushed back the wisps of hair that danced about her face. "What're we doing?"

"Watching for the enemy," Will said.

"Ooooh. See anything?"

"Nothing interesting," Agnes said.

Sadie pointed to a dozen tiny lines that poked up from the distant horizon. "What's that?"

"A convoy," Will answered. "Ten, maybe twelve vessels."

"I don't see no boats," Sadie said.

"That's because they're far away. The earth is curved, so things that are far away are hidden by its curve. Those ships' hulls lay below the horizon. Just their masts are visible."

"They friend? Or foe?" Sadie shielded her eyes with her hand and squinted harder at the horizon.

"Can't tell," Will said.

"If you can't tell, they could be Huns!" Sadie waved her arms at a passing sailor. "Hey! You! Sailor boy! Is them boats Allies or Huns?"

The sailor stopped his dogtrot and stared at the horizon for a moment. "Probably American. You don't gotta worry about convoys. It's the lone ships ya gotta worry about.

"Why's that?" Sadie batted her eyes. The sailor stood a little taller.

"Every legitimate ship has an escort of cruisers or destroyers, like thems out there. But lone ships? They're suspect. German U-boats rig up one or two sails and float on the surface so that they look like harmless schooners."

"Oooh. I'll keep that in mind," Sadie said, suddenly serious. "You know so much! I'm glad I stopped you and not some half-wit rube. What else should we be on the lookout for?"

The sailor snapped to attention, his flushed face showing how flattered he was. It sounded like he was reciting from the official sailor's guidebook. "Floating objects. Barrels, spars, wooden cases, stuff like that. They could be mines. We don't take no chances. Absolutely none. A transport like ours presents a huge target for a U-boat. We ain't called *The Leviathan* for nothing! But we got 12,000 souls aboard, and we pledged to protect them all. Wid our very lives. Our motto is "Safety First."

Sadie cooed. "I feel so much safer, knowing you're watching out for us." She wrapped her arms around the sailor's bicep and gave him a little peck on the cheek. A foolish grin lit up his face and he wandered away, looking a bit punch drunk.

Sadie winked at Agnes. "See? Didn't I tell ya every guy liked a peck on the cheek?" Before he could stop her, she leaned over and kissed Will's cheek. Will didn't wipe the kiss off like the porter had at Penn Station, but he frowned.

"Not everyone," Agnes said in a low voice that made Sadie look at her round-eyed. It bothered her that Sadie kissed Will, but Will's reaction bothered her even more. Time after time he had grown cold and distant with her. Now he was acting the same toward Sadie. Why was he so adverse to attention from women? They silently watched the convoy gradually disappear into the depths.

"Boy! I'm feeling hot! Must be all this sun." Sadie's head leaned over until it was lying on Will's shoulder. Agnes scowled. The sun was low on the horizon, and it was anything but hot on the foredeck. Why was Sadie, who was supposed to be her friend, making a pass at Will? She turned to glare at Sadie. Sadie's cheeks blazed, and the wisps of hair that had been floating in the breeze were plastered to her forehead. Agnes laid the back of her hand on Sadie's cheek. It burned.

"Sadie? Are you alright?" she asked.

"I don't feel so good," Sadie answered.

Agnes leaped into action. Together they half walked, half carried Sadie down the stairs and through the corridors. As the doctor listened to Sadie's chest, she suddenly went green, grabbed a trash can, and threw up the remains of her lunch.

"Well, that settles it. She's got food poisoning. She's case number three. Leave her with me. She'll be fine by morning," the doctor said, and so Agnes and Will left.

"I'm sorry she's sick, but I'm glad it was food poisoning," Agnes said as they walked to the galley for dinner.

Will looked at her. "Why's that?"

"Because I was worried that it was the Spanish flu. There've been cases of it in American training camps on both sides of the Atlantic, and on some of the transport ships. Some, even, on the front lines." Agnes stopped talking before she could blurt that some cases had been deadly. Will had enough to worry about, and so did she. "At least food poisoning isn't contagious."

"I don't know about that," Will said, pushing his tray away from him. "I'm beginning to feel the way Sadie looked."

Agnes walked him to sick bay, where the doctor gave him the same quick exam before having him lie down on one of the last few beds. The entire ward had filled with men and women who were suffering from vomiting and diarrhea. Agnes found Mrs. Abrim and volunteered to work in the sick ward the next morning.

As Agnes entered the sick bay the next morning, Sadie sat up and waved her arms. "Yoo-hoo! Over here! Boy! I'm so glad to have company. It's been so boring lying here, listening to everyone retch."

"You're looking better," Agnes placed a hand on Sadie's forehead. It felt cool and dry. "Feeling better, too."

Sadie grabbed Agnes' hand and held on to it. "My system is good at getting rid of what ails it. I threw up the stuff before it poisoned me. Know what it was? That shit they put on the shingle? It really was shit."

"Then I'm lucky I didn't eat it." Agnes smiled. "Will's in here, too. He got sick right after you did."

"Really? I never saw him." Sadie looked around the ward before she shrugged and lay back on her pillow, patting Agnes' hand. "You're so lucky you have Will," Sadie said. "I wish I could find me a beau."

"No you don't," Agnes said. "Not now, at least. If you get married, they ship you home. Wait 'til the war's over."

Sadie sighed. "I know. Ain't one doughboy or sailor on this fool boat I'd want anyways. I mean, they're fun to flirt with, but I'm looking for a real man. A hero. Someone who'd sweep me off my feet. None of these dopes attract me. What attracted you to Will? Besides his smell, I mean."

"His smell?"

"Sure. Don't think I haven't noticed. Every time you get close to him, you sniff him. You'd think he was a bouquet of roses!"

Agnes laughed. She'd never realized she was doing this. "I guess it's the time he spends in the hold. He smells like horses, and that reminds me of home."

"You like the guy because he smells like a horse?"

"That, and he's dependable and steady. I can always count on Will to be there when I need him. And he's a hard worker. Will knows how to fix truck engines and re-roof houses, mend fences, shoe horses."

"Sounds like you're looking for a handyman, not a boyfriend."

"I'm not looking for either," Agnes said a little too strongly. "I have to get the Sunrise back. After that, I'll think about boyfriends. Now, let me get back to my job. I've got a full ward of patients to check."

She peeled her hand from Sadie's, then worked her way up one side of the room, reading charts and feeling foreheads. When she found Will in the back corner, he was curled up in a ball, his face towards the wall and his sheet pulled over his head as if he was hiding. She placed a hand on his shoulder.

"Will?"

The sheet wriggled. "Go away," it muttered.

"I've got to check on you, It's my job."

Will sighed and rolled over. His face was sullen and closed. "I don't like you seeing me this way. Helpless. Weak. I feel useless."

"We all feel that way when we're sick." She laid her hand on his forehead and, like Sadie's and most of the people in the room, it was cool and dry. "You're mending. You'll be back to your old self before you know it."

"I hope so. And I hope you never, ever see me like this again." Will threw his arm over his eyes. "It's the cattle dog in me. I'd rather be dead than useless."

Agnes' heart lurched. Didn't he know that he was important to her far beyond his usefulness? She didn't like him just because he could fix truck engines, re-roof houses, mend fences, and shoe horses. He made her laugh and relax, and she always felt comfortable and protected around him. He made her feel special.

"Everyone is incapacitated sometime," Agnes said. "If you ever are again, I hope I'm the one who gets to take care of you."

By the end of her shift, Agnes felt exhausted, both mentally and physically. Bending over beds was hard on her back, but assuring sick and scared people was hard on her emotions. It was especially hard when it was Will who needed her. He looked so vulnerable and so miserable, and it pulled on her heartstrings. She walked out onto the deck to get a breath of fresh air and to see the horizon line that never failed to calm her and remind her of the vast expanse of the desert.

It wasn't there. A heavy gray blanket had swallowed everything. She looked over the railing. Nothing. No water, no ship. Gray.

"What is this?" she asked a sailor who was leaning on the railing staring into nothingness.

"Fog." He pulled out a pack of cigarettes, offered one to Agnes, who declined, then took one for himself and lit it. "Extremely heavy fog. And so close to the end! We were planning to make landfall tomorrow."

"Can we still do that?" Agnes asked.

The sailor shrugged and took a long drag on his cigarette. "Depends. It ain't easy to navigate in a fog this thick. Nearly impossible. We've ramped down the engines, almost to a standstill. Christ. It makes me nervous."

"Because you're afraid we'll run into something?"

We're still in the danger zone. This section of water is a hot-bed for submarines. I feel like a sitting duck."

"I see," Agnes said, then suppressed a nervous giggle because in truth she couldn't see at all. She stared at the wall of gray, searching, like the seaman beside her, for something, anything. Agnes gasped when something materialized. She grabbed the sailor's arm, pointing with her other hand. She felt him tense, then relax.

"It's one of our destroyers," he whispered.

The destroyer materialized from the grayness. Pale, ghostly shapes of men lined its railings. An officer on the Leviathan's bridge shouted through a megaphone. "We don't know where we are. Do you?"

"No," came the answer.

"Shit." The sailor stared at the glowing tip of his cigarette, then tossed it overboard. Agnes heard it hiss when it hit the invisible water below. The waves gently slapped the side of the ship and the men aboard the destroyer talked quietly among themselves. Agnes felt herself tensing against the cold, damp air.

A voice called from the destroyer. "Black and white buoy on starboard beam."

The sailor breathed a sigh of relief. "That's the buoy that signifies mid-channel. We're heading directly to Brest. Tomorrow, we'll land."

Agnes stretched her aching back and stared into the fog at the shifting, indistinct figures on the destroyer. Tomorrow everything would change. She and Will would go their separate ways again, and she would begin her duties as a battlefield nurse. Would she be able to handle it? The future seemed shrouded in fog.

Agnes spat over the side and told herself that tomorrow, before they went their separate ways, she would tell Will how much he meant to her. She didn't want a handyman. She wanted him. Body and soul.

Chapter Sixteen

Agnes sat up, slamming her head into the bunk above her for what had to be the thousandth time. Holding her stinging head, she twisted around and dangled her legs over the edge. The girl in the bunk below her gave her heels a playful swat, so Agnes scooted out and dropped to the floor. Around her, nurses shucked off their nightgowns and threw on their uniforms as they jabbered like jaybirds. It was May the second, and the Leviathan was scheduled to enter the harbor at Brest.

Agnes joined the throng of women who bustled to the upper deck. Instead of her first glimpse of France, she stared at the same wall of gray fog that had enveloped her yesterday. Agnes sighed. She ate breakfast, then went to the sick bay. Both Will and Sadie had been discharged.

Agnes' shoulders tightened. She and Sadie would leave the ship together, but when would Will disembark? Where would he go? What if she didn't get a chance to say goodbye? She remembered her vow to tell him how important he was to her, and it made her mad at herself that she had put if off so long. She could rope a steer and shoe a mule. Why was it so hard to say what she felt?

She combed the ship for him, ignoring sailors who shouted for her to go below and pack her pantaloons. She checked far down in the hold, where the transport trucks were stored. She passed through the places where the artillery carriages were securely tied down. She checked the stables. Everywhere she went, someone told her that Will had just been there, but was already gone. Finally, she returned to the nurses' quarters, where she found Sadie happily packing her belongings and jabbering on about how exciting it all was. Agnes threw her few things into her satchel haphazardly as her heart continued to pine for Will.

When everything was packed, Mrs. Abrim herded her nurses topside and positioned them along a railing while they waited their turn to disembark. The lifting fog revealed a slowly developing scene. Indistinct, gray, hunkering shapes became soft-edged, tinged with subdued colors. The sun broke through, and dozens of picturesque fishing boats, their sides painted in colors so brilliant they nearly burned Agnes' eyes with their intensity, came into sharp focus. Agnes gasped. Lovely, tall stone buildings, including a medieval fortress with round turrets and crenelated walls, surrounded the harbor. Beyond the city lay fields of intense green grass dotted with quaint, gray stone farm-houses. The clear blue sky reflected on the deep, blue harbor. Compared with the subtle tans and greens of the desert or the grayed skies and concrete walls of New York, France was brilliant.

"That looks like the kind of castle a princess lives in," Sadie mused. "Will we get to go in it? I never thought I'd be touring castles! Not with a war on. Think we can ask Mrs. Abrim? How long you think we'll be here in Brest before they send us out to the front?"

"I have no idea." Agnes clutched her carpet bag to her chest and scanned the mayhem for a glimpse of Will. Sailors swarming like ants threw ropes around piers and unlimbered the cranes that would transfer loads to the pier. Long gangplanks banged against the port side of the ship, and troops, passengers and cargo began spilling down them. Agnes turned to Sadie. "This is going to take awhile. Ask Mrs. Abrim your questions. Keep her busy. I'll be back soon, probably before she even notices I'm gone and certainly before we get orders to disembark."

Agnes shoved her carpet bag into Sadie's arms and elbowed her way to the starboard side of the ship, where the crew shoveled coal from barges into the ship's bunkers. The two regimental bands that stayed with the ship played jazz band music, adding to the cacophony of boat whistles and shouting men. Just when she had resigned herself that she would never find Will in this crowd, someone placed a hand on her shoulder, and she whirled around to find him right behind her.

"Why are you always sneaking up on me?" she said, with a laugh of relief.

"Why are you always so lost in thought that you don't see me coming?"

"I wasn't lost in thought. I was frantic with worry! Where have you been?"

"Everywhere. And everywhere I went, someone told me that a pretty young woman with a bobbed haircut had just left."

Agnes laughed. "We've been walking around in circles! What a waste of time!"

"We're together now." Will hugged her tightly. "I'll miss you, you little bulldog of a cowgirl. Stay strong. Be brave. You remember how to find me if you need me?"

"Camp de Souge. Burgundy."

"Bordeaux," he corrected.

"Someplace that begins with a B and is a kind of wine! There's too many of them to remember!" Agnes felt her face flush. She felt as ditzy as Sadie.

"It's important," he said, trying to look serious. "Remember it this way: Oh, oh, oh! It's . . "

"Bore-doh!"

"Right. Write as soon as you get an assignment. And wherever I go, know that I'll be fighting for you. You will have that ranch."

"I want you there with me, too, so be careful, Private Bowers." The words slipped out before Agnes could stop them and she felt her face flush, but there they were; she had said it.

Will laughed. "If I can be of use to you, I'll be there. Mending fences, pulling cows . . . "

Agnes took a deep breath and plunged on. "I'm not looking to hire a handyman, Will."

Will's face darkened. "There are things you don't know about me, Agnes. If you knew, you'd know I wasn't good for much more than that."

Agnes shook her head. "I know all I need to know about you. I know you are kind and considerate. Hardworking. And you smell like horses. What more do I need to know?" Will looked like he was going to say something they would both regret, so Agnes got up on tiptoes and silenced him with a long, hard kiss. She filled her memory with his smell, the taste of his tongue on hers, the feel of his muscles tensing. It might be a long time before she would see him again, and she needed this to hold on to.

The ship's whistle blasted shrilly, and they each scurried off to where they were supposed to be. When Agnes got back to the railing, she found it empty. She scanned the crowd on the docks until she saw Sadie frantically waving her arms, then rushed down the gangplank and elbowed her way through the crowd. Agnes slipped into the group of nurses who clustered together, clutching their bags as officers shouted orders and Mrs. Abrim scuttled from one to another, trying to get an idea of where they should go next.

"I been watching that gangplank like a hawk watches a groundhog hole," Sadie shouted in Agnes' ear as she handed over the carpet bag. "What would have happened if you hadn't found us?! Mrs. Abrim's knickers would have been in knots!"

"Did she notice I was missing?" Agnes shouted back.

"Nope. Too busy to count heads. I asked her about the castle. She says maybe we can visit it on leave. Won't that be nice?" Agnes nodded. While Sadie continued to shout, Agnes looked back at the ship. The horses were coming out of the hold now, one at a time, in slings. Will was somewhere nearby, watching after them. She touched a finger to her lips and tried to remember every detail from their kiss, then smiled, pleased with herself that she had finally spoken what had long been in her heart. Until she saw him again, she would work as hard as she could. Someday, she vowed, they would be at the ranch again, and together they would add rays to the lazy D brand. The sun would rise at the Sunrise for another generation of Days.

"Ladies! This way," Mrs. Abrim shouted and gestured, then pressed through the crowd. They followed her, walking through streets of uneven cobbles, down lanes that were so narrow that the houses seemed to touch overhead. The hustle of the port faded behind them.

Agnes' feet began to ache. "I should have joined the cavalry," she muttered to herself. "I wasn't designed for infantry."

Sadie drew in a sharp breath and began limping, her face contorted with pain. "I swear I've turned my ankles a dozen times already. These roads may look like they came out of a fairytale, but I'd gladly go back to tarmac. Or even just plain old dirt."

"Fairy tale or medieval torture device?" Agnes asked, making Sadie laugh. "It's past noon, I think. We should stop and have lunch sometime soon. Maybe you can put your feet up then."

They entered a square crowded with horse-drawn covered wagons. A corporal helped the women scramble into the backs of them. Agnes found herself seated on a bench that ran around three sides of the truck bed. The canvas top flapped as the wagon bumped over cobblestones, then onto a tree-lined lane and out into the country, where the road became dirt that billowed behind them.

Agnes peered out the back flap as the wagon bumped along. The mesmerizing clop of hooves kept time with her heart, lulling her into sleep. She dozed fitfully, waking with a jerk to find her stomach aching with emptiness. Her bottom hurt from bouncing on the hard, flat bench, her neck from jerking in sleep.

She stood up and shuffled towards the back, intending to get out and walk alongside the wagon, but Mrs. Abrim frowned her disapproval and she sat back down. The shadows grew long, then blended into the dusk. Long after dark, the wagons pulled off the road, rocking Agnes to wakefulness.

Sadie lurched to her feet. "About time. I got a bladder as round and hard as a cantaloupe."

A private placed a stool outside the back of the wagon, then reached up to offer Mrs. Abrim a hand. She slapped it away. "What is the meaning of this?" she demanded. "You cannot expect us to sit in a wagon for hours on end with no food and water, and no toilet facilities! It is inhumane!"

"Sorry about that, Ma'am. Next time we'll get you reservations in a conveyance run by the Ritz-Carlton instead of Uncle Sam," he answered in an accent that reminded Agnes of her time in New York. Clearly, this was not the first time he'd been reprimanded by an imperious head nurse for something over which he had no control, and he wasn't going to let it bother him. Feeling as dazed as a cow during round-up, Agnes followed along as he herded the complaining women to the latrines, and then to a large canvas tent that housed a mess hall. She was too tired to complain, too stiff to do anything but follow the line of shuffling women. All day on a wooden bench was far worse than all day in a saddle.

Someone shoved a tin plate of soup, a roll, and a tin cup of coffee into her hands. She ate in silence, lifting the plate to her lips and pouring it into her mouth instead of bothering with a spoon. The coffee revived her enough for her to wonder where Will was and if he was being treated any better than this.

"Ladies! Time for beddy-bye," a sergeant with a clipboard shouted. Agnes dropped her plate and cup into a vat of soapy water and, holding Sadie by the elbow, stumbled along as he assigned groups of four to tents. Inside were four wooden framed camp cots, each with a scratchy woolen blanket and a pillow. Exhausted, Agnes dropped onto her cot without taking off her clothes.

"Thank God that's over," Sadie said with a groan. "I don't think I could take another day like today."

"You'll have to," one of the other two women said. "This isn't the hospital, you know. It's just a way station." Agnes fell asleep wondering if she could face another day like this.

In the morning the nurses got a breakfast of white gravy and sausage on biscuit, and lots of hot, dark coffee. Fearing it was all she would get until night, Agnes ate hers without complaint. She cradled her steaming cup and listened while the others nervously chatted about what assignments they wanted.

"Me? I want to be on the front line," one nurse said.

"You won't be," a second said. "They're not putting women in the field hospitals. The Army's determined they're no place for women. Too much shelling. Snipers. Getting overrun and falling into Hun hands. It isn't safe."

"As if any place else is," another nurse said with a snort.

"Look, you want to be a hero? Ask to go to a Casualty Clearing Station. They're not on the front lines, but they're not out of reach of the big guns. They're only sending the most intrepid nurses there," the second nurse told the first. "But me? I'm hoping for an assignment at a convalescent camp. Those're set up right near the coast. In port cities. So you get to have fun on your time off. And the soldiers there just need time to recover. Their injuries have already been treated."

"I wonder, is there a convalescent camp in Brest?" Sadie whispered to Agnes. "We could see that castle."

Agnes listened to the women discuss why they had come and where they wanted to be placed. Some had seen posters with beautiful women in clean, white nursing uniforms, leading handsome men on the road back to wellness and had decided that they wanted to be this beautiful, this noble, this heroic. Others, like Sadie, had come to escape a staid and boring life. Some, like the one who wanted to join the convalescent camp, had joined to escape poverty, and while they were willing to do their part, they wanted it to be as safe as possible: get the most money out of the least amount of danger. The one who wanted to go to the front had come over to follow her sweetheart. Others hoped to find a sweetheart: heal a man, and his heart will be forever yours. A few wanted to pursue a career in nursing.

Agnes didn't know where she fit in all this. She wanted more than anything to buy the ranch, so she had come for the money. But she didn't want the safest position possible. She craved adventure. And she was, in some way, following Will, but she also wanted to be professional, even if she didn't intend to pursue nursing for the rest of her life. She looked around the table and felt a bond with each and every woman at the table. No matter where they came from or where their lives would take them, they were here now. Agnes was sure each intended to do her best.

Sadie nervously drummed the table. "I thought I wanted a great adventure. Now that I'm here, it seems a little more than I had bargained for."

"You want to go back to Iowa?" Agnes asked.

"And stay on the farm? No thanks. I want to see the wide world. What I hadn't counted on, though, was the confusion. Not knowing what comes next. Back in Iowa, we had a routine. Day in, day out. It was boring, but we knew what was coming."

"You'll be fine once we settle in somewhere," Agnes said, and gave Sadie a quick, reassuring hug.

A corporal came into the mess tent and herded the nurses back to the motor pool, where they found that their trunks had been taken from the Leviathan's hold and delivered. A detail of privates lugged the trunks back to the women's tents and set them up next to the cots, where they served as nightstands and end tables. Agnes watched the other women unpack and set out things, making the tent cozy and home-like. She didn't bother. Mrs. Abrim had already met with various directors and officers and would begin meting out nurses to various camps, hospitals and clearing stations very soon.

"Nurse Sundvuist?" Sadie leaped off her cot, throwing her copy of *Western Story Magazine* into the air. The corporal at the tent entrance blushed. "I'm sorry to disturb you. Mrs. Abrim asked me to bring you to her. She's making assignments."

Sadie grabbed Agnes' hand, a stricken look crossing her face. "Go with me?" she asked in a voice that was so high and tight that Agnes thought it might burst like a balloon. Agnes nodded. Hand in hand, the two nurses walked into the little tent that had become Mrs. Theodora Abrim's office.

The head nurse was seated behind a rustic little camp table that was strewn with papers. A single, bare light bulb dangled by its cord overhead, providing the room with one bright and austere patch of light. Agnes and Sadie, still clutching each other's hands, stood in front of the desk and waited. Agnes could hear Sadie's short, quick breath and feared that the girl would hyperventilate. Her hand felt clammy and wet within her own. She squeezed it for assurance, but Sadie's hand began shaking.

Mrs. Abrim looked up. A scowl crossed her face. "Nurse Day? I don't remember calling for you, too."

"Oh, Mrs. Abrim," Sadie said brightly, in a voice squeaky with nerves, "My friend Agnes, here, is a little nervous about this placement business. She's from out in the desert, you see, and never been away from home. It's all a little strange to her. So, I thought, perhaps, that you could do her the kindness of assigning the two of us together, so I could look out for her."

Agnes tried to keep her face emotionless as her eyes slid sideways so she could look at her friend, who was beaming what she must have thought was an encouraging smile, but looked more like hysteria. She squeezed Sadie's hand until her knuckles ground together. Sadie squirmed. Theodora Abrim's lips pressed together in a prim, white line. Agnes couldn't tell if she was trying to suppress a laugh or was angry at them. She stared at the stack of papers on her desk. Finally, the head nurse looked up.

"I see. Well then. Your selfless devotion to your friend is noted. Your timidity and nervousness are also noted." Mrs. Abrim slipped her glasses down her nose and pinched the bridge of her nose with two fingers. "The American Expeditionary Force has developed a complex system of carefully interwoven parts to deal with its casualties. It is my job to match each nurse with the assignment at which they are best suited. Miss Sundvuist, I do not think you have the nerves to handle the sudden and immense inrushes of cases in the base hospitals, where I had intended to send Miss Day."

Agnes stood a little straighter, proud that the head nurse thought she had steady nerves.

The head nurse continued. "Nor do I think you are well suited for the extreme and raw violence of the wounds displayed in the Casualty Clearing Stations."

"Oh! Yes ma'am," Sadie said. Agnes wondered if, in her nervous state, she had understood a single word the head nurse had said, but she had. Sadie was not a candidate for any position in which quick thinking, calm demeanor, or steely nerves were needed.

"I considered sending you to the recuperation wards, but maybe that's too sedate for the two of you together."

"What about camp hospitals?" Agnes' heart pounded and she tried to keep her face neutral, disinterested. The last thing she wanted was to look over eager.

Mrs. Abrim stared at Agnes over the top of her wire-rimmed reading glasses. "What do you know about camp hospitals?"

"Oh, not much." Agnes struggled to keep her voice steady and casual. "I know the troops train there, before battle. I assume that means there'll be less trauma."

"You'd end up pulling splinters from boys' hands. Checking for colds. Making sure their socks are dry. That kind of thing."

Agnes nodded. "Sadie and I could do that."

"Let's see." Mrs. Abrim studied her notes, "Chateauvillain needs a nurse. So does Bourmont. And Camp de Souge."

"Camp de Souge! Isn't that where. . . " Agnes kicked Sadie's ankle so hard that she sucked in her breath.

Mrs. Abrim looked up. "You know something about Camp de Souge?"

"I think. Maybe. Weren't some of the units from *The Leviathan* talking about it? Maybe the Artillery was going there?" Agnes tried to keep her face from showing the elation that was bubbling in her chest. Camp de Souge was exactly where she wanted to go!

Mrs. Abrim looked down at her paperwork and a smile curled the edge of her mouth. "Maybe, huh? Artillery? Fine. They asked for one nurse, but I'll give them a pair. Talk with Corporal Magee. He is arranging transportation to the various assignments. I believe you'll leave tomorrow morning."

Agnes snapped a quick salute, elbowing Sadie so that Sadie did the same. She hustled Sadie toward the tent flap before her friend could say something that would reveal why Agnes was so happy inside.

"Oh, and Sadie?" Mrs. Abrim called just as they were about to leave.

"Yes, Mrs. Abrim?"

"Thank you for watching out for Agnes. I know you'll take good care of her. And whomever else needs your help at Camp de Souge." Mrs. Abrim smiled and winked, but Agnes was sure the wink was for her. Was she intentionally allowing them to go to Will? Or was she just very, very lucky?

Chapter Seventeen

Agnes peeled back the back canvas flap of the truck delivering her and Sadie to Camp de Souge. The pine forest they had been driving through retreated, and they passed a flat, dusty field surrounded by hangers and huts.

"Airfield," she shouted over the roar of the engine. Sadie nodded, but didn't move. She looked a little green. The gate to the camp came into view next: a thin, metal arch with the name of the camp across it. They passed under the arch and into a camp that was at the same time orderly and chaotic, rows upon rows of wooden buildings that looked like they'd been quickly thrown together by someone who'd never wielded a hammer before, laid out in precise patterns. Incongruously, the buildings looked, at the same time both dilapidated and rawly unfinished. Wooden walkways between them sagged listlessly into seas of mud. The sun shone bright in a soft blue, cloudless sky, making the camp look all the more dreary.

Agnes' eyes searched for Will among the men in khaki who were everywhere, lounging in front of buildings, striding purposefully along walkways, going in and out of doors. As soon as she settled in, she vowed to find him and have him explain why he thought he could be no more than her handyman. What was it in his past that kept him from fulfilling the promise of passion she had tasted on his lips?

The truck screeched to a halt in front of a cluster of buildings whose sign announced it was a hospital. The driver came around to the back and helped the two women out, depositing them on a plank walkway. "There ya go, ladies," he said as he set their trunks next to them. "Just wait right here and someone'll come for youse real soon. And don't never, under any circumstances, step off that wooden walkway."

"Why not?" Sadie shouted after him as he climbed back into the truck.

Without answering the question, he gave them a sarcastic smile, crunched his way into gear, and lurched away.

"Wonder what he meant by that! Golly! An' I thought the ride in the wagon was rough. If I never ride in the back of a truck again, it'll be too soon. Those gas fumes'll kill you." Sadie gazed around and her face fell. "This looks more like the hobo shanty town down near the railroad tracks than a military camp."

Agnes thought of Will hidden away in these hovels, and shrugged. "Doesn't matter what it looks like as long as the people here are. . ."

The door to the hospital opened and a woman came out. She wore a white apron over her plump figure. Ash-brown curls wreathed her round face and blue eyes sparkled behind a pair of round, wire-framed glasses. She smiled, revealing deep dimples in her cheeks. Agnes had a sudden image of Santa Claus' wife, or perhaps what Mrs. Fowler might have looked like a quarter of a century earlier. Hope blossomed in her chest.

"You must be the two new casuals," the woman said in a bubbly voice.

"The what?" Sadie asked.

"Casuals. Nurses from the medical replacement unit." The woman held out her hand. Agnes shook it and the woman's smile drooped into a frown. "Your papers. That's what I wanted." Agnes and Sadie scrambled to deliver their transfer documents. The woman dragged her glasses down to the tip of her nose and studied the papers carefully. "Ah. So, you are Sadie Sundvuist, of Harlan, Iowa."

"Outside of Harlan, actually. I grew up on a farm. We didn't go into town but once, maybe twice a month to get supplies," Sadie began. The scowl on the woman's face silenced her. Agnes decided that, despite appearances, this woman was no jolly old elf.

"And you, I see, are Agnes Day, of Columbus, New Mexico." The woman's head jerked up and she peered at Agnes over the top of her spectacles. "THE Columbus, New Mexico? Of Pancho Villa fame?"

"Yes, ma'am." Agnes didn't bother to add that, like Sadie, she wasn't actually from in town, either.

The woman folded the papers and tucked them into a pocket in her uniform skirt. "Did you serve during that conflict?"

Agnes shook her head. "No, Ma'am. I wasn't certified yet."

"But you saw . . ." the woman's voice trailed off, but the look on her face told Agnes what she was asking. She remembered the mounds of clothing in the street that weren't mounds of clothing at all, the burning buildings, the chaos at the camp, the look of panic on the faces of the soldiers surrounding the machine gun emplacement. She nodded. "A little."

The woman nodded. "That will help prepare you for what's ahead. I am Isobel Chriswell, and I come from Kansas City. My mission here is to relieve the suffering of our heroic boys. Not that these boys are suffering. Nor heroic. Not yet. And when they are, they won't be treated here. That's the privilege of the Clearing Stations and Field Hospitals."

She wheeled on her heels and Sadie and Agnes rushed to follow her. "I am the head nurse, and you will report to me," she said over her shoulder. "You will call me Nurse Chriswell, is that clear? Not Miss. Not Missus. Not Ma'am. My marital status is not relevant. You will work hard, be prompt, and engage in no tomfoolery or, like the women you are replacing, I will send you home."

"Yes, ma'am, I mean Nurse Chriswell," Agnes said. She wished the camp was run by Mrs. Abrim. She would have to be very careful around this new supervisor.

They passed through the front office where a half dozen men and women clattered away at typewriters, and into a narrow, roofed walkway that was flanked by more badly-made buildings. "I know it's not impressive, but we are not charged with doing impressive things. We do what we've been ordered to do, do we not? That building holds our laboratory, which has a few microscopes for determining the types of infection our men suffer from. In there is our x-ray machine for checking broken bones. That's the operating room. That's the dental clinic, and that building, ladies, is our delousing facility."

The walkway led into an open field. Buildings radiated from three sides of the field like rays from the rising sun. "Those are our wards. There are ten of them, each with thirty beds," she said, pointing to each in turn. "Should the need arise, we can create more wards by putting up tents in this open space. But the need never arises. Here in camp, life is pretty stable. It's not like the base camps or the field camps, where the numbers of cases surge after each battle. Those facilities are doing important work."

"Remington!" she shouted at a passing orderly, who froze in place. "Retrieve these women's trunks from in front of the hospital and deliver them to nurses' quarters." The man nodded so deeply that it almost looked like a bow, then hurried down the plankway.

"We've got a staff of ten physicians and, now that the two of you have joined us, ten nurses. Twenty-five enlisted men serve as orderlies, including Remington, there."

"Is the 1st New Mexico Artillery Battery A here, too?" Sadie asked.

Nurse Chriswell raised her eyebrows and lowered the corners of her mouth in a gesture that was both inquisitive and disapproving of questions at the same time.

"That's not what they're called," Agnes said. "They're still Battery A, but they've been rolled into the 66th Field Artillery Brigade."

"Friends of yours?" The head nurse's question dripped with vitriol.

"They were stationed at Camp Columbus," Agnes answered quickly, her heart pounding as she searched for something that wouldn't make Nurse

Chriswell suspicious enough to keep an eye on her. "My parents had many of the officers to dinner."

Nurse Chriswell gave a dismissive harrumph. "Here, the only soldiers we interact with are injured or sick. I'll introduce you to the medical staff after you've had a chance to store your gear and freshen up, but don't expect dinners with artillery officers. Come on. I'll show you the nurses' quarters."

The nurses lived in four rooms set around a central hall. Nurse Chriswell explained that the front one on the right was hers. The other three held three nurses apiece. She pointed to the door in the left back corner.

"That will be your room. You will share it with Ethel Rosenberry. She is an experienced hospital nurse and will be happy to teach you the routine. Now, if you will excuse me, I've got paperwork to do in the front office." The head nurse flashed the happy elf smile that Agnes had noticed when they first arrived, then spun on her heel and left Sadie and Agnes to carry their trunks into their room. Agnes had opened the door and was backing in with the front half of Sadie's trunk when a voice stopped her.

"What the hell do you think you're doing?" It was a woman's voice, husky and deep. Agnes looked up, taking her first look at the room. Three canvas hammocks hung from ceiling hooks. A lone trunk sat in one corner. And a dozen buckets, wastebins and washbasins stood scattered about the room. The lone window was covered with several layers of newspaper, through which the sun shone only dimly. It took Agnes quite a while to find who had spoken. The face that peered out of one of the hammocks was surrounded with a frizzy jumble of dark hair and creased with sleep.

Sadie leaned over the top of the dropped trunk to poke her head into the room. "Sorry! Nurse Criswell didn't tell us anyone was here. Are you Ethel Rosenberry? We're your new roommates. This is Agnes Day. She's from New Mexico, way out west. I ain't never been there. I figured I needed to know more about it, so I bought a couple copies of *Western Story Magazine* before we boarded *The Leviathan*. You can read them if you like. I'm Sadie Sundqvist. I'm from Iowa. What ship did you come over on? Been here long? Is the New Mexico National Guard Artillery Brigade here?"

"The 66th Artillery Brigade. They aren't National Guard any more," Agnes corrected for the second time in an hour.

The face burrowed back down into the hammock. "Oh Gawd," it moaned. "Chriswell's gone and given me a couple of jaybirds."

"They're from Kansas, silly. Iowans are Hawkeyes. And I think New Mexicans are Road Runners. Right, Agnes?" Sadie shoved the trunk forward, gouging the floor in the process. "Whoops. I bet there'll be hell to pay for that."

The face looked out of the hammock again. "That scratch? Nah. These barracks were thrown up quickly, and they used soft, green wood. The stuff scratches if you just look at it wrong. The wood's so warped that wind whistles through. Wear your shoes. Always. You don't, you'll end up with a splinter the size of a knitting needle. Oh, and these hammocks? Temporary until the beds arrive. Which might be next week or next year, depending on which supply clerk you ask."

"Still better than a tent," Agnes said.

"I dare you to say that in a rainstorm." Ethel settled back into her hammock. Agnes and Sadie set the trunk down next to Ethel's, then went back for the other one.

"You work night shift?" Sadie asked when they struggled back into the room.

"Today I do," Ethel said. "Though there's not much to do here at night. It's not like the field hospitals down the line, much to Queen Chriswell's dismay. She wants to be heroic; the most decorated nurse on the western front. It's not going to happen. We don't keep serious cases here in camp. Just the boys who can return to duty after a few days. We don't work twelve-hour shifts like they do at the front. The Queen has us working three overlapping ten- hour shifts: six in the morning till four in the afternoon, two in the afternoon until midnight, and ten at night until 8 in the morning. We rotate, so sometimes we work back-to-back shifts and sometimes we get a whole 20 hours off. It's a pretty sweet deal."

"Queen Chriswell?" Sadie giggled.

"Don't you dare call her that to her face!" Ethel said with a chuckle. "It may be accurate, but still, there'd be hell to pay. Still, keep off her shit list and she can be downright jolly."

"Hey, I got another question," Sadie said. "The guy who drove us here, warned us to never, ever step off the walkway. You got alligators, or what?"

Ethel laughed. "No alligators. This ain't Florida. But you ever hear of quicksand?"

"Yeah?" Sadie said.

"Well, we got quickmud. Step off the planks and you might just disappear forever."

"Where does all this mud come from?" Agnes asked.

Ethel eyed her critically. "Where you from?"

"New Mexico," Agnes said.

"The desert. And how long you been in France now?"

"Just a few days," Agnes said.

"Well, a few days means you've just about used up your quota of rainless days. Before long it's going to start pouring and all that dirt out there? It becomes a bog."

Sadie and Agnes froze as a plane roared over, the sound so loud that Agnes feared it would crash into their barracks.

"Relax," Ethel said. "That's just one of the guys from the Second Artillery Aerial Observation School. They like to let us know when they're back from a run."

"They fly from that field in front of the Camp?" Agnes asked, remembering the hangers she had seen on her way in.

"Exactly," Ethel answered. A new sound filled the air after the roar of the plane died away: the low rumble of distant thunder.

"That's funny," Sadie said. "The sky was cloudless when we got off the truck. Now there's a storm brewing."

"No storm," Ethel said. "Artillery. The wind must have just shifted."

Sadie and Agnes looked at each other. "Artillery? On the front?" Agnes said with a squeaky voice.

"Natcherly," Ethel said. "But it ain't as close as you think. On a clear, still day, the sound travels hundreds of miles."

"Do you know which artillery division?" Agnes asked. "Ours? Theirs?"

"No idea," Ethel answered. "Ask one of the orderlies. They're real Army so they'd know. Me? I'm just a nurse. I don't keep track of who's where except in my own ward."

But Remington the orderly knew. Agnes crossed paths with him later that afternoon and asked if the 66th Artillery Brigade was in camp. He rolled up his eyes and thought for a moment before answering.

"Nope. Their stuff is here, stored in a tent over there. But they were sent to the front just before you got here. Stopping a German drive that crossed the Marne about 50 miles outside Paris."

"When will they be back? Could those be the guns we're hearing?" Agnes' heart pounded. To have missed him by just days! And now Will was at the front line and fighting a battle. She would have to wait for him to return before she could find out what was making him feel like no more than a handyman.

Remington shrugged. "Usually, the men spend four to six days in the front trenches, then move back to the support trenches, and then the reserve ones, so I'm guessing two, three more weeks. Depends on the fighting, though. And that could be them we're hearing. It depends on which way the wind's blowing. Could be just about anybody's guns."

Within a week, Sadie and Agnes had settled into a simple routine. Agnes had expected nursing in France to be physically and emotionally taxing. In reality, she found herself doing many of the tasks she had done under Doctor Pritchard. She diagnosed sore throats and rashes, bandaged cuts, put ice on bruises, and generally mothered a bunch of young men who alternately exhibited bravado and fear of what might be next. Sometimes she worked with Sadie. Other times they didn't see each other even though they shared a bedroom. During her nonworking hours, Agnes kept her uniforms clean, which was an almost impossible job. She ate and slept and wrote an occasional letter home to Ernesto and Lupe or to her Mother in Las Vegas or her sisters scattered throughout the territory. Once she even wrote to her attorney, L.B. Fowler, asking if anyone had shown interest in buying the ranch. And always, Agnes listened for the guns and wondered about Will.

News filtered in from the front, a place called Vaux, some 3 1/2 miles west of Chateau Thierry, neither of which were places Agnes could find on a map. She listened as the shelling intensified, then news came that two American Divisions and a French Moroccan division had moved in behind the heavy barrage, advancing into No Man's Land and capturing the front of the German line. In just a few weeks, the Allied assault penetrated six miles into German territory. After that, she heard that the troops were being relieved. Agnes stood on a walkway and watched fresh, enthusiastic men march out to take their place and wondered when the ones who'd been up at the front would return.

Other news came, too. Letters from her sisters told her about mishaps involving her nephews and their shenanigans. Agnes' mother was settling into life in Las Vegas and enjoying rounds of parties and teas. And Heinrich, in spite all his father's influence, had found himself on the front as a medic.

And then the rains came. The camp, which already looked dreary, took on a gray facade. Sadie, not paying attention to where she was going, stepped off the wooden walkway and one leg plunged all the way up to her knee. She never found her shoe. They also learned why Ethel had scattered buckets, waste bins and wash basins throughout their room. The drip, drip, drip became the sound that lulled them to sleep. In a week, Agnes was sure she'd seen more rain than she had in her entire life in New Mexico.

Agnes was working the shift that began at two in the afternoon when she heard that the returning troops were passing by. She grabbed her raincoat and, holding it over her head, ran to the walkway. Haggard, mud-splattered, bearded men staggered past. Agnes studied each hollow-eyed face.

None of them were Will.

The longer she stood there, the tenser she became. Could he be one of the 10,000 casualties who had been shipped to a Casualty Clearing Station, then another hospital? Had he already been carried into a ship bound for the

States? Would he be able to contact her before he left? She didn't know whom to ask. Worse, she feared that even asking would be grounds for a reprimand. She reminded herself that she wasn't supposed to know any of the soldiers or talk with them unless she was treating them.

She refused to believe that Will could possibly be dead. She would know it if he were: feel it in her bones. He had to be alive, and he had to be coming back to her.

The wards filled with exhausted men. Some needed nothing more than a few blisters tended to. Others quaked for no apparent reason. They complained that they didn't understand how they had calmly endured rats and death and the terrible booming of the cannons and now that they were safe, couldn't stop shaking.

At midnight, Agnes' shift ended. She walked to the ward where Sadie was on duty and waited for her. The rain had stopped, and men's voices droned in the sultry night air. Steam billowed from the wash house. Somewhere an out-of-tune piano played. Perhaps the world was coming back to normal. With rest, perhaps these men could sluff off the dirt and hardship, and become as bright and enthusiastic as the men who had just taken their place.

But where was Will?

Sadie appeared, her pale face glistening with tears. Even in the dim light, Agnes noted blood smeared on the front of Sadie's uniform. "Looks like you had a worse time of it than I did," she said.

"Oh God, Agnes! Oh God!" Sadie's voice shook. She took off down the boardwalk so quickly that Agnes had to run to catch up. "There was this boy," Sadie said in a ragged voice, "So young. He got back into camp, then he used an axe to take off his left hand so he wouldn't have to go back to the front. His buddies brought him in. There was blood everywhere! Everywhere! And that stump! Oh, Agnes!"

Sadie buried her face in her hands. Agnes wrapped her arms around her and rocked her as she sobbed. "That's a terrible thing to see. Could you save him?"

"He's still alive, if that's what you mean. We took him right into surgery. Tied off the bleeders. Pulled a flap of skin over the wound and stitched it together. But what's he going to do now, with just one hand? What kind of a life is that?"

Agnes imagined how Will would feel if he lost a hand. His whole being was tied up in being useful. How would he cope if he wasn't? She pondered just how terrible the battlefield must be if this boy thought losing a hand was preferable to returning to it, and shuddered.

"Come on. Let's go to the mess hall and get some dinner." Agnes nudged her friend along. Dinner wasn't going to erase the horrible images from Sadie's mind, but it would help strengthen her body. Sadie calmed, her sobs softening into little gasps. By the time they passed the Officer's Club, she had quieted.

A young man lounged at the door to the officer's club, silhouetted by golden lamplight from within. He was tall and blond, and as serene and composed as a Greek statue draped in a khaki uniform. A pair of golden wings glittered on his chest. Captain's bars glittered on his collar. Agnes thought of Will mucking around on the front, in the mud, with the terrible roar of his own guns, and took an immediate dislike to this man who flew high above it all, in the pristine, perfect sky.

Sadie let out a low whistle of appreciation, but he was oblivious to her, staring blankly out, his hands shoved into the pockets of his woolen slacks.

"I have to meet him." Awe dripped from Sadie's words as if the man they had just passed was Harold Lockwood or Douglas Fairbanks.

"Why?"

Sadie stared at Agnes. "You have Will. Why can't I have someone to spend my extra hours with?" And before she could stop her, Sadie marched back, with Agnes scurrying behind.

"Well, hello there!" Sadie leaned forward on tiptoes. Agnes had the sudden, almost hilarious thought that if she shoved Sadie, she would fall right into this Greek God's arms. The man's brilliant blue eyes, combined with the slight curl of his lip, showed a chill lack of emotion that made him appear even more as if he was chiseled from marble. He was quite tall, and peered down at the two of them condescendingly.

His eyes moved up and down Sadie, taking in the blood smeared uniform, the puffy eyes, the loose strands of hair coming out of her bun, and he snorted. "Hello, yourself."

Sadie didn't seem the least bit perturbed. "I'm Sadie, and this is Agnes. We're nurses, and we just got off shift. We're going to the mess hall. Care to join us?"

The man's head gave a little twitch that might have been a rejection. "I've already eaten. But if you'd like to come back for a nightcap, I might still be here."

"Perfect!" Sadie said, "See you soon!"

Determined to return to the officer's club before her Greek god got away, Sadie swallowed her stew without chewing it. She tried to get Agnes to do the same, but Agnes was not in the mood. She kept thinking about the boy with no hand, the hollow-eyed men coming back from the front, the boys curled like shaking fetuses, and the fact that Will wasn't among them. "How can you even think about meeting a man after what you saw today?"

"How can I not? Agnes, life is short and brutish. I can't remember who said that, but it was someone famous, and he was right. That gorgeous man could be killed tomorrow, and I'll never have talked with him. Who knows what I might have missed! He might be the love of my life! Did you even take a gander at him? He's as handsome as an Iowa farm boy, but in uniform."

Agnes laughed, surprised by how quickly Sadie's mood had shifted. "If Iowa farm boys look like that, why did you ever leave?"

"See? Now you're talking! He's a dreamboat!"

"He's your dreamboat, not mine. You go. I'm too tired to do anything but go to bed."

Sadie leapt from the bench. "Fine. But you're going to regret not coming with me."

Agnes did regret not going with Sadie, but not because she was missing fun. Agnes worried that Sadie was too innocent and impetuous. That handsome, debonair man could probably talk her into anything. Agnes hung her uniform on a peg, pulled on her nightgown, crawled into her hammock, and listened to Ethel snore. Her mind raced in circles, always coming back to eyes. The eyes of quaking men full of desperation and shame and pain, the haughty, cold eyes of the aviator, the hollow, haunted eyes of the men marching past the hospital, the innocent, cornflower blue eyes of Sadie, the determination in Will's eyes, and the way they had changed when he looked back at her from the deck of the Leviathan. Each pair incriminated her for not caring enough, not saying enough, not doing enough to ease their pain and protect them from disaster. She finally dropped off to sleep somewhere after two in the morning.

Agnes awoke when Ethel's Baby Ben alarm clock danced across the floor at five am. She groaned and dragged herself out of bed. "Ethel. Wake up. You and I are both doing the six to four shift."

"Oh Gawd," Ethel said as she rolled out of the hammock and stood scratching her shaggy black mane. "Why does morning have to come so early? Where's Sadie?"

"Wish I knew," Agnes replied. "Met a guy last night. Never came home."

"Queen Chriswell better not hear about it. Sadie'll be on the next transport out faster than you can say Jack Robinson."

At two in the afternoon, Sadie and the Greek god arrived on the ward just when she was supposed to begin her shift. Sadie was still wearing her disheveled, blood-smeared uniform, but her face glowed. One whiff told Agnes that she was also a little drunk. Agnes scowled, hoping disapproval would sober Sadie.

"Oh, Agnes!" Sadie said with a gush of giggles, "We stayed up all night and just talked and talked. Did you know that the officer's club has a Victrola? And they have oh so many records! We danced and danced and danced. My feet hurt. Come to think of it, my head does, too. But where are my manners? Agnes, allow me to introduce you to Captain Lance Harden. Lance, this is my best friend in all the world. My roommate. Miss Agnes Day. Agnes is from New Mexico, which sounds like it should be a part of Mexico, but it's not, so she's an American."

"Ah! The faithful little lamb of God who keeps our Sadie pure!" Captain Harden's eyes sparkled, the ice in them melted in mirth. He winked at her in a way that made her uncomfortable.

"Lamb of God? Excuse me?" Agnes said.

"Agnes Day. Agnus Dei. Your parents were great punsters."

"Punsters?'

Captain Harden rolled his eyes. "Don't tell me you didn't know!"

"Not only do I not know, I don't care. Sadie is going to be late for her shift, as if she is in any shape to serve at all." Agnes looked at her watch, then the ceiling.

The Captain seemed to sober up. "I take it you're not Episcopalian."

"No, sir, I am not, and I hardly see what that has to do with anything." Agnes took hold of Sadie's arm to lead her away.

"Episcopalians, and Catholics for that matter, would know that Agnus Dei is Latin for Lamb of God. Your name is so similar, I'd assumed that your parents had done so intentionally. A little joke."

"I assure you; my name is no joke. Now, if I can get Sadie a cup of coffee, she might be ready to start her shift." Agnes put an arm around Sadie and was turning her to lead her away when the Captain gave her rear-end a playful pat. Agnes, not wishing to cause a scene or upset Sadie, sucked in a little breath but said nothing. She would deal with his impertinence later.

Agnes dragged Sadie into the washroom, where she dunked her face in hot water. When Sadie came up spluttering, Agnes applied a washcloth full of suds. She ripped off her kerchief and tied it over Sadie's hair, smoothing it as much as she could. Agnes made Sadie drink a couple of cups of scaldingly-hot coffee and they swapped uniforms so that Agnes wore the one with brown, dried blood streaked on it. She would change as soon as she got back to her room, and put Sadie's uniform in a bucket to soak.

She stepped back and studied Sadie appraisingly. "You look overworked and a bit haggard, but I think you'll do. For one shift, at least."

"Where did you learn to manhandle a drunk that way?" Sadie asked with a frown.

"My father used to have to do it to cowboys all the time. I've never seen it done to a woman before." Agnes gave Sadie a curt nod, then left the ward. It was the middle of the afternoon and she was exhausted. She had hardly slept the night before. She hoped that when she reported at ten this evening, she wouldn't look as haggard as Sadie.

Agnes was halfway to the nurse's quarters when she heard the out-of-tune piano playing again. This time, it was playing *The Girl I Left Behind Me* slowly and mournfully in a minor key. Agnes stopped. Was she dreaming? Hallucinating? Hearing nothing but the hope in her heart? She spun around and saw a figure hurrying along one of the boardwalks. It was Remington, who always seemed to be scurrying from place to place like the white rabbit in *Alice in Wonderland*. She called his name and he skidded to a nervous halt.

"Remington, do you hear something?"

"Uhm. Rain dripping? Men talking? Distant shelling?"

"But no music?" Agnes crossed her fingers to ward away disappointment.

Remington tilted his head and listened. "Yeah, I hear it. That piano needs to be tuned, doesn't it?"

Agnes smiled, relieved that she wasn't making this up. "Where's it coming from?"

Remington straightened and rolled his eyes heavenward, thinking. "Can't be sure, but if I had to guess, I'd say the Y hut."

"The Y hut?" Agnes was sure she had never been past it. She wasn't even sure she'd known of its existence. But, of course, nearly every camp had one. The operation run by the Young Men's Christian Association wasn't merely a hut. They were large places for soldiers to while away their time, and usually had food and drink, entertainment and games, and plenty of paper and envelopes to write home with. Y huts were staffed by volunteers, often pretty young, idealistic girls.

"Yup. It's just a row over. You can't miss it. Follow the music."

With her heart thumping, she did just that.

Chapter Eighteen

The music drew Agnes along boardwalks through the maze of buildings. Laughter and the happy hum of conversation compelled her on quicker and quicker. Who else could it be but Will? She found the building with the Y painted on its side and pulled open the door to find men lounging at tables and clustering in small groups. Agnes' eyes followed the music, and there he was, his fingers whipping out a jazzy version of "Your Lips Are No Man's Land but Mine." The sight of him alive and well brought Agnes so much relief that she thought she would burst into tears.

Will's eyes were on the bank of men standing behind the piano, their elbows resting on its lid. He was laughing, obviously having a good time. She elbowed her way through the crowd and was halfway across the room when the men behind the piano noticed her and stopped laughing. Will turned to see what was distracting them. His hands froze on the keys, the lilting tune turning into a long, drawn-out chord.

"Agnes?" Will's face registered confusion, then delight, then concern. He stood up so quickly that the piano bench clattered over.

"Careful, Will. She might slug you like she did during the crossing," a laughing voice called. Agnes pulled her gaze from Will and recognized

Corporal Benavides, the surly dispatch rider who'd gone to her birthday party.

"Look at the blood on her. You been brawling, lady?" One of the men behind the piano asked, and the others started guffawing. It was too much for Agnes. She burst into tears.

Will's forehead wrinkled. "What's wrong?"

"You're alive!" Agnes said through her sobs. The men burst into laughter.

Chuckling, Will took Agnes by the elbow and escorted her out the door and into the late afternoon sunshine, where he folded her in his arms and held her close. Agnes buried her face in his chest, breathing in the scent of him as she said his name over and over. Finally, when she was done crying, he asked her a question.

"I think you're the first person who's cried because I was alive. What are you doing here? And why are you covered in blood stains?"

Agnes looked down at her uniform, then remembered that she had switched clothes with Sadie and was wearing the dress stained with blood from the boy who'd chopped off his own hand. "Nurse Abrim assigned me to Camp de Souge. The blood is . . . oh, never mind. It's a long story."

Will gave a sigh of disgust. "I think we have to give up on the Army's postal system. I would have sought you out as soon as I arrived if I'd gotten it."

Agnes felt tears welling in her eyes, but this time they were tears of embarrassment. "The Army misplaced nothing. I didn't tell you I was coming. I thought I'd see you when I first got here, surprise you. And when I found you were up the line, I kept thinking every day that you'd be back. It's my fault. I'm sorry."

Will kissed the top of her head. "No harm done. Mrs. Theodora Abrim must be our guardian angel, assigning you here, where I can watch after you."

"Sadie's with me, too, and oh! Will! She's found a boyfriend and he's absolutely horrible!"

"Tell me all about it." Will took Agnes' hand and guided her out of camp and into the piney forest. The warmth of Will's hand in hers made her heart pound. She felt flushed and giddy.

"Everything's so strange here," Agnes said. "I don't know any of the plants. These are pines, but they aren't the pinons or ponderosas we had up near Silver City. And I miss the sound of the lark."

Will stopped and cocked his head. "Isn't that a lark singing?"

Agnes stopped and listened. "Maybe it's a lark, but it's not a meadowlark. Not our lark. They're different here. Everything's different here. Even the poppies."

She pointed to a line of poppies that meandered in front of them as if blazing a trail for them. They were blood red, with black centers, not at all like the brilliant yellow poppies of New Mexico. Will picked one and held it out to her, and she took it and tucked it in her hair.

"And what happened to your sunrise patch?" She fingered the patch with the red number one where the sunset patch of the 41st Division's patch had been. She was aware that her conversation sounded like Sadie's rambling blabber, but she couldn't help herself.

"The Army incorporated the 66th Artillery into the 1st Corps, The Big Red One."

"But the sunrise patch is good luck," she said.

Will smiled and fished in his pocket, bringing out the old patch. "It's a sunset, but yes. I thought the same."

They arrived at the edge of the forest. Before them spread the airfield, and beyond that, shrubs dotted a flat, open landscape. Except for a thin line of pale blue at the horizon, pale gray clouds covered the sky. Will sat on a fallen tree and pulled Agnes in close to him. He gestured at the expanse before them. "My first days here, I thought of nothing but you and where you might be headed. I was worried, so anytime I wasn't occupied with the horses or fixing some piece of equipment, I walked. Miles and miles."

"Like you used to do on the Sunrise," Agnes said.

Will nodded. "This became where I went whenever I was agitated. I think it's because you can almost see a horizon here. It doesn't feel as closed in as the camp or the forest. I'd look out over that flat field and imagine you riding across it on Diablo."

Agnes wrapped her arm around Will's waist and leaned her head into the soft place where his shoulder met his chest. "I worried about you, too. All those stories about the trenches. The rats. The damp. The disease." She shuddered.

"I'm not in the trenches," Will said. "I'm artillery. Far back from all the ugliness. You don't have to worry about me."

"Tell me what it is like," Agnes said, but Will shuddered and shook his head.

"There will be plenty of time for that later," he said in a voice grown husky. He drew her to him and kissed her. It was what she had been dreaming of, waiting for so long. Agnes threw her arms around his neck and pressed herself to him. They slipped from the log, onto the soft, mossy ground, with her on top of him. Agnes' breathing came in quick, short bursts. Her heart pounded in her chest. Will's lips left hers and trailed along her jawline, then down the side of her neck. She let out a groan of pleasure.

Will stiffened. Gently, he slid Agnes off him and sat up. "I'm sorry,"

"Don't be. And don't stop," Agnes said, reaching for him. Will gathered her hands between his and kissed her fingers.

"No, Agnes. We can't. I can't."

"But. . ." Agnes got no further. The look of pain and sorrow on his face made tears jump back into her eyes.

Will sighed. "I need to tell you who I am. You have the right to know. You once asked me about the brothels in Mexico, and I told you I hadn't been in a place like that for a long time. I couldn't tell you then, but I will tell you now. I must."

He looked up at the clouds and took a long, shaking breath. "I know about those kinds of places because I was raised in them. My mother was not the kind of woman you would associate with."

Agnes pulled her legs under her and leaned toward him. "No one will judge you because of your mother."

"Oh yes, they will," Will said bitterly. "And they would judge you, too, if word got out that you allowed the son of a whore to paw you. I cannot do that to you. You deserve better than that."

Will's face seemed to cave in on itself. He looked like he was going to burst into tears. "We moved constantly as I was growing up, following wherever there were gangs of men and money. Lumber camps. Oil fields. New railroad lines. And if that's not enough, my mother was a quadroon, from New Orleans. That makes me a Negro. That's a second strike against me. "

Agnes stared at his face, surprised at how different he suddenly looked to her. The cafe au lait skin and khaki eyes suddenly made sense, as did the curl in his short-cropped hair. It didn't matter to Agnes, wouldn't have mattered if he was purple with polka dots. But she realized that it would matter to some people, her mother included. She pulled his head onto her shoulder and patted his back comfortingly. Will had appeared so strong and competent. Now she realized how fragile and wounded he was. She wanted to protect him from anyone who would question his worth. If that meant keeping his heritage a secret, then she would do that.

Off in the distance, a carillon chimed. Will pulled away and listened intently to the sweet chorus as he tried to pull himself together. "Hear that? There's a little church down the road from here. If you're still talking to me after what I've told you, let's go see it sometime."

Agnes heard the nervousness in his voice and was just about to answer when the sun dropped below the line of clouds, the rays hitting her in the face like a spotlight. She felt a sudden stab of panic. "Oh, my gosh. What time is it?" she asked.

Will held out his wrist, smiling nervously. "Look. A watch that fits my wrist. They're really accurate. Nice for coordinating maneuvers. It says it's ten o'clock. On the dot. Isn't it amazing how long the sun stays up here?"

"I gotta go!" Agnes scrambled to her feet and sprinted back to camp. She heard Will apologizing for making her late, but she didn't have breath enough, or presence enough, to answer. All she could think about was how angry Nurse Chriswell would be if she knew Agnes was late for her shift.

She felt humiliated; she had been so self-righteous and indignant about Sadie, but she would look no better in the head nurse's eyes. She could be sent home for this, and then how would she earn the money for the Sunrise!

A light drizzle began as she entered camp, making the boardwalk slippery. The camp was in tumult. Everywhere, officers shouted orders and soldiers loaded crates into truck beds and harnessed horses to the artillery pieces. It reminded Agnes of the docks at Brest, the organization barely containing chaos.

"We'll talk later?" Will muttered under his breath.

"Sure," she answered, and he peeled off towards his unit.

Ethel looked up the moment Agnes rushed to her quarters to change into a fresh uniform. "Ak. You're a mess. But don't bother changing. Just pack up."

"I'm late for my shift!" Agnes said, momentum still dragging her mind forward toward her encounter with Nurse Chriswell.

"No, you're not. We're moving out."

"Moving?" Agnes skidded to a stop, her wet feet nearly sliding on the boards. Her brain, too, skidded to a stop as she adjusted to the change. "Where?"

"North and east. Towards the front. The whole camp is packing up. First Army Headquarters is moving to Neufchateau, on the Meuse."

"The whole camp?"

Ethel shrugged. "Well, not all at once. The nurses who are on duty now are staying to mop up operations and take care of the remaining patients, but the rest of us are following the men. We're leaving under cover of darkness. I couldn't find you to tell you, so I wrapped up some biscuits from the mess hall for you."

"Thanks. I . . ."

"Just pack!" Ethel said. "We'll think about it - and talk about it - later. And maybe then you can tell me why you're covered in blood."

Agnes felt like she was in the middle of a whirlwind. She tried to think, but there was too much confusion, too much noise, too much movement.

Two men arrived to take their trunks. They paced while Agnes threw hers open and tossed in the clothes that had been hanging on pegs and the few things she had scattered about. She and Ethel followed the men out to a waiting truck, where the men loaded the trunks around the edge so that they served as benches for the nurses.

Nurse Chriswell was the last to climb in. Her cheeks glowed and her eyes sparkled. She patted back her wet hair."Finally, ladies! General Pershing's been ordered to straighten out the salient at Saint Mihiel! Our men are going into battle, and we'll be there, right behind the lines! The big push is about to begin!"

The truck lurched into gear and Nurse Chriswell swayed like a flame in the wind. Dozens of hands reached up to steady her and help her find a seat as the truck rumbled out of camp. Now that she was seated, Agnes tried to sort through all her whirling thoughts and emotions. She smiled, thinking how, in all the confusion, Nurse Chriswell had never noticed that she was missing. Why, she was probably never supposed to report at ten at all! How lucky she was. Then a wave of panic swept over her and she lurched to her feet.

"Sadie! We forgot Sadie!"

"Easy there, girlie," Ethel said as she dragged Agnes back to her trunk. "She was on shift. She's one of the ones staying."

"Oh. Good," Agnes said, then realized it wasn't good at all. She was supposed to be watching out for Sadie. She'd promised Mrs. Abrim that she would. Now they were separated. How could she keep Sadie from falling prey to Captain Harden? She didn't trust that man.

They passed a group of men coaxing a team of anxious mules into harness as the rain dripped off the brims of their hats, and Agnes caught sight of Will's strong shoulders among the group. Her heart lurched. He had shared some very private information about himself, and in her frenzy to make it back to the hospital she had not responded, not even to acknowledge him. She remembered how quickly he had switched to the topic of the watch the Army had issued him, how bright his voice had become, and she knew that he thought she was too embarrassed or horrified to speak. Agnes squeezed her eyes shut and fought off yet another round of tears as she considered how he must feel.

Chapter Nineteen

It was close to midnight when the truck stopped at a train depot and everyone climbed out. By the light of headlights, Agnes watched soldiers transfer the nurses' trunks into a cattle car that had the words *8 Chevaux, 40 Hommes* stenciled on the side.

"What does that mean?" she asked no one in particular.

Nurse Chriswell tilted her head back so she could read through the spectacles that hung on the end of her nose. "Eight horses, forty men. It'll do for ten nurses and their trunks. We're luckier than the orderlies, who'll be jammed in with the enlisted men, but not as lucky as the doctors. They get to ride in passenger cars." Agnes was so short that she had to hop to get herself seated on the floor of the car. She swung her legs around, then crawled into the empty car. Mounting a horse was easier than climbing into a cattle car. Headlight beams slanted through the slat walls, illuminating the inside of the car with streaks of light. Some nurses sat on their trunks, as they had in the truck. Others pulled blankets from their trunks and bedded down on the floor. Agnes thought she'd stay wide awake, but she pulled out her blanket to make a pad to sit on as she leaned against her trunk. Finally, the rocking of the train lulled her to sleep.

When she woke, Agnes found herself curled in a ball on her scratchy blanket. It was raining steadily, and the car smelled strongly of wet wool and coal smoke. Someone slid open the doors and they peered out at the fields and forests flashing by in the grey dawn. The train clattered over iron bridges spanning placid rivers. It passed pastoral villages, some with stone farmhouses and others made of what looked to Agnes' eyes like adobe, but with slate-covered roofs. Agnes replayed her conversation with Will over and over. She was grateful that he had shared the little shame-faced boy who lived inside the strong and competent man, but regretted running back to camp without responding to his confessions. Arriving late for her shift seemed far less important now. She wished she had told him that race didn't matter, especially in New Mexico, and especially to her. In her world, whites married Indians, Indians married Mexicans, and no one would care if his mother had some Black blood.

In the early afternoon, the train pulled into a depot at a place where low, wooded hills surrounded broad, fertile fields. Nurse Chriswell, who had snored like a buzzsaw, her head bouncing against Ethel's shoulder, snorted awake. She blinked her eyes and smacked her lips. "Is this a rest stop? Or are we there?"

"You're the head nurse." Ethel rotated her shoulder and made a face that showed how very inconvenient it had been to be the Queen's pillow.

"Right. You nurses stay put. I will investigate." Isobel Chriswell staggered to the door and glared out at the swirl of khaki uniforms. With a grunt she sat down on the floor of the car, slid herself to the ground, then disappeared into the stream of men. Trucks pulled up and disgorged soldiers and supplies. It was almost as hard to hear over the shouts as it had been to hear over the rumble of the train. After a quarter of an hour, the head nurse returned and beckoned to the nurses to join her. As she got to the door, Agnes heard someone shouting "Aggie! Aggie!"

She knew that voice. Agnes looked up and watched Heinrich Dieter part the sea of men with his elbows. He lifted her down, and enveloped her in a bear hug.

"Well, well! I've been pulling strings to get placed near you, and whad'ya know! You come to me! Welcome to Aulnois-sous-Vertuzey! To Mobile Hospital No. 39! Isn't it great! We'll be working together at last!"

"What a coincidence," Agnes muttered. What were the chances that her childhood nemesis would end up in the same camp as she?

"Is this the boy you've been mooning about?" Agnes and Heinrich both turned to see Ethel clambering out of the train car.

"No . . . " Agnes started.

Heinrich crowed in delight. "You've been mooning over me?"

"Not you," Agnes began again.

Ethel smiled cynically and waggled her eyebrows. "OH. Another boy?"

Agnes held up her hands to stop Heinrich and Ethel from commenting. "Ethel, this is Heinrich Dieter. We've known each other since we were children. Heinrich, Ethel Rosenberry. She's a nurse, too."

"Another boy?" Heinrich parroted. "It's not that Private Bowers, is it? I should never have taken him to your birthday party."

He looked so crushed that Agnes felt a pang of pity for him. "Here, help us with our trunks. You know where we're to bunk?"

Heinrich snapped out of his confusion. "Sure do! I'm supposed to help move you in. Well, not you personally! The nurses! Swenson! Crane! Hirsh! Over here!" Heinrich waved his arm and three more orderlies emerged from the crowd and grabbed trunks. Heinrich took a handle with one hand, Agnes' elbow with his other, and waded through the crowd. Agnes looked back at Ethel, who was following, a rather devilish smirk on her face.

"I've been here a month," Heinrich shouted over the hubbub. "Taking pictures to document the whole experience! I'm sending them stateside, to Father, who's getting them published in the papers! Heard you were coming. Well, not you personally, but your unit. We're all set up and ready for business."

But they weren't ready. Far from it. This was the biggest campaign an American force had ever attempted, and General Pershing was determined to show the world what the United States was capable of. For the next five days, troops poured into the camp in wagons, trucks, and on foot. Trains pulled up to the newly-made station and disgorged tons of materiel. The camp swelled. Tents sprouted everywhere. Big guns rolled into town, through the narrow lane, then out the other side. Agnes looked for Will among them, but she didn't see him. It was no surprise, since the artillery rolled through town for hours. The guns were set up five miles beyond the nursing station. Agnes heard the guns frequently. She smelled gun smoke when the wind was right and it drifted back over camp. She knew that the trenches, three deep, started in front of the guns. They were so close. How close became clear that evening, when Agnes and the other nurses were issued gas masks that had to be carried with them wherever they went. She had never seen what gas did to a man, but she had read enough to be scared of it.

The hospital itself was called a mobile hospital, but it was hardly mobile. It had taken 30 train cars to bring all the tents, beds and equipment here, and it didn't look like it would get packed up any time soon. Instead of the hastily-built wooden buildings of Camp de Souge, Mobile Hospital No. 39 occupied enormous canvas tents. Smaller tents housed the staff, including the nurses. Agnes and the others settled in. They prepared for the crowds of wounded that were predicted, but had little to do until the heavy fighting started.

Ethel hung out at the YMCA, serving lemonade and playing checkers with the men. Agnes spent her free time worrying about how abruptly she and Will had parted, and how he might react to her when he finally had the guns in place and returned to camp. She had been so worried about being late that she had said nothing to encourage him. Would that cause him to become distant and formal once again? Over and over, she repeated in her mind what she should have said to him about how race didn't matter, especially in New Mexico, and especially to her.

It was a sunny morning, and Agnes was pegging out her freshly washed uniforms on a bit of string tied between two tents when she saw Will striding towards her, his hat bottom-up in hand as if he were carrying something in it, his face tentative and somber. He looked freshly shaved, and his uniform was clean.

"Whites and Mexicans and Indians and Blacks marry all the time there." She blurted out the words. In the ten days since their walk in the woods, Agnes had mentally argued her point so many times that she forgot that Will hadn't heard it.

Will stopped walking. His forehead wrinkled in confusion. "What?'

Agnes laughed, embarrassed as she realized that she was mid-way through a conversation that Will had no part in. "I'm sorry. Let me back up. I've been thinking about what you told me, and I don't think anyone will care whether your mother was a quadroon or not. At least, not in New Mexico. People of different races marry there all the time. But that doesn't mean we should get married. If we did, I would lose my position, and then I couldn't buy the ranch. So I can't. But it's got nothing to do with your parentage."

Will shifted his feet uncomfortably and kneaded his hat with his hands before he looked up and smiled. "And hello to you, too. I'm glad to see you again."

Agnes felt the tension that had been building in her drain out. She dropped her dress into the mud and threw herself into his arms, laughing at herself. "None of that came out the way I meant it."

"I know. I've been thinking about that conversation a lot, too."

She patted Will's back and felt the stiffness in his posture, the uncertainty. The wounded boy had closed himself off again, but he had come, cleaned up and hat in hand. Didn't that mean he wanted to try again? "What I wanted to say was, what you told me didn't scare me off. I like you, Will Bowers, and your background doesn't change that one bit.

"I'm glad you don't think my race matters, and I like you, too. But you've already turned down my marriage proposal."

"That was a long time ago, and you proposed out of pity for a poor little girl who'd just lost her father and was in danger of losing the ranch. But that's all changed, hasn't it? You don't see me that way anymore, do you?"

Will laughed. "I never did see you that way. You may be little, but I knew you were a spitfire who could take care of herself from the moment I first laid eyes on you. But I agree: we shouldn't be talking marriage, not with the future so uncertain. I just wanted to help then, and I just want to help now. Here. I made you something."

He reached into his hat and brought out a brass shell casing. It was smaller than many she'd seen, a little larger than a drinking glass.

"It's a 37 caliber."

Agnes laughed. "It's a vase. For the next time you bring me poppies. Looks like it'll be around a little longer than those poppies, too."

"It'll be around as long as you want it to be."

Agnes looked into his face and smiled, hoping that the vase and the man would both stay around a long time. She turned it over in her hand, studying how he had worked the metal so that a scene popped out in bas relief. She saw herself and him on horseback, riding through a cluster of poppies in a desert studded with cacti. A herd of pronghorn antelopes ran across the distance. Zia symbols rimmed the top. She smiled up into his earnest face. This is beautiful."

He shrugged. "It can get boring sitting by a gun all day. You know I like to keep busy."

"I'm glad you made it, and I'm glad we'll have time before the battle begins. We have a lot to talk about."

He winced, and her heart constricted. "I've got a lot to do. There are trucks that had their undercarriages damaged on the rough roads. Harness that needs mending. Horses that need shoeing. And the aviators will be flying in later today. Their engines always need tweaking."

"There are people whose jobs are fixing those things," Agnes said.

"Yes, but they could use my help. And they pay me a little for it. You'll thank me for that, later."

Agnes snorted. "How will a little money later make up for time lost now?"

"Every penny's going to count when it comes time to put a down payment on the Sunrise."

Agnes broke into a huge smile. He was thinking about their future! He was saving his money for the Sunrise, just as she was. She remembered Will helping around the ranch after her father died. She remembered all the work he did in the few months he lived with Ernesto and Lupe between the end of the Pancho Villa Expedition and the call up for the Great War. The image of the two of them working hard together gave her a little shiver of delight.

"Do you ever rest?" she asked playfully.

"Do you? We are two of a kind: stubborn, determined, hardworking." He kissed her forehead and went on his way, so she picked her dress out of the mud and went back to the wash house to rinse it. She felt lighter and happier than she had in a long time, and her relief made her whistle *The Girl I Left Behind Me* in an upbeat, major key.

That afternoon Sadie arrived on one of the many trains that chugged into the depot. She threw her arms around Agnes, crying and chattering like old friends who hadn't seen each other in years. They were hauling her trunk down a wooden walkway when a biplane flew over. Sadie dropped the trunk and shielded her eyes with her hand, in what looked like a salute, then jumped up and down, waving. "Oooh! Did you see that? A Dorand AR! And it woggled its wings! I just bet that was Lance, and he saw me!!"

"Lance?" Agnes asked.

Sadie laughed. "Captain Harden! You remember! From Camp de Souge! We've been having such fun the last few weeks! Life around this camp is going to be so much better now that Lance is here!"

Another two two-seater biplanes roared overhead. Agnes watched them pass over and laughed, but it wasn't a happy laugh. "Oh, I bet," she muttered. Captain Lance Hardin was certainly handsome, but there was something about him that repelled Agnes, something shady.

"Sadie, I don't know about this Captain of yours," Agnes said as they dropped off her trunk.

"You're just jealous," Sadie answered, and gave Agnes a playful swat. "Now, if you'll excuse me, I've got to report to the Queen, and if I'm not on duty right away, I'll just go pay a visit to the airfield."

Agnes watched the tent flap fall behind Sadie before she dropped heavily onto her cot. Was Sadie right? Was she jealous? Or lonely? Will was in camp, but he was too busy to spend time with her. Sadie was going to the airfield. Ethel was at the Y. And here she sat, lonely in one of the busiest places along the entire Western Front of the war.

She thought back on her last conversation with Will. At the time, it had seemed lighthearted. In spite of the awful way she had started it, it had ended with him kissing her forehead and her whistling happily. In the time since, however, she had begun to wonder if she really had cause to be happy. After all, he said that they shouldn't be talking marriage, that the only reason he'd asked her was to be helpful. Was that the only reason he was saving money for the ranch now? To be helpful? Agnes wanted to slap her own face. What was wrong with her, that she wasn't appreciating how hard Will was working for her?

Why was she allowing herself to feel neglected? What had Will called her? A spitfire who could take care of herself? Agnes stood up, determined to join Ethel in the Y. A glass of lemonade and a game of cards would be a fine antidote for wallowing in self-pity.

She was on her way there when a tall, blond, captain with brilliant blue eyes stepped into place beside her. Agnes gave him a sidelong glance and noticed the same slight curl in his lip that she had seen that first night. She recognized the pilot who had captured Sadie's heart, and her own heart hardened.

"Hello, my little lamb." Captain Lance Harden cooed.

"Hello, yourself. Now, if you will excuse me."

He stepped in front of her, cutting her off and forcing her to stop. "I'm sorry. We seem to have gotten off on the wrong foot. Was it something I said?"

Agnes sighed and tried hard not to look him in the eyes. He was so very handsome, his eyes such a startling blue. "You might try calling me by my name."

He relaxed and chuckled. "I can do that, Agnes. I'm sorry if my little nickname offended you. I meant it to be friendly."

"Yes, well." Agnes took a step to the side and continued down the walk. Captain Harden kept up with her.

"So, Agnes," he began, "I'm not training other pilots to spot artillery any more, like I did back at Camp de Souge. I'm doing the spotting myself. I fly over the lines daily, protecting soldiers like that boyfriend of yours."

"I don't have a boyfriend," Agnes said, gritting her teeth.

"You don't? That's not what Sadie said. I'm sorry. I must have misunderstood. Anyway, I spotted a place along the lines that is very quiet. A part of the front that's been abandoned. I've rounded up a staff car and talked a corporal into being our driver. Thought I'd pack up a picnic and take Sadie and a few of her friends out on a little souvenir hunt. Care to join us?"

"No," Agnes said firmly, "and I don't think Sadie should go with you, either."

"We can make a party of it. Maybe include that boyfriend you say you don't have."

"I said, no." Agnes crossed her arms and tried to look intimidating. It wasn't easy, since Lance was a foot taller than she.

"Fine," Lance said. "Sadie and I will go alone."

Agnes stopped walking and glared at Lance. "Sadie shouldn't go with you, either. It's dangerous."

Lance shook his head, his eyes rolling to show he discredited her analysis. "I've checked it out, flown low over it. It's perfectly safe. And whether or not you think so, you're not Sadie's boss. She'll go if she wants to, and I do think she wants to."

"Then I'll go, too," Agnes said. Sadie needed a chaperone. Who knows what this man might try to pull otherwise?

"Good. Tomorrow, around nine? I'll have the staff car pick you and Sadie up. You can tell the driver where to pick up that not-a-boyfriend of yours, if you can talk him into going."

Instead of going to the Y, Agnes spent the afternoon hunting down Will. She finally found him in the stables and invited him to go with them.

Will shook his head. "I'll be helping the mechanics with the airplane engines. They've had some problems with the engines stalling. We might drain the lines to see if there's an obstruction."

"You're always helping with something! Horses! Trucks! Now plane engines! Don't you ever want time off? Have fun? Help me?" Agnes asked.

"My idea of fun is being useful, and I am helping you." Will leaned the shovel against the wall of the stable and looked pleadingly at Agnes. "When I was a kid, I had a lot of time to kill when my mother was with clients. Sometimes I hung around with the chauffeurs of the richer clientele, and they propped open the hoods and showed me the engines and how they worked. I started tweaking carburetors, changing oil. It gave me great satisfaction, especially when my mother started bragging that hers was the only establishment in the United States where you could get yourself and your car serviced."

Will winced. "Sorry. You shouldn't have to hear that."

"It's all right." Agnes put a hand on his arm. "You can tell me anything you want. I won't judge."

"That's why I learned to play the piano when I was a kid," Will explained. "I kept the clientele entertained. My mother was always nicer to me when her customers were happy. I think they were nicer to her when they were happy, too."

Agnes nodded. "But that doesn't mean you have to try to make everyone here happy. You don't have to do everyone's job. You could take a day for yourself, go on this picnic with us."

Will shook his head. "I don't want to go, and I don't think you should, either. I haven't been in the trenches. The guns are farther back than that. But I've heard enough stories. There are going to be things you don't want to see there."

"Captain Harden says they've been abandoned quite a while. He's flown over them, and knows."

Will picked up the shovel and slipped it under a pile of horse droppings. "He's seen them at five thousand feet. I don't think you want to see them up close."

Agnes kicked at the pile that Will had raked up. "Actually, I'm not interested in collecting souvenirs anyway. I just want to go to make sure Sadie doesn't get in trouble with this guy. I don't trust him."

Will grinned at Agnes. "So, you want me to choose between meddling in someone else's affairs or working on airplane engines and setting aside a buck or two? Sadie's a grown woman. Let her live her own life."

"But Captain Harden is all wrong for Sadie!"

Will looked up and Agnes saw that he was having a hard time not laughing. "Isn't that what your mother thinks about me?"

"You just don't understand," Agnes said, and marched away, determined to protect her friend whether Will was with them or not.

The staff car ended up being a rickety old jalopy that one of the officers had bought off a local for an exorbitant price. Agnes laughed when she heard it banging and backfiring up the dirt road towards her. She laughed even harder when she saw Corporal Benavides scowling behind the steering wheel, a chauffeur's cap crammed low over his brow.

The car pulled up and Lance leapt out, holding the door and gesturing Sadie and Agnes in. He set a picnic basket on the front seat, then climbed into the back and sat between Sadie and Agnes, his arms draped over their shoulders. "Ah! A picnic, complete with une baguette, foie gras, and champagne, and two beautiful women to share it with. What more could a fellow want out of life?"

Agnes leaned forward and shouted over the sound of the engine. "I didn't expect to ever see you on a joy ride."

"Neither did I," Benavides shouted back. "But the price this moron quoted me will pay for a lot of hay and alfalfa back home. There's a drought there, you know."

Agnes settled back and savored the thought rather guiltily. While she felt sorry for the ranchers, a drought, added to the wariness caused by the Villa raid and the war, might drive away buyers for the Sunrise Ranch. The longer the market remained bad, the more money she could save for a down payment.

For over an hour the car jumped and bumped over a road that was so shelled and rutted as to be almost impassible. They passed a few trenches that Lance said were allied and not worth investigating, and parked the car on the edge of a giant crater. The earth had been churned and frozen into jagged pits and peaks, reminding Agnes of the mud around a watering hole when the hole dried into a shattered wasteland. She had the feeling that nothing would ever grow here again. A strange, sickly-sweet smell filled the air. Agnes sniffed it and the memory of finding a cow carcass putrefying in a bog, spreading its poison in the water made her cover her nose. She was afraid she might be sick.

"Sadie and I will stay here in the car," Agnes said.

"Why?" Sadie asked, looking confused.

"There's something - or someone - out there who's dead," Agnes said.

"Nonsense," Lance said. "I have it on good authority that the medics have been through here and cleaned the area up." He climbed over Agnes to get to the door. After he'd gotten out, he made a gesture inviting them to join him. "Don't worry. Several of the other pilots have done this. They say it's a lot of fun."

Benavides turned off the engine. In the silence, one lone lark sang atop a shattered tree trunk, its song strangely incongruous with the sporadic, distant drum of canon. He pulled his cap over his face and propped his feet on the dashboard while Lance helped Sadie and Agnes pick their way through a cratered field that was littered with brambles of barbed wire.

Lance picked up a German canteen and checked to see that it still had its stopper, cup, and wool cover, then handed it to Agnes, who held it away from her, thinking that the man who once held it was probably now dead. She pushed a few things on the ground around with her toe, but she could not bring herself to pick anything up.

Sadie picked up an officer's sword and slashed it around. "Oooh. Look at this! I'm a pirate queen! But it ain't got no scabbard." She dropped the sword and moved on, picking up something else and tossing it aside.

Lance picked up something that looked like a small telescope. He peered through it for a moment, then tucked it in his pocket. "This is a sight for a maxim machine gun but the gun's not here. A shell must have thrown it here."

"Oh, look! A helmet! I wish it was one of them pickelhaubes. Now that would make a good souvenir."

"They stopped making them," Lance said. "Didn't stop bullets as well as these stahlhelms do." Sadie picked up the helmet. A swarm of flies flew out. Sadie hefted it as if surprised by its weight. She tilted it, looking in, then tossed it away with a shriek. As it hit the ground, a head rolled out. Agnes' stomach convulsed. The thought that Will had to go to a place like this made shivers run up Agnes' spine. If Battlefields were this horrible long after the fighting had ended, what would they be like when the fighting was going on?

She ran back to the car, Sadie's screams following her. Corporal Benavides pushed back his hat, his feet frantically finding the floorboards of the ancient car. His hand came up and Agnes saw that he held a pistol.

She held out her hand, palm forward in a gesture to stop him. "It's okay. We're not in danger. We just found something . . . unpleasant." She scrambled into the car.

"Not surprised," Benavides muttered and turned over the engine. "I didn't think this was a good idea from the start. Wouldn't have consented if the captain hadn't offered me so much."

"I know. There's a drought at home," Agnes said, irritated by his brusqueness.

Benavides looked over his shoulder, a sneer on his face. "And the wife's expecting again. Another mouth to feed."

Lance climbed in, leading the sobbing Sadie, who leaned her face into his chest and howled her horror. Agnes looked at her in disgust. Mrs. Abrim was right; Sadie wasn't level headed enough to handle the horrors of the front line. She was glad that Nurse Chriswell had assigned Sadie to the tent that held the Spanish Flu cases. The flu had a horror all its own, but it lacked the shock of dismemberment.

"What we need is champagne." Lance leaned over the front seat and pulled the bottle from the picnic basket. The sound of the cork popping made Agnes jump. She declined the glass that Lance offered, staring out at the passing landscape. Soon Sadie and Lance were singing and Agnes was near tears. Why had she thought that she needed to protect Sadie? Will was right: Sadie was a grown woman. She vowed to stop being like her mother, meddling in the lives of others. She needed to focus on her own hopes and dreams.

Chapter Twenty

"Can we get some help here?" The voice came from one of three doughboys who'd just come through the tent flap. Agnes looked up from the dressing she was changing and gasped. Two bookended the third, whose face was nearly blue. Even from three beds away she could hear how his breath gurgled in his lungs.

"Not here," a doctor behind her said in a commanding tone that stopped them short. "The isolation tent is on the edge of camp. There." He passed Agnes, blocking the entrance. They backed out and the tent flap dropped behind them, cutting off the afternoon light.

The doctor seemed to deflate. When he turned, Agnes saw the exhaustion on his face. He ran a hand through his hair. "The flu is hitting the same time the big offensive begins. What timing."

The Spanish flu had been around since spring, but had grown far more prevalent and more deadly as summer passed into fall. Sadie, who worked in that tent, told Agnes daily about the soldiers who came in complaining of a headache, back pain, and a feeling of exhaustion which they often shrugged off as battle fatigue and the constant sound of the guns. A dry, hacking cough followed, then loss of appetite and stomach problems. On the second day, Sadie's patients began to sweat excessively. By the third day, many of them felt better. Those that did not, developed pneumonia, their oxygen-starved faces turning blue like the man who had just come in. There were over two hundred like him in the isolation tent right now.

The doctor studied his wrist watch for a moment. "Wasn't your shift over an hour ago?"

"Well, yes," Agnes conceded. "But I thought I'd finish these dressings before I left." They had gone to twelve-hour shifts. Even then, it was hard to get everything accomplished since the battle, and the flu had simultaneously ramped up.

"Finish that one, then be off with you. Nurses need their rest if they're to stay sharp."

"That go for doctors, too?" Agnes wanted to pull back the words as soon as she'd said them. Some of these doctors would consider a question like that insubordination. This one, however, just gave a sardonic harumph and went back to his rounds.

Will stood up from the bench outside the tent when Agnes exited. She held her own hands behind her back and Will did the same. No sense getting in trouble if they ran across Queen Chriswell.

"Hard day?" he asked.

Agnes shook her head. "They seem to be getting harder by the hour. Gunshot and shrapnel wounds. Gangrene and septicemia. Poison gas burns. I'm glad you're here in camp."

"I won't be for long," Will said. "I rotate back to the guns tomorrow. But don't worry. The guns are far back. We aren't in danger like the boys in the trenches."

Agnes nodded solemnly. She'd seen enough artillery men come in to know that what he said was meant to be comforting but wasn't completely true.

"I wanted to tell you something before I left," he said with a heavy sigh that told Agnes that he'd been thinking of how to do this and had not come up with the right way even yet. She walked along quietly, trying with all her might to exude patience and acceptance. Finally, he took a deep, shaky breath and continued.

"I've told you about who - or what - my mother was. I haven't told you about my father - or who I suspected was my father. I've never been told, but I was the only child who stayed with the ladies. There were, on occasion, others born. They were all sent away."

When the silence went on too long, Agnes asked "So, you suspect that . . .?"

Will began walking faster. Agnes scurried to keep up. "Our bordello didn't have a Madam. A man ran the place. He protected all his girls, but it was clear that my mother was his favorite."

"I see." Agnes felt her face flushing. She tried hard to hold her composure so she wouldn't embarrass Will. So, Will wasn't just the son of a prostitute; his father was also involved in prostitution. She tried to imagine growing up under those conditions, but she couldn't. What she could imagine, though, was how her mother would respond if she found out about Will's background. Mildred Day would be scandalized, and she would be no better at keeping that scandal to herself than she had been at minimizing the horror of her husband's heart attack. The whole county would know.

Agnes took a sideways glance at Will, marveling at how normal he was, considering where he had come from. Will Bowers must really, truly be good if he could rise above his upbringing to become the steady, productive man that he was.

Will took another deep breath before he continued. "My mother and the Master of the house sometimes got into terrible rows. I gathered that he sometimes took his pleasures elsewhere. She didn't approve. Once, when I was twelve, I came in when he was hitting her. I was a big lad already; almost as tall as I am now. I defended my mother with a fire poker. But rage overtook me. All the anger, all the frustration. I hit him, even after he was down."

Will stopped walking. He turned and cradled Agnes' forearms in his hands. They were trembling. "When I came to my senses, my mother was screaming for me to get out before the police arrived. I dropped the poker and ran. I've been running ever since."

Agnes gasped. "You think you . . .?"

"Killed him? I do. I changed my name. I moved from city to city. But someday, I am sure, the law will hunt me down."

Agnes leaned into Will's chest. She breathed in his smell and listened to his heart race. Hers, too, beat hard as she tried to make sense of Will's story. She had never seen him raise a hand to so much as a dog, had never seen him angry or even raise his voice. It was hard to imagine him hitting anyone. "You were just a boy," she said.

"Boys have been hung for less," he said.

Agnes thought about the fear he'd lived with all these years. Is that what made him such a quiet person? Did he not want to call attention to himself for fear that who he really was would come out in the open? She wondered that he was so calm.

"You were only defending your mother."

"Who was a whore." Will spoke the words bitterly.

"Who loved you and gave you the best childhood she could manage. You were fed. And clothed. And educated. She tried her best."

Will looked away, his eyes full of hopelessness. "I'm the kind of riff-raff that juries love to pronounce judgement on: a young Negro with a disreputable mother and no father who claims him. They expect my kind to rape white women, rob stores, steal from poor widows. The jury that convicts me will congratulate themselves for ridding society of the kind of scum that threatens it."

Agnes' heart twisted in her chest. Will was the most moral and upright man she knew. How could anyone think these things of him? "No jury would convict you. Not a war hero who's served his country like you have."

Will's lip twisted in a half-smile and he stroked her head. "If I ever do get caught, I hope the jury thinks like you do. But I doubt they will. That's what keeps me moving. What keeps me from settling down."

Agnes looked into Will's stricken eyes. "You cannot run forever. You may not even need to be running now. When this war is over, let's find out. On our way back to the Sunrise, let's stop in . . . where did this happen?"

"Kansas City," Will said.

"We'll stop in Kansas City, then. Together. And we will see."

"Your mother, your sisters, their husbands: they would be horrified to find out you were involved with someone like me."

"Then we won't tell them," Agnes said. "And we make no more plans about the future until we know what happened to your father."

"And you are in firm possession of the Sunrise," Will added. "When you have that, you may find that you have everything you need."

The assault intensified. The future itself seemed less certain. Agnes stopped thinking about money and the Sunrise and worried about life itself. Every ambulance bore in shattered men that she had to help. Some healed and were sent back to the front. Others were mended as best they could, then sent down the line for more surgeries. Many died under her care. Her days and nights became a blur.

Each time an ambulance returned to camp, Agnes fought the urge to search for Will on the arriving gurneys. But Will was not the only person Agnes had to worry about. Heinrich Dieter carried stretcher after stretcher of wounded from rickety ambulances that streamed into camp at all hours of the day and night. Her old friend looked tired and gaunt. He no longer joked or cracked the crazy, lopsided smile that she was so used to. She wanted to comfort him and assure him that everything was going to turn out fine. She couldn't. She wasn't sure herself.

The guns became continuous background noise, so steady that it was hardly noticeable, yet a source of constant anxiety. Ethel, who had grown up by the ocean, said it had almost become as easy to block out as the sound of surf. It was not so easy for the men who'd been closer to the front. Some of Agnes' patients winced with each explosion. Others curled into quivering, screaming balls of panic. Agnes' shifts grew longer, the time when she could drop into her bed and sleep shorter and farther apart. She was exhausted, her hands chapped and sore from the constant scrubbing to keep down the dirt and filth. The sweet, tar-like smell of carbolic acid filled her sinuses.

Agnes had been deep in a dreamless sleep when Sadie shook her awake. It took Agnes a moment to figure out that she was not home at the Sunrise, and that the constant and deep rumble was not thunder. She blinked, clearing the sleep from her eyes and the mental cobwebs from her brain.

Sadie's face hovered over her, tear-streaked and stricken, breath coming in short bursts.

Agnes sat up and brushed the hair from her face. "What is it?"

"Lance. He went on a *rélage*. He didn't return."

"A what?"

Sadie dropped onto the bed and Agnes put her arm around her and pulled her close. "A *rélage*. An artillery adjustment. He flies over the lines and signals back a report to our artillery, then hangs around to note whether the shells are falling in the right place or the gunners need to make a correction. He does them all the time, and says they're a piece of cake. But this time he didn't come back."

"Maybe it's taking longer for the gunners to hit their mark?"

Sadie shook her head. "He's never been this late before. Not ever."

Agnes and Sadie walked down to the airfield. They waited, watching planes come and go. The mechanics eyed them suspiciously and kept their comments to themselves, but Agnes had the feeling that they had given up hope and weren't willing to say it for fear of female hysteria. When Agnes had to report for duty, she left Sadie at the field and walked back alone.

It was the middle of the night and all was quiet in the hospital tent when Agnes heard cheering. She and Remington got up from the chairs they'd been drowsing in and made their way toward the front flap, ready to quiet the mob before it aroused sleeping patients. Before they got there, the flap burst open. A gaggle of French poilu and American doughboys staggered in. They were all smiling, their arms around each other's necks. Some held champagne and wine bottles. At the center of the group, Agnes spied a battered but smiling Lance Harden. One of his eyes was swollen shut, and his forehead was encrusted with dried blood from what looked like a large gash.

Agnes smiled and put her fists on her hips. "Well, Captain, we've been worried about you, and here you are, drunk. What have you got to say for yourself?"

Lance grinned lopsidedly and lifted one finger as if ready to give a lecture. "Thersh a lot more to the shtory than meets the eye! B'leeve me! L'me tell you allll about it."

The men around Lance started laughing and interrupting each other. Agnes cut them off. She gestured towards her chair, and the poilus and doughboys deposited their friend in it before she shooed them out. When all was quiet again on the ward, Agnes tilted back Lance's head so she could examine the wound on his forehead. "Crash landed. In No Man's Land." Lance smiled like a kid who'd found a prize in his Cracker Jack.

"Mmmm hmmm." Agnes pulled back the edges of the cut. "Remington, get me a cup of black coffee for this happy drunk, and some saline solution, carbolic acid, and suture materials. Then let Sadie know that Captain Holden's been found. She'll either be in the nurses' tent or, more likely, still at the airfield."

Private Remington nodded, then scurried to collect her supplies. He disappeared into the night quickly. Agnes laughed. "Remington reminds me of a squirrel; always in a rush, going about some errand. This cut of yours doesn't look too bad. No debris embedded in it."

"Should be clean. Bashed my head against the dashboard when I came down. Owww." Lance winced as Agnes dabbed carbolic acid into the cut.

"You think that's bad, just wait 'til I start stitching that gash up. I'm not going to give you the coffee until it's done. No sense wasting the pain-dampening effects of alcohol."

"You wastch. I won't even twitch," Lance said with slurred bravado.

"So, tell me. What happened? And say it loud enough that your whole audience can hear. These boys need a good bedtime story." Agnes gestured towards the beds. A hundred anxious eyes peered back. Clearly no one had slept through Lance's exciting entry.

"I was doing low work, artillery spotting," Lance said. "The Huns love to take potshots at me when I'm low like that. Usually, they miss. This time, though, a bullet clipped a magneto wire, and the engine stopped. Ouch!

Agnes slipped her needle into Lance's brow and he stopped talking. A dozen patients sat forward in their beds. "Go on," she said.

"I got the plane turned around. Was gliding back towards our lines. But I knew - ouch - that I wasn't going to make it, so I found a flat area with no barbed wire - ouch - to trip me up and no big craters, and I put it - ouch - down in No Man's Land. I start to get out, but a maxim opened fire. Strafed the plane. So, I decided - ouch - to play dead. When it was dark, I climbed down and made a run for it. Once a flare went up, and I must not have - ouch - frozen fast enough, because they saw me and tried -ouch- to take me out, but they missed. I did get this, crawling through some barbed wire, though." Lance held up his hand, and Agnes saw a gash across the palm that was deeper and uglier than the one on his forehead.

"Why didn't you show me that earlier? We'll need to get you a tetanus shot," Agnes muttered as she jabbed the needle into Lance's forehead for the last time. She wrapped Lance's forehead in gauze, then began irrigating his hand.

Lance grimaced, and it looked almost like a grin. He was sobering up, his words becoming clearer, and it was obvious he enjoyed having an audience.

"Anyhow, when the French realized what I was doing, they supported me with covering fire. At least, that's what I'd like to think they were doing. Maybe they thought I was a runaway Hun, and they were shooting at me! If that's the case, they're bad shots.

"Those Frenchies were pretty agitated when I rolled into their trench, and since I don't speak a word of French and none of them spoke English, it took awhile to sort things out. They finally figured out I wasn't the enemy and were so relieved, they broke out champagne. Then they drove me here. And that's about the end of it."

"And that's about the end of it for me, too," Agnes said as she wrapped up his hand. "When Remington gets back, he'll prepare a tetanus shot for you. For now, how about some coffee?"

"I think I've sobered enough, thanks to all your poking and jabbing," Lance said.

The tent flap opened and Sadie and Remington entered. Sadie was in tears, which Agnes knew were tears of relief. She squealed and threw herself into Lance's arms. He kissed her and the patients cheered and clapped as if they were watching one of those new-fangled movies and they were Mary Pickford and Conway Tearle. Agnes sat back and smiled, knowing that a good survival story, especially if it ended with a kiss from a pretty girl, was the best medicine some of these men could get.

Lance came in every day to have his hand and forehead checked. He was always patient and polite, and afterwards he made the rounds among the patients, offering each man a kind word and a little hope. After his story, he had become a celebrity and a hero, but he bore both titles with so much humility and grace that Agnes decided that he wasn't such a bad fellow after all.

The French delivered a new plane for Lance, who said that the French-made Salmson 2 was newer and better than anything he'd flown before. He took it out for a few test runs, then showed up at the nurses' quarters one afternoon when all three just happened to be in.

"What do you think, ladies? Care for a spin among the clouds?"

"Do I? And how!" Sadie didn't take more than two seconds to make her approval known.

Lance looked at Ethel, whose mouth was pursed in consideration. "So, flyboy. You get shot down, then invite us to do the same? What'd we ever do to you?"

"First off, the battle is largely over now. It's much safer to fly now than a week ago. Secondly, I won't be flying you over enemy territory. No one's going to take a pot shot at us, and if, by any little chance of fate we have engine failure and do go down, it'll be in friendly territory," Lance said.

"See?" Sadie nearly crowed the words. "The Captain's thought of everything. Lordy! How many times you're gonna be invited for a joyride in an aeroplane? I say take your chances when you can!"

Lance turned to Agnes. "How about you? I owe you one for stitching me up."

Agnes remembered seeing an airplane for the first time at the Columbus airfield. How she had wanted to go up on that day! Now, here was her chance! But what if Will returned while she was out joyriding? And what if he was injured and needed her. Agnes felt her anxiety rise in her throat. She swallowed it down and put on a brave smile. "Thanks, but I'll take a rain check. Troops are streaming back from battle hourly. Someone's got to stay in case they need help."

"In case a certain private does, you mean," Sadie said with a giggle. Agnes watched Ethel, Sadie and Lance link arms and stroll away. Without them, the nurses' quarters suddenly felt lonely, the air humming with her own anxieties. She decided to walk down to the Y and grab a glass of lemonade. Maybe she'd learn when Will's group was expected in.

She found Heinrich and Remington hunched over glasses of lemonade at a table near the door. Both were hollow eyed and wan, staring into their lemonades without speaking. They looked like two cowboys deep in their cups, and Agnes would have sworn that whatever was in their glasses was higher proof than lemonade if she didn't know better.

Agnes pulled up a chair. "Why the long faces, boys? The battle's over."

"That's the problem," Heinrich said. "The battle's over, so it's time for us stretcher-bearers to visit No Man's Land. We were out this morning. Collecting bodies."

"I bet it was terrible. Did you get some photos to send the papers? They'd want to know about what happens after a battle, all the hard work you do." Agnes rested her hand atop Heinrich's where he clutched his glass. She felt it clench and unclench and feared he would shatter the glass.

Heinrich shook his head. "This isn't the noble war the people of New Mexico want to see pictures of. This is carnage. Some of the bodies weren't all there. Others? Well, they had laid in the sun for a while. They weren't so whole anymore."

"The smell," Remington muttered into his glass.

Heinrich looked up and shuddered. "This sergeant, he tells me to take this man's arms. So I reach down and grab him by the wrists and pull, and the arms pull right off of the body. The sergeant goes berserk and yells that he didn't mean it literally. Someday I suppose I'll laugh at that. It really is kind of funny, in a macabre way. But I don't laugh. Not anymore."

"That's why I wouldn't fight," Remington said. "Wars kill men's bodies, but it kills their spirits, too. None of us will ever be the same."

"You wouldn't fight?" Agnes asked.

Remington nodded. "I registered as a conscientious objector, so they sent me to the medical corps. I keep it quiet. A lot of men think I'm a coward. They like to beat on me when they catch me alone. Makes them feel tough."

Agnes suddenly understood the hunted look in his eyes, the reason he always scurried from duty to duty. He was no squirrel or Alice's white rabbit. He was a man hunted by others' reactions to his convictions. She realized that she had never gotten to know him. She didn't even know his first name. Agnes put her other hand out and squeezed his. "I appreciate what you do. You've saved men's lives."

Remington just stared into his lemonade. He looked on the point of weeping, and it made Agnes' heart ache. She squeezed his hand a little harder, then patted Heinrich's hand again. Neither man responded, but Agnes couldn't pull her hands away. Doing so would isolate them further. She felt trapped, felt the urge to jump into a saddle and ride hard, away from all the pain and suffering and worry, but how could she leave these two, and where could she go?

She was still sitting with her hands covering theirs when Sadie, Ethel and Lance entered. They were bubbly, nearly giddy, and Sadie hugged Lance over and over.

"Oh, Agnes! This was the bestest present I've ever gotten! You wouldn't believe it up there! It's like a fairytale land. Makes the castle at Brest look like an outhouse!"

Ethel nodded in agreement, her laughter filling the room with so much warmth that others looked up from their conversations to watch her. "Agnes, you should try it!"

Lance winked at Agnes. "Why not?"

Agnes looked from Remington and Heinrich's glum faces to the three that were glowing with life and joy. She wanted some of that. She had been so serious, so earnest, for so long. But she couldn't leave Heinrich and Remington to their suffering, and she couldn't leave when Will might be arriving at any moment.

"How about taking Heinrich and Remington. They need it more than I do."

"Sure. Why not," Lance said. "Gentlemen? Want to get above it all?"

Remington pulled his hand away from Agnes' and elbowed Heinrich. "I don't have the energy. You go."

"I'm going to bed." Heinrich pushed himself away from the table and walked, stoop-shouldered, to the door. Agnes watched him go with a sense of frustration and helplessness. She had known him all her life and never seen him be anything but upbeat. He had aged forty years in a fortnight.

"Guess that leaves just you," Lance said. "Last call for the joyride express."

Agnes set her hands determinedly on the table and pushed herself up. "I've wanted to do this since the day I saw my first plane. I guess it's now or never." She allowed Lance to escort her out the door and to the airfield, where her gave her an oversized canvas coat, some large gloves, and a pair of goggles to put on, explaining that while his plane was a lovely piece of machinery, she tended to spit oil, and there was no sense begriming Agnes' nice, white uniform. He helped her into the spotter's seat, then climbed into the cockpit in front of her.

Ground crew turned over the propeller, and they rumbled across the field. Although she had heard them fly over a thousand times, Agnes was surprised just how loud planes were from inside. She wanted to put her hands over her ears, but didn't dare let go of the lip of the cockpit. They taxied down the field, and Agnes noticed men marching along the road that ran parallel. Her heart leaped into her throat. There was Will! Agnes shouted and pounded the fuselage in front of her to get him to stop, but Lance neither saw nor heard her over the roar of the engine.

Agnes waved. His face serious, Will's eyes followed her ascent.

The ground fell away. The huge airplane hangers became khaki rectangles, the line of men on the road, ants on a stick. Agnes watched the dot that was Will until he disappeared into the trees. Lance circled higher, the land became a diagram of itself, a map. The YMCA hut, the hospital tents, the ruined town became dots along the spider's web of roads. They entered a cloud and the scene disappeared. Cool dampness enveloped her, a luminous, shining dimness where nothing seemed to exist except Agnes and the roar of the engine.

The plane burst into a sky so blue and bright that it dazzled Agnes. She blinked at white hills and valleys stretching towards the horizon. Thunderheads rose into shining mesas high above them. Lance pointed to one, then banked the plane and headed toward it. He let the plane bank up its side, then turned and they slid down as if they were in a sled on a snow-covered hill. Agnes found herself in a halo of light. She laughed, but couldn't hear the sound of her own voice. The plane was so completely alone; more alone, smaller than she had ever felt in the desert riding Diablo. After months of being surrounded by others, the solitude was liberating.

Lance banked and the plane descended into the clouds again. When they dropped through to the other side, Agnes could see the camp off in the distance. They made one loop and landed on the field, the ground rising to meet them so quickly that it took her breath away. The plane taxied to a hanger. A ground crew came out to meet them.

"Happy you went?" Lance put out a hand for her, and Agnes climbed down on shaky legs. She hadn't realized how much she had tensed her body during the flight. Now she felt both an exhilaration and an exhaustion, relief that it was over and a yearning for it to go on forever.

"That was better than all the Luna County fairs I've ever been to, all rolled into one! Thank you. I will remember that forever."

Lance laughed and hugged her lightly. Agnes reciprocated with a quick peck on his cheek. She could feel her own cheeks burning with the wind and excitement. She decided he was a fine fellow after all. She excused herself and rushed back to camp to find Will.

Agnes went back to her quarters, hoping that Will would be waiting for her there. She went to the hospital. The bench outside, where he'd sat and waited for her so many times was empty. She checked his barracks. She went back to the YMCA hut, where she found Sadie and Ethel dancing with Remington and Heinrich while the gramophone played a scratchy tune by Smiles Joseph Smith & his Orchestra. At the motor pool she found Corporal

Benavides patching a tire on his motorcycle and asked him if he knew where Will was.

Benavides scowled at her. "Why would you want to know?"

"I saw him march in. I know he's here somewhere," Agnes answered.

"Yeah. He's here. My question is, why would you even care?"

Agnes stared at the corporal, dumbfounded by his surliness. "But I do care. A great deal."

"As much as you do for that aviator?" The anger in his eyes assured Agnes that David Benavides would have hit her if she wasn't a woman.

"Captain Holden? Is that who you mean? I don't care for him at all."

"Sure," Benavides said. "Now if you'll excuse me, I have important work to be doing."

Agnes stepped in front of him, her arms crossed over her chest. She glared at the little man, eye to eye with him. "Not before we settle this, once and for all. I understand you have problems at home, but don't take them out on me. I'm not like your wife. You once made me promise that I wouldn't toy with Will, and I don't."

"I saw you kiss that flyboy!" He shouted the words, spraying Agnes' face with his spit.

"On the cheek! As a thank you for taking me up for a flight. Not that it's any business of yours. Corporal Benavides, you are going to have to stop thinking that I am like your Dolores. Not all women are unfaithful."

Exasperated, Agnes stormed off in search of Will. She finally found him near the stables, currying the tangles out of a horse's tail. He didn't look up when she entered the corral. His face, so serene and composed, gave her pause and she suddenly felt too shy to give him the greeting she'd imagined so many times.

"I saw you march in," she said. "I'm sorry I wasn't there to greet you."

"Yes, well, things change." Will studied what seemed to be a particularly tangled bit.

Agnes studied his face. "Including between you and me?"

Will put down the curry comb. "The smile on your face when you went aloft spread from ear to ear. You looked happier than I've seen you look in a long time. I remembered how you'd wanted to go up back in Columbus, and I thought, I'm holding you down. We can't make decisions. Can't plan for the future. You deserve better than that, and I am selfish to not let you go after it."

Agnes felt her stomach clench. "What do you mean?"

"You want the ranch. That pilot probably has the money to buy it. And he's everything your mother would want for you. Cultured. Educated." He picked up the comb again, gently, intently working on a knot.

Agnes put her hand over Will's, stopping him from currying the tail. "Are you trying to give me away again? Like you did with Sergeant Dobbs?"

"He was a good man, too," Will said.

Agnes felt her muscles clench. Hadn't they been down this road before? She had neither the time nor the inclination to go down it again. She had another road, the road to the Sunrise, and she wasn't going to drag Will down it kicking and screaming. "I don't care a continental about what my mother wants for me, and I don't care about Captain Lance Harden. He hasn't put in an honest day's work in his life and wouldn't know the first thing about ranching. And another thing, Private William Bowers: I may not understand where you're coming from. My childhood was certainly a good part better than yours. But from where I stand, if you want something, you fight for it. You don't sit around thinking how you're not worthy of it. You don't make up excuses for why you don't deserve it. You fight. And you keep on fighting until you get it. Now, if you'll excuse me, I've got a ranch to purchase."

Agnes whirled around and stormed aw

ay, her hands clenched into fists so tight that the fingernails bit into her palms. She was still fuming when she marched into her tent and found Ethel walking out, leading two orderlies who were carrying her trunk.

"There you are," Ethel said. "Another order's come down. The camp's moving again. This time, to the Meuse River.

Chapter Twenty-one

She was still fuming when she slogged through the mud and climbed into the back of an ambulance that was packed high with supplies and equipment.

"Let's get this over with. Where's Sadie?" Agnes shouted over the rain that drummed on the canvas roof hard enough to drown the roar of the engine.

"Left behind again," Ethel shouted back. "Spanish Flu ward isn't moving."

The road to the Meuse River was the bumpiest Agnes had ever been on. Nurses clung to their trunks as if they were life rafts tossed on a turbulent sea. More than one finger or shin was crushed between shifting supplies.

"We could walk faster than this," Ethel Rosenberry shouted over the rain. "How far you think we've gone? Five miles? In what? Five hours?"

"You could miss the potholes by walking, but you'd get awfully wet," another nurse shouted back.

Nurse Chriswell beamed at the nurses, her face aglow with excitement. "This is the least damaged road in this region! German prisoner of war work crews are filling craters in the road with stones from ruined towns just ahead of us."

The ambulance listed to the left, causing the cargo to shift. Nurses screamed, terrified that the vehicle was going over on its side.

"They should have taken the houses apart first before they put them in the holes," Ethel said.

Nurse Chriswell stood, looking like Lady Liberty or a winged Nike. "We are going to be where the action is! In the thick of things! This is history in the making, and we are going to be a part of it." The ambulance rocked to the other side. Nurses screamed. One of them grabbed their leader before she pitched forward.

Agnes cautiously picked her way to the back of the ambulance and peered out the flap. Beyond the curtain of driving rain, the ground stretched, pockmarked and treeless except for shattered trunks. Everything looked gray and worn. They passed through what had been a village but was now just a collection of battered walls and piles of debris. A chicken roosted in a gap that had once been a window, her head tucked under her wing. The tightness in Agnes' chest convulsed into a sob of despair. In Brest, with the band playing and the men marching off the ship, the war had seemed like a grand adventure. But she had always been behind the lines. Now she saw land that had been involved in the fighting. It was blighted. Ruinous. Her heart grieved for the people who had lived in these houses and tilled these fields and for the lone chicken sheltering from the rain in a ruin. "This has got to stop," she muttered to herself.

The front wheels of the ambulance lurched onto something solid. Tire sounds changed from grind to clattery hum thump, hum thump. Agnes noted they were back on one of the plank roads that the engineering corps built over the boggiest stretches of road. Beside the road, she spied an artillery wagon whose mules were balking, throwing their heads about in terror. A man held their harness, his hand reaching up to comfort them.

Will. Despite the rain, she recognized him immediately.

Agnes sat on the lip of the ambulance, then slid onto the road, running with her hand on the ambulance until she caught her balance. The ambulance behind her laid on its horn. She stepped aside, then trudged back through the mud to the artillery wagon. Now that she was away from the roar of the engine, Agnes heard the low rumble of artillery in the distance.

Will glanced at her, a startled look on his face. "What are you doing here?"

"Helping with the hoof stock." Agnes patted the mule's cheek, making a shushing noise that seemed to calm her. "Let's get 'em going again so we can end this war and go home."

"Where's your coat?"

Agnes jerked her chin toward the slowly retreating ambulance. "In there. With the rest of my things."

Chuckling, Will shrugged out of his own coat and draped it over Agnes. "Fool girl doesn't have the sense to come in out of the rain."

"Not when there's livestock that needs helping. Remember that time we pulled the cow from the bog?"

"Good times. These two mollies didn't like the sound their hooves made on the boardwalk. Chose to swerve and bog the wagon. Think we can wrestle it out the way we did that cow?"

"You bet," Agnes said. And that is just what they did.

An hour later they were slogging past another ruined village when she heard someone calling her name. Agnes looked around and saw Ethel striding out of a ruined church.

"Yo! Agnes Day! Over here!" Ethel slipped through the mud, holding her skirts pinched between her thumb and forefingers. "Queen Chriswell says she's going to sack you for disappearing like that. It's my guess we're going to be too busy for her to want to let any of us go, least of all you! You work so hard. Well, hello, Will! You two been wallowing?"

Ethel waggled her eyebrows up and down suggestively, a wolfish grin spreading across her face. Agnes looked down at her mud-spattered dress. She and Will had struggled through mud that almost reached their knees. More than once, she had tripped over his too-long-for-her coat and landed face first in the mud. "It kind of looks like it, doesn't it? But no, I was helping Will get these guns through." Agnes smiled at Will and he smiled back. This is what they were meant to do: face problems head on and work together to find solutions. They were a team.

Ethel snapped a sharp salute at Will. "Carry on, soldier. I've got to get this nurse ready to report for duty." Gingerly, she pinched a bit of Agnes' sleeve between her thumb and forefinger, so as not to sully herself, then pulled Agnes towards the ruined church. Agnes looked over her shoulder at Will, but he was already moving the mules and their load down the road.

"Mercy, Nurse Day! What happened to you?" Nurse Chriswell frowned over the top of a chart she had been studying. Her tone tendered no mercy, despite the words. Beds and equipment were set up in four neat rows, two on each side of the church's center aisle. Most of the beds were already occupied. Behind the altar, a pile of pews looked like a giant game of pick-up-sticks.

"Without her help, the artillery wouldn't have gotten through," Ethel announced. "Agnes is from a ranch, you remember? She's good with horses. You can put that in your report."

Isobel Chriswell tapped her pen against her chin thoughtfully. "It does make us look rather heroic. I bet the press will eat it up. Very well! Go get changed. I'll put you on second shift to give you time to settle in."

"That went better than expected. I guess playing the good press card works on the Queen," Ethel muttered as she dragged Agnes out of the church through a hole that had once been a wall. Shards of brilliant glass, the remains of a window, crunched under their feet.

"We're going to use a ruin as our ward?" Agnes asked.

"Why not? The roof's intact. So's long as the wind doesn't blow too hard, the patients stay dry," Ethel said. "It's pretty primitive here. Maybe we'll improve conditions with time. Maybe the war will end before we manage that. You never know. Here's our quarters. I had Heinrich drag your trunk in. That man will do anything for you."

Ethel pointed to a stone house that still had most of its roof. They passed through a hole that must have once had a door, down a dark hallway, and into a back kitchen whose table had been shoved aside to make way for five cots, one of which had Agnes' trunk next to it.

"Right," Ethel said. "Pump the handle on that sink long enough, you get something that looks like cafe au lait. But it's cleaner than you are. Get some rest. Your shift starts at 6, and from what I hear, we're going to start by being too busy and it'll get busier from there."

The next three weeks proved Ethel right. Cannons roared. Ambulances streamed in filled with wounded. The injuries were far more gruesome than she had seen in the past. Farther back in the hospital chain, the cases had been those who had survived the first few days. Now Agnes got hopeless cases who had but hours to live. For these, she could do nothing except deaden their pain, hold their hands, and be with them as they passed. She lost track of how many deaths she witnessed, lost track of day and night. The smell of carbolic acid lingered even in her dreams.

Surely this level of ferocity couldn't last. Agnes began to believe the rumors that this was the final push that would drive the Germans into full retreat and then surrender. She focused on the tasks at hand, determined to finish strong. All she wanted now was for this war to end so that she could go home, buy the Sunrise and settle into the life that she dreamed of: a life that flowed from one season to another in a predictable pattern, that had hardships and problems, but none that couldn't be solved with hard work and determination.

And as she focused on the end of the war, Agnes stopped focusing on Will. She had no doubt that they would make a good team. They completed each other and supported each other. But she could not drag Will into the future. If he wasn't willing to put aside his fears about the law coming to get him, then he would never be ready to settle down. Agnes wasn't willing to move from place to place for the rest of her life, looking back over her shoulder.

The sound of breathing woke her. She was so deep in sleep that at first, she dreamed she heard what sounded like rushing wind, or someone breathing through a tube. As she rose to consciousness, the breathing continued. She opened her eyes and found an enormous, twisted white face with empty, slit-like eyes hovering over her.

Agnes scrambled to sit up. She opened her mouth to scream, but a hand clamped over it, holding her down.

"Hush! It's all right. It's just me, little lamb." A hand grabbed the face and pulled it up, revealing the chiseled beauty of Captain Lance Holden. Agnes tore his hand away from her mouth.

"What in God's name are you doing here? What time is it?" Constant rain and the steady stream of injured soldiers had turned night and day into one gray, exhausting twilight. She didn't know if it was dawn, dusk, or the middle of another dismal afternoon.

"Like my mask? I made it by myself. For Halloween! You do know that it's Halloween, don't you? Or have you been too busy?"

"Where is everybody?" Agnes looked around at the run-down kitchen. It took her a moment to remember where she was. The pounding of artillery in the distance helped her remember.

Lance sat down on the side of Agnes' bed. "I think the others are at their shift. Or washing. Or something. Who knows? But you're the one I wanted to see. There's a little soiree in the officer's club this evening. Kind of a combination Halloween party and send-off before the big push. Want to go?"

"Big push?" Agnes' heart still pounded from waking up too quickly, and from the fright of the mask. Now it pounded even harder. "I thought we were already in the big push."

"Ah, but it's going to intensify starting tomorrow. This is it: the push to end the war."

Agnes shoved Lance off her cot so she could swing her legs over and get up. She had been so busy that she had lost all sense of time or what was happening beyond the hospital tent. How could things get worse than they were now? How much stress could a person take. Even though she wasn't even sure if he was in camp, Agnes knew she had to find him. She couldn't let Will go into the maelstrom without saying goodbye. She grabbed for her uniform and realized she was still in it. She hadn't even taken off her shoes before falling asleep.

Lance grabbed Agnes by the shoulders, shaking her into focusing on him. "Agnes, my little Lamb. This big push means I go up this afternoon on a final reconnaissance. How's about a kiss? For good luck? And when I come back, we'll go to that party."

"Ask Sadie." Agnes brought up her elbow to break his hold on her. He held her all the tighter.

"Sadie's not here, remember? She's back with the influenza cases. Besides, you are you, Agnes. You have depth. You have drive. Sadie's fun. She's a sparkler on the fourth of July. You're fireworks. Kiss me, Agnes! Kiss me!" He pressed his lips to hers. Agnes struggled. He squeezed her even tighter. In desperation, Agnes bit his lip. Hard. She tasted blood. He pulled back and she slapped his face.

"How dare you! I'm writing to Sadie, telling her what a two-timing snake you are. I never want to speak with you again!"

Agnes stormed past Lance. Halfway down the darkened hall, she crashed into Will. She was so angry that she burst into tears.

"What's this?" Will asked, gathering her in his arms.

"All I did was ask her for a good luck kiss. I'm going on a reconnaissance flight," Lance said as he stepped into the hallway. His hand cradled his bleeding lip

Will's eyes narrowed. "If Agnes wants to kiss you, she'll kiss you. If she says no, she means it. Touch her again, and you'll be answering to me."

Lance laughed. "As if I would ever bother. The bitch bit me!"

Will let go of Agnes. His fist connected with Lance's cheek bone so hard that Lance slammed into the wall. He shook his head, then one hand covering his eye and the other covering his mouth, he rushed from the house.

Will smiled at Agnes as he rubbed his knuckles. "Dang, that felt good! So, the bitch bit him and the bastard punched him. Looks like we gave that flyboy what he deserved. I'm not saying you can't take care of yourself, but if he ever touches you again . . ."

"He wouldn't dare! Not when he has both of us to contend with. We make quite a team, you know that?" Agnes leaned forward to kiss Will, and he pulled her in close.

"I've hardly seen you these past few weeks. We've both been so busy. But there's a big push coming, and my company is ready to leave. I couldn't leave without saying goodbye. Walk me down to the staging area? Even though it's raining?"

Agnes laughed. "Will Bowers! You think a cowgirl cares about a little rain?"

They walked arm in arm, holding each other up as their feet slipped and slid on the walkway planks. "I've been thinking about what you said, and you're right," Will murmured into Agnes' ear as they walked, "How well we work together. When this push is over, let's talk about what we're going to do after the war. Create a plan to buy the Sunrise. Start the herd back up. It's going to be hard, but if anyone can do it, it's the two of us. We are worth fighting for."

Agnes felt her heart leap within her. "Oh, Will! Nothing would make me happier." She leaned her head on his shoulder to stop herself from jumping around like a newborn kid.

They reached the trucks and a dozen men leaned out of the back of one, watching Will and Agnes with mirth-filled eyes. Engine noise and the smell of exhaust filled the air. Will took Agnes in his arms and kissed her and the men in the truck let up a cheer that disappeared into the blast of the horn.

"I've got to go!" Will shouted. He climbed into the back of a truck, and a dozen men pounded him on the back. Will shouted something at Agnes, but she couldn't hear it over the trucks and the men.

"What?" she yelled. The truck lurched into gear and began to move. Agnes ran behind, trying desperately to catch Will's words.

"Just say yes," he yelled.

"What?" The truck was moving faster. She was having a hard time keeping up.

"Yes! Say yes!" Will yelled, giving her a thumbs-up gesture to encourage her.

"Yes!" She yelled, laughing at the absurdity of it all.

The other men in the truck burst into even louder cheer. Many pounded Will on the back. Agnes stopped and put her hands on her knees, panting for breath. What had she agreed to? She turned and ran to the motor pool, where she found Corporal David Benavides packing the panniers on his motorcycle.

"Loan me your motorcycle," Agnes said.

David Benavides laughed. "I can't do that! I've got dispatches to deliver up and down the line."

"I must catch up with Will. It's urgent." Agnes grabbed him by the lapels and shook him.

Benavides gave her a questioning look. "You ever been on one? Know how to operate it?"

Agnes scowled and folded her arms across her chest. "Can't be that hard."

Benavides laughed again. "Now, this I gotta see."

He wheeled the motorcycle away from the rest of the vehicles in the motor pool and gave Agnes a quick tutorial. Agnes hardly listened. She straddled the machine, kicked it alive, then popped the clutch too quickly, causing the bike to lurch. Agnes slipped off the back and landed in a mud puddle.

"You're going to kill yourself before you ever make it to the gun emplacements," Benavides said as he offered her a hand up.

"I've been bucked off before," Agnes said.

"Not by a motorcycle!"

"Then find me a horse!"

The Corporal shook his head. "What in the world is so all-fired important that you would risk breaking your neck for it?"

"I don't know!" Agnes said. "As his truck pulled out, he said something and it was important enough to get a reaction out of the whole truck. I think I know, but I need to know for sure."

He walked toward the stables, shaking his head and chuckling to himself. "You know we both could get court martialed for this."

"We'll let you be the best man at the wedding."

"Some consolation!" He talked a stable hand into saddling one of the officer's horses and she turned it north and rode into the rain, determined to find Will.

Hedges shielded the sunken road that led toward the front. The rain stopped, leaving the world gray and still. A sentry challenged her, but she said she was a nurse on a mission and he allowed her to pass through a group of soldiers sullenly squatting along the edges of the road, their collars turned up against the damp. They looked at her with reverence and awe, as if she were Joan of Arc riding among them.

The sentry explained that the artillery lay scattered along the road, most units hidden among copses of trees. By watching for flashes of light and puffs of smoke, she was able to guide herself to them. Will wasn't at the first gun emplacement she came to, nor at the second. She arrived at the third as dusk settled the world into shadows. Agnes called his name and Will separated himself from the gray group and came towards her, resolving out of the gathering gloom like an apparition.

"Agnes! What are you doing, rushing into danger? This is far worse than Columbus was."

Agnes smiled, remembering him in his long johns at the machine gun emplacement on the day of Pancho Villa's raid. "Finding out what I said yes to. Your buddies in the truck thought it was an awfully big deal."

Will grinned impishly. "It was an awfully big deal. I asked you to marry me."

"And I said yes?" Agnes nearly laughed the words out.

Will's smile gleamed in the gathering gloom. "You did."

"Not fair! I couldn't hear over the roar of the truck motors!"

"But you said yes. And you are a woman of your word, are you not?"

"Oh!" Agnes threw up her hands in a show of indignation.

She swung out of the saddle and tied the horse's reins to a tree trunk. "Will Bowers! You will propose to me properly or not at all! I've waited a long time for this, and I'm not going to tell our children that I missed it when it finally happened."

"Well, all right. If you insist." Will Bowers got down on one knee in front of Agnes and took her hands in his. "Miss Day, I have loved you since the first day I met you and you showed such spirit. You are the woman I want to spend the rest of my life with. Will you marry me?"

And instead of answering, for the second time that day, Agnes exploded into tears. This time they were tears of joy. Will kissed them away.

"All these odd jobs I've had; they were preparing me for everything I need to do at the Sunrise," Will said. "I feel like my whole life has been leading up to this. Finally, I'm ready to face a future. A real future. Tomorrow I'll sneak back to camp. We'll find a chaplain, and tie the knot.".

Agnes pulled back. "We can't do that. "If I marry, they'll send me home. Then how will we afford the Sunrise? Will, we are together. The marriage certificate is just a piece of paper. It can wait."

"The war's nearly over," Will said. "Who's going to care if we leave here married or not?" His lips moved to her throat and her breath caught. His hand trembled as he brushed back her hair and kissed her ear. She couldn't remember a time that his capable hand had ever seemed unsteady.

Agnes trailed her nose across his jaw, inhaling the smell of horse and salt and strength. She stroked his cheek and trailed her lips up his neck. Together they sighed as if they shared breath. Their lips met in an intensity born of fear and desperation. The war with its death and violence and disease disappeared. All that remained was the two of them, holding each other while the world ripped itself apart.

"Yo! Bowers!" a voice called, ripping them from their reverie. "Get that woman out of here and get back to your post. Do you know what time it is?"

Will took a startled breath. "The bombardment! Get on that horse and ride hard. All hell's going to break loose here, and I want you safe and away before it starts"

He pulled her close and kissed her hard. "Until tomorrow."

Chapter Twenty-two

A full moon shone behind the clouds, casting a gray pall over the world that was not much darker than a rainy day. Agnes, deciding that riding the field instead of through a sunken road filled with soldiers would be faster, turned the horse, kicked him hard, and leaned over his neck as he streaked across open land. He was a fine boned, spirited horse, and he responded quickly and with gusto. Agnes worried for a second about prairie dog holes. Hitting one at a gallop could easily break a horse's leg. But she was in France, not New Mexico. There were probably no prairie dogs here, and there were bigger things to worry about.

Behind her, Will's guns opened fire. Other guns fired, too, some nearby and others far in the north. Together they created a thunder so loud that she felt it in her chest, even over the thunder of the horse's hooves. Gunsmoke, thick and acrid, filled the air.

Suddenly the horse was gone and she was flying sideways through the air. She struck the ground hard, knocking the wind from her. Her sight splintered into a thousand fragments, sparks of light and fuzzy dark patches. She struggled to take a breath, but it would not come. Around her the ground erupted in showers of dirt.

Agnes heard shouting male voices. Hands grabbed her, lifted her and she felt herself being carried, then set down on the ground, which shook and jarred as explosion after explosion rocked it. A dozen faces hovered over her. They wore the Brodie helmets that American soldiers wore into battle. Their faces were tense, worried.

"Miss? You all right?"

Agnes tried to answer. Nothing came out.

A man with a medic's cross wrapped around his arm knelt next to her. He smiled encouragingly, and his calmness as his hands moved over her made Agnes feel calmer, too. "Sit her up, fellas. That's a good girl. Breathe. Make that diaphragm work." She tried to suck in a breath. It came in ragged pieces, but it came. "That's it. Just got the wind knocked out of you. No cuts, bruises, lacerations or broken bones that I can see."

"What happened?" Agnes asked, the question coming out croakily.

"We heard you coming," another of the soldiers said. "So, we were watching when the shell hit. You're awfully lucky to be alive."

A number of the men murmured assent. Agnes looked around and realized she was in the sunken road, and these were the soldiers that had looked at her in awe when she passed earlier. She tried to get up, but the medic held her down. "Now, now, missy. Best you wait a bit.

"I've got to get my horse," Agnes said.

The medic shook his head. "'He took off soon's you fell off. I don't think there's any chance you could find him now. Not in this barrage. Boys! Anyone got some water for our guest?" A dozen canteens thrust forward. Agnes took one with a grateful thank you. She brought it to her lips, smelled the warm, grainy smell, and pulled back. "This is whiskey."

"For medicinal purposes, I assure you," the canteen's owner said. "But we have water, too, if that's what you need."

"What I need," Agnes said, "is to get back to camp."

"Not now," said a lieutenant who had just walked up to see what all the commotion was about. "This bombardment makes it too dangerous. Once dawn comes it'll be even worse. You're wearing all white. The road becomes much shallower up ahead. A sniper would get you."

"So what do I do?" Agnes asked.

The lieutenant looked at his wristwatch. "Stay here until nightfall. With any luck, this push will be over and we'll be back to escort you. Anyone want to share some iron rations with this little lady before we go?"

They moved up the road, leaving her with a portion of the emergency foods they carried in their packs. Agnes nibbled the edge of a three-ounce disc and determined that it was a mixture of beef bouillon powder and cooked wheat kernels, and while not appetizing, would probably keep her from feeling faint with hunger. She tucked the three small chocolate bars into her pocket, then got up and began carefully making her way back to camp. While she appreciated the lieutenant's advice and wasn't going to argue with him, she couldn't spend the day hiding. She was getting married.

Agnes stumbled through the darkness, groping along the walls and hiding in the shadow while the ground quaked and dirt rained down. Occasionally the question of how she was going to explain the missing horse and whether Nurse Chriswell would sack her for being absent without leave or if Corporal Benavides really could get court martialed popped into her mind, but it just wouldn't stick. In spite of everything, Agnes' heart sang like a lark on a spring day. She was getting married tomorrow!

Groups of men streamed past her in both directions, and each time she stepped aside and let them pass. Sometimes she saw the whites of their eyes gleaming in the darkness and they seemed to look at her as if she were a specter, the memory of a woman left behind or the foreshadowing of the angel of death. Some reached out and touched her as if she were a good luck charm. She was nearing camp when the roar of a motorcycle made her step aside.

Corporal Benavides pulled up next to her and pulled down his goggles. "You're limping."

"I hate walking!" Agnes said with a huge smile. She was exhausted and sore, but her spirits had never been higher.

"What're you doing here? Where's the horse?"

Agnes smiled. "We're getting married! Today!"

"You and the horse? Come on. Get on." He scowled and shook his head as he patted the seat. Agnes climbed on behind him, her arms wrapped around his waist and her cheek pressed to his back.

"Really! Will's coming back and we're getting married!" she shouted over the roar of the engine. If he responded, she didn't hear him over the roar of the engine. They rode into camp a few hours before dawn. It was quiet, with pockets of business near the officer's quarters and, as always, the hospital, where lights blazed and orderlies unloaded yet another ambulance. The guns in the distance sounded like the roar of surf on the shore. The northern horizon flashed with color. Benavides dropped her off in front of the ruined house that was the nurses' quarters, then roared off with a wave. Agnes limped through the entrance. Every inch of her body ached from the explosion and her impact with the earth, but her mind was a whirl of joy. Today was her wedding day!

"Wake up, Ethel," Agnes said, shaking the lump of blankets in Ethel's cot. "I've got great news! I'm getting married today."

Ethel jerked awake, sitting up with a sudden gasp. "Wha? Where? Ugh! I was sound asleep!"

"I've got great news!" Agnes repeated. "Will proposed, and he's sneaking back into camp today and I'm getting married!"

"What are you, drunk?" Ethel asked as she sat up and scratched her head.

"Nope!" Agnes threw her arms wide as if she wanted to hug the whole world.

"You're acting like you are," Ethel said, grumbling. "Here we are, in the middle of a big push! Men are dying by the droves. And you're talking marriage? When do you go on duty?"

Agnes stopped, thinking for a moment. Her head had been so high in the clouds that she'd forgotten the routine of camp. "6?"

Ethel grabbed her Baby Ben alarm clock and squinted at it. "Right. We've got twenty minutes to sober you up. Where's your nurses' cap?"

Agnes put her hand to her head. Her hair felt stringy and matted. She itched, and she knew she smelled. "Dunno."

"You got an extra in your trunk? Lord, you look like skid row trash from the Bowery. I hate to sound like the Queen, but you made a promise and you're going to stick with it, whether you like it or not. We'll talk about marriage and other such nonsense once this battle's over." Ethel walked Agnes to the sink, pumped the handle and filled the sink before dunking Agnes' face in. Agnes came up spluttering, but Ethel wouldn't listen to protests. By the time Ethel had tugged a comb through Agnes' hair and gotten her changed into a clean uniform, Agnes was somewhat sobered. She rushed off to the ward, willing to do her bit, but waiting for the moment when Will arrived and together, they would search out the Chaplain.

But he didn't come. Not that day, and not the next, when Remington came in leading a line of men, each blindly clinging to the man in front of him. Nurse Chriswell sent them to the showers, to be stripped and washed in hot water and soap to remove the mustard gas from their skins, but enough time had passed that the damage was already done. Men, their bodies covered with blisters, their lungs and windpipes burned, filled the wards with groaning and shrieks.

As she walked bed to bed, Agnes searched for Will's face among the injured, her emotions jumping from dread to relief with each face that wasn't his. She leaned over patient after patient, gently unwrapping the bandages that hid their eyes so that she could irrigate them with an alkaline solution.

"I'm going to bathe your eyes," she explained to one. "It might help the pain."

"Couldn't make it any worse," the man responded, his lips pulling back in something that was part smile and part grimace. "Mustard gas is the devil's own air. I bet it's what they breathe in hell."

"No doubt," Agnes said. "Want to tell me about what happened?"

"It's nasty business," he responded, but Agnes knew that men were distracted from their pain if they talked, so she encouraged him to go on. "I didn't even feel it at first, I was so busy working the guns. And then, I got a whiff of something over the smell of gunpowder. I thought it was garlic. It smelled like the Italians that lived down the hall from me in Brooklyn."

"Guns. You were in one of the artillery batteries?" Agnes' hand shook as she pressed the plunger on the syringe of eye wash, flooding the eye with solution that dripped onto the towel she had tucked beneath his cheek.

"Yes, miss. It wasn't until one of the other men started yelling 'gas, gas' that I noticed the yellow fog drifting through. I looked at him, and he was red, like he'd been running. I put on my mask, but I guess it was too late. Am I blind forever?"

"Probably not. Some men get their sight back in a matter of days. Others, it takes weeks. Which artillery battery were you with?" Agnes tried to keep her voice level and matter-of-fact, but her heart pounded in terror. What was she going to do if he said Battery A, Will's battery?

"At first I thought I was all right: that I'd got the mask on in time. But then I started vomiting. You can't vomit with a mask on! I threw it off, and found my buddies had done the same. We were all red in the face. All vomiting. And then the blistering started." He pulled back the collar of his hospital robe and Agnes saw that his neck and chest were covered with blisters that oozed yellow fluid. "Some of us are covered head to foot. I was lucky: only have it in my elbows and the backs of my knees."

"Very lucky, indeed." Agnes' hands shook so badly that she had to put down the syringe. "What unit did you say you were with?"

"I recognize your voice," the man in the next bed said, his bandaged face turning toward Agnes. "You were there, weren't you? Riding a horse?"

"The nurse on the horse?" another said. "Was that you?"

The pan of solution clattered to the floor and the syringe spun away. Agnes stood up, her hands hiding her face.

"Miss? Are you there?" the man she'd been working on asked.

"Where's Will? Private William Bowers? Is he with you?" Agnes asked.

"Nurse Day? Nurse Chriswell wants you in her office," a woman's voice said. It was not the answer she expected. Agnes pulled her hands away from her face and found another of the nurses looking at her expectantly, her hands flittering about nervously.

Agnes took a deep breath to steady herself. This was it. Once she had come out of the clouds of euphoria, Agnes had realized what a stupid stunt it had been to take a horse and ride to the front. It had only been a matter of time before she was caught and sent home. She wanted to stay and find out about Will, but the longer she kept the head nurse waiting, the more severe her punishment would be. She would come back and talk with the men. They weren't going anywhere. "Very well. Would you be so kind as to get an orderly to mop this up?" Agnes pointed at the spilled basin, then marched to the front of the ruined church with as much dignity as she could muster.

Nurse Chriswell's office was in a small room that had once been the church's sacristy and was still cluttered with colorful robes, silver chalices, and crucifixes and poles. Agnes wondered that a priest hadn't taken them with him, or they hadn't been stolen after he'd gone. The head nurse looked up, scowling over the top of her glasses at Agnes before she set down her pen and folded her hands into a pyramid. "Nurse Day, it has come to my attention that a nurse borrowed a horse. It was not returned. Might you know anything about this?"

"Yes, ma'am," Agnes said, swallowing hard to keep her voice steady. "That was me. I borrowed the horse to run an errand."

Nurse Chriswell frowned. "And this errand? Who ordered you to undertake it?"

Agnes felt her cheeks flush. She stared at her toes. "No one, ma'am."

"I take it this wasn't orders? Not official business?"

"No, ma'am." Nurse Chriswell's head snapped up and her eyes narrowed before Agnes realized that she had compounded her problem by addressing her superior in a way she didn't like. "I mean, no, Nurse Chriswell."

"And the horse is where now?"

"I don't know, Nurse Chriswell. I lost him in the shelling."

"Lost him? In shelling? I don't suppose you have any idea whether it is dead or alive? Or captured by the Huns? Do you have any idea what the punishment is for providing supplies to the enemy?"

It took Agnes a long time to look Nurse Chriswell in the face. She shook her head, unable to speak. Would she be branded a traitor or a spy for this?

"That horse was government property. The price of it will be taken from your pay."

"That's only fair," Agnes said, breathing a sigh of relief. For a moment, she had envisioned an execution squad. Still, every penny taken from her pay was a penny taken from the Sunrise, and horses cost a pretty penny.

"It would only be fair to send you home now, and to make you pay your own passage since you did not complete your contract. But we are too busy at present to do any such thing. You will continue working, but I expect no more escapades like this. Are we clear?"

"Yes, ma'am. Thank you for giving me another chance." Agnes felt weak in the knees with gratitude. She hadn't lost her job after all, after how stupid she'd acted. Now there was still a chance that she'd be there when Will came back.

"Oh, I am not giving you another chance," the head nurse said. "I am giving you the chance to do the work you'd signed on to do in the first place because now is when I need you most. But make no mistake: as soon as this war is over, I will relieve you of your duties and send you packing. Don't expect a recommendation from me. You went absent without leave. You fraternized with men. Exhibited scandalous behavior. Besmirched the image of nurses everywhere."

"Yes, ma'am. Thank you, ma'am. And I'm sorry."

"Sorry does nothing to repair the damage!" Nurse Chriswell's face wrinkled in on itself in the deepest frown Agnes had ever seen. She took up her pen and began savaging the paper with words as Agnes backed out of the little room. She turned around and marched back to the man whose eyes she had been irrigating, her heart wildly pounding in her chest, both from relief that she hadn't been sent home and fear for what she was going to learn next.

"Yes, I am the nurse on the horse," Agnes said loudly enough that all the men in beds could hear. "And I asked a question. Where's Private William Bowers?"

Half a dozen blindfolded heads swiveled back and forth as if searching the rooms with eyes that couldn't see. "Bowers? Yo! You here?" one of them called. He turned his bandaged face towards Agnes. "I don't know, Miss. Maybe still on the battlefield?"

Agnes felt a shudder of horror go through her. She had the impulse to run from the ruined church. She fought it down, picked up another pan of irrigating fluid, and returned to irrigating eyes. She had promised Nurse Chriswell that she would complete her duties, and she would do so, even if it meant burying her emotions and working on blindly and unthinkingly. At the end of her shift, Agnes staggered back to her room, gathered some fresh clothes, then went to the showers. The cold room filled with fog. She wished it would fill her head and block out her thoughts. How could Will be missing now, when they had finally decided to face life together?

As she dressed, she told herself that there had to be an explanation why Will wasn't with his battery. Perhaps he had gotten his mask on in time and was still out there, firing his gun with a group of replacements. Maybe he'd been captured by the Germans and was a POW. Or maybe he'd been sent to another hospital somewhere along the line. In the confusion, had he joined up with another unit? Or gotten lost? Or had amnesia? Maybe he was hiding somewhere. She couldn't give up hope. There was a reason he wasn't here. She had to believe. She told herself that she would get word to Corporal Benavides so that he could make inquiries for her.

Agnes wrapped her hair in her towel and walked back to the half-ruined house. When she got there, she found Ethel sitting on her cot, a writing pad on her lap and a pen in her hand.

"Writing home?" Agnes asked.

Ethel looked up, her face pale and pinched. "Writing to Sadie. Lance's plane went down in flames behind enemy lines."

Agnes collapsed onto the foot of Ethel's cot. "Not Lance. It couldn't be."

"Sentries reported it. They rated his chance for survival as zilch. Here. He stopped by before he headed out. Asked me to give you this." Ethel handed over one of the thin envelopes that the YMCA handed out to soldiers.

"I don't think I want to open this," Agnes said as she fingered the brittle paper.

"I think you better. There might be something in it that Sadie'd want to know."

Agnes sighed and slit the envelope open with her penknife. She scanned the lines of meticulous, finely formed penmanship which lined up, straight and neat, across the page.

> Dear Agnes,
>
> I am writing a letter that I hope you will never have a chance to read, for I would rather apologize in person for my boorish behavior. Last night I had the most vivid of dreams in which I was literally embroiled in the flames of hell. I awoke with a pounding heart and the premonition that this evening's flight would be my last. I am afraid that my fear led me to make unwanted advances against you. Please forgive me, and know that I have nothing but the utmost respect for you and how you've acquitted yourself throughout our acquaintance. I beg you not to mention my brutish lapse to Sadie, for fear of hurting her.
>
> Yours sincerely,
> Lance

Agnes folded the letter and slipped it back into the envelope. "Tell Sadie that Lance's thoughts were with her at the end," she said, then burst into tears. She told Ethel about her meeting with Nurse Chriswell and what she'd learned from the gassed men in the ward. The two held each other and cried until neither had any tears left.

Nine days later, Agnes still had heard nothing about Will's whereabouts when an orderly walked into the ward and waved a sheet of paper in the air. "It's official! The radioman got an announcement at 6:01 this morning. This morning at eleven, hostilities stop along the entire front. So says Marshal Foch, the French Commander-in-Chief. Ladies and gentlemen, the war is over."

Some of the patients put up a feeble cheer. Others stared straight forward as if they hadn't heard the announcement. Agnes looked at the little watch that was pinned to her blouse. It said nine o'clock.

"Two hours to go," she said to the patient she had been tending.

"Pfft. I'll believe it when I see it," he answered. It was doubly ironic since he was one of the ones whose blistered eyes were bound and bandaged in the hopes that they would recover from the gas. The guns in the distance kept firing, if anything at a higher rate than before, as if determined to use up every shell in their huge arsenal in the next two hours. Agnes kept at her work. Even if the war ended and there were no more injuries, she had enough injured men in her charge to keep her busy for a long time to come.

As the minutes ticked by, patient after patient nervously fingered his sheets and asked the time. Agnes kept reading it off her little watch. Nine-fifteen. Nine-thirty-eight. Ten-seventeen. The men kept asking as if they were afraid that they would miss it. It reminded Agnes of New Year's Eve. Did every patient expect a kiss at the stroke of eleven?

A kiss. Agnes' mind wandered back through all the kisses she and Will had ever shared. They seemed so few and far between, too tenuous a thread to withstand the stretch of time. She touched her lips, trying to hold on to the feeling of his lips on hers.

"Miss? What time is it, please?" a man with the stump of his arm wrapped in a white balloon of bandages asked. As Agnes reached for her watch, the shelling stopped, the last booming explosion trailing off like an echo. For a moment the whole ward seemed to be frozen in the stillness and then, from somewhere close by, a lark sang.

Agnes smiled. "I believe it must be eleven o'clock."

The man who had asked smiled wanly, then his eyes rolled back in his head and his body relaxed. His tongue dangled from his open mouth. A flutter of fear crossed Agnes' heart. Had the man survived the war, only to die on hearing it was over? He let out a snore and she suppressed a laugh. Other men did laugh out loud. Some began crying. A few cheered. But there was no celebration. Few, Agnes knew, believed the Armistice would last.

When her shift ended, Agnes trudged back to the ruined house that had been her quarters for the past month. Without the drum of artillery, the night seemed too quiet, as if it were holding its breath and waiting for the war to resume. Groups of men stood around fires, passing flasks and speaking quietly among themselves. They looked up quickly when Agnes passed, their eyes wary.

Ethel looked up from pulling off her shoes as Agnes walked in. "How 'bout that! We survived, and now it's over? Ready to climb out of this hellhole?"

Agnes shook her head. "If the Queen will let me, I'll stay 'til the last patient goes. I could use the money."

Ethel reached out and laid her hand atop Agnes'. It was chapped and dry. Constant scrubbing with heavy soaps had taken their toll, just as the stress and lack of sleep had given Ethel dark bags under her eyes. "He's not coming back, you know. If he were, he would have done so by now." Ethel said the words gently, but they seemed to scream in Agnes' head. She sucked in a staggering breath and looked away.

"Really. I'm staying because I could use the money. Buying the Sunrise is still the most important thing to me." It was a lie, and Agnes knew it. At some point, being with Will had become more important than keeping the Sunrise. She lay down in her cot without undressing, ready in case the war resumed, but she was unable to sleep. The silence, and thoughts of Will lying out there in the darkness kept her awake. Was he in pain? Did he need her? Or was he gone forever? Agnes needed to find out. She wasn't sure if she could go on living otherwise.

The next day Heinrich stopped by the ward as Agnes was working her rounds. He, too, looked tired and drawn, and much older than he had when he got here. Six months in a war hospital had aged him when four years at Harvard could not. "Ethel tells me you're staying until the last patient is transported out. Then I will, too."

Agnes shook her head. "You don't have to do that, you know."

"I do know. But we've been friends all our lives. We got into this together, and we might as well go out of it together."

Agnes sighed and steeled herself to say what she had said so many times before, to no avail. "Thank you, Heinrich. But you know, I'm still not interested in you. Romantically, that is."

"Oh, I know." Heinrich's face softened into a smile that couldn't be faked. "Aggie, ever since that day you sat on me on the playground, you've been like a big sister to me. You've talked to me straight. Forced me to think about what I was doing. Watched after me. Set me straight when I needed it. Please, do me the honor of letting me escort you home. I know you'd rather it be someone else, and I know I can never take his place, but I can do this, to honor both you and him."

Heinrich put out his hand for a handshake. She stared at it for a moment, then tilted her head back and gazed into his eyes. They were so blue and so earnest that she finally gave him the hug he'd been begging for all their life. She rested her head on his chest and felt him tense in surprise before he relaxed and returned the hug. "Thank you, Heinrich," she whispered, "you really are a good friend."

The wards emptied slowly. Some patients died and were buried right outside the hospital. Others grew strong enough to move down the line, back towards the port cities. Staff members left with each departing ambulance. Some patients and staff stopped at the next hospital down the line. Others travelled all the way to the coast, boarded ships, and returned to America. Some were home by Christmas. Sadie sent a note up the line that she was scheduled to be on one of the first ships to leave, and that Agnes and Ethel were welcome to visit any time they were in Iowa. Agnes hoped that she would be happy back on the farm, surrounded by her many siblings. Perhaps she had learned enough about the rest of the world to be ready to return to what she had once spurned.

Agnes checked every list she could get her hands on, searching for Will's name. He hadn't appeared on lists of the dead whose bodies had been recovered, or on any lists of patients being sent down the line. She pestered the clerk in the company headquarters so often that he'd frequently checked before she got to him and knew the answer before she walked in the tent. Will had disappeared, and no one knew his whereabouts or condition.

A week after the Armistice, Corporal David Benavides appeared at the door to the nurses' quarters. When Agnes came out, he took off his hat and smiled nervously.

"Good morning, Miss Day. Is Sadie Sunshine here?"

"Sunshine? You mean Sadie Sundvuist?"

Benavides turned crimson. "I guess it was Captain Harden gave her that nickname. It's what all the men call her."

Agnes smiled. "It's fitting. She always had a smile on her face. But you know she never made it here to the forward camp. She stayed back with the Spanish Flu cases."

Benavides sighed and relaxed. "I only saw her that one time, when we were souvenir hunting. Didn't realize she didn't move up the line with the rest of us. I'm relieved. A crew searching the battlefield found the wreckage of Captain Harden's Salmson. I was going to offer her the chance to see it. Didn't want to. Expected there'd be tears. But it seemed the right thing to do." He sighed and beat the side of his leg with his hat. "Hard to know what to do in a situation like that."

"It is. Thank you for thinking of her. I'm sure she would have derived great comfort from seeing the site." Agnes put a hand on Benavides' shoulder.

His eyes studied hers. "And how're you holding up?"

"As well as can be expected, I suppose. I wish I knew more . . ."

He nodded. "Not knowing is harder than knowing the worst. Maybe we should go out there, for Sadie's sake. We can take a few snapshots if anyone has a camera."

"That would be Heinrich Dieter," Agnes said. They made their plans, then dispersed, he to find a car and she to find Heinrich. When they got back together an hour later, Agnes not only had Heinrich, but Ethel with her. They rode north on a pock-marked road, past no man's land and through the German lines, to the outskirts of a small town that, to Agnes's surprise, still had a few inhabitants. There Benavides stopped the car, got out, and talked with an old woman who was wandering through a field, searching for a few root vegetables.

"She says it's over there," he said when he got back to the car, then jerked his head so that he was pointing with his chin.

"You speak French?" Agnes asked as they started down a rutted track that had obviously seen little traffic. They bumped so hard that Agnes put her hand against the roof of the car to keep her from hitting her head.

Benavides smiled. "Remember Lt. Col. de Bremond? The man who led us into Mexico, chasing after Pancho Villa? De Bremond was Swiss. Taught us all to speak French before he brought us over here. Some of us learned better than others. I was a natural." He took his eyes off the road for a moment, giving Agnes a sardonic look, one eyebrow raised. "I'm not as dumb as I look, you know."

Agnes looked at the man who was little enough to be a jockey, yet brave enough to ride motorcycles between outposts. She knew he was a rancher, but in the three years she'd known him, this sullen man had let her know little else about himself. He'd been fiercely protective of his friend, Will, when he thought Agnes was two-timing him. It occurred to Agnes that wasn't a bad trait to have. "You were smart enough to pick Will for a friend," she said, "That's pretty smart."

David Benavides stole a glance at Agnes, who smiled back. They both had tears in their eyes.

"That must be it!" Ethel leaned forward in the back seat, pointing over Benavides' shoulder to the remains of a plane in a field off to their right. He pulled the car over and they all got out. "The old woman said that they'd given him a good, Christian burial. She said they liked American flyers," Benavides said. The earth around the wreck was blackened, the plane itself just a jumbled metal skeleton that stood up from its nose like a windmill tower. As they neared, Agnes saw a mound of earth, around which stones had been placed to mark the site. The plane's propeller had been buried near the head of the grave, the horizontal blades cut short so that it looked like a cross. Flowers had been planted at the base of the propeller, but now, in mid November, they had withered into dusty mounds. Heinrich took a few snapshots, using the little pen to write the date and location on each picture. When he was done, they soberly walked back to the car.

"When a man dies," David Benavides said when they had passed the village and were on a road again," someone sorts through his things. He distributes the things that others can use: goggles, a compass, a warm helmet, a sweater. He boxes up the things that the folks back home might want and sends them on their way. I did that for Captain Harden. I'll make sure his folks get these pictures, Heinrich, along with his watch, fountain pen, and letters from home. If you have an address for Sadie Sunshine, I'll send her a picture, too."

"I've got her address." Agnes' voice choked. Tears ran down her face. She wiped them with the back of her hand. She hadn't liked Lance from the very beginning, but she had warmed to him over time. Their last encounter had been so negative that she had not felt as sad about his passing as she might have. Now she thought of the people he had left behind and a wave of grief flooded over her. Sadie, she was sure, was deep in mourning. Who else had Lance Holden left behind? Parents? Siblings?

Agnes' thoughts turned to Will, and it occurred to her that she didn't know his mother's name. Did the Army know it? Would the clerk give out that information? Would Will's mother know whether her son lived or had died? "What a hard job that must be, sorting a dead man's things. No one's done that with Will's things, have they? Because he's not been pronounced dead."

"Neither was Captain Harden," David said. "Just missing. Yes, I went through Will's things, too. There wasn't much there, and no one to mail it to. Other than clothes and his kit, this, really, was all there was." He fished in his coat pocket and brought out a packet of envelopes. Agnes recognized the handwriting as hers, the postmarks as Columbus. She turned the packet over, and on the bottom, found the picture that Heinrich had taken on her birthday. Someone had drawn a heart around her face.

Part Three

A Heart A Blaze

1919

Chapter Twenty-three

Agnes walked through the nearly empty ward, enjoying the peace and quiet that last night's merriment had brought on. The few patients left in the bombed-out church that had become a hospital ward had passed several bottles to celebrate the end of 1918. A few pieces of confetti drifted along the central aisle stirred up in the eddies that slipped through the makeshift canvas wall that hung where the stone one had been. Agnes pulled up the blankets covering one of the sleeping men and watched his breath come out in white puffs.

Someone called her name, and she turned to see Mrs. Theodora Abrim, the head nurse who had met her in New York and guided her into this unit, striding toward her. Mrs. Abrim was a little grayer at the temples, but she still held herself upright and rigid, with an undeniable air of authority that Agnes had at first thought would make her a hard taskmaster, but had proved to hide a loving heart.

"Happy New Year's, Nurse Day," she said, shifting her clipboard to her left hand and holding the right out for a shake.

"And to you," Agnes said without much enthusiasm. She absently straightened the blanket over another patient's legs as she drifted towards the front of the church.

Nurse Abrim cocked her head and studied Agnes. "You've lost weight and your skin doesn't have the burnished tan I remember."

Agnes shrugged. "France is a lot rainier than my desert."

"That's what I've come to talk to you about," Nurse Abrim said as she studied her clipboard. "It's time to get you home."

Agnes shrugged again, but she didn't say anything. She stooped to retrieve a wine bottle from under a bed and tucked it into one of the pockets of her apron.

"Sadie went back to the farm in Iowa. She didn't want any recommendations for future placements. That was a disappointment, but I guess every girl isn't cut out for the nursing life. You did a good job keeping Sadie centered while she was here. I'm glad I kept you together."

Agnes shrugged again. "We weren't, really. When the big push came, Nurse Chriswell moved me forward, while Sadie stayed back with the influenza cases."

Nurse Abrim gave Agnes an appraising look. "Nurse Chriswell saw a lot of potential in you. She wrote good things about your competency in your file."

Agnes smiled bitterly. "Really? Did she also tell you I went AWOL more than once, lost a horse, and she was going to send me packing?"

Mrs. Abrim frowned. "She left that part out. I guess, in the long run, she decided it wasn't worth pursuing. So I'm free to ask: A lot of my girls are getting positions in hospitals stateside. How about you? Got plans?"

"I'll think about the future later." Agnes passed to the next bed and mechanically picked up the chart that hung on the footboard, but her eyes stared vacantly beyond it. "Right now, I want to stay until the last man is ready to go home."

"Where's that soldier of yours? From the boat? The piano player?" Mrs. Abrim's tone was soft.

Agnes shook her head. "Went missing. November second."

"What was his name? His unit? I'll see what I can find out about him." Mrs. Abrim reached into her pocket, pulled out a fountain pen and set the nib to her paper. When Agnes had given the requested information, Nurse Abrim capped her pen and tucked it back in her pocket. "I'll let you accompany the last of the patients as they move down the line, but when you get to Paris I want you to take some time off. The Grande Bretagne bar, or the Astra across the street from it are the ones Americans visit. See the Eiffel tower. The Louvre. Notre Dame. You need the distraction. Who knows when you'll ever be back here again?"

Agnes nodded, so Mrs. Abrim went on. "I'll make inquiries about your young man. I hear you're getting more repatriated POWs this afternoon. Maybe he'll be among them."

Agnes brightened, hope rising in her as it had with every batch of prisoners of war that had crossed No Man's Land. The men who climbed out of the backs of the trucks had been pitiable, their frames weak, half starved, and so filthy that they were hardly recognizable as men. Agnes searched their faces for the one she most longed to see. Then, disappointed, she tended their neglected wounds with as much tenderness as if each were Will. With each disappointment, she hoped that there would be one more trade of prisoners, and that Will would be among them.

A week passed. Men passed through camp, some to the burial grounds and some to the hospitals that were further down the line. Agnes hunched over a cup of cold coffee in the canteen when she looked up and saw Heinrich Dieter, hat in hand, standing before her.

"Aggie? Can you spare a minute?" With a flick of her hand, she beckoned him to sit, and he did. "You look tired," he said.

"As do we all," she answered. Agnes had to blink twice at the man who slid onto the bench opposite her. She had known Heinrich so long that she tended to still see him through her memories. She noted that his hair was shaggy, but the acne which had plagued him throughout his childhood was finally gone, replaced by blond stubble. His lean frame had begun to fill out, and he looked less like a scarecrow and more like a man. A very handsome man, with brilliant blue eyes, pale blond hair, and a square jawline. Why hadn't she noticed before?

Heinrich smiled his gawky smile. "I guess that's what wars do to us. Aggie, I know I promised to escort you home, but I've come to say goodbye. I'm sorry. My father wants me back."

Agnes reached out and put a hand over his, which had been nervously drumming the table. "He needs help with the store?"

"No," Heinrich answered. "He's found me a clerkship with the Supreme Court. He thinks it's going to look good on my resume when I begin campaigning for a seat in the senate."

"You're going to Washington?"

"No, silly. Santa Fe. We're talking about the New Mexico Supreme Court, and the New Mexico Senate. I gotta start somewhere. Since I served over here, I got a leg up and don't have to start as Columbus dog catcher."

Agnes leaned over the table and kissed Heinrich's cheek. "It sounds like the perfect opportunity for you. I wish you all the luck in the world. I hope you'll come visit me at the Sunrise."

"I'm sure I'll be campaigning down in Luna country a lot. And I'll be visiting my family from time to time. I promise to come see you." Heinrich's smile grew even bigger and his shoulders relaxed. Agnes realized that he was relieved that she wasn't angry at him for deserting her. She was happy to reassure him, and though she knew it was selfish, she wished for news that would give her the same comfort—for news of Will's whereabouts.

When the forward hospital closed, Agnes and Ethel escorted the last patients down the line in a better train than any they had ridden during the war. This train had special latches that held the gurneys in place, so the men rode as comfortably as if they were in hammocks. Agnes and Ethel sat side by side on a comfortably upholstered bench, each lost in her own thoughts as their shoulders bumped against each other with the sway of the tracks. They were often silent for long periods, but it was a companionable silence.

"Look." Ethel pointed at the sudden splashes of red as they passed a field, "Poppies. Must be spring."

Agnes shuddered. "In New Mexico, the poppies are golden, not blood red. I don't think I'll ever like the color red again."

The train rumbled past the place where their tent camp had been during the Meuse-Argonne offensive. Nothing remained but a barren field and the bombed out remains of the closest village. Agnes felt a hollow ache in her chest as she tapped the window. "That's where Sadie stayed. I guess the Spanish Flu cases cleared out faster. I hope she's doing well."

"Don't worry about Sadie," Ethel said. "She's got a lot of bounce to her, and she'll bounce back. Find a handsome blond Norwegian to marry and have a passel of kids to help around the farm. I'm going to visit her soon: stop in at home, then hit the road. I've seen enough war, but I haven't seen enough of the world yet."

The train pulled into Gare du Nord, Paris' northernmost station.

"This is where I get off, and you switch trains," Ethel said. "You sure you don't want to take a few days here with me before you go?"

Agnes shook her head. "No. You have a fun few days. Your ship leaves when?"

"Next Wednesday," Ethel said. "I still don't understand why you volunteered to go to Camp de Souge. You really want to be the person who blows out the last American light in France, don't you?"

Not knowing how to respond, Agnes shrugged. She felt far more empty and alone than she ever had in the wide-open spaces of New Mexico, but she wasn't ready to go home yet, not until she knew where Will was. She blinked back tears, embarrassed to be so emotional leaving someone she had known for such a short time, but that time had been so emotional that she felt a deep bond with Ethel.

They grabbed their valises and stepped down to the platform, where a couple of stewards waited with their trunks. "I hope we'll see each other again someday," Agnes said as she leaned in for a tight hug.

Ethel gave that sly wink that Agnes had grown so used to. "It'll be sooner than you suppose. I'm planning on coming out to your neck of the woods real soon."

"To visit me?" Agnes asked.

"To visit a Mr. Heinrich Dieter."

"Heinrich? My Heinrich?"

Ethel laughed and waggled her eyebrows. "Yes, that Heinrich. And he's not yours, though heaven knows he would have liked to be. That boy followed you around like a puppy."

Agnes felt her cheeks grow hot. "We have known each other since grade school."

"I like that boy. He's tall. Good looking. And a little gullible, even if he is smart. I think once he's smitten, a girl can get him to do anything for her. And he's got a future ahead of him. Just needs a good woman to manage him. I might just be the woman for the job."

Agnes was still laughing about the idea of Ethel leading Heinrich around like a puppy on a string two hours later, when her train pulled up to Camp de Souge. She climbed out, and the familiarity of the place made her heart ache. This was the camp where she and Sadie had started, the one where Mrs. Abrim had said they'd be pulling splinters from boys' hands, wiping runny noses, and making sure the boys wore dry socks, and it was the camp where Will first stayed. Agnes reached into her pocket and fingered the little wooden horse he had carved for her and blackened with boot polish as she remembered how he liked to keep busy. She was directing a group of soldiers to unload and deliver her trunk and equipment to the nurses' quarters when a carillon chimed a sweet chorus off in the distance. Will had talked of a little church down the road that marked the hours with its bells. Without thinking, Agnes walked out of camp, down the road in the direction of the sound.

She slipped into the tiny chapel and sat in the back pew, gazing around at the simple room. There were no stained-glass windows, no paintings. A small, dark crucifix hung behind the altar, but its features were lost in the gloom of the rainy spring afternoon. The walls were white-washed, just like the little, adobe chapel at the Sunrise Ranch. Agnes closed her eyes and tried to recall her father's voice as he preached in a space like this. It seemed so long ago. She remembered sitting between Sergeant Dobbs and Will, her alto harmonizing with Dobb's bass and Will's tenor. She had glanced over at Will's coffee with cream skin, his light brown hair curling in spite of the close crop of his haircut. His coloring had been so close to that of his khaki uniform that she remembered thinking he looked faded. Now her memory of him really was fading. She struggled to remember details, to bring into sharp focus the piercing clarity of his gaze, the sharpness of his jawline when he set it determinedly, how the tendons in his forearms looked like ropes when he tightened a fence. Every one of her memories was of him doing something, of being useful. She squeezed her eyes tighter together and tried to remember the scent of his skin, the subtle undertones of soap under the slight tang of sweat and horse. But the memories were fading. She could hardly recall the timber of his voice.

When she walked back to camp, Agnes found Theodora Abrim sitting on her cot, waiting for her. Mrs. Abrim looked up and studied Agnes' face. "You look tired. A shame you didn't take my advice about Paris."

Agnes shook her head. "There's been so much to do."

"But you can't fill other people's cups from an empty pitcher, dear. You need to take care of yourself."

Agnes sat down next to the head nurse. The springs in the old cot were worn, and the weight of the two women made the springs sag so they leaned together, shoulder to shoulder. Agnes was tempted to put her head on Theodora's shoulder.

"That soldier you were friends with; William Bowers. His name isn't among the identified dead. It's not among the wounded, either."

Agnes shook her head. "A man can't just disappear. He's got to be somewhere."

Theodora shifted, placing an arm around Agnes and drawing her in close. "Actually, they can. Many have disappeared in this war. Thousands of them. Hundreds of thousands. They've sunk into the mud, been buried in trench cave ins, hit by shells and blown to bits. We may never find Will, but I think you must accept the fact that he is dead. I know that is hard, but it is something you must do."

"But what do I do then?" Agnes said, the words coming out as something between a sob and a plea.

"Go on with life. Do the things you planned. Want to continue nursing? I have open positions back in the states. Some are even in your home state. If you want to continue working with soldiers, Fort Stanton and Fort Bayard both need nurses."

"Maybe later." Agnes sighed and looked at the ceiling of the ramshackle hut. It had been badly constructed the last time she roomed in it, and now it was downright derelict. She wished she had some of Ethel's buckets and wash pans in case it rained. "I first signed up for this war to earn money to buy a ranch. If there's no point in staying here, then maybe it's time to go home and see if I've earned enough for a down payment."

Head Nurse Theodora Abrim nodded solemnly. "I'm glad you have a plan. I'll write in your file that you were honorably released from service, with plans to return home and recuperate. And I will note that you should be brought back into service whenever you are ready."

Agnes nodded. It seemed like a logical plan, and it would keep her options open, even if what she really wanted seemed lost forever.

Chapter Twenty-four

Agnes shook her head. "A man can't just disappear. He's got to be somewhere." Her words echoed off the rocking train car walls, almost bringing her to the surface of her sleep. She was in a half world, where dreams mixed with reality as she dipped in and out of consciousness. In her dream, Theodora Abrim placed an arm around Agnes and drew her close. "Actually, they can. Men disappear. Thousands of them. Thousands. Thousands. We may never find Will. Accept the fact that he is dead."

The train whistle jerked Agnes awake. With the exception of when she'd been asleep, she had been staring out the window ever since the train left Penn station, yet she couldn't say what had passed. Whether waking or sleeping, Theodora Abrim's words filled the space behind Agnes' eyes, blocking everything else.

While the words replayed themselves in a constant loop of agony, gray, industrial cities gave way to woods and rolling hills, then hills to plains. She looked out the window, surprised that creosote, yucca, and ocotillo had replaced the slim green lances of wheat.

"Miss? Next stop, Columbus," the conductor said as he passed by. Agnes noticed the jagged blue line in the distance and recognized it as Florida Peak, the mountain that stood between Columbus and Deming. She was home. But where was Will?

She got up, stretching joints that had grown stiff with sitting, and pulled her satchel from the overhead rack. As the train slowed, Agnes spied Ernesto and Lupe sitting near the station in the gig carriage that was far too small for three people and baggage. Agnes smiled wanly. Diablo was with them. She closed her eyes, remembering what it felt like to have a good horse under her. She pushed away a memory of riding with Will. She wouldn't think of him now. She would concentrate on the here and now, on Lupe and Ernesto and those who remained here on this earth and loved her still.

The train pulled to a stop and Agnes disembarked, falling into Lupe's waiting embrace before the tears had a chance to fall.

"Oh, *mija. Te ves tan flaca.* Didn't they feed you over there in Europe?"

Agnes rested her head on Lupe's shoulder and breathed in the smells of fresh bread and cinnamon and the deep, warm smell of red chile. "Would you believe it? They never cook with chile. Don't even know what green chile is."

Lupe clucked her tongue. "Why would anyone ever go there if they don't know about chile? What's wrong with those people?" Agnes smiled and nodded in agreement. She let go of Lupe and turned to Ernesto, who might never have let her go except Diablo got jealous and forced his nose between the two of them. She hugged Diablo, then mounted while Ernesto helped Lupe into the gig and climbed in after her. With a cluck of the tongue and a flick of reins they were on their way home.

Lupe kept a steady prattle going the whole way home, and Agnes rode right alongside the gig so she could catch up on who had married, who had died, who had moved away and how many babies Doctor Pritchard had delivered in Agnes' absence. Agnes nodded on occasion, but the words flowed over her without sinking in. She forced her eyes to drink in the vast expanse stretched out before her, searching the horizon for the elusive antelopes while trying not to remember Will pointing them out to her on a day long ago. A buzzard hovered in the cloudless blue sky. She studied how its wings rocked and twitched. Staying aloft took work. A fat horny toad lumbered out of the road. Agnes was tempted to climb down off Diablo's back to greet it, to connect with the little things to keep the big ones from pressing in on her. They passed stands of Mexican poppies, their faces more golden than butter. She grinned and pointed at them.

"In France, the poppies are blood red, not golden," she said, interrupting Lupe. "And it rains. All. the. time. Not just during monsoon season."

"More things they got wrong," Lupe said. "No chile. No enchiladas. Red poppies, and rain."

Agnes pointed to a meadowlark who puffed out his pale-yellow chest and sang, as if she had requested it. "Even their larks sing a different song than ours. They look different, too. Ours are prettier."

"Of course, they are," Ernesto said with the confidence of one who had never lived elsewhere. They entered the Sunrise Ranch compound, passing the chapel and the main house, whose drawn curtains made it look as if it were still in mourning for John Day. The memory of Will helping hang black bunting flashed through her mind and Agnes pushed it away and studied the barn and staples. Without the cows and horses, the structures looked desolate. No harmonica music or arguments came from the silent bunkhouse.

Agnes told herself that it had been this empty when she left. Ever since her mother moved to Las Vegas, the Sunrise Ranch had been an empty shell instead of the busy operation it had been when her father was alive. Yet, it was Will's absence that deadened the place now. She looked out at the small plot ringed by a white picket fence which had five fine, granite stones and wondered if she could add a sixth, even if there was no body to lay to rest under it.

"Would you mind if I paid Father a visit?" Agnes watched Ernesto and Lupe glance at each other. Each smiled the same, stiff smile.

"Go ahead, mija," Lupe said in a very quiet voice.

Agnes dismounted at the fence, leaving Diablo to trim the grass that grew green and lush against the pickets. Her father's grave was covered with marigolds that glowed like fire, filling the air with their earthy, sharp scent. His new gravestone listed his full name, birth and death dates, and the fact that he was the beloved husband of Mildred. Agnes dug through her handbag, found a franc, and placed it atop the stone.

When she arrived at the ranch manager's house, where Ernesto and Lupe lived, Ernesto was hauling Agnes' trunk up to her room. She took Diablo back to the stables and put out water and feed. Ernesto had not wanted her doing such things, but Agnes had argued that it was soothing to be working with her hands again. When she was done, she went up to her room and washed her face and hands using the pitcher and basin. She looked at her old dungarees and denim shirts, but they had grown strange and foreign to her. It had been a long time since she'd worn such things. She set the little black horse that Will had carved on her dresser, next to the jar of Peredixo cream that her sister had given her a lifetime ago, then changed into one of the light cotton dresses that she had left behind and went down for dinner.

"So, what are you going to do now, *mija*?" Lupe asked when she had stuffed Agnes full of tortillas, enchiladas and beans and they were sitting on the front porch, drinking coffee. A plate of *biscochitos* perched precariously on the porch railing, perfuming the air with the comforting scent of cinnamon.

Agnes sighed. It was a question she'd been asking herself. The shadow of the earth, a curved arc of inky lavender, crept up the peach-colored east. Agnes pushed back the memory of seeing a similar sky once, long ago, with Will. Somewhere downrange a meadowlark sang out its optimism. She tried to breathe in the sound, to let it fill the empty spaces in her heart. The sky darkened and filled with more stars than she had ever seen in France. Soon, she would have to rebuild her life. For now, it was good enough just to be home again with Ernesto and Lupe, to be fed and coddled and allowed to heal.

"I am tired, Lupe. I want to sleep for a week, and ride the range, and eat your good food."

"*Bueno, mija*. We want to fatten you up and get rid of those black rings under your eyes before Will comes back. We don't want him seeing you like this." Lupe reached out and patted Agnes' arm. When Agnes didn't respond she stopped. Her hand rested, warm and motherly, but to Agnes the touch burned. She watched Lupe and Ernesto's lips tighten, and the whites of their eyes flash as they looked at each other in the gathering gloom. It made Agnes' stomach clench.

"Mija?" Enesto asked. The word hung in the air, a reminder that these two weren't just the caretaker and cook of the Sunrise.

Agnes sucked in a ragged breath and held it, gathering strength. She pulled back her arm and grasped Lupe's hand tightly in hers. "Will won't be coming back, Lupe."

"Mija." Enesto said the word again, but this time it wasn't a question but a statement telling her that, whatever came next, they were there for her. Agnes took another deep breath and continued. They deserved to know. They loved him too.

"He's gone, Lupe. Disappeared in the middle of the last battle. They never even found his body."

"No." Lupe's hand tightened its grip, resolve flowing through her fingers. "Men, they do not disappear. If they haven't found a body, he's out there somewhere."

Agnes shook her head. "Men do disappear, especially in war. I'm told there are hundreds of thousands who did."

"The war, it has given him *bruma de amnesia,*" Lupe said. "He is in a hospital somewhere. When he remembers, he will come back to us."

Agnes nodded, hoping against hope that Lupe was right. She seemed so sure of herself. She wished that she, too, suffered from *la bruma de amnesia,* the fog of amnesia. She didn't want to remember anything right now. Memories hurt. But she couldn't stop remembering, and neither could Lupe or Ernesto. She was not sure who started crying first, the tears seeping out quietly, but the three huddled together, holding each other tightly as the tears came hard and fast and they wailed their outrage and their sorrow into a placid sky that absorbed it in its silence.

When they had all cried themselves out, Agnes excused herself and went back to her room. She pulled out the flower vase that Will had made out of the shell casing and placed it on her dresser next to the horse, turning it until the side that showed the two of them riding their horses faced the wall and all she could see were the pronghorns. She needed to get used to a future without Will by her side. She crawled into bed. Her body buzzed with exhaustion, but she could not sleep. Her mind felt numbed, and she wondered now if she would ever feel anything again. She told herself that Theodora Abrim was right, that she had to go on with life and do the things she had planned. Mrs. Abrim had said that she had open positions back in the states, some as close as Fort Bayard. She told herself that she would check in with L.B. Fowler and find out how much money she needed in order to buy the Sunrise. If she hadn't yet saved enough, she would continue on to the military hospital at Fort Bayard and offer them her services.

Agnes rose before the sun. She hadn't slept much but, hoping that it would make her feel more like herself again, stepped into her dungarees, slipped on a denim shirt and pocket vest, tied a bandana around her neck and stuck her Stetson on her head. If she couldn't feel like a strong cowboy, she could at least look like one.

She tiptoed down the stairs and found her old boots, cleaned and oiled, standing by the back door. She saddled Diablo and rode out to ride fence. She found a few places where the barbed wire had come loose, and she tacked it up even though there were no cattle to fence in. It felt good to be useful. As her own muscles flexed, Agnes thought of watching the lean, ropy muscles in Will's arms. She rode past the old bog and remembered Will wading out of it, covered in mud. Memories littered the ground wherever she rode. She picked each up, rolled it around her mind like a satisfyingly heavy stone in her palm, then tossed it aside to pick up another one. She wished the trail of memories could lead directly to Will.

As she rode in at lunch time, Agnes heard someone plinking on the piano. For a split second her spirits rose as she remembered the evening when she'd come home from working at the refugee camp and found Will at the piano. But this wasn't Will. Whoever was playing really was just plinking randomly at the keys, and no tune emerged. Agnes walked in to find Lupe on the piano bench. Lupe looked up, tears streaming down her face.

"I miss him so much, *mija*! I just can't believe he is dead. *Mi corazon*, it says no."

Agnes wrapped her arms around Lupe's shoulders. "I know. My heart doesn't want to believe, either."

"You are hungry, no? I will make you *huevos.* Ernesto! Agnes *esta aqui.*" Lupe fluttered about the kitchen so distractedly that Agnes knew something was bothering her. She hung up her hat and kicked off her boots, then sat down at the table and waited to find out what it was. A moment later, Ernesto entered the room. He somberly held out an envelope.

"A telegram?" Agnes felt her empty stomach flip. Was it about Will? From Will? She had heard many stories of families getting 'the telegram.' It was always bad news. Agnes dropped heavily into a kitchen chair, her heart pounding in her ears.

"It came this morning," Ernesto said as he handed it to her. Agnes opened it with trembling fingers. She read it silently, then let out a sigh.

"It's from L.B. Fowler, the lawyer in Silver City. He heard I was back and wants me to go up there and discuss business. He wants to send that weaselly law clerk, Mr. Howard, down in his Oldsmobile to get me." Agnes set the telegram on the table. "I'd planned to go up soon, but not this soon. I hope he hasn't gotten an offer and wants me to sign the papers since I'm the closest family member."

"No, mija. It is too soon. You need time to rest, and to mourn. I will ride back into town to send a reply." Ernesto asked.

Agnes shook her head. "I might as well get this over with. One thing's for certain; I'm not going to spend two whole days sitting next to the smarmy Mr. Howard. I'll pack up Diablo and ride up on my own."

Afraid of the bad news she might hear, Agnes took her time riding the eighty miles to Silver City. She spent a night in a Deming hotel that advertised big bathtubs and steak dinners, and she indulged in both as she steeled herself for whatever would happen in Silver City. She thought about her situation. In just a few years, she had lost first her father and then her love and endured the hardship and horror of war. If she now lost the Sunrise, what would become of her? Would she go back to Fort Bayard, as Mrs. Abrim had suggested? To Las Vegas, where her mother now lived with her sister Maude? Or would she leave New Mexico entirely and try to start a new life elsewhere?

By the time Agnes arrived at the tall house with mustard yellow shingles that was her attorney's office, she had convinced herself that her best course of action was to be strong and refuse to accept a negative outcome. She was not going to sign away all her hopes and dreams. If Mr. Fowler told her the ranch had sold, she would make a higher offer. She was not going to let the ranch be wrested from her.

Agnes rang the bell and the same maid in white cap and apron opened it as had the first time Agnes had come. This time, she recognized Agnes. Even though Agnes was dusty and trail worn, she didn't suggest she go around back for a handout. The maid opened the French doors into the office, where Agnes found Arthur Howard, Mr. Fowler's clerk, sitting behind a large pile of papers at the little desk that sat framed by the crimson velvet curtains of the bow window. He looked up, did a double take, then toppled his chair as he scrambled to his feet.

"Miss Day! What a pleasant surprise! We were expecting a telegram . . . "

Agnes held up her hand to stop the flow of words. "I decided neither a telegram nor your chauffeuring services were necessary. What I would like," she said, turning to the maid, 'is a large glass of water. My throat is as dusty as these dungarees." She slapped her Stetson against her leg, throwing up a cloud of trail dust.

The maid gave a quick curtsy and left the room. Agnes watched the clerk right his chair, then run his palms over his slicked-back hair, his little mustache twitching beneath his pointy nose. "Well, if you're sure," he said.

"That I'm thirsty?"

"That my services weren't needed," he said quickly.

Agnes smiled, willing to let him stew in his own juices. L.B. Fowler opened the French doors and stepped back to let the maid bring in a tray that held glasses of water and a plate of Mrs. Fowler's cookies. He wore the same old rumpled suit and string tie, but had less gray fringe on his bald pate and even more in his ears than the last time Agnes had seen him. His limp, the result of an old, Civil War wound, was even more pronounced.

The old lawyer smiled rather jovially as he offered Agnes a seat, then slid behind his enormous desk and sat down. "Miss Day, let me get right to the point of why I asked you here."

Agnes nodded. "I am a bit peeved you made me come all the way up here instead of coming to me, but since I'm here, we might as well get down to business. Mr. Fowler, whatever offer you've been given, I am prepared to beat it. How much money do I need to put down?"

Fowler frowned thoughtfully. "Rest assured, I have good reason for asking you to come here rather than me go to you. As to a down payment, none will be required." He adjusted his spectacles, then picked up a stack of papers.

"None?" Agnes parroted, confused, "It may take me some time to get the money together, but I am determined to keep the Ranch. Now, how much must I put down?"

"There is no need for a down payment. The Sunrise has been paid for, in full, in cash."

Agnes felt her world spinning. "Do you mean it's a done deal? There's nothing I can do to change it?"

"Nothing. The paperwork's all prepared and everything is in order. Now, if you will sign here." He turned the paper, jabbing his finger at a line on the bottom of the page, then slid his inkstand and pen toward her and folded his hands into a neat pyramid.

"No. I won't sign. You can't make me." Agnes pressed her lips tightly together to keep herself from sobbing. She had been so confident that she could buy the Sunrise. She had worked so hard to come up with the money. Now, here at the last moment, someone else had beat her to it. Signing this paper felt like signing her own death warrant.

Mr. Fowler frowned at her. "I don't understand why you wouldn't. Of course, I can't make you, but I advise you to do so. As your lawyer, and as a friend of your family."

Agnes thought about how angry her mother and her sisters would be if she didn't sign and they didn't get the money they were expecting from this sale. What good was money to her? Everything she had ever hoped for had been denied her. But what could she do? The Ranch was sold. She could no more change that than she could bring Will back from the dead. For the sake of her sisters and her mother, Agnes dipped the pen in the inkwell, signed the document, then got to her feet in a desperate attempt to leave the room before she burst into tears.

"Wait until the ink is dry and you can take it with you," Mr. Fowler said.

Agnes stopped, her hand on the doorknob. "Shouldn't the deed go to the new owner?"

L.B. Fowler and his clerk looked at each other before bursting into laughter. "Miss Day, what do you think you just signed?"

Agnes looked between the two men and a spark of hope flared in the ashes of her dreams. Had she misunderstood the whole situation?

"I assumed, since I am the closest to Silver City, that I was acting on behalf of the family in deeding over the property to the new owner. The one who paid cash for the Sunrise."

"Miss Day, the one who paid cash is not the new owner of the Sunrise. You are the new owner."

Agnes looked from one smiling face to the other and felt like she was the butt of a joke that she still didn't understand. "I'm what?" she said in a quavering voice.

"The new owner. The buyer deeded the property over to you. As your lawyer, I advise you to always read paperwork before you sign. This time all is well. Next time, you may not be so fortunate."

Had Arthur Howard not leapt from his chair, knocking it over for the second time that day, Agnes would have collapsed in a heap. He led her back to her chair and helped her into it, then handed her a second glass of water. "I don't understand."

"You've made that imminently clear!" Mr. Fowler broke into a smile that was so broad that it framed itself in wrinkles. "I'm sorry to have caused you such emotional distress by keeping you in the dark. I admit, it wasn't a very nice thing to do. Another party has bought the Sunrise Ranch, paying for it completely with cash. This party then deeded it to you. You have signed the said deed. The property is now yours, free and clear."

"Who did this?" Agnes asked. Her heart was beating *Will, Will, Will,* but how could that be?

"I'm afraid I am not at liberty to disclose that." The twinkle in his eye told her that he knew and considered it amusing. Agnes felt her heart flutter within her chest as the spark of hope flared, twig by hopeful twig.

"But . . . "Agnes began. The attorney put up a hand, stalling her.

"We cannot sit here and play a guessing game. I gave my client my word that I would not disclose his - or her - identity, except under certain conditions, and I am duty bound to keep that promise. Attorney/client privilege, after all."

"What conditions?" Agnes asked. "What do I have to do to find out who did this?"

Mr. Fowler cut her off with a wave of his hand. "We can talk about that later. For now, I suggest we go out to the Palace Hotel and celebrate with a good steak dinner. I think Mrs. Fowler would appreciate that as much as I would. Mr. Howard, do you care to join us?"

The four dined on a salad made with grapefruit and orange slices topped with pimento, followed by sirloin steaks and baked potatoes with cream sauce and several bottles of champagne. Several diners from other tables came over to welcome Agnes back, and when they heard the news, to congratulate her on keeping the ranch. People in Silver City had highly respected John Day and were happy to see the family continuing to work the ranch.

Throughout dinner, Agnes brooded on who might have bought an entire ranch just to give it away. Her heart kept coming back to Will, but it couldn't be him. Will was dead. If he was alive, he would have contacted her. Besides, Will was just a private, and no private earned enough money to pay cash for an entire ranch, even one who got extra pay for being a crack shot and did extra jobs on the side.

Fowler's use of the words *him or her* to refer to her benefactor whirled about in her head. "Did my mother deed the ranch to me? Maybe she realized her mistake in denying me the ranch in the first place? Or she just couldn't get a good price for it and didn't want to admit it was worth less than she'd thought?"

Fowler smiled and patted his pockets. He brought out a fat cigar, but his wife clucked her tongue and he sighed and tucked it away. "Do you think Mildred Day is the kind of woman who would do something of this magnitude and not take credit?"

"Your mother does like to be in the limelight," Mrs. Fowler added.

"And I assure you, she got a good price for it," Fowler said.

Agnes went back to sawing at her steak. It was tender enough that she didn't need to do so, but she was too distracted to notice. *Will, Will, Will,* her heart throbbed, but she ignored it. Suddenly she set down her knife and fork. "Was it Doctor Pritchard? He has no family. Has he decided to make me his heir?"

Mr. Fowler chuckled. "I know Doctor Pritchard thought you made a good assistant, but he's not mentioned adopting you."

Agnes stirred the shredded steak around on her plate before stabbing a piece and chewing on it contemplatively. "Mr. Dieter? In gratitude for my watching after Heinrich in France?"

"No, Florence Nightingale. It wasn't Mr. Dieter," Arthur Howard, Mr. Fowler's clerk said with a smile that looked a little too smug for Agnes' taste.

"Then who?" Agnes asked, throwing up her hands.

"Whom, dear, and we cannot answer that," Mrs. Fowler said, smiling sweetly but a little sadly.

For dessert, Fowler ordered *glaces de fantaisie,* which turned out to be nothing more than chocolate, vanilla and strawberry ice cream frozen hard and cut into little squares.

"I thought, after eating in France, that your tastes would have turned to the gourmet," Fowler said with a chuckle when he noticed the relief on Agnes' face as the ice cream was served.

"I ate army fare over there," Agnes responded. "It's no better than chuckwagon grub. Sometimes far worse. You can take a girl off the ranch, but you can't take the ranch out of the girl."

"True. The Sunrise really is where you belong." Fowler sat back and smiled, obviously delighted by both the meal and the transaction he had been a part of.

Agnes dabbed at her mouth with a napkin, then set it back in her lap. "And it's really mine? I own the Sunrise free and clear? I owe nothing?"

"It's really yours. You're still responsible for yearly taxes. Mr. Howard, here, will make sure they're taken care of for you. He's going to take over my practice, you know. It's time for this old dog to retire and spend some time with my better half. We're planning on going back to some of the old battlegrounds so I can tell Mrs. Fowler exaggerated tales of my bravery as a young soldier." The attorney reached out and took his wife's hand. They smiled at each other so sweetly that it made Agnes' heart ache. She imagined sitting with Will on the front porch of the main house, their hair frosted silver and their cheeks as weathered as old saddle leather. He wouldn't have told exaggerated tales. He probably wouldn't have told any tales at all. Still, she couldn't imagine sitting there with anyone else.

When their meal was finished, Mrs. and Mrs. Fowler walked Agnes back to the house that was both their office and their home. This time Mrs. Fowler didn't have to loan Agnes a nightgown; she had packed one and her toiletries in her saddle bag. Before she tucked herself into the pillowy-soft four poster bed, Agnes drew a bath for herself in the large, clawfoot tub that dominated the bathroom. She sunk down into the steaming water, her muscles relaxing. Agnes closed her eyes and thought about what an emotional day it had been. Since her father's death, Agnes had focused on buying the Sunrise Ranch. She had pursued a career and gone to distant battlefields in order to achieve that goal. She had ridden to Silver City intent on closing the deal, only to think that she had lost the ranch forever, then discover that it was already hers. She had achieved her goal. But was it enough, now that she had no one with which to share it?

Chapter Twenty-Five

Agnes woke up to a room that seemed to sparkle magically. She squinted her eyes against the bright sunshine that bounced off a birdbath in the Fowler's back yard, sending beams through the lacy curtains to cast dancing patterns on the ceiling. It was all too beautiful, and it made the pain in her head more intense. She lay back with her eyes closed and listened to the bustle on the street. She couldn't remember when she had slept past dawn, nor could she remember ever having a headache this sharp. She vowed to never drink champagne again.

She tiptoed down the stairs, clutching the railing with trembling hands. A little coffee would put her world to rights. She found Mr. and Mrs. Fowler lounging in the dining room, he hidden behind a wall of newspaper, and she looking out the window at her garden while absentmindedly swirling a spoon through her coffee. Mrs. Fowler's head turned as Agnes came in. She let go of her spoon and rose.

"There you are! Mr. Fowler thought you might be an early riser, but you slept in! Here, would you like coffee? Cream? I trust you slept well." She beckoned to a chair at a place that had already been set with a lovely, floral-patterned china and silver cutlery, and while Agnes seated herself, Mrs. Fowler poured coffee and moved a basket of muffins closer to her guest.

"I slept very well, thank you," Agnes lied. "I hope I haven't kept you waiting."

Mrs. Fowler waved her hand. "Nonsense. We usually aren't up this early ourselves, but Mr. Fowler thought you'd like to get an early start this morning. Bacon? Eggs?"

"Yes, I believe I would," Agnes answered as she unfurled her napkin, set it in her lap and took a plate of bacon from her hostess.

"How would you like them?" Mrs. Fowler asked, one hand beckoning the maid in.

"What?"

"The eggs, dear. How would you like your eggs?"

"Oh! Scrambled would be fine, thank you." Agnes laughed as the maid left with the order, then brought her hand up to her aching head. "I thought you were talking about when I should leave."

"Well, that, too. I did ask an awful lot of you all at once." Mrs. Fowler sat down and smiled at Agnes. She was a match for her husband, her clothes neat and clean, but rather old fashioned, her gray hair up in a tight bun. Agnes thought Isobel Chriswell would look like this in another quarter century, but never in a million years be this gracious or kind. "Tell me, my dear. Do you have any plans for the day?"

"I don't, really." Agnes picked up her teacup, but her hands were shaking so that the cup rattled. She quickly set it down and placed her hands in her lap. "Everything has changed. I have to wrap my head around owning the ranch."

The attorney looked over the top of his paper at her, frowning. He folded the paper and set it aside. "I'm sure you're quite happy. It's something you've wanted for a long time," he said gravely.

Agnes sat back and considered. She had gone halfway around the world and endured a war to get it. Yet the Sunrise didn't feel like home anymore. The ranch felt lonely, and she felt alone on it. "I know I should be ecstatic. But all I feel is tired."

"That's not unusual at the end of a quest," the lawyer said. "You have been through quite an ordeal."

Mrs. Fowler leaned forward in her chair and stared intently into Agnes' eyes. "Sometimes there's a difference between what you want and what you need. You wanted the ranch. Now that you have it, is something missing?"

Agnes nodded. "I was determined to stay single because every marriage I'd ever seen had taken the woman away from the place she loved. Mother had to leave Las Vegas. Lupe left Mexico. My sisters gave up all their own hopes and dreams to support their ambitious husbands. But then I met a man who loved the same place that I did. I thought we would share the Sunrise, and a life. Every day for the rest of my life I will ride the range and wish that he was there with me.

Mrs. Fowler picked up her napkin and began dabbing at her eyes. The old lawyer looked at his wife and smiled. "Miss Day, do you remember me saying that I had my reasons for asking you to come here rather than me driving down to Columbus? It was to get you closer to Fort Bayard. But before you go, allow me to give you both a warning and a hope. Physical prowess means a great deal to a young man. Having it taken can shake him to the depths of his being. It is a hard thing from which to recuperate. The patience and soft touch of a good woman, though, is a powerful salve."

Mr. Fowler's hand moved to his leg and massaged it as if his old war wound ached, even after all these years. He glanced at Mrs. Fowler, and Agnes recognized not just love, but patience and forgiveness pass between the two. It made her heart ache so much that she had to look away.

Diablo snorted and threw his head as Agnes pulled back on the reins yet again. She'd been alternately galloping and walking the whole six miles between Silver City and Fort Bayard, pushing Diablo hard, then reigning him in.

Her heart had been doing the same thing.

Although the old attorney hadn't given her a name, Agnes' heart was sure that it was Will who was at Fort Bayard, and that he had somehow paid for the Sunrise. In the moments that she thought Will was a miracle, a Lazarus come back from the dead, she raced forward, intent on throwing herself into his arms. Then a feeling of dread would overcome her and she'd pull back on the reins. Questions strung themselves across her path like a barbed wire, cutting her off from her happiness. Why had he left her to think him dead for so long? Why hadn't he contacted her? She slowed to a walk, pondering as her heart pounded.

Agnes had seen enough injured men to know that Will would only be at the Fort if he was badly hurt. Was he missing an arm? A leg? Had his lungs been compromised? His face disfigured? Did he, once again, think he wasn't good enough for her because of whatever disability he'd obtained? He had been so sure that his parentage and his upbringing would dissuade her from loving him. Did he now think an injury would?

Her mind drifted back to the food poisoning incident on the trip to France, when she found Will curled up in a ball, his face towards the wall and his sheet pulled over his head as if he was hiding from the world. He had hated her seeing him that way, had called himself helpless, weak, and useless. She imagined how powerless and helpless he must feel now, and spurred Diablo on. As the land climbed slowly through pinon and juniper, sloping gradually toward the jagged blue line of the Pinos Altos Range, she tried to quell her hope and prepare herself for the worst.

The ground glowed with white evening primrose, yellow desert marigold, fleabane daisies, blue flax and scorpion weed, but it was the poppies, nodding at her like little candle flames, that made her heart soar. She crossed a creek and cut through the fruit orchard, anxious to find Will. Agnes trotted Diablo across the parade ground and tied him to one of the piers that supported the sanatorium's administration building's porch. Edna Gilbert, the competent young receptionist with the finger curls looked up when Agnes threw open the door and rushed into the office.

"Agnes Day! It's been, what? A year? How was France? You looking to get your old position back? We could use you!"

Agnes put up her hand to ward off the questions. "Actually, I'm here to visit one of your patients. Do you know where . . . "Agnes' voice trailed off as she caught the faint sound of a piano. Someone was playing *The Girl I Left*

Behind Me in a minor key, and so slowly that what should have been a march sounded like a dirge.

Edna jerked her chin toward the door. "The day room, first building over. You remember that patients could use the piano there, if they felt well enough. Private Bowers, he talks about you all the time. Well, actually, only in his sleep, and it isn't talk so much as ravings and mumblings. He hardly talks at all when he's awake. Just plays the piano and stares off into space."

Drawn by the music, Agnes left the administration building and crossed to the first ward. The pianist had finished *The Girl I Left Behind Me* and moved on to *After You've Gone,* which sounded even sadder and more wistful. The words played in Agnes' head as she climbed the steps.

Now won't you listen honey, while I say,
How could you tell me that you're goin' away?
Don't say that we must part,
Don't break your baby's heart
You know I've loved you for these many years
Love you night and day,
Oh, honey baby, can't you see my tears?
Listen while I say
After you've gone and left me cryin'
After you've gone there's no denyin'
You'll feel blue, you'll feel sad
You'll miss the dearest pal you've ever had?

Agnes clung to the doorjamb of the day room. The man at the piano had his back to her, but she knew those shoulders, and the short-cropped, curly hair the color of coffee with cream. Even if she couldn't see his face, Agnes knew it was Will.

Will's fingers moved over the keys, creating a dreamy, soft progression that she thought he was making up as he went along. Silently she moved across the floor until she stood behind him, watching his fingers. They stopped, frozen on the keys.

"Why are you always sneaking up on me?" he asked without looking around.

"Me? Sneaking up on you? It's always been the other way around. How did you know it was me?" she asked.

He sat rigid on the piano bench, his back to her. "You smell of fresh air and sunshine, horses, and a sweetness that I was afraid I'd never smell again."

"All you had to do is let me know where you were. I would have been there in a moment. I thought you were dead."

"I thought I was, too. Then I wished I was. But here I am. What's left of me, anyway."

"What do you mean, what's left of you?" Agnes slipped onto the piano bench next to him. He looked whole: two arms, two legs, his face intact. Will turned his head. His eyes did not focus on hers.

"That night." Will took a deep breath, as if trying to steady himself. "You hadn't been gone long when the shelling began. I'd moved away from the gun, trying to watch you. I wanted to make sure you made it back to camp safely. We suffered a direct hit. Direct. Men lay in pieces. But not everyone was dead. Some were horribly mangled. Screaming. Crying. Groaning. I should have been dead, but I was fine. Because I wasn't where I should have been."

Will's shoulders began to shake. His voice broke. Agnes put a hand on his knee to comfort him. "It's all right," she murmured.

"No, it isn't. I rushed around, went from man to man, trying to help. Honest, I was trying. But what can one man do with so much gore?

"And then the gas came. I got my mask on, but not in time to save my eyes."

Agnes blinked. That was why he was not focusing on her. It was the same reason he hadn't seen Diablo outside the window, and why he hadn't turned to look at her. Will was blind.

"Is it permanent? A lot of my soldiers came in blind, but recovered."

"They say I might get my sight back," Will said. "Sometimes it takes six months. I've got another month before they count me hopeless."

"It's never hopeless. Never," Agnes leaned into Will's warm side. He shifted and put an arm around her, burying his nose in her hair, breathing her in her fragrance.

"I couldn't help anyone, not blind like that. And in pain. Burning pain. So, I left. I thought I was walking towards you. I wanted to make it to the hospital. I must have been walking the other way. It's easy to get turned around in chaos. I walked and walked. Shells burst all around me. I know that because I felt the earth rumble and roil. Dirt showered me. Blast waves knocked me down. But I had to get to you, so I kept getting up. Kept walking. Until I couldn't anymore."

Will reached down and massaged his thigh and Agnes had a sudden recollection of Mr. Fowler doing the same thing at the breakfast table. "Shrapnel. Here. The pain was so intense it knocked me out. When I came to, I lay there and tried to think of you. My blinded eyes saw my buddies at the guns, I heard their screams. Maybe it was the screams of others. I don't know. But I decided that I couldn't just lie there and listen. I started crawling, dragging this leg."

Agnes twisted to free her arms, then wrapped them around Will, burying her face in his chest. He felt so strong, even now.

"I was still trying to crawl to you when a French patrol found me. They brought me into a French field station. I was moved down their medical line. The Americans didn't even know my whereabouts until I showed up in a Parisian hospital in mid January."

"That explains why I couldn't find news of you," Agnes said, "but it doesn't explain why you didn't write."

Will nodded. "On the ship, I contracted pneumonia. They said I was going to die. By then, I wanted to. But I didn't die, and here I am. I am too damaged to be useful. I don't want you to marry me out of sympathy. You shouldn't have to settle for a man who can't do everything the ranch needs."

"You don't strike me as a pity case, even if you're having your own pity party right now. Will Bowers, you're not half as terrible as you think you are."

"There are going to be a lot of women who'll resent the men they used to love now that they have to nurse them."

"You won't let me nurse you," Agnes said. "I learned that when you had food poisoning."

Will shifted. "I'm getting stiff. Can we go for a walk, maybe?"

"I know someone who'd be happy to see you." Agnes slipped off the bench, then took his hand and led him out into the sunshine.

Will tilted his head back, basking in the warmth. "I see some blue, I think. It's not all as black as it used to be. Still, it's anyone's guess how much will come back. I'm not the man I used to be."

"You're still Will," Agnes said. She squeezed his hand and together they negotiated the stairs.

"Who's with you?" Will asked. "Lupe? Ernesto?"

But Agnes didn't have time to answer. Diablo had seen them coming and nickered a greeting as he pulled against the reins that held him in place. When Will was close enough, Diablo leaned his cheek against Will's face, nibbling his ear.

"He's missed you," Agnes said. "Want to ride? You can trust Diablo."

Agnes watched Will's face soften, his emotions surge. She helped him into the saddle, then sat on the steps and watched him trot off, sitting tall and riding smoothly. They rounded the building and disappeared, and Agnes smiled, remembering the feeling of getting back in the saddle after too long away. Diablo and Will appeared at the other end of the building and cantered across the parade grounds. Will's face glowed with joy.

"Thank you," he said. "That was the best medicine I've had in a long time. But you know what would feel even better? Riding like we did the day we pulled that cow from the bog." He slipped back over the cantle and pulled his feet from the stirrups so Agnes could climb into the saddle, but this time, Will didn't hold himself stiffly behind her. Instead, he wrapped his arms around her waist and they took off at a gallop towards the old shooting range north of the complex. She felt the assuredness of his body and knew that he didn't need to hold onto her. He could ride at a gallop without the benefit of saddle and stirrups. Even without the benefit of sight.

Despite all that life had thrown at him, he remained strong and competent in his core. They slowed to a walk and Agnes turned Diablo so she could look back down the slope. Up here, the Fort was just a collection of small boxes set among green lines. A hawk circled overhead. The wind rustled through the grasses. Agnes and Will dismounted, and Diablo wandered off, cropping the green spring grass.

"The first time I asked you to marry me, you refused. The second time, you said you couldn't because you might lose your job, and then you wouldn't be able to get the Sunrise, but I talked you into it anyway. It's yours now, free and clear, with no strings attached. Your future is secure."

"How *did* you buy the Sunrise?" Agnes asked. "Privates don't make that kind of money, even if they take every extra odd-job that comes their way."

"It was your idea," Will said. "You told me to check on my mother when I returned stateside. When the ship's doctor said I was dying, he asked who they should contact. I told him to notify her, even though I doubted the last address I had would work. To my surprise, she wrote back to me at Walter Reed, where they put me once the ship landed.

"Turns out, I didn't kill my father. All I'd managed was to give him a good headache. A jealous husband shot him five years later. My mother used her half of the money from my father's life insurance policy to buy the house. She shut down the business, but some of the former ladies, the ones who had no place else to go, stayed on. They created a woman's sanctuary, of sorts. They make pottery, weave shawls, are fabulously happy, and won't let a man on the place. She'd put my half of the insurance aside, hoping to hear from me someday. I used it to buy the ranch.

Will continued. "My future, however, is uncertain. I might never be able to do the things around the Sunrise that need doing, and I wanted you to be able to go on with your life without me if you chose to. But now I know I will never have to abandon you. The law is never going to come looking for me. I am a free man."

"Sounds like a fresh start for both of us." Agnes said in the most serious tone she could muster. Even though she knew he couldn't see it, Agnes tried to hold back the smile that threatened to make her voice sound lighter and happier than she wanted it to sound. She hadn't had anyone to kid in a long time, and kidding Will was fun, especially when she was sure of the outcome. "Let's get down to business. Now that I own a ranch, I'll need a manager. He must know a lot about a lot of things: roofing, construction, motor maintenance, cattle, how to pull bog.

"What if he knows how to do those things but can't actually do them anymore?"

Agnes shrugged. "The war is over. There'll be a lot of young bucks looking for jobs. I can hire a few to do the actual work as long as my manager is experienced, knowledgeable, and has a level head."

Will smiled. "I've got that. Think I should apply for the job?"

"No, I don't," Agnes said and smiled as Will sagged a bit before she added, "I've got another job I think I'd rather see you take."

Will cocked his head. "And what's that?"

"Do you remember the first time you met me?" Agnes asked.

"Like it was yesterday," Will said.

"You know the reason you were invited, don't you? My mother was looking for marriage prospects for me, and I was determined to stay single. I'd seen what happened to women who married. Their desires, their hopes, their dreams all became subservient to those of their husbands. I didn't want that. I've changed my mind on the marriage issue, though. I've decided that I do want a husband, but one who shares my interests and isn't bothered if I have an active part in running the ranch. I want a man who loves the land as much as I do, one who won't make me give up my dreams for his. He has to be level headed, a good dancer, a better kisser, and he has to smell like sunshine, horses, and hard work. That's the position I think you should apply for."

Will crossed his arms over his chest and frowned, but Agnes could see that he was enjoying himself as much as she was. "I've already asked you twice. The second time you even made me go down on one knee."

"You know what they say: third time's a charm. Besides, as you've said yourself, conditions have changed. I'm a free woman now, and a landowner.

If I'm going to accept, I want to accept you under the present conditions, so you know I really mean it."

Will rolled his eyes. "You wouldn't let me kneel in a cow patty, would you?"

Agnes looked down. "All clear, Romeo."

He got down on one knee and turned his face up towards her, his vacant eyes drilling into her soul. "Miss Day, I've been running from my past and running towards conflagrations for far too long. The only fire I want to kindle now is the one between us. I've never felt good enough for you, but I promise to spend the rest of my life working hard at making you happy. Will you marry me?"

Agnes had planned to tease Will some more, but his words and the look on his face were far too earnest. She found herself overwhelmed with emotion that clogged her throat. Agnes took his hand and felt its warmth and strength. "Yes," she whispered, and hoped that she could make him as happy as he had made her.

Chapter Twenty-Six

Agnes rubbed the last of the Peredixio cream into her face and slapped her cheeks until they glowed. She trailed her hand lovingly along the mirror's frame, remembering a lifetime of sitting before it, brushing the knots out of her hair. It had been a long time since she'd been in her bedroom in the old house. Returning felt comforting.

When she was sure she was ready, Agnes picked up the bouquet of yellow and red crepe-paper poppies and came down the stairs, stopping a couple of times to pound her heels on the stairs. The low, ribbon-tied pumps she wore were lovely to look at, but pinched her toes.

Halfway down the stairs, Agnes heard a burst of male laughter floating up from the parlor. She smiled, pleased that Ernesto Bernal and L.B. Fowler were enjoying each other's company. They looked up as she entered the room. The expressions on their faces were gratifying.

"Mija," Ernesto murmured approvingly.

"Isn't she a sight?" the lawyer agreed. "Miss Agnes, you clean up quite well." Agnes hooked arms with both men. They left the house and made their way to the chapel, which was even more packed than it had been for

John Day's funeral. This time, everyone was smiling. Agnes smiled, too, when the organist began the hymn that had been played the first day Will had visited the chapel.

Be an overcomer, only cowards yield
When the foe they meet on the battlefield;
We are blood-bought princes of the royal host,
And must falter not, nor desert our post.

Never yield a step in the hottest fight,
God will send you help from the realms of light;
In Jehovah's might put the foe to flight,
And the victor's crown you shall wear at last.

Be an overcomer, forward boldly go,
You are strong enough if you count it so—
Strong enough to conquer through sustaining grace,
And to overcome every foe you face.

They passed Doc Pritchard, whose mustache was definitely doing its best to hide a smile, then Frederick Dieter and his wife Sophie, still over-dressed, even for a wedding. Heinrich was with them, and at his side sat Ethel, who waggled her eyebrows at Agnes as she passed. Agnes smiled at Octavio and Miguel, Ernesto and Lupe's sons, who both wore their best suits, then at several of the old cowhands who were working at other ranches in the area. All of Agnes' sisters, their husbands and children crammed into two pews. The nephews looked like stuffed sausages, wearing suits that had been purchased for their grandfather's funeral. They had grown, as boys do. In the front pew, Mildred Day, dressed in a gown that was even whiter and more showy than Agnes', dabbed dramatically at her eyes while Lupe bawled like a baby. Across from them sat Will's mother, Rosette Laveaux, a very stylish lady in a lavender dress that complemented her dark complexion and black, glossy hair.

And there at the front stood Will, tall and proud in his uniform, his new, thick-lensed glasses gleaming back a picture of herself. Next to him stood David Benavides, who had swapped his Corporal's uniform for a very dapper suit. Agnes noticed the plump woman with a brilliant smile sitting in the front row, who must be his wife. She had a red-headed baby in her arms. Half a dozen other kids crawled over her lap and sat at her feet.

Agnes placed her bouquet into the brass artillery shell vase that sat on the altar. She turned and smiled at her mother, who had argued that roses were the appropriate flowers for weddings. Poppies had blazed the long road that led Agnes here. They needed to be on the altar, even if they were out of season and she had to make do with home-made ones.

"You look beautiful," Will murmured in her ear after the two men who had stood in for her father handed her over to the man who would soon be her husband.

"When your eyes improve, you'll see I'm the same, dull mouse I've always been," Agnes whispered back.

"You're no dull mouse. Never were. But my eyes are good enough to see that you're limping almost as much as I am."

"Whoever decided that brides needed to have a penny in their shoe was cruel. I can't wait to get back into my boots."

"Soon, love. Soon."

The chaplain cleared his throat, so they stopped their private conversation and let the ceremony proceed. Dazed by the heat and the press of well-wishers, Agnes mumbled her way through the ceremony and was surprised how quickly the chaplain pronounced them man and wife. The chapel filled with thunderous applause as Mr. and Mrs. William Bowers walked back down the aisle.

The Daughters of the Confederacy's local chapter had laid out a huge spread of fried chicken, coleslaw and an enormous wedding cake in the barn, where everyone who was anyone in southwestern New Mexico held a brimming plate and an Army band played "Let Me Call You Sweetheart." Agnes smiled bemusedly at David Benavides, who was dancing with four children at once while Frederick and Sophie Dieter dragged Heinrich and Ethel about, working the room as if this was a political event.

"Aggie!" Heinrich said when they got to the head table, "Have I got a story to tell you! Ethel came to visit me up in Santa Fe, and I took her on a tour of the Supreme Court building. On our way up the stairs, we accidentally played a bit of tanglefoot. We both fell, and guess where Ethel ended up?"

"Sitting on top of you?" Agnes asked.

Heinrich's crow-like guffaw was loud enough to turn heads. "That's right! And that's when I knew that Ethel was the girl for me! We're engaged! Show her the ring, Ethel, dear."

"Well! Congratulations, Heinrich!" Agnes said.

Ethel held out her hand, displaying a substantial diamond. "Only it's not Heinrich anymore. Too German for politicking these days, right Henry?"

"Of course, dearest," Heinrich said as his father pulled them away to shake yet another hand.

Agnes smiled at Will. "I suppose there's someone for everyone in this world."

"You're the only one for me," Will said, and he took her hand and led her to the center of the room for their first dance as man and wife.

The End

About the Author

Jennifer Bohnhoff was born in Las Cruces, New Mexico, in the southern part of the state close to the Mexican border. An author and former history and English teacher, she has always been interested in history. She now lives high in the mountains of central New Mexico with her husband, a devoted Rottweiler named Panzer, and a petulant cat named Pepé le Pew who doesn't care one bit for his mistress' writing.

Check her website at jenniferbohnhoff.com for more information, to join her email list, or to contact her. Joining her email list will allow you to receive information on her upcoming books and promotions. She would appreciate it if you followed her on Facebook, Twitter, or Pinterest.

Any reviews on Goodreads, Bookbub, Amazon, in blogs and on social media would be appreciated.

More Books by Jennifer Bohnhoff

The Bent Reed: A Civil War Novel about Gettysburg

It's June of 1863 and Sarah McCoombs feels isolated and uncomfortable when her mother pulls her from school and allows a doctor to treat her scoliosis with a cumbersome body cast. She thinks life can't get much worse, but she's wrong.

Physically and socially awkward, 15-year-old Sarah feels her life crumbling. She worries about her brother Micah and neighbor Martin, both serving in the Union Army. She frets over rumors that rebel forces are approaching the nearby town of Gettysburg. When the McCoombs farm becomes a battle field and then a hospital, Sarah must reach deep inside herself to find the strength to cope as she nurses wounded soldiers from both sides. Can she find even more courage to continue to follow her dreams despite her physical disabilities and her disapproving mother?

Code: Elephants on the Moon

As D-Day looms ever closer, a girl in a small town in Normandy joins the Resistance, where she learns some dark family secrets that allow her to follow her own conscience and to understand the coded messages on the radio.

Swan Song

What if the Beowulf assigned to be read in High School English classes is just the first written account of a much older story - a story that stretches back to the dawn of time?

While Helen Bowie asks this question, Hrunting, daughter of Unferth, the mage of Heorot, lives it. Both women are content with their lives until a man enters and changes everything. Ben Wolf and Beowulf are two powerful men in two very different times. Each is a hero, with the power to change society, perhaps for the better, perhaps not.

This dual narrator contemporary/historical novel spans 25,000 years. It asks the reader to consider who determines who is human and who is not: who stands outside society and who belongs at its center.

On Fledgling Wings

Nathaniel Marshal is a bully with a short temper and an empty place in his heart left by the mother who disappeared when he was a baby. The spoiled boy can't wait to leave boring Staywell and begin training so he can become a knight like his father, the cold and distant Sir Amren. But when he arrives at Farleigh, he finds himself in a place of death and danger.

Set in the period of Richard the Lionheart, this is a coming-of-age story about a boy who must confront issues that many modern boys will recognize: the need to control one's temper and destiny, the quest for acceptance, the desire for fitting in, and the awakening of love.

Made in the USA
Middletown, DE
28 October 2021

50968740R00172